# RIP CREW

ALSO BY SEBASTIAN ROTELLA

*The Convert's Song*

*Triple Crossing*

*Twilight on the Line: Underworlds and Politics
at the U.S.-Mexico Border*

# RIP CREW

## Sebastian Rotella

**MULHOLLAND**
**BOOKS**

Mulholland Books
Little, Brown and Company
New York  Boston  London

Mulholland Books / Little, Brown and Company
Hachette Book Group
1290 Avenue of the Americas, New York, NY 10104
mulhollandbooks.com

First edition: March 2018

Mulholland Books is an imprint of Little, Brown and Company, a division of Hachette Book Group, Inc. The Mulholland Books name and logo are trademarks of Hachette Book Group, Inc.

The publisher is not responsible for websites (or their content) that are not owned by the publisher.

The Hachette Speakers Bureau provides a wide range of authors for speaking events. To find out more, go to hachettespeakersbureau.com or call (866) 376-6591.

ISBN 978-0-316-50553-6
LCCN 2017949756

10 9 8 7 6 5 4 3 2 1

LSC-C

Printed in the United States of America

*Para Carmen, mi amor.*

"There ain't no clean way to make a hundred million bucks," Ohls said. "Maybe the head man thinks his hands are clean but somewhere along the line guys got pushed to the wall, nice little businesses got the ground cut from under them and had to sell out for nickels, decent people lost their jobs, stocks got rigged on the market, proxies got bought up like a pennyweight of old gold, and the five per centers and the big law firms got paid hundred-grand fees for beating some law the people wanted but the rich guys didn't, on account of it cut into their profits. Big money is big power and big power gets used wrong. It's the system. Maybe it's the best we can get, but it still ain't any Ivory Soap deal."

—Raymond Chandler, *The Long Goodbye*

"Hunger is a powerful thing."

—"Border Patrol Push Diverts Flow,"
*Los Angeles Times,* October 17, 1994

# RIP CREW

# Prologue

Valentine Pescatore encountered the Beast while hunting a smuggler of humans.

The Pakal-Na neighborhood was about fifty miles northwest of the line where Guatemalan jungle flowed into Mexican jungle. Hundreds of migrants filled the shack town surrounding the freight yards. Most of them were Central Americans. Their presence on Mexican soil made them illegal. But no one in law enforcement seemed to be around or interested.

Pescatore trudged through trash and weeds. The jungle heat made it feel like wading in a swamp. He was sweating and unshaven, and he had a hangover. His short curls were appropriate for Washington, but down here he worried about looking like a cop. Imitating a migrant beggar he'd seen on a roadside, he removed his black T-shirt and draped it over his head like a kaffiyeh. His bantam muscular frame had acquired a few scars over the years. His crucifix necklace fashioned from braided black thread was a talisman purchased long ago from a street vendor in Tijuana. He wore scuffed hiking boots and jeans. Hopefully, his look evoked manual labor, street life, jail time. He didn't need to play this role for days, just hours. Just long enough to get within striking distance of the smuggler known as Chiclet.

Emerging from an alley, Pescatore beheld the Beast, a rusty behemoth at rest. The freight train had stopped in Palenque en route to Vera Cruz. Migrants swarmed the train like flies on a buffalo. They pulled at door handles. They peered between slats. They climbed ladders affixed to boxcars. A few men had staked out rooftops. They withstood the afternoon sun in caps, hats, sunglasses, and bandannas.

Corporate names on the boxcars—Cemex, Pemex, Ferromex—competed with gang graffiti: *Mara Salvatrucha, 18th Street.* In addition to fearing rape, robbery, extortion, and abduction, the illicit riders had to worry about falling off, getting run over, losing limbs. For those who survived the trek across Mexico, another task awaited: sneaking into the United States. A rough crossing that had gotten rougher since Pescatore had left the U.S. Border Patrol.

It was Pescatore's first time at the line between Mexico and Guatemala. The mission had stirred old instincts and dormant emotions from his years in the Patrol. But he was in the private sector now. He had come to Palenque in the state of Chiapas as a contract investigator for the Department of Homeland Security. It was a sensitive, off-the-books assignment. Not officially an undercover operation. Right now, however, he was doing his best—strange as it felt—to impersonate an illegal immigrant.

Feeling self-conscious about his bare-chested piratical getup, he passed a basketball court where migrants dozed on the blacktop, their backpacks and laundry hanging on the chain-link fence. He walked through a low-slung corridor of houses and shops painted in peeling blues, greens, and yellows. Migrants crouched by the tracks, drank water, talked on cell phones, and eyed signs offering the use of toilets and showers for a fee.

4

Pescatore approached a grocery stand. Flanked by a cobbler's hut and a bike-repair shop, the open-air cubicle did brisk business. It seemed like a good place to start. A sign proclaimed ALMACÉN DOÑA ALMA. The proprietress barely fit among her wares. She had chubby cheeks and black braids and wore a frilly white blouse with floral designs.

Pescatore bought a bottle of water. He leaned on the counter.

"*Oiga,* señora, please," he said. "I'm looking for a guy named Chiclet."

He spoke softly, politely, like a gentleman hard-ass, and faked a Cuban accent. A lot of Cubans came through here. Pescatore had talked that morning to a genial muscleman from Bayamo named Nelson. Nelson had followed a well-traveled route via Ecuador. After working in Quito for a while, he had headed north, knowing he had a shot at refugee status if he could just present himself to border inspectors at a port of entry in Texas.

The accents Pescatore could best imitate by virtue of his ethnicity and experience—Argentine and Mexican—were not relevant. But he could pull off Cuban. He tried to mimic the sugary cadences of Nelson from Bayamo and Isabel Puente's cousin Dionisio from Miami, a car salesman who said *oiga* and *oye* a lot.

"*Oiga,* they call him Chiclet," he said, glancing around. "Honduran. He's a guide. Helps people go north. Please, señora. Can you give me a hand?"

Doña Alma studied him. Beads of sweat glistened on her high forehead. He wondered if she was Maya. Her earrings were silver crucifixes. Maybe the TJ jailbird cross on his chest would score points with her.

Finally, she said: *"No sabría decirle."*

The wariest response possible. Worse than "I don't know."

It literally meant "I wouldn't know what to tell you." It really meant "I'm not going to say anything about anything, and your questions frighten me, so please go away forever."

Or not. Doña Alma did an interesting thing. Her eyes widened and did a slow shift to the right. Her gaze fixed itself on a point over his left shoulder, paused, then lowered demurely.

*"No sabría decirle,"* she repeated.

Once again, her eyes traced the same parabola. Her look lingered on the spot beyond his shoulder. A hint of a grin flickered across her face.

*"Oiga,* no problem, señora," he said, raising his voice for the benefit of anyone in earshot. "Thanks much just the same. God bless you."

He turned casually, swigging water. Doña Alma had eyeballed a boxlike structure near a curve in the tracks. Getting closer, he saw it was a diner called Delicias Hondureñas. The faded walls were painted blue and white, the Honduran national colors. The corrugated metal roof was off-kilter, like a carelessly worn hat. People congregated on the front patio around white plastic tables and a Honduran flag on a pole. Honduras was drowning in dysfunction. It had one of the highest homicide rates in the world. Hondurans were becoming soldiers in Mexican cartels. Joints like Delicias Hondureñas were popping up in places like Palenque.

A bald, shirtless guy lounged at an outdoor table. Three tattoo-covered hoodlums drank beer at an adjacent table. They looked like *mareros*—members of the *maras,* the Central American street gangs born in the United States and bred into transnational killing machines. A dozen migrants hovered in clumps of two and three, supplicants waiting at a respectful distance from the gatekeepers of their future.

Pescatore joined the migrants. He leaned against a tree and gulped water.

*God, is it hot. God, am I hungover.*

Two teenagers were the center of attention. They stood in front of the shirtless man. Pescatore concluded that his nickname was La Rana (the Frog) when, in an indolent voice, he said, "La Rana decides who rides. As of now, you're not going anywhere."

The boy told La Rana that his name was Oscar. He was about sixteen. His fashionable red high-tops struck Pescatore as a bad wardrobe choice for the trek, like a sign proclaiming ROB ME. Oscar had a peak wet-combed into his hair. He wore designer jeans and a striped polo shirt. His build suggested that he'd done some weight lifting but he hadn't filled out yet. His sister was long-legged and doe-eyed. Her hair hung down over a pink backpack decorated with images of the Powerpuff Girls. She stayed behind her brother.

Oscar's diction, lack of tattoos, and frequent mentions of God led Pescatore to think he was an evangelical Christian. The boy explained that his parents had already paid the entire fee, cash money, door to door, from San Salvador to Las Vegas. Nobody had mentioned a supplemental charge in Palenque.

"Well, they should have," La Rana said. "Two spots on La Bestia will cost you five hundred apiece. Babysitting snotnosed kids on top of that train is a pain in the ass. Cops all over. Hey, *muñeca,* how old are you?"

The girl peered out from behind her brother.

"Fourteen." Her voice was barely audible.

La Rana considered her. His fists clenched the short towel around his neck. His physique was indeed froglike: round belly and shoulders, stumpy legs below baggy cutoffs.

"What's your name?"

"Nelvita."

"Don't be shy, let me get a look at you. What grade are you in?"

7

"Ninth," she said in that wisp of a voice. As if fearing the answer was insufficient, she added, "I didn't finish, because we left."

"*Ay,* what a shame, you didn't finish. Don't worry, we've got a lot of teachers around here. We can teach you all kinds of things."

Chuckles from the *mareros.* Nelvita took refuge behind Oscar, who mopped his forehead with his arm.

*Look at these scumbags,* Pescatore thought. *Smacking their lips over a fourteen-year-old.*

La Rana told Oscar to come back with cash. Or some other form of payment. The teenagers sidled off, looking lost, whispering heatedly. Pescatore could imagine their story. The parents had migrated to Las Vegas, probably leaving the kids in the care of grandparents. The parents had stayed in touch via Skype, WhatsApp, Facebook. They had earned enough for smuggling fees to try to reunite the family, but Oscar and Nelvita's relatively decent upbringing had not been the best preparation for the journey.

*Those two are going to get eaten alive,* he thought.

He forced them out of his mind. He scanned the people around him. No one was clamoring for the next audience with La Rana.

Pescatore took another gulp of water. He removed the shirt-headdress. He poured the rest of the bottle over his head, pasted his hair back with his hand, and pulled the shirt down over his torso. Undercover or not, he intended to show these thugs some dignity. He entered the patio of Delicias Hondureñas with a jaunty walk — what Cubans call *tumbao.*

"What's up, brother?" he said.

La Rana's beady eyes did, in fact, remind him of a frog's.

"*Oye,* I'm with the Eagles," Pescatore continued. "My name is Dionisio. I was told to ask for Chiclet."

Nelson from Bayamo had explained the drill. At each stage of the migrants' journey, smugglers provided them with a new code name and contact. Upon arriving in Palenque, Nelson's group of migrants had been told to call themselves the Eagles and meet Chiclet.

*"Cubano,"* La Rana grumbled.

Cubans were regarded as pushy and crafty. Still, they tended to have relatives in the U.S. with deep pockets. They weren't first-class cargo like Indians, Africans, or Nepalese, but Cubans were good value.

"That's right, *chico,*" Pescatore replied. "And proud of it."

"Where are you going?"

"Chicago, Illi-noise."

La Rana dried his pate with the towel. He asked questions about the trip from Cuba. Pescatore described an odyssey through Ecuador, Colombia, the tropical wilds of the Darién Gap. His answers appeared to be satisfactory.

"Come back later," La Rana said. "Seven o'clock."

*"Oye,* will Chiclet take care of me then?"

La Rana repeated the words "Seven o'clock" and told him to scram.

Pescatore killed time. He bought another bottle of water. He walked through the freight yards and the shantytown. He sat on a crate on a hill with a view.

The shadows lengthened. The groups around the train grew. He took deep breaths.

The Guatemalan border was like a return to the battlefield, a flashback to the Line in San Diego. Working in the Patrol had overwhelmed him. He had felt too much sympathy for the migrants, too much hatred for the criminals. It had messed with his head.

At about six thirty, two men approached the diner below. The shorter one had a pile of black hair and wore a guayabera-type shirt. Even from a distance, he looked very much like Chiclet. La Rana accompanied them inside.

Pescatore called Porthos. They settled on a plan.

At seven, Pescatore crossed himself and raised his crucifix to his lips. He walked down the hill. His gun was with Porthos, who had been reluctant about this improvised undercover gambit. Isabel would not have approved either. But Isabel was counting on him.

The setting sun shone off the metal roof of Delicias Hondureñas. He squinted. The outdoor tables were empty. There was a mural on the wall: a figure in a poncho, the face shrouded by a wide-brimmed hat with a black band. Painted below was the word *Catracho,* a nickname for Hondurans. He hadn't noticed the mural earlier.

He reached for the handle of the screen door. Time slowed down. He thought about the places he had been during the past months: Buenos Aires, Paris, Washington, San Diego, Tapachula. Travel had left him in a daze, always alert, always weary. So many miles covered to reach this remote corner of the world, this destination that seemed somehow inevitable—a den of cutthroats in Pakal-Na, Palenque, Mexico.

There were a dozen tables in the dim interior. A freezer whirred. Rotor fans spun. Flies dive-bombed plates.

La Rana wore an orange T-shirt now, but his fists still clenched the towel around his neck.

"Right on time, eh? Wait here."

La Rana passed a table occupied by the hoodlum trio—still drinking beer—and muttered with two men at a table in the back. He returned to fetch Pescatore.

The one sitting by the wall was definitely Chiclet, aka Héctor Talavera. The pompadour confirmed it. Like in the mug shot: A prodigious head of high-maintenance hair. A castle of hair. Combed in swirls and levels. String-thin sideburns extended along the jaw to the chin.

*No doubt about it,* Pescatore thought. *I got you.*

The face showed damage and dissipation, especially in the flat nose. Protuberant teeth chomped gum—probably the origin of the nickname. The gum-chewing worked the sinews of a short trunk of a neck encircled by gold chains. Chiclet tilted his head back against the wall. His bloodshot eyes focused on Pescatore from the depths of a hostile stupor.

"*Buenas tardes,* Señor Chiclet." Pescatore tempered his bouncy manner with deference. "I am Dionisio. From Bayamo. A pleasure to meet you."

He extended his hand. Chiclet's face twisted as if Pescatore had offered him a stool sample. Chiclet let the hand hang.

"Sit," La Rana growled, poking Pescatore in the ribs.

The table held three cell phones and a bottle of rum. Chiclet's tablemate was a long-armed bruiser whose straw hat recalled the Catracho mural.

Pescatore was just starting to speak when music blared: the ringtone of a phone on the table. A bachata guitar riff, then the falsetto croon of Romeo Santos: "*Sooo nasty!*"

Chiclet picked up the phone. His end of the conversation consisted of profanities and monosyllables. He swigged from the bottle.

While Chiclet talked, Pescatore scoped him. Rolex, gold bracelet, a wad of cash swelling a pocket of the pale blue shirt. Smells came off the man in waves: sweat, cologne, hair gel, cheap rum, chewing gum.

La Rana walked past the counter to a bathroom in back. Chiclet finished the call. Pescatore explained his situation, his hopes of reaching Chicago. Chiclet listened, drank, fiddled with his phones, and avoided eye contact. Pescatore realized that the smuggler wasn't capable of having a civil conversation with him. Chiclet saw him as human freight, merchandise, a commodity to be bought and sold, shipped from here to there after extracting maximum profit.

"Fucking Cubans," Chiclet said. "Why don't you take a boat to Miami instead of coming all the way here to break our balls?"

"The sharks, *hermano*. I'd rather take my chances on dry land."

"The sharks." Chiclet swigged from the bottle. "Not enough sharks to eat all the *putos* in Cuba. *Mucho puto* in Cuba, no?"

"Compared to where?" Pescatore heard himself retort. "Honduras?"

His accent had wavered. His mask had slipped. Not that he really cared. He'd had about enough of this humiliating little dance.

Chiclet's jaws worked the gum harder. In his line of business, people didn't talk back. They obeyed orders, kissed ass, begged and pleaded. The sudden impudence had put him on guard.

Pescatore planted his feet, ready to move.

*He's gonna curse me out and slap me around,* he thought, *or tell me I've got* cojones *and offer me a drink.*

He never got a chance to find out. The door opened. Two men entered, silhouetted against the evening light. Pescatore gave thanks and praise. He felt a jolt of the confidence that had enabled him to stroll unarmed into Gangsterland. It came from having two of the baddest cops in Mexico as backup. Ex-cops, really, but he wouldn't have traded them for Wyatt Earp and Wild Bill Hickok.

Porthos was the muscle. Serious wingspan, and an excess forty pounds that made him even more imposing. Athos was four inches shorter and pushing sixty, but his marksman's stare emanated menace. Both men wore baseball caps and camouflage vests. They gripped the guns in their belts but did not draw.

"*¿Que onda?*" Chiclet growled. "Those *cabrones* are *judiciales*."

Pescatore didn't waste time. With all the command presence he could muster, he declared, "Absolutely correct. They are *judiciales,* and so am I. And you are under arrest, Héctor Talavera. Stand up, turn around, and put your hands behind your back. Right now."

Frozen in disbelief, the smugglers and the *mareros* looked back and forth between Pescatore and the newcomers. Pescatore slid to his feet, producing a pair of handcuffs from a pocket. He grabbed Chiclet by the arm and pulled him up. To his surprise, the smuggler complied, rising like a sleepwalker.

*This is gonna work,* Pescatore thought. *Smooth as silk. Easy as pie.*

The first cuff had clicked onto the first wrist when he heard a toilet flush. In a kind of slow-motion delayed reaction, he turned to see La Rana emerge from the bathroom. La Rana took in the scene. His mouth and eyes opened wide. Before Pescatore could order him not to do anything stupid, he did something stupid.

La Rana charged, his legs pumping, his bald head lowering. Reluctant to release his captive, Pescatore managed at the last moment to duck and pivot, minimizing the impact. The tackle took him down and overturned a table. As they grappled on the floor, he heard a brawl break loose. Shouts, curses, bodies colliding, furniture crashing.

Pescatore was in better shape than La Rana. The urge to hit someone had been building in him for days. It didn't take him long to roll on top of his assailant and punch him senseless. He gave La Rana an extra shot between the eyes. From his crouch, he saw Porthos doing damage with windmill arms, blows resonating, men dropping. He saw Chiclet contorted over a table, the handcuffs dangling from his wrist. The smuggler had the barrel of a pistol in his ear. Athos had pinned Chiclet's head to the table with the pistol and appeared intent on driving the barrel into the ear and through the skull into the wood below.

Athos looked up. When he spoke, his voice was loud enough to cut through the racket but calm given the circumstances.

"Everyone settle down! Or I blow this monkey's brains out."

Chiclet shrieked at his men to obey. Gradually, the commotion came to a stop. Pescatore scrambled to finish handcuffing Chiclet and retrieve the phones. Pescatore, Athos, and Porthos rushed the prisoner outside and into a black Suburban. Their driver sped along unpaved lanes. The vehicle banged over potholes and rocks, raising dust in its wake.

Sitting on the prisoner's right, Pescatore frisked him. He breathed through his mouth to ward off the smells. Porthos pulled a burlap sack over Chiclet's head. The Suburban bounced onto a main road.

Pescatore gripped Chiclet's arm. The pulse hammered against his fingertips, echoing his own heartbeat. Beneath the burlap, the captive made a kind of humming sound— between a moan and a sigh.

Fifteen minutes later, the two-lane road had brought them to the outskirts of town. Migrants hiked on the shoulder of the road. Pescatore stared through the orange glow of dusk in his window.

"Wait a minute!" He lunged forward and grabbed the driver. "Pull over! Pull over here, please."

The driver hit the brakes. Pescatore reached into Chiclet's breast pocket and removed the wad of bills. The prisoner remained inert. Pescatore lifted the shirt and rifled through the fanny pack he had found while frisking him. Another roll of cash, mostly U.S. dollars.

"What are you doing?" Athos demanded.

"Forgive me, Comandante, I'll be right back." Pescatore poked Chiclet. "Mr. Talavera, I'm confiscating these funds for official business."

He got out and sprinted down the road. An evening breeze ruffled bushes and palm trees. His foot speed had been useful in the Patrol. When he thought back, he remembered the chases most of all. Night after night of running all out, full tilt, hell-bent.

A bus stop took shape in the dusk. Oscar stood in front of the hutlike wooden shelter. Nelvita sat inside. Oscar had a duffel bag over his shoulder, and he held his sister's pink backpack as well. He gestured, apparently imploring her to get up. She huddled on the bench.

"Excuse me, Oscar." Pescatore spoke his usual Spanish inflected by Buenos Aires, Tijuana, and Chicago. "I need to talk to you."

The teenager whirled. He backed up, positioning himself in front of his sister, and confronted the latest specter in the horror movie that his life had become: a disheveled madman with a strange accent who had come tearing out of the shadows and addressed him by name.

"Who are you?" Oscar demanded. "What do you want?"

Hands on knees, Pescatore panted. After the hangover, the fight, and the sprint, he was winded. Oscar inserted his hand into the duffel bag. Maybe he carried a knife or a club, showing he had a little street sense after all.

"Sorry to startle you." Pescatore straightened. "I was at the Honduran place today in Pakal-Na. That's how I know your name."

Oscar stared at him. A truck rumbled by. Pescatore glanced back at the lights of the Suburban waiting down the road.

"Where are you from?" Oscar asked. "Are you a, uh, guide?"

"No."

Pescatore advanced cautiously into the bus shelter. He looked around before extending the pile of cash to Oscar. There was blood on Pescatore's knuckles—a souvenir of the capture. He tried to avoid staining the bills.

"Take this," he said.

Oscar didn't move. Nelvita stood up, pushing her hair back. Her eyes were riveted on the money.

"Seriously, take it," Pescatore said. "About six thousand dollars. If I were you, I'd go home to El Salvador. Use it for college. Start a business. What you're planning to do is against American law, and I don't like it. But if you really want to go north, call your parents. Tell them you've got cash. You could fly to Sonora, or take a bus. They could send someone for you. You have options now."

He placed his free hand on Oscar's shoulder and offered the cash again. The youth accepted it, head down.

"Whatever you do," Pescatore whispered, "promise me you won't let that girl near that goddamn train."

Oscar called him "señor," asked God to bless him, stammered his thanks.

"You're welcome. Now get off the street quick."

Pescatore ran back to the Suburban, propelled by pure exhilaration. He slid into his seat.

"All set."

The vehicle swung onto the road. Athos turned. In a low voice, he asked, "What was all that, muchacho?"

Pescatore remembered a phrase he had heard Leo Méndez use.

"Redistribution of wealth."

The motel was outside of town. Pescatore had rented three rooms and the presidential suite, whose only conceivable qualification for that designation was its size. Porthos installed Chiclet in an upright chair. Athos and Pescatore pored through the prisoner's wallet, cell phones, and pocket litter.

Porthos removed the sack from Chiclet's head. The smuggler blinked. His pompadour was a mess. Shudders racked him. His lips moved without sound. The sneer had evaporated. His eyes darted among his captors.

Chiclet surely imagined that a roster of time-honored torments awaited him. Beatings. Cigarette burns. Head-dunking in the bathtub. Carbonated liquid sprayed up the nose. Electric shocks to strategic anatomical areas.

In reality, Pescatore had never tortured a suspect and wasn't about to start. As deputy chiefs of the Diogenes Group of Tijuana, Athos and Porthos had embraced a gospel of humane policing.

But Chiclet didn't know any of that.

"All right, *guey*," Pescatore snapped. "We don't have time to fuck around. Nobody's hurt you yet. You still have full use of your limbs and organs. That'll change fast if you don't talk. I want to skip the part where you whine and bitch and lie and tell us we've got the wrong guy, you don't know what we're talking about, all that shit. We know who you are and what you did. It's time to get with the program. Otherwise you'll wish you were never born. Understood?"

Chiclet made the humming-moaning sound. His eyes teared up.

"What do you want?" he croaked.

"I want to know what happened with those African women in Tecate."

# PART I

# Chapter 1

On the day Pescatore returned from Paris, Isabel sent an intriguing invitation.

The e-mail appeared on his phone when his flight landed at Dulles. He had spent a week visiting Fatima Belhaj. It had not been restful.

Isabel proposed Saturday lunch at the Argentine restaurant he liked. She wanted to discuss a "business matter."

The words bounced around in his head overnight. His move from Buenos Aires to DC in the spring had been a business decision. His Argentine boss, Facundo Hyman Bassat, had decided that the private investigations firm needed its American employee, Pescatore, based in Washington to handle international clients. Meanwhile, Isabel had been promoted again at Homeland Security, where she now oversaw operations related to the Mexican border and Latin America. If she wanted to, she could open doors for the new U.S. branch of Villa Crespo International Investigations and Security. After all, Facundo had worked for her before. Pescatore had worked with her and almost married her. After teaming up again on a terrorism case, Pescatore and Isabel had established a cautious friendship. She worked nonstop, though, and he was reluctant to hit her up for business opportunities on the rare occasions when he saw her.

But maybe, he told himself in the morning, she had decided to steer something his way: a lead, a client, a contract. He wasn't sure what to wear. He put on a cotton pullover shirt and jeans, then changed his mind—too casual. The dress slacks and blazer he tried next looked stiff and goofy. He settled on jeans, a button-down white shirt, and a lightweight gray sports jacket.

Pescatore had found an apartment near Western Avenue, the boundary between the District of Columbia and the state of Maryland. An Israeli friend of Facundo's was subletting him a furnished one-bedroom in a 1970s-era complex. The imposing lobby and red-carpeted hallways recalled an aging hotel. The residents were young professionals, senior citizens, foreign diplomats. One way or another, they were passing through. Like him.

At 1:00 p.m., he steered his black Impala past empty sun-baked sidewalks. After the tumult and swagger of Buenos Aires, this upscale frontier of the U.S. capital seemed desolate, as if the government had ordered an evacuation and forgotten to tell him.

Wisconsin Avenue became Rockville Pike and carved north through a prairie of malls, chain stores, and fast-food outlets. The CD player cranked Springsteen. "Death to My Hometown."

The restaurant was tucked between a martial arts school and a discount clothing store in a shopping plaza. Isabel Puente was already at the table. Ever since San Diego, when she ran him as a reluctant Internal Affairs source in the Border Patrol, she had arrived early for meets to do recon, scan the clientele, check the exits. He knew from experience that the purse hooked on the right side of her chair held her Glock.

"Back to the wall, packing heat," he said, kissing her on the cheek. "Taking no chances in Rockville, huh?"

"It's not just physical threats," she said. "I can't afford to sit near some nosy bureaucrat. Or a foreign government official. Or a sneaky journalist. Washington is a small town. You can commit career suicide by opening your mouth in the wrong place."

"Your secrets are safe at El Patio."

The restaurant was like a hidden outpost in the suburban moonscape. The narrow deep interior was painted in warm gold tones. The sound system played the gravelly baritone of Alberto Marino singing a tango. On the walls were amateur paintings of Carlos Gardel, the waterfront in La Boca, the Obelisk on Nueve de Julio Avenue. A grocery area in back offered dulce de leche, *mate* tea, pastries, wine. The clientele were mostly families, Argentine and Central American, immigrants and expats. Many had their eyes lifted to a Spanish-league soccer game on the overhead screens. A large family, probably Salvadoran, occupied a nearby table. The mother used one hand to push a stroller back and forth, quieting a baby girl who wore an elaborate pink ribbon around her head like a gypsy princess. Two small boys dueled in the aisle with sword-shaped balloons, making a racket that nobody minded.

"This is like my little hangout," Pescatore said. "A bona fide neighborhood joint. Except there's no neighborhood."

"You miss Buenos Aires."

"In BA, I missed San Diego."

"In San Diego, you wouldn't stop talking about Chicago. Mr. Nostalgia." She studied him. "You look tired."

He could have said the same about her. But Isabel always looked good. Her black hair had grown long and hung down her back. Diagonal zippers adorned her black dress, which narrowed at the waist to accentuate her curves and showed the right amount of thigh and cleavage. She wore the usual high heels that pushed her above five five.

"I'm jet-lagged," he said. "I got back from Paris yesterday."

"Oh. How's Fatima?"

"Good. How's Hasselhoff?"

"Good." Her smile was playful. "And his name, my friend, is Howard."

"Right. Sorry."

Isabel was dating a high-powered lawyer. Pescatore had run into them strolling arm in arm in Georgetown and endured introductions and sidewalk small talk. Howard was tall, tanned, and toothy, reminding Pescatore of a young East Coast version of the former *Baywatch* star.

"Are you still taking college courses?" Isabel asked.

"University of Maryland. If I bear down, I'll have my degree in a year."

They ordered empanadas and a grilled-meat platter for two. To his surprise, Isabel hit the wine pretty hard. Toward the end of the meal, she asked about work. He told her that Facundo Hyman's U.S. expansion had produced its first case. Pescatore had spent time guarding an executive in Venezuela and overseeing his move to Florida.

"I was going back and forth to Caracas," he said. "It got rowdy—threats, anti-Semitic graffiti, a kidnap attempt. Thugs on motorcycles chased us one night. These *cabrones* wear red berets, call themselves revolutionaries. Buncha criminals."

"Are you busy now?"

"Not really."

"Lots of competition."

"Yep. Seems like every ex-spook, ex-agent, ex-anybody in town has something going: investigations, consulting."

Isabel surveyed the surrounding tables. She sipped cappuccino, her oval wide-set eyes hovering above the cup. In Washington, her beauty had acquired an air of solitude.

*Here comes the business matter,* he thought.

"Do you have time for a case?"

"Of course. You bet. Absolutely." He sat up straight. "For who? ICE? Homeland Security Investigations?"

"You'd report to me." She leaned forward. "It requires travel. The border, Mexico. Maybe Central America."

He nodded, restraining the impulse to ask questions.

Her hands tore at discarded sugar packets on the table, reducing them to tiny squares.

"I need someone I can trust," she said. "Someone who knows the Line. And Latin America."

*"Para servirle."*

"Are you familiar with the case of the off-duty Customs and Border Protection officer who disappeared in Tijuana a couple of weeks ago?"

"Little bit."

"And the massacre in Tecate? The female aliens in the motel."

"Yeah. Awful."

"The cases are related."

"Jeez. I didn't hear that."

As was her habit when angry or pensive, she put her thumb to her teeth.

"It's unconfirmed intel." She signaled the waitress for the check. "Why don't you come to my office, take a look at some material?"

"Now?"

"You should start ASAP."

He dropped his car at his place and they rode downtown together in her Mazda sport sedan. During the ride, she asked about his personal life.

"I don't want to pry," she said, "but you looked unhappy about Paris. We're friends, Valentine. You can talk to me if it helps."

He stared at the ornate facades of Embassy Row. He wondered if this line of questioning figured in her assessment of him for a job that was urgent, hush-hush, and involved working directly for her.

"Basically," he said, "long-distance relationships suck."

"I see." She glanced at him through her sunglasses.

"Look, I grew up in one place. You know that. Same neighborhood, same house. From Chicago straight to the Patrol. Culture shock. Craziness. Then I moved from the border to Buenos Aires. I barely got settled. Now I'm here. Meanwhile, Fatima's from Paris, she's French, and that's the bottom line."

"She wants you to go live with her?"

"No. And I wouldn't expect her to move here."

"There's no real solution. That's why you're depressed."

He grimaced. "Tell you the truth, turns out another guy is in the picture."

"Oh, I get it. *Típica francesada.*"

The tone of "typical French situation" spurred him to Fatima's defense.

He told Isabel what Fatima had told him days ago. She had met Karim when they were nineteen-year-olds in the housing project—a brief but intense romance. Karim joined the French army and became a commando. Fatima became a cop. She hadn't heard from him again until he transferred to a tactical unit of her counterterror agency and they ran into each other one day after almost twenty years.

"Did you break up?"

"Not yet."

"What does she want?"

"She doesn't know. She needs to think. I told her, 'Listen, I'm not comfortable with this whole *Jules and Jim* situation.'"

Isabel pulled into the garage of her headquarters near the National Mall. She showed the guard her ID, then turned with a sardonic look.

"Who and Jim?"

"It's a French movie."

"This relationship sure has expanded your horizons."

A big quiet building in the big quiet of a downtown Saturday. Their footsteps echoed on marble in the lobby. Recognizing Isabel as a boss, a duo of drowsy security guards roused themselves in a hurry. They waved Isabel and Pescatore through the metal detector with a cursory glance at Pescatore's ID. In a reception area on the tenth floor, a more alert guard at a desk relieved Pescatore of his cell phone and put it in a small locker.

Isabel briefed him in her corner office. Plaques. A Miami Heat poster. Souvenirs from foreign law enforcement agencies. Family photos: nieces and nephews in baptismal and communion finery, men in U.S. military uniforms. Work photos: Isabel with agents in raid jackets. Isabel shaking hands with a cabinet secretary.

Pescatore had a stomach full of meat, a head full of Malbec. The espresso had barely dented his jet lag. He wanted nothing more or less than a nap. But he kept his eyes on the image freeze-framed on the screen of the desktop computer.

"San Diego Border Patrol Sector," she said. "A few miles from the Line."

"Looks familiar."

"A smuggling corridor. It's calmed down since our day. The whole border has. But they still move OTMs and SIAs now and then."

The grainy black-and-white image had been filmed from above by a security camera. A twenty-four-hour convenience store occupied the top of the screen. The lone parked vehicle was a white Chevrolet Express cargo van facing the building. The lights of the store were halos in the night.

"So we think the missing CBP inspector was involved," he said.

"The van drives through his lane at the port of entry half an hour earlier."

He noted the numerals on the screen: 2:57 a.m.

"This part," Isabel said, clicking the mouse, "is hard to watch."

At the bottom of the screen, a Suburban pulled into the lot. Doors opened. The two gunmen wore Stetson hats and long coats. He knew the look: Sinaloan Badass. Some border gunslingers favored trench coats or slickers at night, partly for style, partly to conceal weapons.

The coats billowed around the men like capes. Their movements were smooth, coordinated, almost balletic. One crept up on the passenger side of the van. The other flared left. He padded up to the driver's window. He aimed—a slow unfurling of the arm. He fired twice.

The shooter yanked open the driver's door, hauled out his victim, and did a half spin like a disdainful matador. The black-clad corpse tumbled past him onto the concrete, limbs splayed.

The shooter slid behind the wheel of the van. His partner climbed in on the other side. The van sped away. The Suburban followed.

It was 2:58 a.m.

Isabel stopped the video. She looked at Pescatore.

"Damn," he said.

"There were ten aliens in the back."

"According to your unconfirmed intel."

"Correct. These women are already scared. Now their *pollero* gets his head blown off in front of them."

"Cold-blooded."

"That's what the rip crews are like. Worse than narcos, worse than human smugglers. Pure predators."

Pescatore looked at the documents on the desk—the cell phone records of Mario Covington, the Customs and Border Protection inspector who had gone missing soon after the shooting. Last seen at a bar in Rosarito Beach.

"I bet this Mario got whacked," he said. "A dirty inspector deals with smugglers, okay. But an inspector working at the same time with smugglers and a gang that rips off smugglers, setting up the ambush and everything? That's crazy."

Along with the video, the phone records and photos from the border ports established a timeline. After starting his overnight shift at the San Ysidro port of entry on August 5, Covington had received calls on his cell phone from a convicted alien smuggler, a U.S. citizen residing in Tijuana. The smuggler was the driver of the van. Each time the driver called Covington en route to the border, the inspector called a burner cell phone in California. He called the burner for the last time just after he waved the van through his lane into San Diego at 2:20 a.m. Cell-tower data put the burner phone in the vicinity of the convenience store when the gunmen killed the driver. An hour later, they took the van back south to Tecate, Mexico, about sixty miles east of the San Diego–Tijuana port of entry.

Grim-faced, Isabel described the events in Tecate. The crime scene was a motel used by smugglers to stash loads of high-priced clients known in law enforcement parlance as "special interest aliens" (SIAs). The "special interest" referred to the fact that they came from Somalia, Syria, Pakistan, or other havens of terrorism. As opposed to OTMs, or "Other Than Mexicans": Latin Americans from places where mayhem, massacre, and decapitation were driven by business imperatives, not religious ones.

At five thirty a.m., sustained gunfire had been heard from the second floor of the motel. The police discovered the bodies of ten women shot execution-style. They were Somali, Ethiopian, and Eritrean. The ages ranged from early twenties to mid-fifties. Some of the women had not yet been identified. Three Mexicans guarding them had also been killed. The men had records for crimes typical of rip crews: robbery, kidnapping, assault.

"The descriptions of two male victims match the shooters in the video. The Mexican police claim they don't have any leads. They have frozen us out. They won't give us access to evidence that could connect the incidents. No U.S. jurisdiction. None of our business."

"Do we have confirmation that the women were in the van?"

"No. But Covington's girlfriend knew about his activities. He told her a load vehicle was coming through with migrants from Africa. Big payday. Africans aren't smuggled at San Ysidro that often. This can't be a coincidence, not when you factor in the resemblance between the van shooters and the dead guys at the motel, the phone traffic, the van going to Tecate, Covington disappearing."

He thought about the workmanlike brutality of the shooting. Hours later, someone more brutal had killed the killers. And the women.

"What are you thinking as far as motive?" he asked. "Retaliation? The rip crew steals the load and the smugglers track 'em down. But they wouldn't kill their own clients. Africans pay thirty thousand bucks apiece, right?"

"Maybe a third gang hit the motel."

"This is some complicated, sinister shit," he said.

Isabel stretched in her executive chair. He caught himself looking at her lush compact body, recalling its contours.

"There are conflicting theories," she said. "People say it was done to send a message. Or interfere with business. Make a mess on enemy turf."

Pescatore thought back to the brief news reports he had seen in France about the massacre. His attention had been on his drama with Fatima.

"This must be taking up all your time," he said. "The FBI's involved, the inspector general, you name it."

"That's right."

"I gotta ask you: If the Bureau's working it, and all your troops"—he waved at the empty cubicles and offices beyond the glass—"and your attachés and vetted units in Mexico, what do you need me for?"

"I should clarify," she said in a fierce tone. "The FBI took over. We were ordered to stand down. Even though it's our turf. Even though we opened a corruption case on Covington before the incident."

*Another surprise,* Pescatore thought. *This is getting wilder.*

"That's why I need you," Isabel continued. "For a discreet, unofficial inquiry into one angle of the case. A specific, focused lead about a missing individual."

"The inspector?"

"No. A guy who's a witness or an accomplice, it's not clear which."

"You want me to track him down."

"Exactly. He knows a lot about what happened."

"Okay."

"It needs to be confidential. I'm encountering interference."

"Inside the U.S. government?"

"Yes. People who have been trying to make my life impossible."

"Really? Who?"

She used both hands to sweep her hair out of her face, tilting her head back, hands lingering behind her neck. "Now is not the time to get into it."

Her high-powered job came with high-powered hassles. Her agency functioned in a perpetual cross fire from Republicans, Democrats, the news media, foreign governments, pro-immigrant and anti-immigrant activists. Although lately she had been dealing with congressional hearings and political pressure, he hadn't thought the problems were unusually serious.

"You can't tell me?"

"I'll say this: I'm not winning the battle right now."

His eyes widened. Although she was only five years older than him, her rise had been swift. She was a workaholic, an instinctive leader, good at cultivating allies and deflecting rivals. Now, despite all the personnel and resources at her disposal, she had turned to him. It showed trust. It also showed she had run out of options.

"Isabel." He patted her hand. "Whatever you need. If you want, I'll work no charge. Pro Bono Pescatore."

"That's not necessary. I've got a discretionary budget. Your firm has a proven track record with the U.S. embassy in Buenos Aires."

"But you and me were engaged to be married. How's that gonna look?"

"I'll take that chance. I want to get to the bottom of this. It's not just about my work situation, the politics. *Esas pobres mujeres…*"

She paused. She rarely spoke Spanish with him, especially about work.

"I want to know who murdered those women," she said. "And why. There have been worse massacres, higher body counts. But not on my watch."

Slowly, she pushed a folder across the desk. The moment had the weight of ceremony: the silence, the afternoon shadows, the thick folder with official stamps. She was opening a door into a secret world. Sealing a covenant with him.

The photos from the crime scene were not especially bloody or lurid. Not sadism, just extermination. The scene was a dingy motel room. The women had been lined up and mowed down. Corpses were crumpled on a frayed brown carpet, slumped against walls, sprawled across a bed whose cover was decorated with images of tropical birds.

Pescatore gritted his teeth. He propped his head in his hand as he reviewed the pictures. A multicolored hooded scarf, tribal-looking, evoking faraway lands. A sandal near a child-like foot. A fist gripping prayer beads. A gold hoop earring entwined in braids. The striking and delicate features of the victims reminded him of the East African immigrants who were plentiful in Washington.

He swallowed. Isabel's eyes glistened.

*She's my client now,* he thought. He looked down at the photos. *And so are they.*

"Sorry to drop this on you," she said.

"Don't be. Now I know what kind of animals we're dealing with."

"Valentine, you don't have to take the job."

He puffed reproachfully, as if blowing the idea away from him.

"Have you thought about reaching out to Leo Méndez?" he asked.

"Of course. But he's a full-time journalist now. I can't take the risk."

"I won't tell him anything if you don't want, but if I'm gonna go poking around down there, he could hook me up with some guys I'd like on my side."

"Who's that?"

"His musketeers."

# Chapter 2

Méndez had imagined his death many times, many places, many ways.

Méndez was morbid by nature, nationality, and profession. He had survived ambushes and gunfights. He had studied the tactics and semiotics of assassination. His list of enemies was long and ominous.

In nightmares and daydreams, the ever-changing film of his anticipated demise ran on a constant loop. He had been immolated like the Italian judge Falcone in Palermo, explosives erupting through asphalt to hurl cars and bodies heavenward. He had been shot point-blank like the Mexican presidential candidate Colosio in Tijuana, the gunman surging out of a crowd, grabbing his arm, and putting a gun to his head, an instant of human contact heralding obliteration. He had been shredded in a drive-by fusillade—car to car, pickup to car, motorcycle to car—like late Latin American colleagues in journalism and law enforcement. He had been set afire, flayed alive, dismembered, disemboweled, and decapitated like the narco-grunts in the violence-porn YouTube videos that the cartels used for psyops.

The one scenario Méndez had not imagined was that the

end would come at a children's soccer game in La Jolla, California, U.S.A. And that the hit men would wear suits and ties.

An August weekend: warm sun, mild breeze, the park gleaming green. The summer league held its games on Saturdays at eight thirty a.m. Méndez and his wife were night owls. They did not understand why American soccer parents deprived themselves of sleep after a hard workweek.

*Demented puritans,* Estela declared. *You won't catch me vertical at that beastly hour.*

So Estela stayed home with Renata, their three-year-old. Méndez took his son to the games. Although Méndez's command of the language had improved, his English was still—in the words of the singer Celia Cruz—"not very good-looking." He was uneasy among the soccer parents. They were loud and cheery; he was quiet and reserved. They wore shorts and sandals; he stuck to his jeans and gym shoes. They drove shiny vans and sport-utility vehicles; he had bought his brown Chevrolet Caprice from a friend in the San Diego Police. Their mansions overlooked canyons; he rented a bungalow in flatlands south of La Jolla. They were investors, executives, lawyers. He was a journalist-turned-advocate-turned-cop-turned-journalist: a refugee, dangerous and endangered, from the fog of war at the border.

He gravitated to the foreigners, a courtly Chilean economist and a dour Eastern European who retreated to the parking lot to smoke. Neither had shown up today. Méndez paced the sideline alone, watching his son.

Juan was eleven. He was fast and skilled, though he insisted on using only his left foot. Méndez blamed himself. Juan had inherited an obsession with Diego Armando Maradona, who remained his father's all-time-favorite player despite an apocalyptical Argentine slide into squalor. When Juan was little,

Méndez had mentioned that Maradona worked his magic almost exclusively with his left foot. Back then, Juan didn't get many opportunities to talk to his father, so he soaked up everything he said. And he had quietly decided to emulate Maradona's one-footed style.

Playing wing, Juan served up sharp crosses. He narrowly missed a shot on goal. He flashed a smile as he ran by, his black hair askew. His face was thin and solemn, resembling Méndez's, but his eyes and hair were his mother's. Méndez returned the smile.

"Good one, *m'ijo*," he called. "That's the way to do it."

During much of his son's life, Méndez had been the state human rights commissioner of Baja California and then the chief of the Diogenes Group police unit of Tijuana. He had missed most of Juan's sports events and school activities. They had finally begun to spend meaningful time together in the two years since their hurried move to San Diego.

*A fringe benefit of exile,* Méndez thought.

That was when he noticed the two men across the field.

*Guaruras,* he thought at first. Bodyguards. Human Dobermans. Slabs of muscle in dark suits.

Looking incongruous, the duo stood behind the opposing team's bench. They glanced around, men on a mission. They weren't guarding anyone; they were hunting someone.

As he watched, he got the distinct impression that their stares had come to rest on him. Like dogs spotting a squirrel.

The burly one nudged the bearded one. They set off toward the end of the field. When they rounded the corner flag heading toward his side, Méndez felt a stab of concern. They walked purposefully, robotically, arms wide, their eyes on him.

It occurred to him that they might be detectives or federal agents. Perhaps the Americans wanted his help with an emergency. But he didn't know any cops in Southern California who wore suits and ties on Saturday morning. Unless they were attending a funeral.

When the men passed behind the goal, it became clear to him that they were not American. The bigger one seemed Mexican, judging by the helmet of hair, the mix of fat and muscle, the dutiful gait.

The other one looked stern and agile. His beard was black and close-cropped, his head jutted forward, and his shoulders spread the suit. Méndez had seen him before, perhaps in an intelligence report or a mug shot. The realization caused an icy sensation in his stomach.

*Not bodyguards. Not cops. Not Americans. What does that leave? Hit men.*

Méndez owned a pistol. The DEA and DHS had helped him get the permit. Federal agents and the San Diego Police updated him regularly on threat information. For months, their assessment had been consistent: no sign of danger as long as he stayed out of Mexico. His pistol was locked in his glove compartment. He hadn't thought he'd needed it to watch the game, for the love of God.

Athos, his former deputy at the Diogenes Group, had taught him about firearms. He could see Athos shaking his head. *A gun is only as effective as the man who carries it, Licenciado. You have to be ready to use it.*

The duo gathered speed. Their stares stayed on him.

He told himself it was crazy to think that his enemies would kill him in broad daylight north of the border in front of witnesses. Then he told himself: *No, this is exactly how they would do it.* The more brazen, the better. It all seemed part of a macabre choreography: the setting, the undertaker suits, the presence of his son. As he had written in more articles than he cared to remember, Mexican assassins paid attention to detail.

Instead of walking around the flag, the men cut diagonally

across the corner of the field. This double infraction—spectators weren't supposed to change sidelines or enter the field—raised the ire of a soccer mom.

"They're walking on the pitch," she declared somewhere on his left. "They're walking on the pitch!"

Her scolding nasal voice startled him into action. Spectators and players were in the line of fire. He needed to move.

Méndez strode toward the corner the men had passed but veered to his right, away from them. His heart hammered. There were bushes and trees near the parking lot. He could reach cover among the cars and retrieve the gun.

*A doomed and pathetic plan,* he thought.

The main thing was to draw them away from the others. From Juan. He cursed himself for wearing glasses rather than his contact lenses. If he had to fight or run, the glasses might fall off. A sleepy decision in front of the bathroom mirror had worsened his meager chances of survival.

The men changed course to intercept him. The burly one undid a button, his right hand reaching over his belly into his suit jacket.

Méndez stopped and locked eyes with the man. Too far to attack, too close to escape.

The moment had arrived. The fact that he had imagined it so many times did not make it easier.

*Here I am, miserable cowardly sons of whores. Do your worst. Fuck your mothers. See you in hell.*

It was a good thing he didn't say it out loud. The burly man produced a business card from an inside pocket. With a deferential grimace, he extended his arm as he closed the final distance between them.

"Licenciado Méndez!" he said in a rumbling Mexico City accent. "Licenciado Méndez, forgive me, please."

Méndez stood very still. His reaction intensified the man's

discomfort. Despite his girth, he seemed boyish up close. Sweat seeped from his sideburns and glistened on the folds of his neck around the tie knot.

"The secretary — forgive me, the ambassador — would like to speak with you," the man stammered, sausagelike fingers still proffering the card. "Very urgent."

The bearded one stood with his hands crossed over his belt buckle. His brow was dry. His gaze did not waver.

*This one always looks at people as if he's about to kill them,* Méndez thought.

He placed the face. Mexico City. Gálvez, Galindo, something like that. A federal police commander who had been fired for torturing suspects then recycled into the intelligence service as a chief of internal security. His reputation for brutality and honesty had appealed to his boss, who had once been Méndez's boss — and who was the last person Méndez had expected to drop by for a visit.

Méndez exhaled. His legs trembled. Relief and embarrassment flooded through him. His first instinct had been correct: bodyguards. His mind had run away from him. The incident had unleashed all the paranoia, all the demons, lurking beneath the surface of his placid new life.

*Nadie muere en la víspera,* he told himself. No one dies before his time.

He glared at the business card, at the men. Finally, he reached out and took the card. He studied the words, then turned it over and examined the back, as if the blank white rectangle contained a hidden message. After a long moment, he looked up.

"As far as I know, he is no longer a secretary nor an ambassador," he growled. "He can wait. The game is not over."

Méndez sat in a suite in a pink Colonial-style hotel that had crowned a cliff in La Jolla for a century.

Sunlight bathed the pastel interior. The picture windows offered a view of the ocean beyond palm trees, a row of slender sentinels. Through the screen door of the balcony, he heard the waves on the rocks and the bark of a sea lion. Suites at the hotel cost a thousand dollars a day. Méndez wondered who was picking up the tab. Mexico's ruling political party, perhaps, or a company that studded its board with names from the power elite. His host had retired from government service, but Méndez would always think of him by the title he had held while commanding a chunk of the Mexican national security apparatus: the Secretary.

Méndez had done his best to make the Secretary cool his heels. He had watched the rest of the game, then told the Secretary's bodyguards that he had to take his son home. While the bodyguards waited outside his house in their Escalade, Méndez had showered, put in his contact lenses, and exchanged his blue LAPD T-shirt for a button-down with red and white stripes. He had gone to the kitchen and, forcing himself to keep a leisurely pace, made himself a cup of coffee. Leafing through the newspaper as he drank, he noted that there were no developments in the investigation of the massacre of African migrants in Tecate. Even by the standards of a nation awash in cadavers and cruelty, it was a heinous crime. After covering the breaking story for U.S. and Mexican newspapers, Méndez's reporters had run into a wall of silence and moved on to other things.

Méndez had little appetite for an encounter with the Secretary. The veteran national security bureaucrat had been his best source before becoming his boss. He had been the political mind and muscle behind the Diogenes Group, unleashing Méndez on an anti-corruption crusade and placing him at the helm of a handpicked unit. The experiment had ended in betrayal. They hadn't talked since.

Sitting now with a cup of tea at the glass-topped table, the Secretary projected an air of beatific patience. A breeze from the balcony ruffled strands of hair on his domelike skull. He had always reminded Méndez of a priest. Today, he looked like a hunched and aging cardinal.

*Cardinal Richelieu. Without the whiskers or women, but with the intrigue and ruthlessness.*

The Secretary still maintained the formality that he had always imposed on himself and his entourage, even on weekends. His gray slacks, silver tie, and blue blazer looked like purchases from Bond Street in London, one of his favorite spots for shopping. He had no doubt indulged himself there during his recent ambassadorship to a small European country—the anticlimactic final chapter of an eventful career.

"Life in the embassy was quiet, pleasant, dull; a perfect environment for writing, if I had been inspired," the Secretary said. "By the way, I must say you look well. Grayer, but healthier."

Méndez nodded. Another by-product of exile: he was sleeping, eating, and exercising more than he had since his university days. He was still thin, but he had developed strength and endurance. He sipped orange juice, stealing a glance at the unmarked manila envelope on the table. The old scoundrel had staged the reunion with his usual wiles. The swoop into town. The summons from the bodyguards. The detail intended to hook any self-respecting cop or reporter: documents.

"You have returned to your original métier," the Secretary said. "I often read your column in the Mexican press. I understand you publish in English as well. A quixotic website venture?"

"It is an investigative news site. Bilingual. In partnership with Mexican and American media."

"A tiny operation, I imagine. How do you earn a living?"

"Donors. Grants. Foundations. Some freelance fees."

"A very American concept. Even agitators need benevolent moguls."

The Secretary looked toward the entrance of the suite, the sun glinting off his glasses. He produced a cigarette, eyes rolling, enacting a caricature of furtiveness, and struck a match.

"I assume you won't denounce me to the cigarette police," he said. "Do you know the anecdote about Franco and smoking?"

Méndez waited. The Secretary blew smoke at the balcony. He said, "The *generalísimo* held a cabinet meeting. A minister next to him lit a cigarette. Franco looked around and asked, very innocently, very gently, 'Oh, do they permit smoking in here?'"

Méndez smiled. The Secretary continued, "It was at that moment the Spanish minister realized his career had peaked."

The Secretary crossed a bony ankle over a bony knee.

"Leo," he said. "I know it's not every day we chat. It was urgent for us to talk face to face. Let me start with a question. How informed are you about the current status of the Ruiz Caballero organization?"

Méndez took a breath. It was the topic he had expected and dreaded.

"Obviously, I live in San Diego due to the fact that remnants of the Ruiz Caballero mafia want to do me harm, though they are fragmented and weak. I am kept up-to-date by friends and sources. I know Junior has appealed his court convictions, which seems fruitless. I know that his uncle, despite his unsavory past, has gained control of the Senate."

"A reconfiguration of alliances. You have heard no other rumblings?"

Méndez scowled. The pomposity was starting to get on his nerves. "I'm not sure what you mean."

The Secretary inhaled smoke. "What I tell you now is off the record, of course. A political, economic and criminal operation is under way that will benefit Junior and his uncle. It might liberate Junior."

"Impossible."

The bloodless lips tightened. "Impossible, you say."

"It would be a political disaster. Junior was arrested and prosecuted with the participation and support of the U.S. government."

"In the history of Mexico, the U.S. government has pursued a number of our political figures for serious crimes. Some of them walk the streets and enjoy their riches today. They run for high office."

"A leading newspaper in the United States published articles about the investigation. It got great attention."

"Yet Senator Ruiz Caballero dominates the legislature. I'm afraid that journalists have an inflated view of their power. In the end, you are voices shouting outside the palace walls. You are scribblers on the margins of history. You—"

"I get it," Méndez snapped. "I still don't see Mexicans or Americans letting a notorious and savage drug lord walk out of prison."

"What can they do? Interfere in our national sovereignty? Seek extradition? They made a strategic choice to return him to us and aid our prosecution rather than charge him themselves."

"You really think this could happen?"

"Yes."

Méndez ran a hand down his face. He was thinking about contingencies. About exile. About his family. He had an impulse to call Estela but he shook it off, chiding himself.

*Put it in context. Consider the source. He's pumping up his importance.*

The Secretary reached for the envelope.

"I think you will find this instructive," he said.

The Secretary put a flourish into handing over the document. His manner said, *I am the repository of knowledge and, therefore, power. I have made the magnanimous decision to share a little piece of that power with you.*

Méndez had the feeling the man missed this kind of thing.

The report bore the logo, seals, and other authentic markings of a Mexican intelligence agency. It read like an executive summary, nine pages divided into three sections.

The first section assessed Junior Ruiz Caballero's mafia. The organization had begun to recover from years of disarray, becoming "a lean, mobile, well-armed force that taxes, extorts and robs criminal industries, especially smugglers of drugs and migrants."

The second section analyzed the political machine of Senator Bernardino Ruiz Caballero, Junior's uncle, and his faction of the ruling party, a mix of gnarled bosses and young hardliners.

The third part was the most surprising. A U.S. firm called the Blake Acquisitions Group was in talks to absorb a Mexican conglomerate. Fortunes were at stake. The founder of the U.S. company, Walter Blake, was an old friend of Senator Ruiz Caballero. Blake and his son Perry, who oversaw the corporation day to day, had clout. Although there was opposition to the merger in Washington and Mexico City, Senator Ruiz Caballero had assured fellow leaders of his party that the Blakes could seal the deal with his able assistance. Everyone would get paid handsomely.

The report discussed the roots of the alliance between the Ruiz Caballeros and the American executives. The Blakes had opened doors for the senator in the United States years ago. The senator had steered money into banks in the U.S. Southwest that were connected to the Blake Group. Law enforcement had detected money laundering, but investigations had produced few results beyond a couple of low-level indictments.

The report cited the pending U.S.-Mexican merger as a reason to look into recent shady dealings. Mexican intelligence had begun a discreet inquiry with U.S. agencies. But the document concluded, "It is unlikely there will be meaningful results. Contacts in the United States inform us that the latest federal investigations of the Blake Acquisitions Group have run into aggressive political interference."

Méndez looked up at the Secretary. "If an analyst had written this for me, I would have told him it lacks specifics."

"Unfortunately, Leo, analysts no longer write for me. The administration has not seen fit to give me an opportunity to serve the fatherland. I am a dinosaur to the reformers, a reformer to the dinosaurs. I am relegated to a role I abhor: elder statesman."

The Secretary sighed theatrically. He said, "I can add a fresh item. Something transpired recently that has caused concern among the Blakes and their Mexican allies. Something in the United States. A leak, a whistle-blower, an internal problem. It is unclear."

Méndez put the folder on the table.

"Interesting," he said. "But I must ask: Why am I here?"

"Well." The Secretary's brow furrowed. "There are grave implications for your safety and the safety of others, myself included. These people do not forgive and forget."

"Did you come all the way to San Diego just to tell me this?"

"I felt it was my duty to warn you."

"I don't mean to sound ungrateful, but you seem to have forgotten how badly things ended between us."

"I never forget anything."

Méndez showed his teeth in a smile that was not a smile. His wife called it his Tijuana-wolf look. "You just told me the Ruiz Caballeros are impervious to the, eh, impotent scribblers of the press."

"Correct."

"So?"

The cold little eyes gleamed behind the glasses.

"This battle can only be won north of the border. The American angle is different, powerful. If someone investigated the Blake Group, their dirty history, their links to Mexico, their roots in money laundering, that could have a real impact. On Wall Street, in Washington, and, of course, in Mexico City. The story would have repercussions. Perhaps enough to scuttle this transaction and keep Junior where he belongs."

"Frankly, I don't accept the scenario with Junior. His uncle doesn't want that kind of heat. I think Junior will remain in prison regardless."

*In fact,* he almost added, *I think it's a red herring. I think you've exaggerated the likelihood of his release and the whole Ruiz Caballero angle to manipulate me into looking into this for other reasons related to politics and finance. Supreme conniver that you are.*

"It is still an exceptional story," the Secretary said, unruffled. "Do you know much about the Blake Group?"

"Not much."

"I am sure they will appeal to your crusading instincts. I read that column you wrote about how, when it comes to white-collar crime, there is more impunity here than in Latin America."

*If you want to stroke a journalist, quote his work,* Méndez thought.

"I didn't say there was more impunity. I wrote that I have

spent my career investigating gangsters, politicians, corrupt cops. When I see what has happened in the United States since 2008, the inability to punish those responsible for the economic collapse, I wonder if I pursued the wrong criminals all these years."

"An excellent premise for a hard-hitting exposé on the Blake Acquisitions Group."

"My website covers border issues. I have a handful of collaborators. I don't have the resources to take on a multinational corporation."

"Your reports appear in important media. You just won an award from Columbia University. You have contacts, credibility. People in U.S. law enforcement trust you. I can't think of anyone else, American or Mexican, who is better suited."

Méndez finished his juice, watching a seagull circle above the palm trees. The old schemer had access to current information. Despite his lament about being in limbo, he was probably acting as an emissary for a political faction.

"You would have to join forces with American media," the Secretary said. "If I am not mistaken, your English is weak. And a collaboration would heighten the impact. You turn the usual narrative upside down. A Mexican journalist exposes a U.S. corporation in cahoots with the narco-politicians of Mexico. At last, the truth some of us have known for so long."

Méndez raised his eyebrows. The man was pitching him a story.

"Let's pretend for a moment that the proposal is realistic," Méndez said. "The fact remains, I have moved on. I spend time with my family. I write my column. I direct projects. Reporters do the street work. I am safe, tranquil. Why the devil would I want to involve myself in a kamikaze crusade?"

The Secretary smiled victoriously.

"Two reasons," he said. "First, you are spectacularly bored. You are not content in this antiseptic pseudo-paradise. These Americans—"

"Don't presume I share your resentments and biases. This country has given me refuge. I am profoundly grateful."

"Nonetheless, you need a true challenge. You miss the past, you miss the Diogenes Group, you miss the violent emotions of police work."

It took a moment for Méndez to subdue his impulse to get up and leave. The reason for his indignation was simple: the Secretary was right. No sense in denying it, at least not to himself.

In a low, dry voice, Méndez asked, "And the second reason?"

"You have just been informed that our enemies are going to attain even more power. That will put them in a better position to do what they have always wanted to do: fuck you."

The words startled Méndez. The Secretary had an aversion to obscene language. Yet he had deigned to use a classic profanity: *chingar.*

The Secretary crushed out his cigarette.

"And you are not the kind of fool who will sit around waiting for that to happen," he said. "You know you have to fuck them first."

# Chapter 3

The last time they had seen each other, Leo Méndez had given Pescatore a handsome edition of *The Three Musketeers*.

During the phone call Sunday, Pescatore told Méndez he had liked the book, the swashbuckling and swordplay. He had a new appreciation for the nicknames of the former deputy chiefs of the Diogenes Group.

"You called him Athos because he's so serious, right?"

"Exactly," Méndez said. "As for Porthos, have you ever met a Mexican who looks more like a Porthos?"

"He'll do, that's for sure. Speaking of which..."

Pescatore said he had a job proposal for Athos and Porthos. Méndez gave him their phone numbers and promised to tell them Pescatore would be in touch. The situation reminded Méndez of *Twenty Years After*, the sequel to *The Three Musketeers*.

"D'Artagnan recruits his old friends for a new adventure," Méndez said. "They are retired in the countryside, but they are bored, so they join up."

"If I'm D'Artagnan, who are you?"

"Aramis. When he was a soldier, he dreamed of being a priest. When he became a priest, he missed being a soldier."

"I hope I'll have time to see you in San Diego."

"Unfortunately, *mi querido* Valentine, I don't think I will be here. I am planning a trip to the East Coast. It has come up, eh, rather suddenly."

In a way, Pescatore was relieved. Isabel had given him strict orders to avoid discussing the case with Méndez.

Pescatore spent Monday getting ready. He talked to his boss in Buenos Aires by Skype. Facundo congratulated him on landing their first DC contract.

On Tuesday, Pescatore flew to San Diego. He rented a car and drove to a Coco's diner off the freeway near the Mexican border.

Athos and Porthos waited at a corner table. There were big hugs all around. The three of them had seen action together years back. After an uneasy start, the adventures had ended in friendship.

The conversation was in Spanish. Athos, whose real name was Ramón Rojas, wore a baseball cap over his balding pate. His goatee had grayed. He had retired after four decades of police service. He divided his time between "your house" in Tijuana (a courtesy meaning Pescatore was always welcome) and the U.S. suburb of Chula Vista, where he had an immigrant son who worked as an engineer. Athos explained, "It's like George Bush *padre* once said: I'm in the grandfather business."

Porthos, aka Abelardo Tapia, was as affable and cheerful as Athos was laconic and somber. After the Diogenes Group, Porthos had landed a plum job as director of the security force at a factory in Tijuana.

"It's honest money, more or less," Porthos said, lifting a jumbo hamburger. "My wife doesn't miss trying to raise four kids on a police salary. She says it was a vow of poverty."

Porthos sported gold chains, fancy-toed cowboy boots, and

a collarless leather jacket. In his early forties, he had a broad face and a thick neck and looked as strong and well fed as ever.

Pescatore described the assignment and pay. He said it was a confidential mission. He didn't mention Méndez. He knew they wouldn't tell their former chief about the case unless he asked. And Méndez wouldn't ask. Although he had gone back to journalism, he was a man of honor.

"Any questions? If you guys need time to think about it, check your schedules, we could talk again tomorrow."

They looked at him blankly.

"Shouldn't we get started?" Porthos asked.

"What about your job?"

"They owe me weeks of vacation."

"So you're on board? Just like that?"

Porthos clapped him on the back.

"Valentine, it's all set," he said. "Licenciado Méndez said you need help. Sounds like it involves travel, visiting half-ugly places. We can't let you do that all by yourself. We are at your orders."

Pescatore smiled. If Méndez asked a favor, these two treated it like a command.

He told them he had a lead on a survivor of the massacre in Tecate, a Salvadoran or Honduran known only as Chiclet. A street-level service provider, Chiclet operated drop houses where smuggling crews stashed illegal immigrants. The overnight clerk at the motel had recognized him from past stays with groups of migrants. On the afternoon of the murders, Chiclet had rented two rooms under an alias that turned out to be the name of a dead Honduran migrant. Late that night, he had returned to the front desk, rented a third room, and bought a bottle of liquor from the clerk. Chiclet had not been among the corpses found in the first two rooms. The third room had been empty except for the half-finished bottle.

That was the intelligence Isabel's Homeland Security agents had been able to gather despite Mexican interference.

"He might've escaped," Pescatore said. "Or he might've been a traitor working for the killers."

"You have only a nickname?" Porthos wrote notes on a legal pad. His mug of Coke burbled as he slurped with a straw.

"Yes."

"This massacre..." Porthos said. "A strange affair. That's the talk in the cantinas where the cops go. Usually, as barbaric as these things are, the motive makes sense. To the criminals, at least. Who was killed, when, where, how. Who gains, who loses. It all has meaning. Like a language."

"And this one?"

"This one seems like pure killing for the sake of killing."

A few minutes later, Pescatore watched the two men climb into Porthos's fully loaded GMC Sierra pickup truck. He had no doubt they would take care of business. Porthos had been a star homicide investigator before joining the Diogenes Group. Athos was more of a weapons and tactics man, but he had sources too, and an elephantine memory for names, cases, and faces.

Pescatore had booked a room in a corner hotel on India Street in Little Italy. He wanted to roam the city, visit Border Patrol stations, pick up scuttlebutt. Isabel had instructed him to stay low profile, however. He spent most of the first day in the Italian café on the ground floor of the hotel, where he set up his laptop by a window and reviewed the case file. He drank espresso, ate lunch, drank espresso. He watched the tourists, office workers, downtown hipsters, valet parkers— and a few actual old-school Italian-Americans who looked like they had mixed feelings about gentrification. He went for a run on the waterfront. San Diego was where he had first joined law enforcement, first killed a man, first fallen in love.

During his years living with Isabel, it had started to feel like home.

Wednesday dragged on without word from Athos and Porthos. Idleness got him thinking about Fatima Belhaj. Distracted by the assignment, he had resisted the urge to call her. She hadn't called him either. Five days now.

After a failed attempt at a nap, he called her cell phone. Her recorded voice was throaty, confident, with the slightest percussive hint of her Moroccan origins: *"Je me trouve dans la impossibilité de vous repondre…"*

He remembered kidding her about that message. *"I find myself in the impossibility of responding." What kinda highfalutin nonsense is that? How about "I can't answer the phone right now"?*

He didn't leave a message. Angry with himself, he redialed. The recording again. It was evening in Paris. Maybe she was working. Maybe she was with Karim. Drinks, dinner, a stroll. Back to his place. Or hers…

The bottle of wine Pescatore drank with dinner did not make him sleepy. Sometime after midnight, he couldn't sit still any longer. He retrieved his rental car, an Impala as usual. A Tijuana radio station played "La Flaca," a moody cut teaming Carlos Santana and Juanes, the Colombian singer. Pescatore cranked the volume. He sped through the amphitheater of the city beneath the stars. The elevated freeway curled south past the Coronado Bay Bridge, a ribbon of lights shimmering on the water. He had a vague plan to drive to the border and cruise through his old patrol area. After a few minutes, he realized he was near the scene of the murder-kidnapping. Surely Isabel wouldn't mind if he took a look.

He pointed the car at the exit ramp. The convenience store appeared, an island of light in a semi-industrial area. He pulled into the space where the van had been parked during the shooting he had watched on the video at Isabel's office.

Green and red neon glowed on his windshield. The uniformed clerk, a heavyset Latina, was intermittently visible behind the counter.

The radio played banda music, wailing horns and rat-a-tat drums. He imagined the last moments of the driver of the van. Maybe he had been grooving to a song. Then, *bam-bam.* Two in the head. Lights out. End of story.

His phone beeped. A missed call from Fatima. He cursed. It was nine hours later in Paris. She had probably called before work. To his relief, she answered when he called back.

"Valentín." She used the Spanish pronunciation. Café noise in the background.

He asked how she was doing.

"I am at Les Deux Palais," she said quietly.

The century-old brasserie on the Île de la Cité was across the street from the stone sprawl of the Palace of Justice and near Paris police headquarters, which explained the "two palaces" in the name. Pescatore and Fatima had once drunk champagne at Les Deux Palais while she narrated the revolving-door menagerie: cops, prosecutors, lawyers, judges, bureaucrats, defendants, reporters, and other big shots and dirtbags.

"Where are you?" she asked.

"On the road, working a case."

"Very late."

He closed his eyes, concentrating. She was the chief of a counterterrorism squad. She probably had a court hearing or a meeting at the Palace of Justice.

"It's not a good time," he said. "But we need to have a conversation."

"When you like."

He frowned at his red and green reflection in the windshield.

"I gotta say, I'm kinda disappointed you didn't call."

"You didn't either."

"Yeah, but I'm not the one who dropped a bomb. I'm not the one who got all complicated. I'm the one waiting for your decision."

"Wait." To someone else: *"Deux secondes."*

The echo of voices and china gave way to street sounds, a passing two-tone siren.

"We will talk later," she said calmly. "But do not have expectations."

"What does that mean?"

"You want a decision." She said it almost like a question.

"Yeah. As far as us. If you choose him or me."

She made an exasperated clicking noise. "I have said it already. I find this impossible. It is not like choosing between, eh, two sofas."

"Well, you can't…"

Motion in his side mirror distracted him. A vehicle had entered the lot, almost hidden in his blind spot, about twenty feet behind him. The same position as the killers' vehicle before the murder. He saw it was a green and white Chevrolet Tahoe with roof lights. The Border Patrol.

"Goddamn it…"

"Valentín?"

"Fatima. Sorry, I'm in the middle of an operation. Something just happened. I gotta go."

"Oh." She sounded surprised. A pause. *"Au revoir,* then."

He hung up. His train of thought sped toward disaster. He saw himself through the eyes of a Border Patrol agent: *Male Latino, early thirties, reasonably hard-ass-looking. Talking on the phone in a parked car at one a.m. at a known smuggling location. And the scene of a recent 187. What've we got here? Possible alien smuggler, drug runner, stickup man, auto thief. Watch him. Run his plate, call for backup.*

Pescatore kept his eyes on the mirror. The Tahoe didn't

move. Minutes later, another Border Patrol Tahoe nosed to a stop next to the first one.

Ordinarily, he would have enjoyed talking to brother PAs. The problem was that he had become a minor celebrity in the San Diego sector after the Ruiz Caballero investigation. Agents knew he had been engaged to Isabel, and that he had become a private investigator. Word would spread that he had been skulking around the scene of the rip-crew murder. That was the kind of trail Isabel didn't want to leave. It could end up burning her secret inquiry. He cursed himself for not staying in his hotel room where he belonged.

Vehicle exhaust mixed with mist. While he watched in his mirrors, Pescatore held the phone to his ear as if still having a conversation. The PAs might decide to question him and search his car. But this wasn't a checkpoint or a port of entry; mere suspicion wouldn't do. If the agents didn't articulate a good reason, he could refuse to cooperate. He could go "California asshole," as agents called it, on them. Curse, complain, threaten to sue. *¡Pinche migra, discriminación basta ya!*

Most PAs wouldn't back down, though. The agents would call in a supervisor or request assistance from local police. Or haul his uppity ass out of the car and throw him on the hood.

He considered going into the store and buying something. His fingers closed around the door handle. He hesitated.

Another minute passed. He figured they weren't sure what to do. They were waiting for him to make a move.

He placed the phone in his jacket pocket. He put the car in reverse. He backed up. Slowly. Smoothly. He shifted, turned left, and rolled past the Patrol vehicles toward the exit of the parking lot. He braced for lights, sirens, amplified voices.

Nothing happened. He kept the radio off. He respected the speed limit all the way back to the hotel.

He fell asleep at dawn. An hour later, Porthos called.

Twenty-four hours and two thousand miles after that, the hunt had moved to southernmost Mexico. A Chevrolet Trailblazer rolled down a jungle road in the state of Chiapas.

"Sure you know where you're going, Comandante?" Porthos asked.

Athos allowed himself a grin behind the wheel. "I have done raids in this region, Comandante. Fugitive apprehensions. When you were in diapers."

"You're old, but not that old," Porthos said.

"You wore diapers until you were fifteen, no?"

Pescatore turned up the air conditioner. Like the others, he wore a lightweight vest. The shoulder holster under it contained a Glock that the Mexicans had handed him on arrival.

Athos and Porthos had identified Chiclet thanks to contacts in the Baja police's homicide unit and the smuggling underworld. Pescatore stared at the mug shot of the fugitive: Héctor Talavera, twenty-seven, a Honduran with a decade-long record of arrests related to smuggling. First at the Guatemalan border, then in northern Mexico. His girlfriend in Tecate had told police that after the massacre, Chiclet had come home to grab clothes and money. He had said he was going to Honduras. Athos and Porthos believed a more likely destination was the state of Chiapas, where he had lived in the past. Wherever he was, whether he was a survivor or an accomplice, the Mexican authorities were not looking for him.

The Trailblazer approached a bridge over the Suchiate River between Ciudad Hidalgo, Mexico, and Tecún Umán, Guatemala. No walls, fences, or fortifications. The border bridge disgorged Mexico-bound buses, cars, scooters, bicycles, and pedestrians in a stream of energy and color, rust and sweat. In the background, a swan fluttered up off the bridge. A shimmering apparition in the sun, the white bird flew low over piles of garbage, riverbank huts, and vending stands, over the waters dotted with rafts ferrying people and contraband in both directions. Athos turned left, cruising northeast along the international boundary demarcated by the river.

*The new front line,* Pescatore thought. Because of the drop in Mexican immigration and the rise in Central Americans, most U.S.-bound migrants crossed this border first. The humidity, vegetation, and tumbledown architecture made the place seem sleepy, but the smuggling industry flourished at high noon. Pescatore watched the riverine advance of a raft assembled from truck tires. It carried a family and luggage. A smuggler swam alongside in his underpants, steering the vessel. Further on, a cable stretched from the roof of a three-story Guatemalan building to a tree on the Mexican riverbank. Men clustered on the rooftop. When they stepped aside, a woman whizzed into view seated in a ski-lift-type contraption attached to the cable. The aerial chair slid down the zip line slanting across the river and landed by the tree. A man in a baseball cap and sunglasses helped the passenger dismount. He hurried her into the brush.

"I thought I'd seen every trick in the book," Pescatore said.

"Air Chiapas," Porthos said.

Rather than blocking the border, the Mexican police concentrated on strategic choke points, intercepting illegal crossers in and around the freight yards. The police pulled Central Americans off the trains in droves and deported them—an enforcement campaign encouraged and assisted by Washington.

The Trailblazer rolled through congested streets. Pescatore and his companions visited an old address for Chiclet. Then they met with sources—an immigration official, a bartender in a dank club where squat women in shorts sat along a wall. No results. But Athos and Porthos had high hopes for their meeting that evening with Padre Bartolomeo, an Italian priest who ran a refuge for migrants in nearby Tapachula.

The drive into the compound took them uphill past banana trees, dormitories, a dining hall, a pink chapel. Two South Asian women in saris walked close together in the dusk. African kids chased a soccer ball. Latin American youths clustered at a picnic table. Some sat facing outward, like inmates in a prison yard.

Padre Bartolomeo greeted his visitors in Italian-accented Spanish. He served them glasses of chilled grappa from his home region in the mountains near Venice. He had met Athos and Porthos during a visit to the Diogenes Group in Tijuana, where his religious order operated a shelter for northbound migrants as well as deportees from the United States.

"Do you remember we took you on a ride-along, Padre?" Porthos asked.

"How can I forget? You made an arrest while I was there, a corrupt federal officer who was extorting migrants. Exhilarating. Leo Méndez created a police experiment full of hope and grace, a mystique of service and idealism. To the Diogenes Group!"

Padre Bartolomeo downed his drink. He shook his gray cropped head with gusto, his prophet's beard bobbing. The four of them were sitting on a patio behind a one-story structure housing the priest's office and living quarters. Pescatore glimpsed a cell-like enclosure with a hammock. Birds warbled in a palm tree above the table. Pescatore was tired. The night was steamy. He was drinking mainly from thirst. The grappa had a kick to it.

The priest reached across the table—the rock-knuckled hand of a bricklayer—and refilled Pescatore's glass.

"*Salute, giovanotto.* Are you of Italian origin?"

"Italo-Argentine."

"Like His Holiness Papa Francesco."

"Mexican-American too."

"Better to drink it all at once. It burns less that way."

Pescatore glanced blearily at Porthos, who beamed as he downed his shot. Athos had turned his baseball cap backward like a catcher or a sniper. The Mexicans were comfortable with the interview becoming a drinking session. And they were being deferential. Porthos called the priest "Father" every time he addressed him. Pescatore, however, made a point of omitting the title. He repeated the question he had asked moments earlier.

"Yes, my son, I have been thinking about it." Padre Bartolomeo's eyes widened as if he were going into a rapture. "I think there are some Talaveras who operate to the north. Honduran smugglers in San Cristobal and Palenque. My staff will ask among the migrants. We must be prudent. Anything resembling the police frightens our guests. They live in fear. They breathe, eat, drink fear. It smothers them, it crushes them, like the heat."

Pescatore had seen the priest on Spanish-language television in his Franciscan-style robes, the thick hands waving, accusing, imploring, as he thundered about the plight of immigrants, the dangers of La Bestia (the trains known collectively as the Beast), and abuses by mafias and security forces. Porthos had said earlier, "It's a wonder no one has put a bullet in *el padre*."

"All that fear, all that tribulation," the priest continued, lighting a cigarette. "Yet the migrants, especially the Central Americans, have such faith. A deep, pure, profound faith. An absolute intensity of faith that I, for example, do not have. A wondrous—"

"So you think we should go to the smuggling corridor at Palenque?" Pescatore wasn't in the mood for a sermon.

"I do." Padre Bartolomeo squinted through smoke. "First of all, Chiclet may well be related to the Honduran Talaveras. Also, there is a large police presence here in the southwest corner of the border. Military and intelligence activity. Pressure—media, political, diplomatic—to crack down on people riding La Bestia. Palenque is a better place to hide, especially from the repercussions of a case as notorious as the killings in Tecate. *Salute!*"

Pescatore returned the toast and polished off his grappa, blank-faced. They had not said why they were looking for Chiclet. He wiped his brow.

"What makes you think we're working that particular matter?"

"*Allora.*" The green eyes turned roguish. "A process of deduction. I ask myself: What would such high-caliber investigators be looking into? Two veterans of the Diogenes Group and an American pursuing a minor smuggler from Baja California, the scene of a recent massacre—close enough to the U.S. border to perhaps interest the American government."

"The father gathers a lot of information in this place," Porthos said. "When he did us the honor of visiting us in Tijuana, I told him he had the instincts of a first-class intelligence analyst."

The priest shrugged, raised his glass, and sent another shot of atomic Venetian grappa down the hatch. He was average size, but sturdy. He sure could hold his liquor. Pescatore drained his glass, eyelids heavy. In a flash of disturbing clarity, he recalled the photos of the crime scene in Tecate.

"Without confirming or denying," he said slowly, the words thick on his tongue, "I can tell you the facts of that case are nasty."

"I don't doubt it, my son. And yet it is one small chapter in a litany of cases. An epic saga of horror. The cartels have built an economy based on exploitation, brutality, barbarity of every imaginable variety. They inculcate it in the youth gangs they use to expand their empire. A business model."

The priest started telling stories. He puffed rhythmically on the cigarette. Pain shone in his eyes, as if he were seeing the cruelties he described, reliving them. He talked about torture and murder. He explained the term *body card:* migrant women pressured into paying their way with sexual favors, like a credit card. He described how gangsters had killed a migrant and forced his companions to eat pieces of his flesh.

The priest's work had filled him with the suffering of others, Pescatore realized. Padre Bartolomeo felt a duty to express the agony, chronicle the atrocities, bear witness. Pescatore listened. He drank. His head spun.

Then the priest recounted the deaths of a Guatemalan mother and her baby at the hands of human traffickers in Tamaulipas. And it was too much.

"Oh God," Pescatore exclaimed. He shook his head, jaw clenched, wanting to banish the image that had just been burned into his brain forever. "Oh God, a little baby? That's the worst thing I ever heard in my life!"

He slumped. Athos's head hung low. Porthos wiped away a tear.

*We are all very drunk,* Pescatore thought. *A bona fide* borrachera.

He turned to Athos and demanded, "Isn't that the worst fucking thing you ever heard?"

The web of wrinkles around the ex-cop's eyes made him look old and mournful.

"One of the worst," Athos said. "One of the worst."

Pescatore contemplated the idea that Athos lived with the knowledge of something even more atrocious. The priest patted Pescatore on the wrist. Pescatore withdrew his arm.

"You see," Pescatore said. "You see, that's why I don't go to church. Because of shit like what you just told us."

Padre Bartolomeo's eyes were sad now, and attentive.

"Is that the reason you don't go to church, Valentine?"

"Well, since you ask, it's more than that. Tell you the truth, I'm disgusted with the clergy. Priests in general. I have been for a long time."

Porthos was trying to get his attention. Pescatore plowed on, hearing himself as if from a distance.

"I know you do good work in this place, and my colleagues here admire you and everything. But I think ninety percent of priests are tainted. Child molesters or corrupt or both. Or they protect the ones who are child molesters or corrupt or both. A giant ongoing criminal conspiracy. A mafia. I expect smugglers to be animals. Like narcos, politicians, businessmen. But priests are supposed to help people. Like cops."

Eyebrows raised, mouth open, Porthos stared in consternation. He said, "Valentine, one moment. There are bad people in all professions. You—"

The priest waved his cigarette, smoke swirling. "Please, Comandante, don't worry. I admire this young man's candor."

The green eyes had locked in on Pescatore, who looked down and ran a hand through his curls.

"When I was a kid in Chicago, I went to church every Sunday," he said. "I read the Bible stories in these little picture books—the prodigal son, Jonah and the whale. I liked the images, the rituals. I was gonna be an altar boy. It was a mixed parish, Italian and Mexican. They brought in this new priest, Father Rogelio. Young, slick, smooth talker. From Mexico City. A total predator."

Porthos rose, planting his hands to push himself up off the table. He muttered something about finding the facilities and lumbered away.

The priest nodded at Pescatore to continue.

"Father Rogelio never did anything to me and my friends," Pescatore said. "No, he was too crafty. He went after new kids, from immigrant families. It went on for a while, rumors and stories. Sure enough, the police caught him at his place with a twelve-year-old. But they didn't press charges. The archdiocese transferred him out to some monastery in the desert in California. The Antelope Valley."

"Outrageous," Padre Bartolomeo said.

Pescatore toyed with his glass. "When Father Rogelio said hello—on the street, at Mass—he'd take your arm. He'd ask if you'd been good. That snotty *chilango* accent: '¿*Has sido buenooh?*' I didn't become an altar boy. I stopped going to church."

"Do you miss it?"

The question surprised him. "I guess I do. In the States, you know, we move around a lot. Families separate. Neighborhoods change. It would be nice to have something to hang on to. I still wear this cross around my neck. But I stay away from church."

"Listen, my son," the priest said. "If His Holiness Papa Francesco in his infinite wisdom were to put me in charge of *internal affairs*"—he said it in English—"I would be a twenty-first-century Torquemada. Heads would roll. Monsignors, bishops, cardinals. Arrests, punishment, prison. Dante's Inferno!"

"*Infernal* affairs." Pescatore chuckled.

"*Assolutamente sì.*"

"You got some cop in you, you know that? Here's to you: Detective Torquemada."

They clinked glasses. Porthos returned and sat down.

Athos raised his head. His red-streaked eyes focused.

"*Mi querido padre,*" he said. "I would like to ask a great favor."

"Of course."

"I would like to ask you to give your blessing to us. And to our mission."

"It will be an honor."

Athos and Porthos stood up. They bowed their heads and crossed their hands over their belt buckles. As Pescatore rose, the world reeled. He concentrated on keeping his balance.

He didn't know why all that stuff had come pouring out of him. The liquor, of course. The tension. The facts of the case. And something about Padre Bartolomeo that invited trust, that almost made him want to believe.

The priest's hand traced shapes over Pescatore's head. The voice was a soothing rumble.

Pescatore said, "Thank you...Father."

# Chapter 4

Estela called the staff of the website "Leo's garage band." The Méndez family barely fit in the one-story house, so he had converted the garage into a work space. Computer stations, filing cabinets, bookshelves. A photo of Méndez, Athos, Porthos, and the Diogenes Group occupied a place of honor among journalism prizes and framed articles. There were posters of Carlos Santana in concert, Al Pacino as Serpico, and the Sinaloan reporter Javier Valdez Cárdenas, slain by cowards in Culiacán, smiling beneath his trademark straw hat.

This was the "newsroom" of the website known as Line of Investigation (Línea de Investigación). On Wednesday night, Méndez sat at his computer enduring a lesson from Santiago, a twenty-eight-year-old with a ponytail and a scraggly beard.

"You see, Don Leobardo?" Santiago leaned over his shoulder to tap the keyboard. "Now the file is encrypted. Just don't forget the password."

"Bless you," Méndez said. "What's on the pen drive?"

"Your material," Santiago said, referring to the secret document from the Secretary. "And everything we found on the Blake Group: articles, public records, court files, interview notes."

"Good. Before I forget, on a separate matter, anything new on the massacre of the African migrants?"

"I'm afraid not, Don Leobardo. A few days ago, I button-holed my best source in Tecate, a *comanche* in the municipal police. He got all nervous. He told me, 'Listen, *cabrón,* that case is too hot to handle. The American *federales* were sniffing around, and nobody talked to them either.'"

"The Americans?"

"That's what he said."

"Interesting. Well, don't worry about it. One story at a time."

Méndez could imagine Santiago cornering the police commander. The mellow manner and bohemian-cholo wardrobe masked a fearless reporter. Luz, Santiago's bespectacled girlfriend, was the website's other reporter, a dynamo who wrote and talked at high speed. Luz sat at a computer with Karen, Méndez's assistant and the staff photographer. A blonde from Santa Barbara, Karen had served in the Peace Corps in Peru. She had abandoned her graduate studies at the University of California after convincing Méndez to hire her as his Sancho Panza for this venture into the new frontier of journalism.

In addition to doing investigative projects, the team occasionally covered breaking stories for news outlets, which—along with Méndez's syndicated column—helped pay the bills. His family was never far. Renata sat on a tricycle by the door to the kitchen, wearing pajamas. Juan stopped in to ask about new soccer cleats. When Estela returned from the university where she taught Latin American studies, she maneuvered through the fray distributing coffee and cookies.

By the time the work was done, goodbyes said, and children in bed, it was eleven. Méndez had to leave for the airport at dawn. He sat behind his desk with a Coronita. Estela sipped a glass of red wine across from him. The Pacific rumbled faintly in the distance. On the computer, Maná played a rock cover of "Somos Más Americanos" (We are More American), the immigrant anthem by Los Tigres del Norte.

"*Ay, mi amor,*" Méndez said, reclining in the high-backed rolling chair. "All this effort, and frankly now I'm wondering if the trip will be worth it."

"We already had this conversation," Estela said.

"I know. But it won't be easy. And I'm feeling lazy."

"Lazy? You?" Estela pushed a tangle of black hair behind her ear. She had put on weight since Renata's birth and her face had gotten rounder. At forty-five, she retained a sweet, good-humored energy, a counterpoint to his tendency to brood.

"It has been a great summer. Calm, predictable. Regular meals, exercise, soccer games, the playground. Even"—he raised his eyebrows—"the occasional amorous interlude."

"Beast." She scowled. "I used to complain that your work separated us. Now I've got you prowling around the house behind me all the time."

"As Robert De Niro said in a movie, isn't that the final irony of life."

She crossed her strong brown legs in the summer dress and waved a mocking goodbye at him.

"*Ándale,* go to Washington. Take advantage of this opportunity. But come back soon. And talk to your son."

"Why?"

Her smile faded. "Juan has been asking about the visit from the Secretary's bodyguards."

"He has?"

"It made an impression on him, Leo. He said you seemed very sad and very angry."

Méndez sipped beer. "Well, I was. Also frightened."

"He asked me yesterday if he should learn to shoot a gun."

She lowered her voice. "So he can defend the family when you are away."

"For the love of God. My brave boy. I will talk to him."

"I assured him this trip will be totally safe."

"The only danger, if it is fruitless, will be to my pride."

The next afternoon, he checked into a hotel on L Street where the FBI had lodged him once when he gave a lecture on police reform in Latin America.

The contrast between capitals never failed to impress him. Mexico City was a monster metropolis, a swarming, roaring, squalid labyrinth. But he understood it. He knew how to maneuver in it. The urban grid of Washington was clean, orderly, startlingly quiet. The stately gleaming facades hid a different kind of labyrinth, the vast apparatus of American power. This wasn't his turf. He needed guides.

Daniels had suggested the basement bar of a 1920s-era hotel near the White House. Méndez descended into a grotto of chandeliers, mahogany, and red velvet. He slid into a corner beneath a framed caricature of a jowly senator from the Nixon years. Méndez liked the sense of place and history, a respite from the generic spaces that filled the U.S. landscape. The bar was half empty. Television news had reported on the president's vacation, the official peak of the summer doldrums.

A text message buzzed on his phone—an apology from Daniels for running late. No problem. Méndez's return to journalism had reminded him that some reporting skills were simple. One was to keep your mouth shut and listen. Another was to be patient.

Daniels had been the highest-ranking American official Méndez knew. As a federal prosecutor, he had worked with Méndez and Isabel Puente on the Ruiz Caballero case. More recently, after the assassination plot that had forced the

Méndez family to flee Tijuana, he had won Méndez's gratitude. Daniels had made sure that federal agencies provided them with everything from security to green cards. Now he was a partner at a powerhouse law firm. Isabel Puente predicted that he would end up in politics—if he got bored making money. Although Méndez hadn't communicated with him for months, Daniels had replied quickly to the e-mail and had agreed to meet without asking the reason.

Méndez reviewed the notes he had jotted down on the plane. After the Secretary's visit, he and his team had done research and telephone reporting. He was convinced that the Mexican intelligence document was genuine. But he needed confirmation at a high level in Washington. It was time for Line of Investigation to make its mark north of the border.

"We'll have to confiscate that notebook, Mr. Méndez," a jovial voice said. "In your hands, it qualifies as a lethal weapon."

Daniels had made this affectionate corny joke in the past, but he had the flair to pull it off. Méndez laughed. They exchanged hugs and Mexican-style double backslaps. They talked about travel, family, weather. Drinks arrived— Absolut for Daniels, a Coronita for Méndez.

"Mr. Daniels, let me say again how happy I am to see you," he said. "The private sector treats you well."

The lawyer's sleek looks reminded Méndez of Duke Ellington, though Daniels was in better shape and lacked the mustache. He wore a tapered pin-striped suit, dapper rather than flashy. His close-cut curls were sprinkled with gray.

"A true pleasure to see you, Mr. Méndez." He pronounced it "Mend*ez*." "But please, call me Sylvester."

"Then call me Leo." Embarrassed about his accent, Méndez hoped the beer would loosen his linguistic inhibitions. "I appreciate that you make me the favor now that I am again a journalist."

71

"When I see your byline—you all are writing good stuff, by the way—I remember that case. It was special."

"I must thank you once more, Sylvester, for protecting my family."

Daniels gestured gallantly with his glass. "Do you ever wish you were still a cop?"

Méndez smiled. "It was a masquerade."

"You were damn good at it."

"You are generous. I miss the Diogenes Group, the solidarity. Perhaps I miss the, eh"—he remembered the Secretary's phrase—"violent emotions. Also, it is more easy to investigate when you have a pistol and a badge."

"No doubt."

"Do you miss the Department of Justice, Sylvester?"

"Not the measly paychecks. Or the bureaucracy. Now, do I prefer locking up bad guys to defending them? Affirmative." Daniels stole a glance at his watch. "So what brings you to town, my brother? I'm glad you caught me. I'm only back from Cape Cod to help my daughter pack for Swarthmore."

"A possible story. With some connection to our old enemies." Méndez gave a simplified summary, omitting the Secretary and the intelligence report. Daniels signaled the waiter for another round.

"I would like to know this history of narco-money and the Blake Acquisitions Group," Méndez said. "To understand the Blake family, their relations to the senator and others in Mexico. And the accusations that the Blakes have political protection now."

Daniels paused while the waiter set down drinks. He used the waiter's departure to glance at the tables around them.

"A high-value target, Leo. As long as I can remember, the Blakes have been a white whale."

For Méndez, speaking English was like reading in a cave by

candlelight. Sometimes the candle flickered. He first thought it was a racial allusion, then realized it was a literary one.

"Collectively, for the federal government, you understand," Daniels continued. "I avoid obsessions. They cloud one's judgment. Yet and still, I've devoted my share of time to the Blakes. Heavyweight players. Too dirty to ignore, too big to fall."

"Is it true Blake Senior met the senator in Mexico buying racehorses?"

"That sounds right. They also have a shared taste for vintage cars."

Méndez asked about the past investigations of the Blakes.

"Variations on a theme," Daniels said. "A U.S. attorney gets a phone call from main Justice. His boss is fired up. He says, 'Okay, about that Blake case—those suckers are going down. Man the torpedoes, full speed ahead.' The prosecutor is stoked. He puts his team to work. Weeks go by; the boss calls from DC again. All wimpy, like he just got a first-class ass-whipping. 'Forget it. Stand down. Leave them be.' Last time, the boss on the phone was yours truly."

Méndez laughed. His instincts had been good. Bingo with the first source. Daniels knew the topic. He had authority and credibility. Méndez wondered if he had kept files.

"The allegations are true? They laundered money for Mexican narcos?"

"Well, that depends how you define *true*." Daniels's brow furrowed. "Leo, I've never spoken about this to the media. We're on deep background here. I'm only talking to you because, well, you're my *hermano*."

"*Muchas gracias.*"

"As you know, banks paid fines. Employees were prosecuted."

"But minor figures. The Blakes, father and son, were not touched."

"As I recall, the investigating agents felt the Blakes had

approved this systematic enterprise. The intel indicated the senator steered associates to the U.S. banks. Mexican drug proceeds, dirty political money. East European, Middle Eastern mafias. All looking to wash cash."

"What happened?"

"Lack of proof, smart lawyers, political muscle. Witnesses and suspects disappeared, reversed themselves. One or two got popped. In Mexico."

"The Blakes ordered murders?"

"Whoa." Daniels leaned back. "I didn't say that. Never saw evidence of it. I doubt they gave explicit orders."

"I see."

"We couldn't prove an overarching conspiracy. Assistant U.S. attorneys and supervisory agents ran into career problems. The fines were a mosquito bite for the Blakes, a footnote. People stopped talking about it. The group diversified into finance, real estate, hotels, you name it. Staggering wealth, my friend. Stratospheric."

"And the federal government considered other charges? Evasion of taxes, insider trading, selling bad financial instruments?"

"Yep. The Blake Group always played it close to the line. But so do a lot of companies. These complex financial cases are difficult to prove up. There's a fear juries won't convict, and we look like we're persecuting success, sticking it to Wall Street. Of course, it was hard to convict John Gotti too, back when I was a rookie AUSA. But we didn't wimp out on that one."

"Perhaps the Italian Mafia does not have so many friends."

"Perhaps."

Méndez thought about the intelligence report in his briefcase. He started to ask about it in a roundabout way, but when he said "new investigation," Daniels raised a hand to cut him off.

"Before you go any further, Leo. So far we've been discussing matters from my tenure at Justice. Historic, adjudicated, public-record cases. Regarding current events, I can't help you."

"Why?"

"The influence of the Blake Group touches many people and entities in this city. Case in point—colleagues at my firm represent them. A big client."

Méndez tried to hide his alarm.

Daniels sighed. "Do you know the joke about lawyers and rats?"

"No."

"Turns out scientists have decided to use lawyers instead of rats in lab experiments. For three reasons. Number one, there are more lawyers than rats. Number two, there's no fear that lab assistants will develop sympathy for the lawyers. And number three, there are certain things rats will...not...do."

They both chuckled. Méndez thought fast. Would Daniels talk to him again? Had Méndez inadvertently tipped off his targets?

Daniels continued, "One thing I will not do is provide services to dirtballs like the Blakes. Yet and still, since they're clients of my firm, it's inappropriate for me to discuss. See what I mean?"

"Of course."

Méndez hadn't asked his reporters to check if Daniels's law firm worked for the Blake Group. The possibility hadn't occurred to him—an embarrassing sign of his naïveté about the machinery of Washington.

Daniels glanced at his watch again. He typed a text message on his phone.

*Now comes an excuse to leave,* Méndez thought.

He was wrong. The lawyer leaned forward. The debonair face filled with concern.

"Leo, you are the last person I need to lecture about risks. You've gone toe to toe with giants. You've faced danger with remarkable courage. What I'm trying to tell you is, if you pursue this story, please watch yourself."

The sun spread violet hues on the Potomac River. The taxi cruised south past bikers and joggers, picnics and sailboats. Méndez admired the low skyline across the water, spotting the rectangular bulk of the Kennedy Center, the cupola of the Jefferson Memorial, the apex of the Washington Monument. Unlike New York or Los Angeles, with their legions of European and Asian visitors, Washington was full of American tourists. He could see why. Although time and wisdom had extinguished his anti-Americanism, he remained cynical about patriotic clichés. Yet he found the vista inspiring. If it had that impact on him, for Americans it was a physical celebration of their dream. And a way to forget the damage done to that dream.

Méndez took stock. The golden source was awkwardly close to the enemy camp. However, Daniels had confirmed key points. The story had become real, human, tangible. Méndez was fairly confident that Daniels would not divulge anything to his colleagues at the law firm. His distaste had seemed genuine. His warning had sounded heartfelt. And familiar. Countless times, Méndez had been urged to back off stories and investigations by friends, enemies or ambiguous intermediaries. It was an uneasy exercise with a vocabulary all its own.

*You are stepping into hazardous terrain, Licenciado. You are messing with heavyweight people.* Peces gordos, gente pesada, tipos chingones. *Fat cats, heavyweights, tough guys. Delicate*

76

*interests are involved. Go slow.* Aguas. Cuídese. *Watch yourself, Méndez.* No le pise la cola al león. *Don't step on the lion's tail.* Te vamos a cortar los huevos. *We are going to cut your balls off.*

It had not stopped him in Mexico. He would be a poor excuse for a reporter if he let it stop him in the land of the free and the home of the brave.

The taxi left him on a tree-shaded street near the genteel bustle and red-brick sidewalks of Old Town Alexandria. Isabel Puente lived in a three-story unit in a row of attached town houses.

Always the workaholic, she had just arrived home from the office. She opened the front door wearing a blue pin-striped pantsuit and sunglasses propped in her thick black hair.

"Leo!"

They embraced. He hadn't seen Isabel Puente in more than a year. When he was chief of the Diogenes Group, they talked or met several times a week. Seeing her now drove home how much he missed her, missed working with her, missed that life of nonstop action. Overcoming a moment of emotion, he kept his manner amiable and relaxed. He handed her the bottle of Albariño wine he had brought as a present.

"Isabel, what a pleasure to see you again. What a lovely home."

"Thank you. You should have brought your wife and kids, I don't know what to do with all of this room."

She installed him in an armchair with a glass of wine, then put on a disc of Gloria Estefan singing standards in Spanish and English. Before setting the table, she took off her jacket and removed her holstered gun from her waistband. She was not the type to stop carrying a gun because she worked at headquarters. Méndez had never seen her without it.

"I hope you don't mind takeout Thai food," she called from the kitchen.

"Not at all." He was grateful to speak Spanish again. "I hate to impose."

On a table holding framed photos was a picture of a young Valentine Pescatore in his Border Patrol uniform. Méndez wondered if her renewed friendship with Pescatore might lead to romance again. They both had hot tempers, and their breakup had been uncomfortable for friends in the cross fire.

During dinner, Méndez said, "I heard from Valentine the other day."

"You did?"

"Just briefly. I put him in touch with Athos and Porthos. He's doing an investigation for Facundo in Mexico."

"Mexico?" She refilled his water glass, eyes on him, tone mild.

"Yes. I don't know anything more. Do you see him much?"

"Not often. But he's doing well. Working hard. Studying too."

"An impressive young man. I don't mean to sound paternal."

"He brings out that quality in people."

The upturned white collar of Isabel's blouse highlighted her cinnamon-colored skin. When Méndez had first met Isabel, she had dazzled him. Working side by side with her, sharing risks and secrets and sorrows, he'd had moments when he felt attracted to her—and guilty about it. Now he was fifty, and she was in her mid-thirties. The dynamic had changed. He felt paternal toward her as well.

She asked about his website or, as she put it mischievously, "That left-wing media thing of yours."

He feigned indignation. "We are a model of Anglo-Saxon objectivity."

"What are you working on?"

"I had an unexpected visit from the Secretary."

He rarely revealed sources to anyone, but Isabel was an exception. In fact, he wanted her to know. Just in case.

"The Mexico City Machiavelli. How is he?"

"Perverse as ever. He brought me a gift."

He put the intelligence report on the table. She read it, toying with her hair, winding it tightly around her fingers. She flipped back a page and reread something. Finally, she looked up at him, feline and intent.

"You plan to write a story about this?"

"Possibly."

She enunciated in a legalistic tone. "Our ongoing arrangement is we talk on background, and you quote me as a 'senior law enforcement official' or a 'senior national security official.' Usually, that's fine."

"Not this time?"

"Consider this truly off the record. Way off the record."

"Isabel, my first desire is to protect you at all costs."

"If there were a leak investigation…"

The corridors of power had made Isabel more cautious, he thought. It was unlike her to worry about an internal investigation, much less admit it. He asked if the report was authentic and accurate.

"You've seen more Mexican government documents than I have. I don't doubt the authenticity. As for accuracy…parts of it are consistent with my understanding of events."

He grinned. "Which parts? What events?"

"Tell me your assessment, Leo."

"The Blake Acquisitions Group was involved in money laundering years ago, with the help of the senator. It was a decisive moment in the company's growth. They got away with it because your Justice Department did not pursue the case— a problem of political will."

He paused. Isabel nodded.

"And I believe today, because of activity related to this merger, there is a new effort to investigate the Blake Group and the senator. And new interference."

"I wouldn't push back on that," she said.

"The Secretary suggested this might involve a side deal with the Ruiz Caballeros. For the release of Junior from prison."

Isabel frowned. "And?"

"It's unlikely. I think he used Junior to whet my interest."

"I think you're right. The drug connection was important years ago, when the Blakes needed an infusion of cash. Allegedly. Nobody wants Junior back on the street, including the senator. This is a different kind of business. A different level."

"Is Senator Ruiz Caballero a target of a U.S. investigation?"

"Off the record?"

"Yes."

"He's a conspirator. A fixer. He'd get a big kickback. But he's not one of our top targets."

"What about Walter Blake? Or Perry Blake, the son? They must be top targets."

Her eyes hardened. "That's a logical conclusion. They've drawn a lot of investigative effort. But will it amount to anything? The answer depends on the issue you mentioned before. Political will."

"So the obstacles are really north of the border. This is more an American affair than a Mexican one."

"I suppose."

"The report is not clear about the new investigation. I am inclined to believe it concerns money laundering. But the way you are looking at me makes me think I should expand my analysis. Bribery, other forms of corruption?"

"I've always respected your analytical abilities."

Méndez refilled their water glasses.

"As you often remind me, I am a Latin American intellectual of a certain age and ideological provenance. When it comes to American magnates, I start from a premise that an inmate in the penitentiary of Tijuana once described to me as 'the Napoleon law': guilty until proven innocent."

"That kind of silly attitude has made Cuba and Venezuela models of democracy."

"The point is, I want to understand the Blakes."

"If you've seen pictures of Walt Blake, he is pretty much what he looks like: big, crude, and mean. Also smart enough to talk anyone into anything."

Méndez recalled the file photos of a bearlike figure with a bald head, a pointy white beard, and a look of barely restrained rage.

"One of my reporters interviewed a former manager at the Blake Group. He said Walter Blake looked happiest when he was calculating how many thousands of employees he could fire at companies he took over. He liked to sit with the consultants to make the lists. What about the son?"

"He has a better image. Media-savvy, good-looking. But don't forget, Perry Blake was the one directly involved in the dirty banks. The father had the connections, but the son oversaw the actual laundering. Allegedly."

Méndez and Isabel talked for another half hour. As he left the house, he said, "The more I hear, the more I like this story."

She kissed him on the cheek.

"Good luck finding a way to tell it."

The cabdriver who took him back to the District of Columbia was an aging African in a skullcap. He was listening to a talk show on National Public Radio. Méndez lolled his head back, almost asleep, the low cultured voices murmuring a blur of words.

What a day. He had learned a lot. But he didn't have much he could use. He didn't know whether to feel hopeful or defeated.

The cab sped through the moonless night. There were few streetlights. Trees and bushes deepened the darkness of the suburban highway.

He had forgotten about all the greenery in metropolitan Washington. The rolling parkland, the urban forests. Deer wandered in yards. Raccoons raided trash cans. Eagles hunted along rivers. The wilderness was never far.

# Chapter 5

Chiclet wanted a drink first. Tequila, if they had it. Or rum.

Pescatore told him this wasn't fucking happy hour on Avenida Revolución. They had already removed his handcuffs out of the goodness of their hearts. All he was going to get was water.

Chiclet gulped from the bottle. He patted his disheveled pompadour.

Pescatore sat in his chair with his elbows on his thighs, fingers intertwined. He had strapped on his shoulder holster over his black T-shirt to emphasize his change in status from undercover captor to chief interrogator.

Early that morning, Pescatore, Athos, and Porthos had returned to the Catholic shelter in Tapachula. With Padre Bartolomeo's help, they had talked to some Cuban migrants. The Cubans had heard of Chiclet. Their smugglers had instructed them to meet a contact with that alias in Palenque, but a police sweep had scattered them back into Guatemala. The Cubans had eventually entered Mexico via Tecún Umán instead.

It was Saturday night. The hunt for Chiclet in Palenque had produced results fast. Pescatore's hangover was a distant memory. He felt sharp and poised and in sync with his partners. Porthos stood on the prisoner's right, casting an ominous shadow. On the prisoner's left, Athos stepped back to film the interrogation with his phone. Chiclet's wallet and phones lay on the coffee table in front of Pescatore.

Pescatore started with basic questions. Chiclet explained that he had arrived weeks earlier by car from Tijuana and had taken charge of the smuggling ring in Delicias Hondureñas. His uncle had bought the diner at the southern border a year earlier with money Chiclet had sent from the northern border.

"I own it," he said with sullen pride. "I'm going to buy another one."

"Wonderful. You're so enterprising. Tell me about Tecate, *guey*."

Chiclet made the humming-moaning sound. He slouched, his thick legs akimbo. His jowls, wide neck, and weak chin created the impression that his head sprouted directly from his shoulders. His face looked even worse than it had in the dimness of the diner. A drunkard's face. His words slurred the way a drunkard's do, even when sober. He still had a Honduran accent, but over the years it had absorbed the slang and intonation of northwest Mexico.

"I don't know much," he muttered. "The business is spread out in cells. Drivers, gunmen, money collectors. All I do is run safe houses. I don't know where the foreigners go."

"Who were you working for?"

"A gang. El T's gang."

"What do they do exactly?"

"*Tumbes.*"

"Rip-offs?"

"They are *tumbadores.*"

*Central American slang,* Pescatore thought. "Meaning what?"

"They rob loads from smugglers. Drugs and immigrants. Hold the *pollos* for ransom."

"A rip crew." Pescatore said it in English. Chiclet nodded. Pescatore asked in Spanish: "Who's El T?"

"A mafioso. A *chingón*. A killing machine. He'll kill you as easy with his hands as a gun."

"What else?"

"Everyone's scared of him. Even the *federales*. He was in the military."

"The military? He's like a Zeta or something?"

"I don't know."

"Mexican or American?"

"I don't know."

"Where does he live?"

"I don't know."

"I'm getting tired of hearing you say that."

"He has cells in Tijuana, Tecate, Nogales."

"What about north of the Line?"

"Probably."

Chiclet didn't know what the *T* stood for. He described the gangster as tall and with a crew cut, late thirties, light-skinned. El T's gang terrorized smugglers, robbing them or demanding transit "taxes" and robbing them anyway. The rip crew used Chiclet to house kidnapped migrants and provide intelligence on smuggling rings, which he also worked for now and then.

"El T paid well," he said. "I gave quality information."

*You were in the backstabbing business,* Pescatore thought.

A week before the massacre, a guy in the rip crew had asked Chiclet if he knew about any African women coming through the smuggling pipeline.

"Specifically African women?" Pescatore asked.

"Yes." Looking befuddled, he mispronounced nationalities: "Eritreas, they said. And Ethiopias."

"Why?"

The noisy air conditioner in the threadbare presidential suite was doing a poor job, yet Chiclet hugged himself as if he were cold.

"I don't know," he said. "I didn't hear anything again until the day of the, uh, thing. El T called me."

"Was that normal, him calling you?"

"Not at all."

"Then what?"

"He wanted me to take care of a load. I didn't have a drop house available so fast. We decided on the motel. Two rooms for a couple of nights."

Chiclet claimed not to know that a corrupt U.S. border inspector had helped the migrants cross while tracking them for the rip crew. El T had called Chiclet several times. Chiclet was waiting at the motel in Tecate when the henchmen arrived about four thirty a.m. with a van load of women.

"How many?"

Chiclet hesitated. "Twelve."

Although Pescatore kept a poker face, his adrenaline flared. There had been only ten female corpses. To his surprise, though, he had found photos of twelve women on one of Chiclet's phones. The individual face shots had been taken in the motel room—Pescatore recognized the decor, the images of birds on a bedspread—before the murders. The women's faces, some encircled by hoodlike shawls, were terrified and exhausted. Their stares searched beyond the camera for a sign of hope or humanity.

"Twelve," Pescatore said. "You sure?"

Chiclet nodded.

Pescatore told him to go on.

The Honduran knew the kidnappers from previous jobs. They were Mexicans. Ramiro and El Nightowl were the gunslingers in cowboy hats and coats. Escuincle was a young flunky. Once the migrants were installed in the motel room, Ramiro and El Nightowl went into the adjacent room to rest. El T had given them orders to get some sleep because the job would last a few nights. Escuincle and Chiclet stood guard over the load.

El T phoned again. Another odd request: He ordered Chiclet to photograph each woman and send him the photos by text. Chiclet obeyed.

"What happened next?"

Chiclet cleared his throat messily. He gulped water. "Could I please get a real drink?"

"Hell no. What happened next?"

Chiclet had gone in search of liquor. The desk clerk sold him a bottle of tequila, and he rented a room in which to drink it. The room was across the courtyard from the others and one story higher, on the third floor.

"You left Escuincle in charge of the migrants by himself?"

"He had a sawed-off shotgun." His lip curled disdainfully. "They were women. Scared shitless. He could handle it."

"Why the new room?"

"I was tired. I thought I'd sleep. Or watch TV."

*He's lying,* Pescatore thought. *But I'm not sure why.*

"Then what?"

At about five thirty a.m., Chiclet heard noise, gunfire, horrific screams. The angle from his window didn't allow him to see much. He spotted a body in a cowboy hat, probably El Nightowl, sprawled in a doorway, and gunmen storming down the second-floor walkway outside the rooms.

"I didn't waste time," he said, his voice lifeless, his chin resting on his chest. "The window in the bathroom opened onto a roof. I went through the window. I ran and kept running."

Pescatore rose. He picked up a phone from the table and showed photos to the prisoner.

"Are those the women?"

"Yes." Chiclet slouched down even farther, arms folded.

"Sit up! There were only ten bodies, *guey*. Explain that."

"I don't know. Two must've got away."

"How? They overpowered a hit squad?"

"I wouldn't know what to tell you."

*No sabría decirle.* What you say when anything you say could be dangerous. Pescatore flipped to the two faces he had not seen in the crime-scene photos.

"Are these the missing ones? Are they still alive?"

Fear bulged in Chiclet's eyes. "Could be."

Pescatore examined the faces again; they were the prettiest of the group. He looked at Porthos. The Mexican's frown was eloquent. He was wondering what was taking Pescatore so long to figure things out.

"Oh, you lying piece of shit," Pescatore snarled. "Fuck your mother. I know why you rented the room. You had yourself a little party, didn't you? A threesome. That's what animals like you do. Am I right, you repugnant despicable son of a bitch?"

Chiclet cowered, shaking his head. Pescatore stood over him. On his right, Athos moved closer to keep filming. Pescatore contemplated methods of inflicting pain: breaking fingers, stomping organs, cracking an arm over his knee. As if watching through the lens of Athos's phone, he imagined handheld video footage of himself beating Chiclet to a pulp. The temptation was tangible.

Pescatore shouted, "You raped them, didn't you?"

Chiclet buried his face in his hands. Growling, Porthos grabbed his collar, wrenched him upright, and swatted him across the head. An open-handed blow, but it promised plenty more where that came from. Chiclet whimpered. He took a while to shake it off. Reluctantly, he looked up into Pescatore's eyes. The smuggler's stench was a physical force.

"It's not true," he wailed. "I mean, it's true I wanted to. But I didn't. It all happened too fast."

"I'm right on the edge with you. Tell me the truth, Chiclet. Before something bad happens."

Chiclet nodded repeatedly, wiping his eyes and nose.

"I was drunk. When I drink, I lose control."

He had slipped twenty dollars to Escuincle to keep him quiet, then taken the two women with him to the room.

"This one was Brazilian," he stammered, pointing at the photo. "*Mulata*. The only one who wasn't from Africa. She spoke Brazilian. The other one was from Eritrea."

Chiclet had ordered the women to drink with him. The shooting outside started minutes later, just when he was telling them to take off their clothes. He bolted out the bathroom window without looking back, forgetting his watch and money clip in his panic. He had no idea if his captives followed him, went out another way, or stayed in the room. But he was convinced they had escaped.

"What makes you so sure?"

Chiclet's sidelong look made him resemble a trapped animal. El T had phoned after the massacre. Furious, he demanded to know what had happened, who had attacked the motel. And where the two survivors were. Chiclet lied. He said he had left to buy himself a bottle, so he didn't know anything. El T wanted to meet right away. Instead, Chiclet fled town.

"You see, I didn't hurt the ladies. If you think about it, I saved them."

"Yeah, you're a real hero. We should give you a medal instead of a gigantic ass-kicking."

Pescatore sat down. He was breathing fast. His heart was pounding. He had to find the two survivors. He had to tell Isabel. He had to get to the bottom of this.

In a calm but menacing voice, he asked, "Do you know their names?"

"No."

"Did you see their passports?"

"No. The smugglers take their papers. If they get caught, it's harder to deport them."

"Do you remember details? What they said? A way to identify them?"

"The Eritrean seemed educated. She spoke some Spanish. English too. The Brazilian was from Rio de Janeiro. She begged me to let her call her family. I said I would later if…she behaved."

Pescatore gritted his teeth, restraining himself. He waited.

"She gave me a phone number in Rio," Chiclet said. "I put it in my phone. It should be in there."

Pescatore exchanged glances with Athos and Porthos. A lead.

"So why did this happen? Some hard-ass went to war with El T's crew?"

The Honduran looked at the floor, shaking his head. "No. He's *el mero mero*. Top dog. Too strong. No one would dare."

"Then who slaughtered thirteen people?"

Chiclet snuffled, tears spilling. He spoke in a hoarse, halting voice: "I've been thinking and thinking. I come back to the same thing: El T must have done it. To his own guys, his own load. Don't ask me why."

"What makes you think that?"

"All the weird things. Him calling so much. The photos. The timing. It felt like a setup."

*Sounds sincere,* Pescatore thought. But he kept up the pressure.

"Why would he organize a butchery like that? Take money out of his own pocket, cause himself grief? It doesn't make sense."

"I know." Chiclet slumped again. "And no matter why it happened, I'm dead meat."

Pescatore regarded him: a picture of abjection. Weak with the strong, strong with the weak. He sighed in disgust, then turned to Porthos.

"Cuff him up again and put him in the bedroom. We need to talk."

It was a real-life three-dimensional chess problem. Pescatore had to figure out how to hang on to his prisoner, how to keep him alive and, ultimately, what to do with him. Pescatore and his team conferred into the night and consulted by phone and encrypted messages with Isabel in Washington and Facundo in Buenos Aires.

Although Chiclet's captivity was essentially a kidnapping, it was also—as Pescatore explained over breakfast in the suite the next morning—the best thing that could have happened to him. Chiclet needed to cooperate with his captors, whom Pescatore described—truthfully, if omitting caveats—as a joint team of U.S. and Mexican investigators. The Honduran did not care as much about their affiliation as he did about the fact that they hadn't tortured or executed him yet. He perked up at Pescatore's use of the term *protected witness* and promised to be on his best behavior.

"No drinking, no bitching, no sneaky moves," Pescatore warned.

Chiclet slurped coffee, raising the cup with both hands. He had bathed and shaved. He looked relatively presentable in the morning light.

"Your confession could be your death sentence or save your life," Pescatore continued. "Depends how you play it, *guey*. You are going to help however you can. To save your ass. But you're gonna do it for another reason. You listening?"

Chiclet raised his head. He blinked but made eye contact. "Yes, Comandante Valentine."

Pescatore didn't know where the *comandante* came from. He let it go and pointed across the table.

"You've done evil, horrible shit. This is a chance to rise above yourself. Do something good for once. You promise to do that?"

"Yes, Comandante Valentine. I promise."

"*Orale.* You better not be saying that just because it's what I want to hear. Don't think we won't fuck you up."

The second problem, keeping the witness alive, required immediate action. After breakfast, they transported Chiclet to Tuxtla Gutiérrez, the state capital. The five-hour drive wound through remote spectacular country: jungles, mountains, waterfalls. They rode in silence, on alert for bandits, police, or soldiers.

That night, two trusted officers from Porthos's security force at the factory in Tijuana—hired urgently over the phone—flew in to Tuxtla Gutiérrez to reinforce the team at their new hotel.

The third problem: what to do with the witness. Pescatore had discussed scenarios with Isabel before his departure. On the phone, though, it became clear she hadn't decided the next step. The interim solution was that Athos, Porthos, and the two new men would drive Chiclet to Mexico City and guard him in a discreet apartment-hotel. Pescatore would fly to Miami to meet with Isabel, then continue to Rio de Janeiro to chase the Brazilian lead.

Waiting for a taxi in the hotel lobby Tuesday morning, Pescatore told Porthos and Athos, "I hope you don't have to babysit this lowlife too long. Keep him away from the booze."

"No problem," Porthos said. "He will be clean and sober and well behaved. Or else."

The taxi arrived. Pescatore fended off Porthos's attempt to carry his suitcase. He embraced his friends.

"Good work, muchacho," Athos said.

"We remain at your orders," Porthos said.

Speeding away without the musketeers, Pescatore felt alone and unsafe.

Miami always had a pleasant effect on Isabel Puente. Her voice got livelier. She smiled more. She relaxed.

Granted, this was a whirlwind visit. No family feasts in Hialeah or Coral Gables, no dance clubs or beach expeditions. But she was home. She looked radiant in a sleeveless blue top and white jeans. Pescatore watched from the kitchenette as she took a break from her conversation with him and, pacing back and forth, led a phone meeting with field offices about a mul-tistate drug takedown. Although she had a lot going on, his secret mission was important enough for her to zoom down from DC for the day to meet with him.

The high-rise one-bedroom apartment in Miami Beach had a view of Biscayne Bay. Isabel had inherited the place from a widowed aunt. She predicted she would retire there one day, alone, like her *tía* Lupe and all the other old ladies.

Isabel sat down next to him at the table. On the laptop, they watched the video of Chiclet's confession in Palenque.

"Okay, that's what he's like under stress," she said. "With preparation, how good a witness could he be?"

"Look, he's telling the truth. You can tell from the way it went down. He's cooperating in good faith. But he's an animal. No jury is gonna fall in love with him, if that's what you're asking."

She pushed her thumb against her teeth. "The priority is finding those two women. If they're still alive."

"It's hard to imagine them hiding out for weeks in Mexico."

"I want to put out a lookout for them somehow. The prob-lem is, we can't trust the cops and we don't want to tip off the bad guys…Here, have another cup."

He savored the sweet Cuban coffee. "Give me a couple days in Rio."

He showed her the evidence he'd retrieved from Chiclet. The phone numbers for the rip crew matched numbers called by Mario Covington, the missing U.S. border inspector.

"That's a direct connection right there," Pescatore said. "You've got your cross-border linkage between the Tecate and San Diego shootings."

"We know a lot about what happened now. But not why."

"Yep. Even if you believe Chiclet's theory that El T pulled some kind of bizarre hit on his own outfit."

Isabel swept back her hair. "You said you had a hunch about this El T?"

"Athos did. He's like a crime encyclopedia. The description reminds him of a suspect in some cartel killings a couple years ago. There was scuttlebutt about a hit man with a nickname like that. Former military. Not clear if Mexican or American, but a veteran."

"And?"

"I got to thinking. Chiclet pronounces it 'El T'—'the T' in English. Short for *tiger* or *toro* or something. But what if he heard it wrong? The guy's ex-military, a serious badass. The alias in English could be the initials *LT*—slang for *lieutenant*. In Spanish you'd pronounce that 'ele T,' which sounds almost the same. Or it could stand for 'El Teniente.' The Lieutenant."

"It's a thought," she said.

"Maybe you could get Chiclet with a sketch artist when he's in custody."

"We will. Nice work, Valentine."

Pescatore stirred the sugar granules at the bottom of his cup. Although her praise thrilled him, he was uneasy. When they lived together, they had visited this apartment during vacations. He had memories of the place. Vivid memories. His relationship with Isabel had swung between hot and cold, love and war. Their Miami trips had been on the hot side.

Rogue flashbacks harried him. Isabel walking in from the balcony, stunning in a black bikini, her slow smile making him a promise. Isabel's arms and legs wrapped around him in the shower, water pounding down on them, her back against the wall. The two of them getting spontaneous on the couch a few feet from where he sat now.

*Enough,* he thought. *Get it under control. When was the last time you thought about Fatima, much less called her? Of course, she hasn't called you either. Anyway, stop thinking nonsense about Isabel. No matter how close to her you feel. Or how good she looks right this minute.*

"Hey," Isabel said.

"Huh?"

"I lost you."

"Oh. Sorry. I was just thinking…about Athos and Porthos in Mexico."

"You trust them?"

"Absolutely. Those guys'd take a bullet for me. And I'd take one for them. I'm worried about how long they have to wait, how we resolve that."

"I'm working on it."

Isabel's plan was to engineer a handoff. Chiclet would "surrender" to federal agents at the U.S. embassy in Mexico City. Athos and Porthos would fade away, erasing the tracks of Pescatore's operation.

"The timing depends on what you find in Rio," Isabel said.

"You're gonna have to finesse some political dynamics on this, huh?"

"Oh yes."

"I gotta tell you, Isabel, this is kinda refreshing."

"What is?"

"We're in the middle of a wild caper. And for once, it's not my fault."

Her smile was conspiratorial. "You're right. It's all mine."

"I'm not complaining. So, how's Howard doing?"

"Hasselhoff?"

They laughed.

"I haven't seen him in a while," she said. "How's Fatima?"

"No news. I guess we agree to disagree."

Isabel went to the refrigerator to get two bottles of water. He was aware of her perfume, the sculpted outline of her bare shoulders, the tight white jeans. He was all worked up in a jumble of euphoria, fatigue, and desire. He realized what was going on. He and Isabel were falling back into their old roles, handler and agent. Except better—no wariness, no manipulation. She was in charge, but they were partners.

"Isabel," he said. "Remember what you told me? About your job, the pressure from up high? I've been thinking about that."

"Save your energy." She handed him a bottle of water. "That's a whole separate matter. At least no one's shooting at me."

"I don't want to get in your business but...can you tell me what's going on?"

She shrugged. "Look, it's sensitive. Basically, I'm part of a group of supervisors and prosecutors working a case against a corporation. The executives, anyway. The original investigation was connected to Senator Ruiz Caballero, believe it or not."

"That *tremendo hijo de puta*."

She grinned. It was an expression he had picked up from her. "That *tremendo hijo de puta*." She continued, "Back then, our American suspects slithered out of it. Now there are new leads, mostly related to the Foreign Corrupt Practices Act. But it's hard to develop solid evidence connecting them to bribery in Mexico. And we're getting pushback. The suspects have unlimited resources—lawyers, lobbyists, friends in Congress and the administration."

"Is it okay to tell me who they are? Your enemies are my enemies."

Arms folded, she studied him. Her expression was tender. Her big-eyed gaze lowered for a moment. He wondered if she was having the same memories, the same guilty stirrings, as he was.

"The Blake Acquisitions Group," she said. "Walt and Perry Blake. Have you heard of them?"

"No."

"Well, forget the Ruiz Caballero cartel. These guys take *hijo de puta* to a whole new level."

Hours later, he went to the Miami airport for his overnight flight. Entering the terminal, he thought about calling Fatima. But it was three a.m. in Paris. He'd wait until Rio.

His phone rang while he stood in line at the check-in counter. He fumbled for it. *Fatima can't sleep. Fatima's thinking about me. She wants to talk.* But it was a Mexican area code.

A jovial Italianate voice. *"Giovanotto."*

"Padre Bartolomeo. How you doing?"

The priest had heard news from Palenque. It regarded the abduction three days earlier of a Honduran smuggler known as Chiclet in a brazen raid on a diner. The three culprits were thought to be either police or gangsters.

"Interesting," Pescatore said. "Is that making some noise down there?"

"This morning, our sources in the community say a convoy of vehicles arrived. A group of armed men in civilian clothes. They spent time in the Pakal-Na neighborhood by the train yards asking about what happened to Chiclet. The description could once again correspond to the security forces or mafiosi."

"It's a fine line."

"The chief of the unit was an intimidating northerner. Possible military. A lieutenant, they said."

Pescatore took a step to the side. He cupped a hand over his mouth. "That was his rank? That was how he identified himself?"

"I am not sure."

"Did he have credentials?"

"My understanding is that he was described as a lieutenant."

"This is kinda important, Father. Could it be an alias? El Teniente?"

"I suppose so."

"Did he have an accent?"

"I do not have that level of detail, *caro.* I will inquire further, now that you have inspired me with the specificity of your questions."

"I'd appreciate that."

Pescatore hung up. He dialed Isabel. His hunt had flushed out new prey. And they were acting a lot like hunters.

# PART II

PART II

# Chapter 6

A s the Amtrak Acela rounded a bend and the towers of
Manhattan came into view, Méndez finished the article.
He had written and rewritten, honing and trimming and
tightening. In rhythm with the train, feeding off its energy, he
tapped slow emphatic strokes.

> Instead of demonizing the police, the Left in the United States
> should focus on the true structural problem: the impunity of the
> elite. Bankers, financiers and corporate executives get away
> with predatory, destructive and criminal behavior. It recalls
> Steinbeck's phrase about business in America: "a curious ritu-
> alized thievery."
>
> As the secret Mexican report we have obtained indicates,
> the Blake Acquisitions Group allegedly embodies this culture
> of lawlessness and impunity. Finally, investigators in the United
> States and Mexico are trying to do something about it. Let's
> hope the rule of law prevails. And that this is just the start. The
> time has come for "stop and frisk" on Wall Street.

Period. Graf. Send.
He reclined in the window seat. The morning light glinted

off approaching skyscrapers. He reread the piece. After Karen in San Diego translated it into English, both versions would be ready to post on the website and send to Mexican and American newspapers, magazines, and websites that published his regular column.

Méndez had been away from home for a week. His family was giving him grief. After seeing Isabel, he had visited editors in Washington, including friends with whom he had exchanged favors in the past. The editors had all rejected his proposal to collaborate on an investigative project. They were demoralized by budget cuts and didn't have the resources or the attention span. The subject matter crossed turf lines: foreign, business, national. The Blakes were influential and litigious. The editors insinuated that Méndez was not the ideal harpooner for this whale hunt. In their view, his past as a police chief blurred the line between journalist and protagonist.

In fact, Méndez realized that his law enforcement experience had changed him. Even as a reporter, he had felt instinctive solidarity with police officers—at least the honest cops, like Athos and Porthos. He shared their code of discretion, loyalty, and honor. His tour of newsrooms had reminded him that his appetite for the company of journalists—especially American ones—had diminished. In more ways than one, he was a man without a country.

During the cab ride from Penn Station, he called Fred Weinstein, a human rights lawyer in Los Angeles who was his website's pro bono adviser. Méndez had sent him a copy of the Spanish version of the column.

"Licenciado Fred," Méndez said. "How does it look?"

"Fine, *compañero,* but I need to see the English version."

"It is being translated. Come on, your Spanish is excellent."

"My Spanish is only good enough to get me into trouble. I

think you're fine. You added the *allegedly*s, fixed the problematic language. They'll squawk, but you're fine."

"Thank you for troubling yourself with this."

"Remember, if you give interviews, stick to the wording of the story. Careful with off-the-cuff comments. Cite the document."

Méndez had been driven partly by developments. Over the weekend, he had learned that the Blakes had scheduled a press event for Wednesday in New York to promote the Mexican merger. He had decided to pull the trigger using the ammunition he had. And he would attend the press conference to assess the results.

Mindful of his travel budget, he had asked Karen to find a bargain hotel. The place on Lexington Avenue in Midtown was musty, the carpets mangy, the wood chipped. It was nonetheless packed with Europeans. He remembered visiting New York for the first time in the 1980s, seeing drug dealers and chain snatchers prowl in daylight, the police all but hiding in their patrol cars. Today, it was as if someone had waved a wand over the metropolis. Tourists strolled at all hours, thronged Central Park, made excursions to Harlem. Unlike Latin American cities, the crime rate had plummeted in poor neighborhoods too. He wasn't sure if New Yorkers—especially the chattering classes—appreciated what the police had achieved.

The cramped, stuffy room overlooked a ledge full of bird droppings. Méndez turned up the air-conditioning, flopped onto the bed, and pulled the comforter over him. He needed a nap. He hadn't stopped working since Saturday, when he had called the Secretary from Washington to inform him of his new plan. The Secretary took it in stride. He agreed to be quoted as an unnamed former national security official. He offered trenchant comments about the irony of Mexican intelligence sounding the alarm about the misdeeds of a

U.S. corporation. Méndez had reached out again to Isabel, who relented and told him he could write that a senior U.S. official had confirmed the accuracy of the Mexican document. At the Justice Department, a spokesman gave him a tight-lipped "We neither confirm nor deny."

The resulting column was artfully constructed and rather brief. Its weight rested on his credibility, Isabel's confirmation, and a key line in the document: "Contacts in the United States inform us that the latest federal investigations of the Blake Acquisitions Group have run into aggressive political interference."

On Tuesday afternoon, he had called and e-mailed the Blake Acquisitions Group asking for comment. No response.

Drifting off, he thought, *You're about to find out who we are,* cabrones…

The ringtone of his cell phone—"Corazón Espinado" by Santana and Maná—woke him. Karen sounded excited and apprehensive.

"A lot of reaction, Leo," she said. "Everybody's picking up the story or writing about it. AP, Bloomberg, Notimex."

With effort, he sat up. He had slept deeply.

"Anything from the Blake Group?"

"Not yet."

"The governments?"

"That's why I'm calling. Senator Ruiz Caballero in Mexico City just said the story is 'absolutely false.' He says the intelligence report doesn't exist."

He experienced a twinge of unease. Could the Secretary have fed him a bogus document? He shook it off. Isabel's word was rock-solid.

"I'm not surprised," he said. "Are you?"

"No. But we are getting calls from Mexico questioning the story."

"Fine. Post the intelligence report."

"All of it?"

"Yes."

Refreshed, showered and changed, Méndez arrived at the hotel near Columbus Circle at four p.m. His reflection approached in the glass of the hotel entrance: a thin graying fifty-year-old with a lined face. His black shirt under the tan sports jacket was the last clean one in his suitcase. Méndez straightened, self-conscious about his habit of coiling forward as he walked. He felt calm. He had been in situations like this before, though never on foreign soil. And it was strange to see himself alone on the street. In Tijuana, he had almost never ventured outside without a driver, bodyguards, Athos and Porthos, his family. He was still getting used to operating solo. American-style.

The hotel was a glass tower wrapped in a steel skeleton, a chilled and scented haven. The ballroom on the mezzanine was filling up. High windows showed the treetops of Central Park. Tables for investors and shareholders surrounded rows of chairs for the press. A giant screen stood by a stage. A voice called out to him in Spanish.

"Do my eyes deceive me? Hey, Daniel, what are you doing in the lions' den?"

Fulgencio Ayala darted into his path and clapped a hand over his mouth in consternation.

"A pleasure to see you, maestro." Méndez's tone was dry, but he felt relieved to run into someone who spoke Spanish, even Ayala.

"Likewise, Licenciado, likewise. You are looking wonderful. Though I am not sure how long that will last. What have you done, Leo? *Híjole.* You are a marvelous and delirious madman. Oh, the emotion, the excitement. My heart's all aflutter."

As always, Ayala was breathless and jocular. As always, the

rotund, bowlegged newsman looked natty, encased in a maroon double-breasted suit. Ayala was the New York correspondent for a Spanish-language television network. He had spent his career shuttling between jobs in newsrooms and in the press offices of Mexican companies and government agencies.

Ayala took Méndez by the arm and walked him away from the stage. Glancing around conspiratorially, Ayala congratulated him.

"You are the man of the hour," he said. "You have put your rinky-dink nonprofit scam on the map. And the best way to culminate this glorious moment is to give me an exclusive interview."

Having known Ayala since they were rookie reporters in Tijuana, Méndez knew he couldn't trust him. Yet he made Méndez laugh. He was a ball of energy. There was a kind of purity to his cynicism, his inability to take anyone or anything seriously.

Méndez suggested they find seats.

"Yes, yes, good idea, the vultures are circling." Ayala wheeled, still gripping Méndez by the arm, and hurried him to the front. Méndez sat in an aisle seat. Ayala made a production of sliding his ample butt to the right, leaving an empty chair between them.

"In case they start shooting at you." He chortled. "Sorry. I know you are a fearless *pistolero*. But me, I am a poor wretch with three ex-wives and five children to support."

Five executives took seats at a table onstage, Perry Blake in the middle. Walter Blake was not present. Ayala whispered side-of-the-mouth commentary about the likely price and designer of Blake's suit, the combined net worth of the Americans and Mexicans at the table. Méndez recognized one of the Mexicans—comb-over, withering stare, mega-mustache—as a crony of the Ruiz Caballeros: Jorge Monroy, the founder of

Monroy Enterprises, where Ayala had once worked as a press adviser. Despite his antics, Ayala was plugged in on this story.

"Who's the American *guarura* with the shaved head?" Méndez asked.

"His name is Krystak. Chief of security for the Blakes."

The bodyguard hovered behind the executives. His eyes swept the room.

"They must feed him meat."

"With a shovel. He's a North American mastodon, look at him."

A willowy blonde in a green dress put a binder in front of Blake; he took her arm and whispered to her, her hair cascading close to his face. When she walked to a lectern to check the microphones, his gaze followed her.

Ayala clutched his chest as if going into cardiac arrest.

"*Híjole, híjole,* now that's a first-class assistant. Like a young Sharon Stone. I bet she gives him plenty of…assistance. And there's a reason I say that word in English."

"Shame on you, Fulgencio. You've got a daughter her age."

"You're right. I'm a beast. I don't know how I live with myself."

Méndez glanced at him. Ayala stared penitently at the floor. After a moment, he made sidelong eye contact. A grin filled his baggy face.

Lights dimmed. Music began. The logo of the Blake Acquisitions Group—an image resembling the offspring of a supernova and the starship *Enterprise*—appeared on the screen. A video described the Blake Group and the Mexican conglomerate and their combined holdings: banks, hotels, railroads, real estate, insurance companies. Charts and statistics attested to the might of the firms and the colossal benefits their deal would bestow on investors, shareholders, Mexico, the United States, and the human race. The screen spewed words: *dynamic, visionary, diversified, high-impact, growth-friendly, profit-intensive, forward-leaning.*

Méndez studied Perry Blake, whose face flickered in the light of the screen. Blake was in his forties and had a strapping, long-limbed physique. His upswept hair stood off his head like a rooster's crest—a boyish touch. Méndez went through his mental file. Blake had attended a Big Ten university and played tennis, lacrosse, and golf. He had belonged to a fraternity. He had shown fierce drive in academics, athletics, and whatever else he put his mind to. He was known for wearing out his employees with round-the-clock work binges. When the lights went on, Méndez saw impatience in the face and body language. Not a man who liked to sit and listen. Méndez recalled the photos and video of Blake's father, his shambling frame and profane tirades. The father and son were said to have a close but difficult relationship.

A spokesman named Ross took the lectern. He was silver-haired and pigeon-chested and came off like an anchorman who didn't know or care that the antiquated style of locution he favored had spawned a satirical genre. Swiveling, squaring his shoulders, and raising his hands high, he led the audience in a round of applause for the presentation.

*I hadn't realized it was possible to clap pompously,* Méndez thought.

Ross opened the floor to the reporters. The blond assistant walked the aisle with a microphone. A reporter asked for comment on the article by Méndez. The reporter suggested that federal investigations could be an obstacle to the merger. Ayala poked Méndez in the ribs.

Ross frowned. He referred the reporter to a statement that had been released earlier. The Blake Group denied any wrongdoing and had always cooperated with the federal government.

"We are not going to dignify this fake news, these debunked

allegations, with further comment," he said. "The Blake Group is in discussions with legal counsel about a decisive, proactive response to this outrageous attack."

Ayala wiggled all ten fingers at Méndez as if he were making a spooky gesture at a child.

"Good thing your bank account is empty," he whispered. "They are going to trample you like Godzilla."

More reporters asked about Méndez's story, one addressing Blake directly. Ross insisted there would be no further discussion of the topic.

"You spoiled the party, Leo," Ayala whispered. "The plan was for the executives to speak, but they will wrap it up fast. Don't strain yourself raising your hand. That hot *güerita* isn't coming near you with the microphone."

Blake jerked his head at the spokesman. Blake rose, the others following. Reporters shouted questions at the departing group.

Méndez had an idea.

"Do you want to interview me, Fulgencio?"

"Of course!"

"A gentleman's agreement, then. You have access to these Americans through Monroy. Tell them I am here and I want a comment, face to face. If you can convince them it's their opportunity to respond to me in person, scold me for my transgressions, they might do it."

Ayala savored the proposition like a wine taster.

*He's figuring out the best way to play both sides,* Méndez thought.

Ayala slapped Méndez's knee.

"Follow me, my valiant soldier. When I give the sign, you make an apparition like the Virgin of Guadalupe."

The TV reporter darted out of his chair and slalomed through the crowd, his footwork surprisingly agile.

Ayala did not disappoint. Half an hour later, Méndez sat in a hastily arranged conference room down the hall. In basketball terms, he had shown up for a one-on-one while the other side brought the whole team. Ross glared across the table, anchorman as enforcer. He was flanked by the blonde in the green dress and two public relations men for Monroy Enterprises. A bespectacled, sharp-faced American occupied a chair at the far end. A lawyer.

As far as Méndez was concerned, the most interesting person in the room was the spectator. Krystak, the security chief, had propped himself against the wall by the door.

*About the size of Porthos,* Méndez thought. Less stomach, but similar girth in the back and shoulders, similar outsize hands. In color and consistency, the shaven head resembled granite. The nose was prominent and fleshy. Krystak wore a black suit and an earpiece with a wire. He acted as if he had a two-part directive: (1) memorize this pesky Mexican's face; (2) put a scare into him while you do it.

Méndez jotted notes as Ross spoke, the bass voice reverberating with the undertone of a Texas accent. Méndez had gone way too far, Ross said. His article was irresponsible, unprofessional, and inaccurate.

"Which part is inaccurate?"

"The so-called Mexican intelligence document is a fake."

"Excuse me, we have made public the classified report. Verified by impeccable sources. The only person who says fake is Senator Ruiz Caballero, a possible target of investigations and friend of the Blakes. If not for politics, the senator would be in prison long ago. I have personal knowledge of this aspect."

"That's the whole problem. It's personal for you. A Mexican political vendetta. A crazy extremist crusade."

"I will report your criticisms as promised. But I have questions."

Ross shook his head, his blunt polished features tight with indignation. "It doesn't work that way. You don't get to write that crap and come in here and ask questions. You wanted our response. I'm giving it to you."

"I would like to interview Mr. Perry Blake."

Everyone glared except the blonde, who looked sad and distracted.

"Don't hold your breath," Ross said.

"Very well. Is there anything you wish to add?"

"You'd better start writing a retraction. Your story's falling apart. There's no proof of money laundering and there never has been."

Méndez scribbled dutifully. He recalled Isabel's hint.

"What about bribery?" he asked. "What about obstruction of justice?"

"Listen, pal," Ross boomed, reddening. "I don't know what you consider yourself—a journalist, an activist, a freelance investigator? You and your, um, outlet are bound by the same rules and ethics as everyone else. I speak as a professional person with decades of broadcast experience. You can't write whatever you want and get away with it. This isn't Tijuana."

Méndez frowned. He glanced at one of the Mexicans, a reedy young man with glossy black hair, then back at Ross. Méndez let the silence lengthen. Ross swallowed.

Méndez smiled coldly.

"I know where I am," he said. "And who I am dealing with."

The corporate contingent bustled out. No one told Méndez to leave, so he stayed in the room to go over his notes. He reviewed the e-mails and messages, mostly interview requests, that had inundated his phone. He called his office. Finally, he called his wife.

"You've caused a ruckus, Leo," she said.

"I hope you say that as a good thing."

"I do. My wolf strikes again. What now?"

"We'll see. Perhaps it will lead somewhere, catch fire. Perhaps not. Regardless, I intend to be on a plane tomorrow night."

"About time. School starts on Monday."

"I know, Estela."

"Juan has his last game of the summer on Saturday."

"I promised I would be there and I will. The days of sacrificing family for work are over."

Méndez checked his watch. He had agreed to do the interview at Ayala's studio in an hour.

As he hurried down a hall toward the elevator bank, an elevator door opened. Perry Blake emerged. He was deep in conversation with Ross, who hustled to keep up with the younger man's strides. They were accompanied by the bodyguard, the blonde, and the lawyer. The group was about fifty feet away. Krystak spotted Méndez first and stepped in front of Blake. Ross looked flustered. The group muttered among themselves as Méndez closed the distance. The bodyguard glanced over his shoulder.

Blake snapped, "No, I want to."

Krystak moved aside. Méndez found himself face to face with Blake.

"Mr. Blake," he said, extending his hand. "I am Leobardo Méndez."

The executive had alert blue eyes. Up close, his features had thickened compared to younger photos Méndez had seen. The hairline had receded, enlarging the rectangle of the forehead beneath the crest of light brown hair. Blake's groomed eyebrows seemed perpetually raised, as if he were reacting to big news. He cocked his head with an expression of grudging interest—*This is the loser who ruined my day?* A jaw muscle bulged. He was chewing gum.

Méndez stood with his hand out. After letting a second

go by, the executive shook it. His sudden, seemingly genuine smile caught Méndez off guard, a display of the charisma Isabel had described.

"Leo."

"I would be honored if we could speak, Mr. Blake."

"You're being used, Leo. You're attacking a project that has massive historic economic benefit to your country. To your own people."

The voice was crisp. The tone was chiding but controlled, as if he knew Méndez would come to his senses if he just listened.

"With respect, Mr. Blake, your history is not a guarantee of progress for Mexico."

"Lookit, you think you're sticking it to the Man. But you're being used, Leo, and you know it."

Blake's stare bored into him. The chiseled jaw worked the gum. Méndez was aware of Krystak breathing like a mastiff on a leash.

"An interesting analysis," Méndez said. "I am at your disposal to speak."

"I'm glad." Blake cracked another shiny smile, looking down at Méndez in a way that accentuated the height difference. "But I'd rather talk to the boss than the errand boy. By the way, are you packing right now?"

It took Méndez a moment to remember the meaning of the slang term, which he had heard American police officers use. And to digest the fact that Blake had asked a strange and aggressive question with the charming smile still in place.

"Not in this moment." Trying to match the nonchalance, Méndez flubbed the preposition. "Why?"

"Just curious." Blake spoke with exaggerated care, as if concerned Méndez wouldn't follow. "I understand you were in law enforcement."

"I was, yes."

"Interesting. You don't meet reporters with that kind of background. They're usually all bullshit, no action. Not exactly tough."

"For better or worst, Mr. Blake, I am from a tough place."

"You are indeed." The smile disappeared. "Have a good one, Leo."

Blake walked away. His phalanx followed. Méndez pulled out his notebook to record Blake's words verbatim. Blake had asserted that Méndez was being used. A good quote, and Blake's best defense. Méndez knew that some of the political interests the Secretary represented were nefarious. The encounter with Blake had been unsettling: his contained intensity, the hovering security man, the scared blonde. And, of course, the offhand question about whether Méndez was carrying a gun.

After the TV interview with Ayala and a bite at a Japanese restaurant, Méndez returned to his hotel. The story had hit major media websites. U.S. officials confirmed the gist of his column. Articles revisited the Blakes' history of alleged links to money laundering and to the Ruiz Caballero clan.

He turned on the television. On the Spanish-language network, Ayala gave Méndez screen time, though the report put too much emphasis on his past at the Diogenes Group, showing irrelevant footage of cadavers and raids. A Mexican corporate spokesman described Méndez as an agitator.

Before going to bed, he glanced at his e-mails. There was one from Fred Weinstein in Los Angeles.

Leo:

Great story, compañero. What a coup. Congrats.

This might interest you. A colleague in New York called. Immigration/labor lawyer. I don't know him, but he knows I work with you. He's got a tip related to the Blake Group about the janitorial staff at their headquarters getting fired. Twenty illegal immigrants. I think it would be worth talking to him. In person.

The e-mail ended with contact information for a legal-aid clinic in Spanish Harlem.

It was Wednesday night. Méndez had a flight booked for the next evening. His plan was to devote Thursday to writing a follow-up story. He didn't want to waste time on an opportunistic lawyer chasing headlines.

However, Méndez respected Fred's judgment. He would check out the tip, make a trip uptown. He would still have time to finish his work and catch the flight to San Diego. His son would be happy to see him on the sideline of the soccer game.

# Chapter 7

S o that's our guy, huh? The local bookie."
"Pernambuco."
"He's named for a state?"
"A nickname. He's really from Ceará, the state next door."
"Like he's from Oklahoma, but they call him Tex."
"Like that."
"How long do we wait, Facundo?"
"He knows we're here. Let him finish the lunch rush."

Pescatore and Facundo Hyman Bassat watched the street from a Formica table in an open-walled *lanchonete*. The eatery smelled like coconut and burned toast. It occupied a corner across from an industrial compound and the entrance to a favela called Jardim do Fogo (Garden of Fire) on the outskirts of Rio de Janeiro.

Pernambuco did business on the sidewalk by the factory. He sat, regally, in a folding chair at a folding table. On the weather-beaten wall behind him rose a mural of a ninja, a masked crouching figure holding a scimitar. Beneath the ninja, a cluster of bettors allowed glimpses of Pernambuco: cannonball head, red shirt and shorts, thick calves. His clients wore green industrial coveralls, or white button-down shirts with name tags, or the unofficial favela uniform of flip-flops and cutoffs.

"Business is booming," Pescatore said, chewing a cheese-flavored roll.

"The *jogo do bicho* is an institution," Facundo said. "There are three thousand spots like this in Rio. They're called *pontos*."

The *jogo do bicho* — the animal game — was an illegal lottery. It sounded to Pescatore like the old numbers game in Chicago that had died out in the 1970s. In the Brazilian version, pictures of animals on lottery slips represented numbers and were related to dreams and superstitions. The game earned billions and employed thousands. The gambling bosses, or *bicheiros,* were mobsters involved in shootings and scandals. Facundo had once done security work for a legitimate company owned by a *bicheiro*. They had become friends.

"If Pernambuco is a sergeant, my friend is a general."

"A bona fide mafioso, huh?"

"Yes and no." Facundo wiped his mustache with the back of a hairy hand. "He's a patron of the Samba schools, the ones that perform in Carnaval. Once he invited me to Carnaval — the VIP section in the Sambadrome. The *bicheiros* are chummy with politicians, celebrities, billionaires, soccer stars. And why not? The game runs like clockwork. Winners always collect. The *bicheiros* pay good wages and benefits. If Pernambuco gets arrested, they handle the legal fees. If he dies, they take care of his family."

It was Thursday. When Pescatore arrived the day before, Facundo had just identified the Brazilian survivor of the Tecate massacre: Tayane Pires. With the help of a source in the Rio state police, the cell phone number obtained from Chiclet had led to her family in the Jardim do Fogo favela. Facundo's friend the gambling boss had directed Pernambuco to find her.

Facundo finished his melon. He put money on the table and

got up, adjusting the gun in his belt beneath the Hawaiian-style shirt.

"Good thing we have an intermediary," he rasped. "We can't just go strolling into Jardim do Fogo like a couple of schmendricks."

Like his boss, Pescatore wore a loose short-sleeved shirt with the tails out over his pistol. He followed Facundo across the street. Facundo knew Brazil, having worked for a long time at the triple border of Brazil, Argentina, and Paraguay. He spoke Portuguese. With his jaunty manner and rumpled, swarthy look, he fit in.

Pernambuco's ink-stained fingers counted cash into the hands of an elderly black woman in knee-length cutoffs. She patted his unshaven cheek.

"Keep dreaming, Pernambuco," she said.

"I have good dreams," the bookie said. "My dreams make money."

Although they had only spoken on the phone, Pernambuco and Facundo greeted each other like long-lost friends. The bookie had a gap-toothed, slit-eyed smile. His gaze rose skyward as he mentioned "the Chief" and "our mutual friend." Like Facundo, he was in his sixties. A fringe of gray hair encircled his sun-reddened dome. A crucifix on a ropelike chain hung over his chest. He closed a flat wood box containing money and betting slips and tucked it under his flabby left arm. He told a shirtless young man leaning on the wall—a lookout or runner—to keep an eye on the *ponto*. The narrow-waisted, bushy-haired guy appeared to be taking a vertical nap.

Pescatore recalled Fatima Belhaj's term for loiterers in the Paris housing projects: *hitistes. Hit* was "wall" in Arabic; *hitistes* leaned on walls. He hadn't talked to Fatima since the interrupted phone call in San Diego. At dinner last night, he had discussed his romantic woes with Facundo. Facundo had given him a loud, lengthy lecture. The gist: Based on his forty-three years of marriage, Facundo believed Fatima's ambivalence amounted to rejection in slow motion. He had recommended that Pescatore act accordingly.

Pernambuco had a rolling, deliberate walk in his white clogs. He led the way across a footbridge over train tracks. Pescatore understood most of what he said. It was possible to enter the favela by car, but the route was roundabout. Pernambuco did not want the local drug traffickers to mistake them for the police or enemy *bandidhos.*

"We walk in nice and easy, nothing to hide," he said, puffing as he descended metal stairs.

Pescatore had never been in a favela. During past visits to Rio, he had seen the slums topping the green hills above the beachfront high-rises. The favelas of the coast were alive with vivid colors and panoramic views. They were the sites of police pacification campaigns and economic revitalization programs. Their feral mystique inspired music, movies, even tours.

Jardim do Fogo was a long way from the beach. The warren of dusty streets spread in a flatland enclosed by the tracks, an elevated highway, and a lagoon with a sulfur smell. Dogs trotted. Kids scampered. A radio blared Brazilian funk. A hairdresser did a woman's braids at an open-air beauty shop. Men drank standing up at the window counter of a grocery. They called out, "Oy, Pernambuco!" and "All good?"

"All joy." Pernambuco raised a hand high with the palm turned inward, like a politico acknowledging the crowd at a rally.

Pescatore noticed that the walls around him were pock-marked. He recognized the spatter of impacts from automatic-weapon fire. Someone had used the bullet holes to paint connect-the-dots flowers on the walls.

Pescatore had trouble figuring out Rio. He compared it to

places like, say, Detroit. Detroit looked the way it was: cold, mean, and ugly. Rio fooled you. It was breathtakingly beautiful. The people mixed together in a kaleidoscope of races and colors—friendly, relaxed, sexy. But the city was dangerously divided between *o asfalto,* the asphalt enclaves of the well-to-do, and *o morro,* the hill—the unpaved combat zones of the favelas.

"Epah," Facundo said. "Here we go."

Two youths on bikes rolled toward them, raising dust in the haze. The cyclists wore caps, shorts, and T-shirts. Pescatore spotted walkie-talkies and pistols in their waistbands. They were too young and thuggish to be cops. His hand strayed to his shirttail near his gun while his eyes searched the lane for cover. No cars, no trees, nothing.

The cyclists came to a stop. They sat on their bikes watching the outsiders advance. The stiffness in Pernambuco's stride indicated that he didn't have much clout with the teenage triggermen of the drug trade. Facundo ran a hand through his salt-and-pepper hair. Pescatore resisted the urge to draw. Facundo was fond of quoting a line from *My Darling Clementine,* his favorite Western: "When you pull a gun, kill a man."

The cyclists made eye contact with Pernambuco. Barely a nod. Once the visitors had passed, the duo glided off again.

Facundo exhaled.

Pescatore said, "I'm assuming that wasn't the neighborhood watch."

"Hah. The narco watch. The traffickers rule this place."

They rounded a corner and came across three boys lugging buckets.

"Youngsters," Pernambuco exclaimed. "Say hello to my visitors. High-class people, refined people. Show them what you've got there."

The tallest boy was about eight. He had a sand-colored

Afro. Grinning, he hefted his bucket. It was full of used bullets and spent cartridges.

"Tell them where you take those," Pernambuco said.

"The sculptor!" the boy said. "At the House of Solidarity."

The boys hurried off. The bookie explained that the children of the favela retrieved bullets after firefights. A sculptor at the community center paid a penny a bullet and used the bullets in his statues.

Pernambuco shrugged. "Life where the asphalt ends."

Tayane Pires lived on a slight rise known as the Heights. The homes were bigger and better-kept. The Pires house had a satellite dish. Pernambuco said the two-story hodgepodge of colors and materials had been built in stages by the woman's father, who was a line supervisor at the factory across the bridge. That made sense to Pescatore. For many inhabitants of the favelas, the concept of foreign travel—passports, visas, planes—was like going to the moon. The relatively few Brazilians who migrated illegally to the United States were not the poorest of the poor. That group was too busy just surviving. The immigrants were, by Brazilian standards, at least lower middle class.

Tayane Pires answered the door. As Chiclet had said, she was a *mulata*—a blend of African and other. Her eyes were golden green, her hair golden brown, her skin copper gold. She had dressed for the visit in a velvety jacket, purple slacks, and sandals. Silver earrings framed her round open face. Tall and on the heavy side, she moved with casual grace.

"I speak a little English," she said. "I was living near Boston."

Pernambuco introduced Pescatore and Facundo as the important personages from the United States he had told her about. After assuring her she was in good hands, he left. He didn't know the particulars behind the visit, and he didn't want to know.

Tayane served the obligatory coffee—she called it *cafe-zinho*—in an enclosed porch on the second floor. When Facundo admitted he had quit coffee for medical reasons, she went to get him a papaya juice instead. Pescatore used his forearm to brush away the ants marching across the plastic tablecloth toward the sugar bowl. He had heard and seen adults and children in the cluttered maze of a house as Tayane led them upstairs. Because of the Latin American tendency to receive guests in groups, he had thought relatives would be present for moral support, but Tayane was handling this alone.

Although Facundo was fluent, he had decided Pescatore would be the lead interviewer. He knew the case and was, Facundo said, *More simpatico for the ladies than a grumpy old moishe*.

When Tayane came back with the juice and sat down, Pescatore pulled out his notebook. He took his time. He wanted to put her at ease.

He started by apologizing for his Portuguese. It was a stew of Spanish, French, and Italian spiced with Portuguese phrases and intonation. His success at communicating in Brazil mystified him.

"I understand you," she said. "Just speak slowly."

*"Obrigado."*

At his request, Tayane spelled her name.

"I'm named for Princess Diana," she explained. "My parents improvised the spelling."

Pescatore said he was investigating a murder-kidnapping in California and a multiple homicide in Mexico. He had reason to believe Tayane was a witness and a victim and had narrowly escaped being a casualty. Knowing it was traumatic for her, he was sorry but he had come to ask for her help.

Her golden eyes reflected the sunlight sliced by bars on the window.

"I have not told anyone, not even my family, the whole story," she said. "It has been eating me up inside. I am glad you are here. Frightened too. But I am glad I can finally talk to someone."

"The U.S. government will make every effort to protect you," he said. "There's a chance you could be brought to the United States to testify. If you're willing."

He added the last words when he saw her flinch at his mention of testifying.

After a moment, Tayane started talking. Her voice was husky, her gaze direct. She was twenty-five. She had married four years ago. Her husband, Leandro, wasn't from the favela. He had more money than she did, and how he made it wasn't entirely clear. He had Brazilian friends who had gone to Boston, and he wanted to try his luck there. The couple traveled on tourist visas and remained illegally. Except for the harsh winter, Tayane had enjoyed the adventure at first. She found a job in a supermarket. Leandro schemed and hustled.

"Sure enough, he got me in big trouble," she said.

One night in the spring, the police pulled her over. The car turned out to be stolen and her husband had left a bag of marijuana in the trunk. Tayane refused to implicate him. She agreed to a plea deal: deportation instead of prison time. She was sent back to Rio. Leandro laid low and avoided arrest.

"You must think I'm a fool, taking the fall like that," she said.

"No, ma'am," Pescatore said.

"Who can criticize a faithful wife?" Facundo dried his brow with a napkin. "Unfortunately, Leandro was a bit of a *malandro*."

She laughed ruefully, her first laugh since their arrival.

*Nice one, boss,* Pescatore thought. *Malandro* was slang for a trickster or con man. Facundo was a comforting presence in interviews, a big shaggy uncle who forgave human frailties.

"I should have stayed away from him," she said. "I let him sweet-talk me over the phone. He convinced me to go back to Boston, he said that we could still share a life there. Mainly, I just wanted to be with him."

Leandro wired her money to hire a smuggler, a Somali based in Rio. The Somali handled a thriving market in East Africans; there were more of them coming through Brazil than there were Brazilians going north. In early August, Tayane flew with six African women to Mexico City. Mexican smugglers took them to Tijuana, where another five African women waited at a safe house. The conditions were uncomfortable, but the Mexicans did not mistreat them.

"The driver of the van looked like a bandit. He was okay. A joker. When we crossed, he made a production of it. 'Ladies, welcome to the United States!'"

"Exactly how did that happen, the crossing?" Pescatore asked.

Tayane shrugged. "They just put us in the van. They didn't really hide us. It was arranged with an American border policeman. We stopped. I heard the driver speak English, show papers. We kept going."

She had been talking with her head down. She looked up into his eyes.

"The driver...he got shot right in front of me. It was horrible."

"Take your time, Tayane."

"Living here, I've been around guns, shooting. But not like this. The driver stopped at a store. He was looking at his cell phone. All of a sudden, his head exploded."

After commandeering the van in San Diego, the two gunmen in cowboy hats terrorized the twelve women, screaming threats, ordering them to duck down and cover their eyes. Tayane didn't realize they had crossed back into Mexico until the women were herded into a motel room. Chiclet took charge. She described the smuggler's pompadour and bat-tered, leering face.

"A drunk pig," she said, shuddering.

Pescatore felt a pang of regret at not having thumped Chic-let when he'd had the chance. He said he knew this was difficult. She could take a break if she wanted. She shook her head. Her composure impressed him.

The second woman whom Chiclet pulled out of the room with Tayane was named Abrihet, an Eritrean in her thirties.

"When he ordered us to go to another room with him, we did what we were told. We were petrified."

Tayane's account was consistent with Chiclet's. She had pleaded with him to let her call her family. He dialed the Rio number into his phone and promised to let her call later. He ordered the women to drink with him, then started paw-ing them, but the barrage of gunfire outside interrupted. After he escaped through the window, the two women hud-dled on the floor.

"The shooting ended. But we could hear them walking out-side, banging on doors, yelling. Abrihet said we had to get out of there. She said the killers were looking for us. She heard them calling her name. Then she noticed the drunk had left a money clip and his watch by the bed. About five hundred dol-lars, thank God."

Eventually, Tayane and Abrihet fled through the window, across the roof, and down a back stairway. As they ran, they saw a half a dozen police cars parked in a street behind the motel.

"No lights, no rush, just sitting there like they were waiting for the killers to finish," she said, closing her eyes. "They were all in league together."

Tayane looked up as a woman came into the room. The woman looked like an older, shorter, lighter-skinned version of Tayane. She put a plate of coconut cookies on the table.

Facundo thanked her effusively, eliciting a shy smile as she retreated.

Tayane resumed the story. She said she and the Eritrean stumbled through dark streets at six a.m. No identification, no phones, no jackets, nothing except Chiclet's cash and watch. They didn't know exactly what had happened at the motel. They didn't know what city they were in. Every noise frightened them, every shadow. Tayane was hysterical. Abrihet calmed her down.

"A small girl, but strong in her body and mind," Tayane said. "She was educated. The others were kind of, you know, from the countryside. Abrihet spoke good English, and Spanish mixed with Italian. It seemed like she knew Mexico. She figured out we were in the city of Tecate."

"How?"

"She saw a big sign on a factory. They make a famous beer there. The sun was coming up, and she said we had to leave. The *bandidhos* would be hunting for us."

On a roadside lined with early-morning commuters, the two found a station-wagon taxi that charged thirty-five dollars for a ride to Tijuana. They shared the taxi with four other passengers. An hour later, they were eating sandwiches at a counter in the Tijuana bus station. A television showed the motel in Tecate, emergency vehicles, news bulletins about thirteen corpses.

Tayane studied her bright purple nails. Her voice was slow and hollow.

"All dead. I almost fainted from the shock. Abrihet kept saying we had to stay quiet, the police would spot us. She said we had to split up. She gave me money for a bus ticket to Mexico City. I didn't want to go. I wanted to go to the border and turn ourselves in to the American police, tell them everything. She got angry. She said the Americans were involved with the bad guys too. We had been kidnapped on the U.S. side. We couldn't trust anyone. She told me to go to the Brazilian embassy in Mexico City and ask for help."

She paused. Pescatore thought she had stopped talking because she was choking up. But she didn't cry. He exchanged glances with Facundo.

Finally, Pescatore said, "What did Abrihet do? Where did she go?"

"She didn't say. The important thing was for me to get away from her."

"Why?"

"Safer for me, she said."

"And the Brazilian embassy flew you home eventually?"

"Yes."

"Did the Brazilian police interview you? Contact the Mexican police? Take a statement about the killings, that kind of thing?"

"I didn't say anything about the killings."

"You didn't?"

"No. I said I was abandoned by smugglers in Mexico, nothing else."

"Tayane, I gotta ask you: Why didn't you tell them about this horrible experience you'd been through?"

She raised her chin, her full lips pursed in a look of defiance and fear. He realized that she was shaking.

"Abrihet asked me not to."

After buying the bus ticket for Tayane, the Eritrean had taken her aside, embraced her, and talked in an urgent whisper.

"Abrihet said it was all her fault. She was convinced the killers had been looking for her. She had gotten in trouble with some very powerful Americans in New York, at a place where she worked. These Americans had sent people to hunt her down. 'I am the reason this happened,' she said. I said that was crazy. She said she didn't have time to explain, but it was true, that was why they took our pictures. That's why the killers called her name."

"Did you say the gunmen at the motel spoke Spanish?"

"Yes. From what I could tell, they looked Mexican."

"Who were these Americans, then? What was that all about?"

"I don't know. She asked me to keep quiet. For my sake and for hers. I made a promise and I kept it. I am telling you the truth now because Pernambuco says you are good people. And Pernambuco has known my family since I was little."

Facundo's elbows were propped on the table, a half-eaten cookie forgotten in his hand. Pescatore wasn't sure what to do. He put his phone in front of Tayane and asked her to look at some pictures.

She identified Chiclet and the three dead kidnappers. Next came the photo of the Eritrean woman.

"Abrihet," she said.

Tayane picked up the phone and mimed a soft kiss, her lips almost touching the screen. The gesture caught Pescatore off guard. He felt a lump in his throat.

"My sister," she said. "I don't even know her full name, but she's my sister now. May God protect her."

Pescatore did his sad duty. One at a time, pausing on each face, he showed her the photos of the ten dead women.

"Yes," Tayane said. "I recognize them."

And then, at last, she wept.

The moon glowed blue over Copacabana.

On the sound system of the rooftop bar, the rich somber voice of Virginia Rodrigues serenaded the moon with *"Lua, Lua, Lua, Lua."*

Pescatore surveyed the bay, thirty stories below. Traffic

flowed on the beachfront avenue. Lights glittered like diamonds in the hills, on the water, and along the urban reef formed by high-rise buildings. Barefoot soccer players shadow-danced on the sand. The games had been going on in front of the hotel all day. He wanted to go down and play, sprint in the surf, lose himself in the simple pleasure of sport.

He signaled the waiter for another round of *caipirinhas*.

"This fucking case," he said. "It's getting to me, Facundo."

"You said Isabel was pleased."

Pescatore had briefed Isabel by phone. She was getting ready to move. The first step was to hand off Chiclet to the embassy in Mexico City. The next would be to arrange for Tayane Pires to give a formal statement. Isabel wanted Pescatore to come to Washington and make plans. She had other hassles. Her politically sensitive white-collar-corruption case was getting media attention. Leo Méndez had shaken things up with an article, she said.

"Yeah, she's pleased," Pescatore said to Facundo. "Everything's falling into place. We've got a confessed accomplice, a bona fide victim, and a lead on the other victim."

"What's the problem, then?"

Pescatore slouched, his muscular arms folded on his chest.

"That horror story we heard today. It's bad enough Tayane lives in that shooting gallery of a neighborhood. She's gonna have nightmares the rest of her life. And who knows what happened to Abrihet. Meanwhile, we're sitting high on the hog in Copacabana."

Bushy eyebrows raised, Facundo watched him drink.

"Not enjoying our good fortune will not improve their bad fortune," Facundo said.

"It's just fucked up, that's all."

Pescatore told himself to go easy on the booze in front of his boss. And in general. He sat up and asked, "What about that bizarre stuff the Eritrean lady told Tayane? The rip crew gunning for her, big-shot Americans wanting her dead?"

Facundo sipped his drink. "One could say it sounds preposterous. Delirious. We have to remember that these young women endured enormous psychological trauma. And we only know part of it. Noooo. The Eritreans are a desperate diaspora. Thousands drowning in the Mediterranean, thousands tortured for ransom by smugglers in the Sinai. A friend in the Israeli border police has told me things that made my hair stand on end."

"You're right. No wonder she started raving."

"On the other hand…"

"What?"

"Eritreans are tough. They do military service. The women too, like the Israelis. This young lady Abrihet thought on her feet, one fast decision after another. Clearheaded."

"And?"

"She didn't necessarily act like someone suffering paranoid delusions."

"Wait. You're saying it could be true?"

"I'm just saying I hope we find the young lady. Alive and well."

"*Salud* to that."

"*L'chaim.* Let's order some food with all this beverage, Valentín. We need to keep our wits about us."

# Chapter 8

It was a blessing and a curse: Méndez had become famous on the streets of Spanish-speaking New York.

A curse because he preferred anonymity. A blessing because it aided his search.

He was accustomed to public attention in Mexico and, to a lesser extent, in Southern California. On the East Coast, he felt invisible—or he had until Fulgencio Ayala's report hit the news. Spanish-language television wasn't just information and entertainment for Latin American immigrants. It was identity, community, a survival guide to their new world, a lifeline to their old one. Some people he encountered knew exactly who he was. Others treated him like some kind of real-life action hero. En route to the legal-aid office Thursday, he had walked out of a subway station into stares and greetings in Spanish Harlem. After he went from there to Flushing, the Ecuadoran tenants at the house he visited insisted on helping him canvass the neighbors.

And now, as he manned his stool at the window of the pizza place on First Avenue, the youthful Sinaloan counterman with the fledgling mustache brought him a Coke and a *cannolo*— on the house. He addressed Méndez with the friendly street abbreviation of the title *licenciado*.

"No, *Leek,* it's my treat, please. I'm in charge on Sundays."
The kid's lordly wave took in the empty tables around them.
Patting Méndez on the back, he said, "I hope you have more
success today, *Leek.*"

"Me too, *hijo.*"

*Because if I'm not in San Diego tomorrow,* he thought, *I might
not have a home to go home to.*

By staying in New York, Méndez had missed Juan's soccer
game and enraged his wife. Yes, she had encouraged him to
go on the trip in the first place. But she had no patience for
broken promises. So fuck his excuses. And fuck him. Estela
hadn't sounded this angry in a long time. The wounds of their
years of living dangerously had reopened.

Still, Méndez was swept up in the rush of reporting. He
kept telling himself it would all be worth it in the end.

The legal-aid lawyer in Harlem said he had received a call
in July from a Guatemalan immigrant named Zoraida Padilla.
She had been the supervisor of the night janitorial crew at the
corporate headquarters of the Blake Acquisitions Group. The
crew were a mix of Latino and African immigrants. They had
lost their jobs when the Blake Group abruptly dismissed the
firm. Padilla said it was the result of an "incident" involving
an executive and a cleaning woman.

"Zoraida sounded scared," the lawyer told Méndez. "She
said there was a lot to tell, but not on the phone. I said we
could talk in person. But that was it. I've tried to reach her a
couple of times. No luck."

The tip appealed to Méndez for several reasons. Four days after his exclusive, things were clearer. The Justice Department
had confirmed, on background, that the federal case was about
suspected violations of the Foreign Corrupt Practices Act. Investigators believed the Blake Group had used systematic
bribery to expand in Mexico (*Shocking,* Méndez thought) and

lay the groundwork for the merger. The prosecutors weren't sure they had enough evidence for indictments, though. U.S. newspapers had reported that developments were not imminent or even likely.

Meanwhile, Zoraida Padilla offered a story for which Méndez had a rare competitive advantage over the U.S. press, linguistically and culturally—a story with a human face.

If he found her. If she was telling the truth.

Méndez ate the *cannolo* slowly. It tasted like cardboard. His view consisted of an Irish bar, a laundromat, and a fruit-and-vegetable market across the street. Sparse midday traffic flowed north on the avenue.

Padilla had moved from Queens to the Upper East Side of Manhattan, an area Méndez thought of as wealthy. Her building, though, was an old walk-up, faded brick and rusting fire escapes above a pet store. He had managed to slip inside behind a mailman. The hallways were gloomy. The residents looked indigent, elderly, damaged, or some combination of the three. A fourth-floor one-bedroom here was not ideal for a single mother and three children who, until recently, had been living in a rented bungalow with berry trees in the yard.

The neighbors in Flushing said Padilla's move had been hurried. She hadn't told them where she was going. The neighbors gave Méndez a cell phone number, an e-mail address, and a photo of Padilla. He wrote to her and left text and voice messages. On Friday, he returned to Flushing and, after a long stakeout, coaxed Padilla's new address out of a neighbor who hadn't wanted to talk in front of the others. On Saturday, he went to the Manhattan apartment, buzzed from downstairs, knocked on the apartment door after following the mailman in, and slid a note and a business card beneath it. He hung around for hours. If she lived here, Padilla was staying low profile.

For the stakeout today, he again chose the pizza place next door. It was a shotgun space with a row of tables against one wall. He kept watch from the counter at the front window. A mirror on his right enabled him to see the sidewalk on his left in front of her vestibule and down to the corner.

He checked the time. He had to leave for the airport in a few hours. He had reserved the last flight of the night. If he missed it, he wouldn't be home in time to take Renata to her first day of nursery school. And there would be hell to pay.

In the mirror, Méndez saw a boy come around the corner. The boy was Latino, a year or two younger than Juan, with wet-combed hair. He resembled a miniature provincial gentleman in his oversize suit.

Méndez toyed with his phone, tempted to call his son. Last night, Juan had sounded sad that his father had missed the game and worried that his mother was furious. Yet he had given Méndez a breathless play-by-play of the goal he had scored with a back-heel shot off a corner kick, a move they had practiced together. Méndez had teared up when he heard that. Now he was tearing up again, like a maudlin fool.

Then he saw that the boy in the suit had stopped a few feet away. A woman and two small girls rounded the corner.

Méndez stumbled off his stool toward the door.

*It's her. She has a nine-year-old son and twins. It's Zoraida Padilla.*

Seeing Méndez appear on the sidewalk, she came to a stop. She clutched the hands of the adorably identical girls, who were about five and wore matching skirts and bows in their hair. Méndez slowed himself down. He approached with a soothing smile. Padilla was diminutive with hunched shoulders. She wore makeup, a violet dress, and a necklace with a golden Saint Anthony medallion. Her hair had dyed blondish streaks and was carefully brushed and arranged.

"Señora Padilla," he said. "Please forgive me for bothering you. I am Leo Méndez, the journalist who has been trying to reach you."

Recognition rearranged her features, then relief.

"I saw you on television," she said.

They ate sandwiches in a booth at the Irish tavern.

Beneath big screens showing baseball, football, and soccer, a few grizzled regulars huddled at the bar as if it were a ship in stormy seas.

Zoraida Padilla had a habit of ducking her head as she talked, looking up at him out of the heavily painted corners of wary eyes.

"Thank you very much for lunch, Licenciado Méndez," she said gravely.

"My pleasure. I hope I am not delaying the children's meal."

"No, I took them for pancakes after Mass. I always do."

She had polished off the sandwich, though. He suspected that she hadn't eaten any pancakes herself because she had to watch every penny. She hadn't invited him up to the apartment when she left the children there, probably because it embarrassed her. Her fragile dignity heightened his discomfort about having stalked her. He disliked the way many reporters treated people, especially working-class people, bellowing questions in public, browbeating, bullshitting. He always told young reporters that being a journalist didn't excuse you from the human race. You had the power to invade lives, walk through walls. It came with an obligation to behave with manners and decency.

"How about dessert?" he said. "A drink? Something Irish?"

She glanced around. An unfamiliar, intimidating setting

for her. She had said he was the most famous person she had ever met.

"I drank Baileys Irish Cream once," she said timidly. "It was sweet."

"Good idea," he said. "I take mine with ice. It's a hot day."

"Me too, please. Thanks very much."

As he ordered at the bar, he checked the time. She had told him about herself, her life in Guatemala, her new job as a barista in a coffee shop. She said she was living in fear. She had avoided Méndez because she thought it might be a trap, someone posing as him. He let her talk, hoping she would circle around to the real topic on her own. But she had barely touched on it.

Back in his seat with the drinks, he said, "Señora Padilla. In order to help you and the others, I really need to know about this 'incident.'"

Ducking her head, she said, "What does 'off the record' mean, exactly?"

"I don't mention your name. I don't quote you, even anonymously."

"So what do you do?"

"It's up to me to find sources who confirm your story. Then I can write it based on their accounts."

She sipped her drink, took a deep breath, and nodded.

"What was the name of your colleague who was the victim?" he asked.

"Abrihet Anbessa."

"From Eritrea, you said?"

"Yes."

"Where did she live?"

"Queens. Not far from me."

"She was a supervisor as well?"

"Not officially. She didn't have papers. I was the only supervisor. I have a green card. But I persuaded the boss to give Abrihet extra responsibility and pay. She was such a good worker. She had gone to the university in her country. She worked at night and studied during the day at community college to be a nurse."

"Impressive."

The executive floor caused a lot of hassles. Perry Blake and his staff worked late, often overnight, requiring the crew to maneuver around them. The executives were demanding and impatient. They complained about cleaners who got in the way, made noise, didn't speak English. Padilla assigned Abrihet Anbessa to handle that floor because she was poised and professional.

"She did a good job. No more complaints. But it was a strange environment there at night. Sometimes the executives were working hard; other times it was more like a party. Drinking, maybe drugs. Abrihet felt uncomfortable around Mr. Blake. He was a night owl, that one, always there."

"Perry Blake?"

"Yes. The younger one."

"When did the incident happen?"

"In July." Head and voice low, Padilla scanned the room. She said, "The shift ended at five in the morning. I was leaving for the subway. Abrihet ran up to me in the lobby, very upset. She said something happened."

Abrihet told her the story on the subway ride out to Flushing. They sat close together in the corner of a near-empty car, the elevated train clattering past cemeteries at dawn.

Perry Blake had sexually assaulted her, Abrihet said. They'd struggled. She escaped.

"She said he was staggering, acting crazy. Like an animal."

"My God."

"They were fighting, wrestling around, for several minutes. She finally got away."

"Did he rape her?"

"She said he didn't. She fought him off."

"Was she hurt?"

"Yes. When we got to my house and I made her coffee, she showed me. She had a bump on her head, under her hair. Her jaw was scraped. And she had a big bruise on her left side, the ribs, where he kicked her."

"Did you take pictures of the injuries?"

"Yes, with her phone. She has them."

Méndez did not have a physical memory of putting his notebook on the table, but he was scribbling away, trying to record every word. He was picturing the victim telling the story, imagining the crime itself, assembling the narrative, examining it for gaps and flaws.

Elbows on the table, Padilla clasped her hands and rested her chin against them. There were mottled circles under her eyes.

*Her life was hard enough already,* he thought. Someone else's misfortune had wrecked her job and home, piling on another burden. Nonetheless, she had done her duty. She urged Abrihet to go to the police and offered to accompany her. The Eritrean didn't want to. She was an illegal immigrant, she was poor, no one would believe her.

"I told Abrihet that wasn't true. Here it's not like in our countries, I said. Reporting it might actually help her immigration status. I've heard of the American government giving green cards to victims of rape or abuse. Remember that French politician and the maid in the hotel? The New York police arrested him, pulled him off a plane. The maid got a lot of money in court. Now she owns a restaurant. She was African too."

Abrihet had reminded her that the hotel maid in that case had been humiliated, her life exposed, her reputation trashed. What's more, Abrihet said, Perry Blake hadn't actually raped her. The attack would be even more difficult to prove.

"Abrihet was a sweet girl—bright-eyed, always with a smile, a laugh. But when I insisted about the police, she got a tough, bitter look on her face, a look I had never seen. She said that man was a monster and he was going to destroy her."

Abrihet said she was going to run, leave the country via California to Mexico and Europe.

"She couldn't fly out of the United States without papers. She thought she could find smugglers in Mexico to help her. You see, she came here originally by traveling through South America and crossing from Tijuana. Your hometown, Licenciado."

Padilla allowed herself a faint smile. Méndez smiled back. She said, "She didn't have any family here. Few friends. She was so busy all the time. Her plan was to go to Italy, where her brother lives. He migrated to Italy on a boat, like you see on television—the Africans who drown?"

"Yes. They land on the island of Lampedusa. And Sicily."

Abrihet left Padilla's house. Later that morning, Padilla got a visit from Louis Krystak, the chief of corporate security.

"The big bald bodyguard," Méndez said.

"He and another. They were angry. They said Abrihet had stolen valuable property. From the security cameras, they knew she had left the building with me. They asked about one of those little computer sticks, you know."

"A pen drive. Did Abrihet mention anything about that?"
"No."

The security men searched Padilla's house. They grilled her. She told them about the Eritrean's accusations against Perry Blake. They said Abrihet had lied because she had been caught stealing. Krystak warned Padilla not to talk to the police and ordered her to call him immediately if Abrihet or others contacted her about the matter.

"The next day, we all got fired. The company we worked for were subcontractors of subcontractors, and the building got rid of them. I called the legal-aid lawyer, but I was scared. I changed my mind."

Jobless and frightened, Padilla was forced to move. She lived for a while with a friend on the Lower East Side, jammed with her children into a tiny spare bedroom. The children were devastated; they missed their house, their yard, their friends. Moreover, Padilla was convinced that Blake security officers were doing surveillance on her.

"Two men—one white, one black—and a woman. They take turns. Sometimes on foot, sometimes in cars. I see them here, at work, at the playground."

Padilla wiped away tears, shoulders high. Méndez sighed sympathetically. Still, he could not rule out the possibility that she was being melodramatic or paranoid.

Quietly, he asked, "Why would they be watching you, Zoraida?"

"To find Abrihet. Listen to this: She called me from Mexico. I think they tapped my phone. They started watching more closely after the call."

His eyes widened. "When?"

"Late July, early August."

"How many calls from Mexico?"

"Just one."

Abrihet had said she was in Tijuana. After talking to her brother, she had changed her mind about trying to join him in Italy. Instead, he would wire her money for Mexican smugglers to sneak her back to the United States. She intended to return to New York.

"She said I was right about telling the police. She had decided to do it, so she asked if I would be a witness for her, back up her story with the authorities if she denounced Mr. Blake."

"And?"

"I said I would. She said she was glad she had listened to me. She would get revenge. She had information, and she was going to use it against him."

"Information? From the pen drive?"

"That was what I presumed. She didn't say."

"What happened?"

"I don't know. There's a lot of Border Patrol at the Line. It's very difficult. Chances are they caught her. I never heard from her again."

Méndez and Padilla talked for a while longer. When they were done, he walked her back to her building. She startled him by taking his arm as they crossed the street. She gripped it hard.

"Licenciado," she murmured. "One of the cars that follows me. At the end of the block, by the bus stop."

He smiled and nodded as if they were making small talk. He didn't look until they had reached the sidewalk near the pet store.

"A blue Crown Victoria," he said. "Two men."

"One white, one black." Her voice shook. "I don't see them together a lot. Maybe they are here for you."

"I should take their picture, ask them what they are doing. Give them a fright."

Her fingers dug into his arm.

"Please, Licenciado. I don't need any more problems."

"Don't worry, Zoraida. You have an ally now."

He followed her into the vestibule, which smelled vaguely like cat litter. She stared up at him, looking small, exhausted, and miserable.

"Thank you, Zoraida," he said. "You are a good and brave person."

"You think so?" Her eyes gleamed with shame and anger. "It hasn't brought me any luck."

Méndez hesitated. "The important thing is that you tried to help."

Zoraida shook her head. Avoiding his eyes, she said, "Licenciado Méndez, I really don't know if they tapped my phone. But Mr. Krystak came to see me again several times. The last time was two days after Abrihet called. He said he could cause many problems for me. Have the government look at my taxes, tell my employer bad things, endanger my green card. He demanded to know if I had heard from Abrihet."

Méndez waited. He knew what was coming. *What a brute,* he thought.

"So I told him," she continued, unable to meet his eyes. "About the phone call, that she was in Tijuana, what she said about the information and revenge. Everything I knew. And he gave me five hundred dollars. And I took it. That's how good and brave a person I am, Licenciado Méndez. I took the money."

Méndez tried to console her. He told her not to be hard on herself. He gave her a brief hug when they said goodbye and said to call him immediately if anyone bothered her.

Méndez walked a block south to hail a cab. As he passed the Crown Victoria, he clicked off a burst of photos with his phone aimed at the windshield and the license plate. The men inside wore baseball caps. They stiffened but otherwise didn't react.

*Maybe they are here for you.*

Or maybe there was a second team shadowing him. In the taxi, Méndez turned in his seat to see if he could spot a tail.

Until this moment, working north of the border had felt like operating in a bubble of security. The bubble had burst.

*Probably better,* he thought. *If you feel safe, you drop your guard.*

He worked during the flight. He transcribed the interview, adding every detail he could remember. He wrote a list of questions, items to double-check and follow up on. He recalled his encounter with Perry Blake, juxtaposing it against the grim tale he had heard in New York. He did not find it hard to imagine Blake as a predator. However, the image of Blake unhinged surprised him.

Remembering something, Méndez searched in the background files that Santiago had prepared for him. He found notes from an off-the-record interview with a businessman who had gone to college with Blake. There was a section about Blake's fraternity — binges, brawls, injury lawsuits, run-ins with campus police. And a rumor: A fellow student had accused Blake of raping her at a party. The Blake family threw its weight around, the source said, and the rumor went away. Only three sentences, an anecdote from twenty-five years ago, nothing that Méndez had thought he could use. But now it was a possible precedent for a kind of crime that was almost always repeated.

Méndez closed his eyes. The triumph of the day was wearing off, giving way to doubts. He had been building a story about complex, sophisticated, white-collar impunity. The narrative had veered in a way that was dramatic and problematic. He wasn't sure how to go about proving this tale of cruelty, brutality, and abuse of power. Unless he found the Eritrean. Perhaps she had landed in an immigration detention center in the Southwest. Perhaps Mexican police had picked her up. Or smugglers had kidnapped her. Then there was the supposed theft of the pen drive. Did she really have compromising information?

Méndez remembered another detail. When the Secretary

had given him the Mexican intelligence report, he had said there was a rumor that the Blakes were concerned about a problem. Some kind of internal leak or whistle-blower.

After New York, San Diego seemed impossibly calm, clean, and empty, the palm trees backlit by the moon, the breeze a welcoming caress. When Méndez arrived home, Estela was standing at the front door, eyes narrowed.

"So," she said. "You are back."

He found himself unable to sleep that night. On Monday morning, the Méndez family functioned with Prussian precision. Estela's mood was Prussian as well. Her silence was ominous. She had left for the university by the time he got back from dropping off Renata. He decided to deceive his body by acting as if he had arisen from a regular night's sleep. He showered and shaved. He put on jeans and a Team Mexico soccer jersey with the name of Chicharito, a star forward, on the back, then took a mug of coffee into his garage-newsroom. No one else was there. The sun shone. Birds chirped.

Isabel Puente answered his call on the street, walking and talking fast.

"I've had you on my mind, Leo," she said. "You've pretty much dictated my schedule, in fact."

"My apologies. I hope, at least, there were positive repercussions."

"We'll talk. I'm running now."

"How does it look?"

"Now is not the time."

"Give me a hint, Isabel."

"Your story forced high-level people to engage on this issue. You shamed the bad guys, which is nice. But the bottom-line dynamics haven't changed."

Méndez rubbed his eyes. What had the Secretary said about

journalists? *In the end, you are voices shouting outside the palace walls.*

Isabel started to hang up. Méndez interrupted to say he needed a favor.

"Information on a name," he said. He didn't plan to mention a Blake connection unless or until Isabel did. "An illegal immigrant."

"Can this wait?"

"I'm afraid not."

He waited while she found a spot where she could write it down.

"Go ahead," Isabel said.

"An Eritrean immigrant. Abrihet Anbessa. I have—"

"Repeat the name."

"Abrihet Anbessa." He spelled it.

"Eritrean? Illegal?"

"Yes."

A long pause.

"Hello? Isabel?"

"Go ahead."

The edge in her voice took him aback. He read her the date of birth and last known address Padilla had given him.

"I'd like to know if she is in any databases," he said. "If she was detained by the Border Patrol. Possibly a recent arrest in California."

"What makes you say that?" Her whisper was urgent.

"Well, the last information I have puts her in Tijuana with plans to be smuggled across the border."

"When?"

"Early August. Eh…are you familiar with this name?"

Silence. Finally, she asked, "Do you have a photo?"

"In my laptop. One moment, I will send it to you."

Zoraida Padilla had taken the picture at an employee picnic.

Abrihet sat at an outdoor table, glancing up at the camera. Slim, early thirties, windblown hair, but her face was visible. An engaging smile. Delicate, fine-boned features. As Padilla had said, she had bright, animated, resilient eyes.

After confirming that she had received the photo, Isabel hung up without asking anything else.

He was perplexed. Isabel could have conceivably learned about Abrihet through a source inside the Blake Group, perhaps a wiretap. But if so, why hadn't they jumped on it, bringing in the New York Police Department to investigate the assault? And Isabel would have mentioned something, at least obliquely, if she had that kind of artillery against Perry Blake. Méndez told himself that he might just be imagining things about Isabel's reaction. Maybe she had never heard the name; maybe she was just tired and exasperated.

That afternoon, Méndez tucked his daughter in for a nap. Renata regaled him with an account of her adventures at nursery school. Although he was desperately sleepy, he sat enthralled by her big eyes, her round cheeks, her crisp little voice sliding between Spanish and English. He had missed her.

In violation of his wife's naptime policy, he read to Renata from a picture book about Clifford the Big Red Dog. Curled up at his side, she corrected his pronunciation in English now and then. He wished he had his daughter's talent for languages, her ear for mimicry. After repeatedly viewing the Disney cartoon film *Peter Pan,* she had taken to calling him "Father" in a disconcertingly British accent.

*It's like having a little bilingual extraterrestrial scampering around the house,* he thought.

"Father," Renata said drowsily. "Go like this: Hem-hem. Hem-hem."

After a moment, he figured it out. His voice was hoarse; she wanted him to clear his throat. But she didn't know the phrase in Spanish or English.

"Like this?" He made a production of clearing his throat.

"Yes. *Muy bien.*"

He kept reading. He wasn't sure which of them fell asleep first.

His cell phone woke him. Isabel.

She wanted him to come to Washington right away.

# Chapter 9

Leo Méndez had always reminded Pescatore of a streetwise professor.

Although his hair had grayed, Méndez looked better now that he had put distance between himself and all his would-be assassins in Mexico. He had lost the pallor, the stooped and haunted look.

As Méndez told his story, Pescatore took notes. He copied information from the whiteboard that Isabel had set up in the dining room of her town house in Alexandria. Two columns on the board, one devoted to the Tecate killings, the other to the Blake Acquisitions Group, listed names, dates, and events. Each column ended with Abrihet Anbessa, the name that had caused the cases to intersect. Pescatore was still getting his head around the whole thing.

Isabel stood at the whiteboard, running the show. Her black hair was piled up and pulled back with barrettes. She wore makeup and a blazer over a skirt. She had taken the afternoon off to host the meeting at her home. Pescatore and Facundo faced Méndez, who was flanked by Athos and Porthos. The two veteran cops were behaving as if Méndez was still the chief of the Diogenes Group and they were still his loyal deputies.

Méndez had dropped a bomb. While reporting on the Blake Group, he explained, he had stumbled onto an allegation against Perry Blake. An employee had accused him of assaulting her, but the victim, an illegal immigrant from Eritrea, hadn't gone to the police. She ran to Mexico with information stolen from Blake's office, planning to use it against him somehow. Then she decided to come back. Méndez had traced her whereabouts as far as Tijuana in early August. Her name was Abrihet Anbessa.

In return, Pescatore told Méndez about his own investigation. Abrihet Anbessa had surfaced as a survivor of the Tecate massacre. She had told a Brazilian witness that she thought powerful people in New York had engineered the multiple murders in order to kill her. The photos and facts matched. Pescatore and Méndez were looking for the same person.

The group had spent the afternoon talking. Where was Abrihet? What was in the pen drive she had taken? Was there a connection between the Blakes and the killings at the border?

"If there isn't," Méndez said, "it means coincidence is the most powerful force in the universe."

"We don't have proof," Isabel replied. "Suspicion. Logic. A potential motive. But we don't have proof that the Blakes, or someone acting on their behalf, were involved."

"What other explanation is there?"

"Leo, immigrants get killed all the time. Here's a question: Why kill the others if she was the target?"

"We were talking about that..."

Méndez glanced at Athos. The grizzled cop had taken off his baseball cap; his remaining strands of hair were combed neatly across his brown scalp. He sat with his fingers interlaced in front of him.

"Based on past experience, Licenciada Puente," Athos said, "it could be the triggermen lost control, or improvised. The young wolves out there today are totally crazy. Another scenario: it could be a mafia tactic to hide the true target of the crime."

"I suppose. But that's convoluted. What do you think, Valentine?"

"You're right—we can't prove it. But I gotta think Blake's involved. Maybe they got their pals in Mexico to send shooters after her. I wonder if there's a link on the U.S. side through the missing border inspector, Covington. Maybe he was helping them look for her. Did he ever turn up?"

"No. The word is he's dead."

Isabel turned to Facundo and asked for his opinion.

Facundo sipped a San Pellegrino lemon soda.

"I think this is a real *quilombo,* that's what I think," he growled.

"Translation of folkloric Argentine term," Pescatore said drily to the others, "'a big complicated mess.'"

"I would venture to say," Facundo said, "that it is unusual for American titans of finance to hire Mexican assassins to rub out African migrants."

"Extremely unusual," Isabel said.

"It would help to know more about the leader of this gang—El T. And any conceivable connection to the Blake Group."

Isabel opened a folder. "Well, we have a sketch, for what it's worth. Based on Chiclet's description."

Two days earlier, Athos and Porthos had delivered Chiclet to the front gate of the U.S. embassy in Mexico City. With the Honduran smuggler in the custody of Homeland Security agents based at the embassy, Isabel had reinserted her agency into the official investigation, which the smuggler's confession would point toward Tayane Pires in Rio de Janeiro.

Isabel distributed copies of the sketch. It was a reasonably detailed likeness of a strong-boned, clean-shaven face. A Latino in his thirties with grim eyes and buzz-cut black hair receding at the temples.

After putting on reading glasses, Athos studied the image.

"He looks familiar. It would help to show this to certain people."

"By all means do that, discreetly," Isabel said. "We haven't come up with anything."

"With all respect, I would bet on the *comandante* against your databases," Porthos said. "He remembers everything. And he is older than Moses."

It occurred to Pescatore that the group at the table were the people he most trusted and admired. The woman he had almost married; a boss who was like a father to him; three staunch friends with whom he had battled bad guys. Heart-warming, but also kind of sad. The breakup with Isabel still cast a shadow over their relationship. He and Facundo were based in different countries now. Despite Pescatore's bond with the Mexicans, he didn't really know them that well. It made him realize how alone he was in the world. Especially now that his so-called romance with Fatima Belhaj had sunk into radio silence.

"One thing," Pescatore said. "El T is former military. Didn't you say the Blakes have a veteran running security, Leo?"

"Yes," Méndez said. "A large surly individual named Krystak."

"Major Louis Krystak," Isabel said. "Veteran of Afghanistan. Close to the Blakes, especially the father. We can look for a connection. But we don't even know if El T is American or Mexican."

She turned to Méndez. "Except for you, Leo, everyone in this room works for me—and therefore the U.S. government. But we are old friends, and you've made an extraordinary contribution today. I'm ready to incorporate you into the team if you'd like. Unofficially—as an unpaid consultant, let's call it—on the condition that you don't write about this again unless you have my approval."

"Ideally, I will write something in the future," Méndez said. "When the timing is right."

"That might never happen." Isabel showed her teeth without smiling. "The timing might never be right."

She had made a calculated choice to have this conversation in front of witnesses, Pescatore thought. She had to protect herself. Even though this journalist had once been a police chief—and had handed her a breakthrough on the case.

"Fine." Méndez sighed. "The important thing is to get to the bottom of this. And to find that young woman—if it isn't too late. I surrender my reporter's badge to you, Isabel."

"Good."

"Temporarily."

"Understood."

Méndez glanced at Pescatore, who flashed him a grin in response. *Way to get with the program, amigo. Welcome back to Cop-World.*

Isabel laid out the game plan.

"Facundo, you have to return to Brazil and make sure Tayane is safe and cooperative. She's our only victim-slash-witness."

"Very good," Facundo said. "I will leave tonight."

"What about Zoraida Padilla?" Méndez asked. "She is a valuable witness too. I am concerned about her."

"I'll assign New York agents to protective surveillance," Isabel said. "They'll be told she's a source in a sensitive smuggling case. Anyone shadows her, my guys shadow them."

"Thank you," Méndez said. "I will tell her to rest easy."

Isabel turned to Athos and Porthos. She wanted them to fly to Tijuana and start a search for Abrihet.

"At your orders, Licenciada," Porthos said.

*Good plan,* Pescatore thought. *But what about the third musketeer?*

He raised his hand. "Isabel. Shouldn't I go down there too?"

"You're going to work another front. With Leo. In Italy."

The Mexicans left. Pescatore walked with Facundo to the Argentine's rental car. They conferred on the sidewalk. Facundo bowed his head pensively, hands stuffed in the pockets of his off-white linen suit, feet planted in pointy two-tone shoes. The outfit made him resemble the owner of a Caribbean nightclub in a 1950s film.

Facundo urged Pescatore to watch himself. Things were moving in a dangerous direction.

"This is uncharted terrain," Facundo said. "Although I have great respect and affection for Isabel, she is playing a tricky game on multiple levels. We are in a vulnerable role, scouts out in front of the official inquiry. Her bosses don't know about us, do they?"

"Uh, no. We're off the books, as far as I can tell." Pescatore hesitated. He hadn't told Facundo much about the secret nature of his mission or Isabel's troubles in her agency. In a hopeful tone, he added, "It's worked so far."

"How she handles it is her decision. She's the client. Sooner or later, though, operating in a gray area could be a problem. Be careful, son. Are you going home now?"

"Not yet. Isabel wants to talk privately."

"Ah."

Facundo raised his eyebrows. He thumped Pescatore on the shoulder, told him again to be careful, and left.

Pescatore knew that Facundo had been on the verge of making another comment. At the dining-room table, the Argentine's calm alert eyes had moved between Pescatore and

Isabel. Perhaps he had noticed the feeling that had rekin-
dled between them. Unspoken, a glimmer, but it was there.
Facundo's discretion was a vote of confidence that Pescatore
could handle such entanglements on his own.

*I hope he's right,* Pescatore thought.

Isabel had changed into jeans, a denim shirt, and some kind
of fashionable-looking open-toed ankle boots. She suggested
he stay for dinner. He said he didn't want to impose.

"Why eat alone when we can eat together?" she said. "We'll
get some work done at the same time."

"Good point. Can I help in the kitchen?"

"Not unless you've learned to cook."

Isabel prepared *ropa vieja,* rice and beans, fried plantains.
She kept their glasses filled with Rioja. He hoped it would
calm him down and help him sleep. So much for his resolution
to stay away from alcohol. Isabel was knocking back the wine
right along with him.

Ladling seconds onto his plate, she asked, "More *maduros*?"

"Absolutely."

"You always liked them."

"I'd eat fried bananas for breakfast if you let me."

"You'd weigh two hundred fifty pounds."

Her grin faded. She said she was going to share information
with him in confidence.

"Not because I don't trust the others, but they aren't U.S.
citizens. Bottom line: this trip to Italy is really crucial."

"It's all riding on Leo's source, I guess."

"Right. If we don't find Abrihet, if we can't corroborate her
account and make a connection to Tecate, the Blakes could be
in the clear."

"What about the corruption case? Didn't Leo's article get
things moving?"

"Yes and no. I met with the FBI and Justice. The State

Department got involved. There's White House interest. Many equities."

"What does that mean?"

"DC-speak for a lot of players throwing their weight around."

"Huh. Did they finally decide you've got enough for indictments?"

She grimaced disdainfully. "They decided not to decide. Until after the elections. This administration doesn't want to tangle with the Blakes. Or interfere with a big international merger."

"That sucks."

"I'd like to find Abrihet, or find out more about her, before I contravene direct orders and accuse Perry Blake of being an attempted rapist and murderer."

After dinner, Pescatore and Isabel took a walk. It had been their evening ritual in San Diego. Pescatore preferred the Pacific to the Potomac, but he liked Alexandria's historic district with its Colonial facades and cobblestones. Twilight softened the blanket of September heat. They strolled past a World War II–era torpedo factory converted into a riverfront center for art galleries. The wooden marina was half empty on a Wednesday night. In the park, a family of ducks waddled across the grass. Pescatore felt full and tipsy. He imagined Isabel taking walks here at dusk, sometimes with Hasselhoff, mostly alone. He pictured her living in that big town house all by herself.

A message pinged on her BlackBerry.

"Leo just reminded me," she said. "Blake is on TV tonight. A counterattack to the article last week."

"For our viewing pleasure."

Back in her living room, Isabel took off her ankle boots and slid onto the couch. She curled up on her side, knees drawn up, in the feline TV-watching pose that Pescatore remembered.

Resisting the impulse to join her on the couch, he sat in an armchair at an angle to the television.

A financial network was broadcasting a profile of Perry Blake. Tall and lithe, he strode across a stage to accept an award. He conferred with guys in hard hats. He escorted a supermodel out of a helicopter in the glow of rooftop spotlights. He tossed a football during a charity event.

"Throws a nice spiral, I'll give him that," Pescatore said.

The camera did a quick tour of Blake's duplex by Central Park and his mansions on the East and West Coasts, in the Hamptons and Bel Air. He also kept an apartment upstairs from his headquarters office because he pulled so many all-nighters. The interviewer was a star of the financial network and had a folksy, brassy style. She power-walked with Blake down a glass-walled hallway, the canyons of Manhattan rising and falling behind them. She called him Perry. She asked how he kept up his bicoastal, round-the-clock pace.

"Is this a commercial?" Pescatore demanded. "Is she gonna mention the freaking federal case against him? What is this bullshit?"

No answer. He glanced at Isabel illuminated by the screen, the sleek sculpted lines of her face brought out by the pulled-back hair. Her eyes glowed in the shadows. Pescatore scrutinized Blake as he would a suspect he wanted to remember: rooster crest of hair, crisp pointy jaw, tight impatient mouth. His office commanded a view of the Hudson and East Rivers flowing together at the prow of the island, the Statue of Liberty a midget in the background. Blake reclined at his desk in a salmon-colored polo shirt that showed off his biceps. When the interviewer got around to asking about "recent media reports," he smiled narrowly. His long arm executed a sweeping, dismissive gesture.

*I bet that's the same office where he tried to rape the cleaning lady,* Pescatore thought.

"The federal government has a job to do," Blake said. "Lookit, I understand that."

His Midwestern accent reminded Pescatore of home; heavy consonants, a nasal tone adding a *y* to vowels.

"Frankly," Blake continued, "they are wasting energy and money on us. Not for the first time. You'd think they'd learned their lesson. Is it possible there were administrative errors, corners cut as we grew in Mexico? Sure. It's a complex and dynamic market, as you know, Sophia. But this talk of bribery and corruption is outrageous. It's bull. It's insulting. Lookit, at the end of the day, this fuss will amount to nothing. Here's your headline, Sophia: 'Another Win for the Blake Group. And for the U.S. Economy.'"

Pescatore shook his head. Isabel pointed the remote at the television and killed the power. They sat in sudden darkness. It made him uneasy. Isabel remained silent. Pescatore peered at her. He considered turning on a light, but it wasn't his house. In the faint glow from the windows, he saw Isabel's thumb pushing at her teeth. He realized that she was seething, as angry as he had ever seen her.

"Hey," he said. "You okay?"

He got up and sat on the couch at arm's length. She pursed her lips and exhaled slowly. She turned, as if noticing him next to her for the first time.

"I'm okay," she said.

"It's hard to watch him talk that shit, am I right?"

She nodded. She reached to her left, away from him, and turned on a lamp.

Pescatore tried to sound optimistic. "Blake's playing all cool, but he's worried. I can see it in his eyes. He knows what he did. He's gotta know the survivors are out there, and it scares him. When criminals get scared, they make mistakes."

"I hope you're right."

"I gotta tell you, Isabel, I've never seen you like this. Taking it so personal, I mean. Breaking rules, running ops on your own. Like you don't care who you piss off, what the consequences are."

"I've had it," she snapped. "I spent months on the Blakes, getting nowhere. Then Tecate happened. Horrible, but simple. Somebody killed these people; we need to solve it. Then I got blocked again. And now it all turns out to be connected. It's too much. I can't stop thinking about Abrihet."

Instinctively, Pescatore took her hand. "However you wanna play it, I'm with you a hundred percent."

She squeezed his hand.

"I know."

Her voice was a near whisper, her eyes wide and melancholy. He was unsettled by the nearness of her, the swells and slopes of her curves in repose. Her breathing was agitated. He couldn't tell if it was due to anger, or sadness, or the same urge he was resisting. Or all of that at once.

It would have been so easy to lean across the space between them. Let himself go, reach for her, find her mouth with his. But he didn't budge. The voice in his head wouldn't shut up.

*What the hell are you doing? What's the matter with you? This is not the time or the place.*

With great effort, he disengaged. He pushed himself up off the couch. Trying to act nonchalant, he retrieved his notebook from the dining-room table.

"Okay, great," he said. "I better get home and pack. Thanks for dinner."

She caught up with him at the door, moving with small-footed quickness.

"What's wrong?" she asked.

"Nothing."

"Nothing? One minute we're having a serious conversation, the next minute you bolt."

She was shorter without her heels. She stepped close, like a flyweight boxer slipping inside his reach. His back bumped against a closet door.

"What's wrong, Valentine?"

"It's just...I'm trying to keep things professional."

"Meaning?"

He looked away. "Tell you the truth, I've been having some unprofessional, inappropriate thoughts when I'm around you."

"Inappropriate."

"In a romantic sense."

"Oh."

"I'm sorry to mention it, but that's the way it is."

"What happened with Fatima?"

"Nothing. I decided something, though. Her not making a choice is a choice in itself."

She nodded.

"Isabel," he said. "I don't want to mess things up between you and me. Too much life-and-death stuff going on right now."

She put her hands on his shoulders and looked into his eyes.

"The important thing," she said, "is that we're friends. Good friends. We have to watch out for each other."

"You're right about that."

"Give me a hug before you go."

They kept the hug brief and safe. He turned toward the door.

"Valentine."

"Yeah?"

"When this is all over...we need to have a conversation."

She said the words deadpan, a statement of fact. Yet he had the sensation that a gate had swung open—a gate he'd thought was closed forever.

Driving north on the wooded road through Rock Creek Park, he turned up the music. Springsteen was still in the CD player: "We Take Care of Our Own."

*You did right,* he told himself. *It wasn't the easy thing. Which means it was the right thing. But now what?*

In the final months of their relationship, he and Isabel had fought like cats and dogs. In spite of everything, though, he had always believed that they would get married. The breakup was the main reason he had gone to Buenos Aires. Then he had met Fatima. Things with her were more relaxed. The long-distance aspect helped. They didn't fight, not even in Paris when she had told him about Karim.

He steered the Impala up the exit ramp to Massachusetts Avenue and went northwest. At Wisconsin Avenue, he headed north in sparse traffic on a moonless night.

He was only a few blocks from home when he noticed that the configuration of headlights in his rearview mirror hadn't changed for some time. He peered at the mirror. The sedan behind him was a Ford Interceptor, a model used often as a taxicab or police car. A light-colored van trailed it. The vehicles had remained in position, keeping a moderate distance from him, while others had passed him or turned off the avenue.

He considered slowing down or stopping to see what they would do. By now, though, he was too close to home. A surveillance team would probably know where he was going and avoid blowing their cover. He looked in the mirror again. The driver's hat obscured his face. When Pescatore turned off the avenue, the sedan did not. But the van followed Pescatore. Coincidence? A synchronized move? He decided to pass his apartment building rather than pull into the garage driveway. The van stayed with him. He took a hard right into the dimly lit residential streets behind the apartment towers. The van kept going and disappeared from view. He circled back to his driveway.

In the elevator, he berated himself for dropping his guard. He had been absorbed in his thoughts. He couldn't pinpoint when he had become aware of the vehicles, but he had the uneasy sense that they had been behind him for a while. Maybe there had been a stakeout outside Isabel's house. His first guess: Blake security goons, like the ones Méndez had seen in New York. Watching the watchers. Another scenario: What if they were federal agents? HSI or FBI? Maybe Isabel's rivals in government had gotten wind of her little freelance global op and were gathering evidence to squash her good. Along with her associates. He resisted the impulse to call her.

*What are you gonna say, exactly? The wine went to your head and you hallucinated spies on your tail?*

His two-bedroom apartment was on the eighteenth floor. It offered a view of dense treetops and single-family houses stretching west toward Virginia. Nice, but no comparison to the rooftop place where he had lived in Buenos Aires. His Washington landlord, Facundo's Israeli friend, was a former pilot for El Al. The paintings and decor were dominated by motifs of airplanes, travel and Israel. Pescatore had added art and souvenirs from Chicago, the Mexican border and South America.

Pescatore checked his phone and discovered an e-mail from Fatima. The brief note said she was very busy; French counterterror cops were on high alert for attacks. He decided he had to talk to Fatima in person. Before anything else happened with Isabel, good or bad, verbal or physical. Maybe after he got done in Italy, he could take a day or two off and go to Paris. Otherwise, chances were that he'd end up losing Fatima and Isabel both.

He packed a suitcase in his bedroom. Then he went into the

study that served as the DC operations center of Villa Crespo International Investigations and Security.

Pescatore's father had grown up in Sicily, immigrated to Argentina, and eventually made his way to Chicago. When Pescatore was in kindergarten, his family visited his father's hometown near Messina. Pescatore remembered old ladies in black. Sheep crossing the road. Eating an *arancino* on the ferry crossing from Calabria—just a fried rice ball, but he'd never tasted one so good before or since.

He was excited about going to Italy, but it was brand-new turf. He had been able to converse in Italian since childhood, and he'd taken a college course. Still, he was far from fluent. He would have to be on his game. He wanted to read up on organized crime, immigration, smuggling.

Opening his laptop, he glanced at his shoulder holster lying on the desk. He would have to leave the gun behind. Unlike in Mexico, he didn't have contacts in Italy who could arrange to score him an unofficial gat.

*This is gonna be the kind of situation*, he thought, *where it would come in handy.*

# PART III

# Chapter 10

The aging turboprop plane banked steeply toward the Mediterranean, causing police helmets and riot shields to clank together.

The island came into view, all twelve square miles of it, an apparition, a clump of rock and earth interrupting the endless expanse of turquoise.

Méndez saw a port, villas on hillsides, the rectangular slab of the approaching runway that bisected a corner of the island. He saw a fortified institutional compound that had to be the detention center. He did not see corpses floating in the water, nor had he expected to. Migrants drowned by the thousands en route to the island, but usually out at sea, out of sight, out of mind.

His vertigo was the result of the rapid rattling descent of the Alitalia flight from Palermo. And anticipation and uncertainty. And the impact of seeing Lampedusa for the first time. A place that was so far away yet had such resonance for his life's work.

Across the narrow aisle separating the single-seat rows, Pescatore gazed out of his window like a bombardier. He leaned toward Méndez, raising his voice over the throb of the engines.

"Guys like us just can't get away from the border, huh, Licenciado?"

Méndez smiled, nodded, and gave him a thumbs-up.

They disembarked with a squad of Italian riot police lugging blue helmets and Plexiglas shields. The burly, bronzed officers were reinforcements for the overcrowded detention center, a powder keg that exploded now and then. East Africans versus North Africans, Muslims versus Christians, everyone versus the cops.

*Poveri diavoli,* the mustachioed sergeant had said. Poor devils. *But if one of them bashes in your head with a fire extinguisher, it doesn't matter how sorry you felt for him.*

Pescatore had struck up a conversation with the sergeant standing at the bar at the Palermo airport. Soon they were all talking and drinking espresso. With smiles and backslaps, the officers celebrated Pescatore's improvised, Spanish-inflected Italian and his Sicilian ancestry. Pescatore and Méndez avoided discussing the reason for their visit, and the cops didn't ask. All kinds of foreign VIPs passed through Lampedusa on vaguely important pilgrimages.

In the terminal, Pescatore picked up Méndez's suitcase. Méndez wrestled it away.

"I'm not a grandfather yet, Valentine," he said.

"No offense intended. It's just I figure you're the brains of the operation, and I'm like the bodyguard."

In some ways, Méndez thought, the young American hadn't changed much. Years ago, Pescatore had been a rookie Patrol agent who had infiltrated a drug cartel thanks to his undercover skills and sheer wildness. He still had curly hair, hard eyes, and a compact, powerful frame. Beneath the thuggish look, though, he was serious and respectful. Hard to believe that he and Méndez had despised each other when they first met, a loathing that had culminated in violence. Pescatore never mentioned that incident. He was unfailingly polite to Méndez and spoke to him in Spanish. As Isabel had said, Pescatore had matured. He spoke more clearly, chose his words more carefully. During the flight, he had been reading a book by an Italian journalist who had traveled with African migrants across the Sahara to the Tunisian coast, then posed as a shipwrecked Bosnian to do undercover reporting in the Lampedusa detention center.

"He calls it 'the New Slave Route,'" Pescatore said. "Good book, Licenciado. I'd read faster in English, but this way I practice a little bit."

The taxi drove past palm trees in a small drab downtown. Dogs slept in front of a city hall with a low clock tower and smudged pink walls. The people on the streets were mostly police, soldiers, sailors, bureaucrats, medical personnel, aid workers, and others involved in handling the influx of smuggling vessels and human cargo.

"More like a movie set than a town," Méndez said.

"What's the population, maybe ten thousand?"

"At most. It has some tourism. But it's a long way south."

"I think they used to exile mafiosi here."

"And political radicals like me."

"Could be worse, exile-wise."

Their hotel had a beach, a nautical motif, and a view of boats bobbing in a marina. Méndez and Pescatore checked in, showered and changed for the meeting that had required eighteen hours and three flights to reach this speck of Italy near North Africa.

Two days earlier at Isabel's house, Méndez had suggested searching in Italy for Abrihet Anbessa's brother. Zoraida Padilla had told Méndez the bits and pieces about him she recalled from conversations with her Eritrean coworker. The brother was older than Abrihet and had a wife and two children. He had been a policeman or soldier before he and his family sailed illegally to Lampedusa about five years ago. While Abrihet was on the run in Tijuana, she had called him in Italy to ask for money to return to the United States.

Isabel wanted her investigation to stay secret, so she couldn't ask for help from the U.S. embassy in Rome or from the Italian authorities. Méndez had proposed an alternative. He knew the director of a nonprofit aid organization in Lampedusa.

Annelise Hald met them on the windswept terrace of a bar overlooking the sea. Upturned nose, golden tan, cherubic features beneath short, tousled blond hair. She was in her late thirties but could have passed for a student. She wore a jean jacket with the collar up and laminated credentials on a cord around her neck.

After the greetings and introductions, Hald said, "You have come a long way to visit, Mr. Méndez."

Her smile had the Scandinavian serenity he remembered. She looked happy to see him, but there was also concern in the slate-gray eyes. Mindful of the need for discretion, he had sent her a cryptic e-mail inquiring about the possibility of locating one of her "clients." She had responded by saying that she could help him next time he visited her. He understood; this kind of thing required a conversation in person. He had said he would be there the next day. That had no doubt caught her off guard.

"Yes, indeed." His laugh sounded a bit forced. "And what a lovely spot. After all, last time you came all the way to Tijuana."

He had met her at an international conference on migration at a think tank in London, an oak-paneled, stone-columned, nineteenth-century sanctum. It was soon after he had become chief of the newly created Diogenes Group, an experiment in border policing that had made him a minor celebrity at the conference. He had participated with Annelise Hald on a panel about comparative border experiences in the Americas and Europe. She presented her project of counseling refugees on Lampedusa and training the Italian police, navy and coast guard on how to treat victims of trauma. Despite her youthful sweetness, she'd struck him as tough-minded and pragmatic. Over drinks with her, he was flattered to learn she knew a lot about his work and its relevance to the surge in migration and the backlash in Europe. They had kept in touch, and a year later, he saw her again when she toured the Mexican border region. He had referred her to friends in law enforcement and human rights groups to ensure that she stayed safe and was not fed nonsense by government mouthpieces.

So he had seen her only twice in his life. He felt it best to ease into his request. He asked how she had held up under the summer's refugee-smuggling onslaught.

"Last week was bad," she said. "Twenty-four-hour days. Forty dead. Dozens of boats, thousands of passengers, mostly departing from Libya."

"Smugglers prefer failed states."

"The anarchy is extraordinary." She spoke confident English with a British tinge. "When I began here, Gaddafi's regime controlled the smuggling. His colonels were greedy sadists, but things were clear. Today, no one is in charge. Soldiers, warlords, Islamists, men with guns—all of them victimizing the refugees, taxing the smugglers, making money. It's a feeding frenzy."

"We are seeing the atomization of mafias, as in Latin America."

She tilted her head. "In what capacity are you here, Mr. Méndez? Reporter? Human rights advocate? Policeman?"

"All three, I suppose."

Stirring his espresso, Pescatore said, "International man of mystery."

Hald grinned. She appeared comfortable with the American, though Méndez could tell she was trying to figure out who he was and why he was there. Méndez had introduced him as a colleague.

"Our visit is unofficial, off the record," Méndez said. "I am here as an investigator, not a reporter. I would like to impose on you for a favor."

He explained that they wanted to find an Eritrean refugee who could lead them to a witness in a U.S. criminal case. The witness was the refugee's sister, who was in imminent danger. Méndez gave her Abrihet's full name; he didn't have the first name of the brother. He omitted contextual details except to mention the link to the Mexican border, which he thought might pique her interest. He described what he knew about the brother.

"Not much to work with," she said. "It is quite possible the family left Italy. Many Eritreans continue to Sweden or the UK."

Méndez gestured at Pescatore, who pulled a notebook from the pocket of his leather jacket.

"Actually, ma'am, we are pretty sure they're in Italy," Pescatore said. "We have phone traffic with Italian numbers. I can help narrow it down as far as time frames and locations."

Isabel Puente had obtained the records of a cell phone belonging to Abrihet Anbessa. Not with a judicial request, because Isabel didn't want the obligatory explanations and paper trail just yet. Méndez believed she had gone to a friend in an intelligence agency.

The records showed calls to and from Italy over four years. Pescatore said the first phone number was in a town in Sicily that housed a government shelter where refugees were transferred after landing in Lampedusa and being processed. The subsequent numbers were in the south of the Italian boot around Naples. An analyst in Isabel's office had traced the numbers to migrant centers, pay phones, and cell phones. Abrihet had made her final calls—one on the day after Blake attacked her—to a cell phone without a registered owner in a coastal town north of Naples. After Abrihet's escape to Mexico, her phone and the phone in Italy went dark.

"I think he's living somewhere around that town," Pescatore said. "We'll go there next. But it sure would help to know who we're looking for."

Hald drank her tea impassively. The phone data Pescatore had outlined gave off a distinct whiff of secret government machinery in action. The enthusiasm of her greeting had all but evaporated.

"It improves the chances to identify him," she said.

"Excellent," Méndez said. "I—"

"But you put me in a difficult position." She interrupted him, her voice soft and steady. "There are rules and laws governing privacy and confidentiality. My organization, the Italian government, the European Union, the UN—they all have rules and laws. Also, I do not know where this information will go. A newspaper, an intelligence service?"

"I apologize, Annelise," Méndez said. "I will be careful and discreet."

"Can you tell me why you must talk to this man?"

"I am afraid not. It is a very serious case. Terrible, remarkable, like nothing I have seen before. If I could explain to you the facts, you would understand."

"What will be the consequences for him if I disclose his identity? Will he be dragged into an international police investigation? Will it bring him a great deal of public attention?"

"I would like to avoid all that, but honestly, I am not sure."

"Would it put him and his family in danger?"

"Possibly. But his sister is already in danger. If she is still alive. I cannot imagine he would not want to help."

She stared at the sea.

*She doesn't want to harm people she's supposed to protect,* Méndez thought. *And she could lose her job. Her calling, her obsession. More than most people, I know what this kind of work means to her. And I am asking her to risk it.*

"I need to know more," she said. "Trust works both ways."

Méndez glanced at Pescatore, who widened his eyes to indicate he would follow the Mexican's lead.

"Very well," Méndez said.

He told her about the massacre in Tecate and about Abrihet. Although he didn't mention the Blakes, he said the investigation had led in unexpected directions and implicated powerful figures. When he finished, Hald said nothing for a moment. One hand lay flat on her collarbone, her thumb and forefinger bracketing her throat.

Her eyes glistening, her voice firm, she said, "Meet me here tonight at eight."

The plan for the afternoon was to get some rest and then go for a run.

Méndez dozed for a few unsatisfying minutes. He got up and paced. He hoped Annelise could deliver. That depended not just on her willingness but on the vagaries of record-keeping and communication in underfunded, overworked government agencies and nonprofit groups.

Meanwhile, Méndez was having regrets about his deal to give Isabel veto rights over his article. His nostalgia for police work had gotten the better of him. He had surrendered to his eagerness to join the hunt, get inside the investigation, and regain the power—at least figuratively—to kick down doors. In the larger scheme of things, what was one newspaper story more or less? That's what he had told himself in Washington. Now, though, he pictured the young faces of his staff in San Diego—who knew only that he was chasing a lead overseas—when he tried to explain himself. He had used the website's funds to pay for a trip that might not result in a story. Annelise's question echoed in his head: *In what capacity are you here?*

Méndez stood on the balcony holding his phone. Seagulls cawed. Yachts and fishing boats bobbed in their berths. He checked the time. At this hour, the kids would be in school.

His marriage was in crisis. After Isabel Puente called, it had been a harsh task to inform his wife that he wanted to turn around and leave San Diego again. The best approach, he had decided, was full disclosure. He had told Estela about his breakthrough in New York and Isabel's mysterious summons to Washington.

Worse than rage or tears, Estela reacted with icy indifference.

*When we left Tijuana, you promised to make sure our life as a family was your priority again. Finally, after all that sacrifice and pain, we would come first. What you are saying now, no matter how reasonable and compelling it sounds, shows you weren't telling the truth.*

Méndez recalled the aloof goodbye at the airport, her grudging acceptance of his kiss. He didn't have the energy to talk to her right now. He sent her a text message to say that he had arrived, told her to give his love to the children, and promised to call when he could.

Two minutes later, she called him.

Her tone crushed any hope that her mood had improved. Her words sent his stress level soaring. She was being followed.

"I noticed the day you left," Estela said. "Coming back from the airport, I saw a gray truck behind me, a Suburban. I thought I had seen it when we left the house. Then I spotted it again yesterday taking the kids to school, and again going to the university. So I did one of the maneuvers we learned: I exited the freeway and got right back on. They stayed with me the whole way."

Porthos had taught Méndez and his wife evasive driving, how to spot and lose a tail, how to thwart a carjacking or ambush. Estela was levelheaded and didn't tend to imagine things.

"This is serious, *mi amor*," Méndez said. "How about this morning?"

"A black Jeep when I dropped Renata off. It followed me part of the way home."

"Do you see anything strange on our street now?"

"No."

"Have you called the number they gave us at the federal building?"

U.S. agents had set up emergency protocols, including a phone number the family could call day or night.

"No, Leo. I did the logical thing and called you first."

Méndez banged a hand down on the balcony railing. It was the worst possible moment for this to happen. The vault of cloudless sky above him worsened the sense of being marooned and out of position.

"Call them right away. Even if nothing else happens, it's important that we document this."

"You call them."

"What?"

"You call them."

"Estela. I am halfway around the world on an island in the middle of nowhere. In the middle of an investigation."

"Don't tell me about your problems."

He was infuriated by her coldness, her use of the potential danger to worsen his guilt feelings. Composing himself, he said, "Fine. Of course, they will just turn around and call you, and probably pay you a visit, so be ready for that."

"Fine."

"Call me again if anything happens. If you have even the slightest sense of danger, call 911 right away."

"Fine."

"Tell me when you hear from them. Kisses to you and Juan and Renata. Please take care of yourself, *mi amor.*"

She hung up. Méndez dialed the emergency number and was relayed to a San Diego police detective on the federal antidrug task force. The detective promised to look into it. Méndez called Isabel Puente in Washington and got her voice mail. He left a message explaining what had happened and asking if she could check with her people in San Diego. He called his wife again. It was a short conversation.

Any lingering notions of taking a nap had disappeared. Méndez put on sweatpants and a T-shirt and went to the small, marble-floored lobby. He found Pescatore at the bar hoisting yet another espresso. Pescatore's green Border Patrol T-shirt and baggy shorts emphasized his tanklike physique. He ordered coffee for Méndez and asked what was wrong.

"Is it that obvious?"

"You look upset, that's all."

Méndez described the call from his wife. Pescatore's eyes widened.

"You think it's connected to the Blake security guys tailing the Guatemalan lady in New York?"

"It occurred to me."

"The other night, after we met at Isabel's house, I could have sworn I spotted vehicles following me."

His stomach tightened. "Really?"

"Yeah. But I wasn't on the ball like your wife. I wasn't able to confirm it. Can't jump to conclusions."

"The situation is conducive to paranoia."

"Absolutely."

"Another possibility is that Mexican operatives related to this somehow are doing surveillance on Estela. Also, I have accumulated an assortment of other enemies for other reasons."

"I don't like any of those scenarios."

"Me either. Let's get some exercise."

At first, the run was a welcome release. Pescatore led him on a route through hills above the rocky coast. They ran past sumptuous villas, vacation bungalows, and older, flat-roofed dwellings of stone and wood. A resort lifestyle juxtaposed with a national security outpost, a penal colony, in a limbo between north and south. Living in Lampedusa was a bit like living in the Playas de Tijuana neighborhood near the beach during the years when the migratory madness at the Mexican border was at its peak, Méndez thought. Enjoy the view—if you can ignore the despair.

After two miles, Méndez began to suffer. Although Pescatore was taking it easy, he was too young, strong and fast. The sun beat down. Méndez poured sweat. He had difficulty breathing. Silver spots swam in front of his eyes. An itching sensation buzzed through his arms and torso. It escalated into a burning.

As they labored up an incline in open land, the pain narrowed and mutated into a spear jabbing into his belly. The silver spots accumulated, obscuring his vision. When he reached the top, his legs gave way. He avoided total collapse by sitting down abruptly against a boulder. He experienced an overwhelming desire to sleep...

"Leo! Leo, are you all right?"

Pescatore shook him. Méndez blinked. He drank from the proffered water bottle, seeing alarm in the tough earnest face floating above him.

"Don't fret, Valentine," he said, gasping for breath. "I will live to fight another day."

"I overdid it, pushed you too hard."

"Not your fault." *The runner stumbles,* Méndez thought. *The embarrassment is worse than the pain.*

Pescatore tried to encourage him. "The time zones, the jet lag, it's wearing me out too. You okay?"

"I would like to sit a moment."

"Sure."

Méndez pulled himself up and sat on the boulder. Pescatore joined him. They passed the water bottle back and forth, silent except for the sound of Méndez's breathing returning to normal. Pescatore nudged him.

"Leo, isn't that the detention facility?"

Méndez looked. A chain-mesh fence topped a ridge. There was a warning sign in Italian and English. The hillside dipped to reveal a corner of the compound: high walls, floodlights, a courtyard. Laundry hung from barred windows, multicolored African garments like banners festooning a white-walled dormitory. Knots of people ebbed and flowed. Shirtless youths kicked a soccer ball. A murmur of voices reached Méndez on the wind.

"Looks calm," he said.

"The sergeant at the airport said things can get nasty, though. When they riot, they burn mattresses, throw broken glass, rip up furniture for weapons."

Méndez drank more water. Pescatore spoke up again.

"You think we have a chance of locking up these guys, Leo?"

"Who?"

"The killers. The masterminds. Everybody involved."

"I don't know, Valentine. I almost prefer dealing with drug lords. That may sound strange. I don't romanticize them at all, but at least drug lords have personality. And physical courage. And, occasionally, something of a code. Do you remember when they caught Chapo Guzman?"

"Which time? He escapes so much, I lose track."

"The last time. In Sinaloa. He was running from the police. He and a henchman carjacked a woman. The woman left her purse in the car, but before they took off, the henchman reached out and gave her the purse."

"Why?"

"Because he was a narco, a killer, at that moment a car-jacker. But he was not a thief. Do you think Perry Blake would do the same thing in that situation?"

"Good question."

"We have had perverse good luck—Perry Blake has trouble controlling his vicious impulses. Otherwise, I wouldn't have much hope."

"Why not?"

Méndez used his shirt to mop sweat from his face.

"I have learned how much these people get away with. Not just ruthless, unethical business practices—nobody cares about that. No, I mean demonstrable crimes. I wrote an article about it, and I was naive enough to think it would have an impact."

"Isabel said your article was great, it shook things up. But her bosses don't want to mess with Wall Street *chingones*."

"Those *chingones* have more impunity than drug lords or terrorists or politicians. And they run your country, my friend."

Pescatore shifted uncomfortably. "I respect your politics and everything, Licenciado. But China and Venezuela and Cuba are a hell of a lot worse."

Méndez grinned.

"I detect the influence of a certain charming Cuban-American conservative."

"Compared to Isabel, I'm more of an independent. But I gotta tell you, I know a guy from my neighborhood. His father made money in the produce business. The son made a fortune in finance. Family man, treats his employees right. He's a CEO now. They're not all animals."

"Of course not. It's not a question of ideology, it's a question of justice. When I was your age, Valentine, I thought capitalism had to be abolished. Now I have a simpler solution. Put handcuffs on the gangsters. Including the ones in business suits."

"Doesn't sound radical to me."

The wind had picked up. The temperature had dropped.

Méndez buttoned his tweed sports jacket and raised the collar. Annelise Hald wore a Palestinian scarf furled around her neck with the dexterity of someone who had actually seen Palestinians wear scarves. Behind her, the sunset had left slashes of red and orange across the sky and sea. She occupied the same spot on the terrace as before. Inside the bar, a table of half a dozen officers of the Carabinieri—red stripes on black pants, white diagonal sashes over blue shirts—watched a newscast on a big screen. Their postures suggested they had plenty of time and limited recreational options.

Pescatore's slouch was more alert. His fingers toyed absently with the black-thread crucifix around his neck. Like Méndez, he eyed the laptop computer on the table.

Hald sipped a glass of red wine, her face half hidden in shadow. It appeared to Méndez that her serenity was back and that her misgivings had been offset by curiosity about why this particular name had materialized out of a tsunami of suffering.

"I think I found him," she said. "I had to do research. And make phone calls."

Méndez nodded appreciatively, not wanting to slow things down with a comment. He was still recovering from his exertions that afternoon. The fog in his head had not entirely cleared.

She opened the laptop. The glow of the screen illuminated strands of blond above the youthful features. She read in a businesslike voice.

"Solomon Anbessa. Age forty-six. Accompanied by a wife, seventeen-year-old daughter, ten-year-old son. From Asmara. They were rescued four years ago by the Italian coast guard. They sailed from the Libyan coast near Benghazi. One hundred eighty-seven people on a fishing boat built for twenty. Eritreans, Somalis, Nigerians, a few Syrians. The smugglers chose Mr. Anbessa to steer. He has no maritime experience, but he is a computer technician and a military veteran, a former captain in the army. He seemed capable to them. They gave him a short lesson on how to use the tiller and a satellite phone programmed with the number of the Italian coast guard. He was told to sail for twenty-four hours, then call, ask for help, and pray."

She raised her head, glanced around at the terrace and the bar, and resumed.

"The boat began to leak. Mr. Anbessa called the coast guard. He steered the best he could. They had no food or water. The sea became rough. Two children fell overboard and drowned. Four children, a woman, and an elderly man died of exposure and dehydration. They were rescued on the fourth day. The boat was so crowded there was no room on deck for the rescuers. Most of the passengers suffered third-degree burns."

"A fire?" Méndez asked.

"No. Burns caused by the sun, leaking gasoline, urine, saltwater, chemicals in clothing. The toxic mess mixes together, and they sit in it for days."

The horizon had turned black. The wind blew cold. Méndez imagined an armada of ghost ships piled with cadavers sailing through the night, souls swirling in the sky like an aerial escort. He shivered.

"Is there mention of a sister?" he asked.

"No. The family applied for political asylum for the usual reasons: they feared the daughter would be forcibly conscripted and abused in the Eritrean military."

Two years later, Méndez thought, Abrihet Anbessa migrated as well. But she, for whatever reason, had chosen a separate path and gone to the United States. He asked Annelise if she was confident that Solomon Anbessa was their man.

"The timing, the facts and the geography fit the data points you gave me. The first phone number in Sicily is near the Catholic shelter where the family went from here. The most recent residence I can find was in government-subsidized housing—a converted hotel in the Campania region you mentioned. And his face looks something like the photograph of her you showed me, though that is not conclusive."

She dictated the details to Pescatore, who took notes. Méndez asked if she had brought a photograph.

She handed him an envelope. Pescatore leaned forward. Méndez staved him off with a look and tucked the envelope into a pocket.

Méndez thanked Annelise again. They sipped their drinks. The wind ruffled his hair. He ached. He was cold. He was concerned that he had created problems for Annelise, or damaged their friendship, or both. He was worried about the safety of his family and the future of his marriage. But at this moment, he was happy.

Annelise Hald closed her laptop. She rolled her shoulders. From the refuge of her scarf, she gave him a brief smile.

"It was a pleasure to see you again, Mr. Méndez. If the situation were different, I could have taken you on a tour. We could have talked to refugees, accompanied a rescue patrol."

"Another time. But I am at your orders for any favor you might need in the future."

"There is a favor you can do for me."

"Name it."

"Please get off this island as soon as you can."

# Chapter 11

In the glory days of Rome, the emperor Domitian built the coastal road to connect the capital to the commercial and military ports of the Bay of Naples.

The Via Domiziana belonged now to the Camorra, the Naples mafia. A seaside drag running through criminal empires. Because Neapolitan gangsters disdained prostitution, the Camorra had ceded the racket in the bleak towns north of Naples to the Nigerian mafia—for a fee.

On the outskirts of Palazzo di Sabbia, African women appeared. A Saturday-night parade of silhouettes in shorts, miniskirts, knee-high boots, multicolored braids, posing and strutting and staggering. Pimps sat on walls, crates and beach chairs. Drug dealers prowled among stopped and slow-moving cars. The rented Fiat passed polluted beaches, trash dumps, empty stores, and car skeletons.

"Reminds me of Stony Island Avenue back home," Pescatore said. "All torn up."

Pescatore drove through a neon-lit corridor lined by the hulks of faded motels with fanciful names. The helter-skelter architecture dated to the 1980s, when a construction frenzy had enriched the Camorra and its cronies. Grandiose notions of a tourist Riviera didn't materialize. The hotels and motels had served mainly to shelter victims of an earthquake. Some of the establishments had been abandoned. Others had become cheap housing for immigrants and refugees, mostly from sub-Saharan Africa.

Pescatore saw men alone with time on their hands. They congregated in the pallid glow of cell phone shops, money-transfer outlets, a storefront chapel, a business called Makalele Exotic Fashions Boutique.

"Remarkable," Méndez said. "For a century, Italy was a sending country. So many Italians migrated to the Americas, to northern Europe. And in a few decades, it has transformed into a receiving country."

"Migrants or not, this place has always been wild," Pescatore said. "It's where the *latitanti* hide out."

"The what?"

"Camorra fugitives. The police take years to find them in their own neighborhoods. My uncle Rocco says people in this part of Italy have trouble with rules, so it's a good place to hide. And to be an illegal alien, I guess."

"Are we getting close?"

"A few blocks, I think."

They had spent two days driving up and down the Via Domiziana. The information from Annelise Hald had led to a town near Palazzo di Sabbia and a converted motel with small satellite dishes dotting windows and balconies of units occupied by multiple families. Pescatore and Méndez found an apartment where the Anbessas had lived, but the family had moved. The search led to previous workplaces for Solomon Anbessa—a ranch where he had cleaned up after buffalo that produced milk for mozzarella cheese, then an Internet café where he had put his computer skills to use. A Ghanaian at the café said Solomon was managing another Internet spot in

Palazzo di Sabbia. The Ghanaian and others they talked to, African and Italian, harmless and hard-ass, hadn't been enthusiastic about outsiders asking questions.

The atmosphere aggravated Pescatore's paranoia, which had amped up after the news about Mrs. Méndez being followed in San Diego. He checked his mirrors again. He hadn't spotted surveillance, but that didn't mean much in a region full of eyes and ears. By now, a lot of people knew they were looking for Solomon Anbessa.

"Look." Méndez pointed. "Dar es Salaam First Class Internet Service."

"That's the one," Pescatore said. "They said the owner is Tanzanian."

He pulled to the curb. The cybercafé across the street was the only open business in a strip of shuttered or boarded-up locales. The barred windows cast a peninsula of light onto the street. Pescatore backed up. He wanted to see without being seen.

"Now what?" Méndez asked.

"I think we should scope it out a minute, Licenciado."

"Very good."

Reclining behind the wheel in his leather jacket, Pescatore scanned the landscape. Past the commercial strip, human and canine shapes meandered in the gloom of an overgrown vacant lot. The area gave him a bad vibe. And he was worried about Méndez. Pescatore had joked in Lampedusa about feeling like a bodyguard, but he was acutely aware of the fact that Méndez lived under threat. He had been alarmed when Méndez almost fainted during their run. The Mexican sat now with his head back, wearing glasses and a rumpled tweed jacket. He looked beat. He had made a comment about troubles back at home.

*You and me both, brother,* Pescatore thought. *Except I don't have anyone at home. Just troubles.*

He heard the vehicle before he saw it. African hip-hop thundered from the yellow Maserati convertible that pulled up in front of the Dar es Salaam cybercafé. The driver sported a 1970s-style brimmed cap. The passenger wore wraparound shades on a shaved head. Both men looked better fed, better dressed, and more thuggish than the Africans Pescatore had seen up until now.

Two women emerged into the light from the thigh-high weeds of the vacant lot. They tottered on platform heels, statuesque in minidresses, long hair swirling. They greeted the men, making a provocative show of leaning into the car for hugs and kisses. The taller woman did a twirling dance step on the sidewalk, arms wide like she was flying.

After a few minutes of raucous conversation and pounding music, the door of the cybercafé opened. Méndez and Pescatore sat up in unison.

"Now that's what I'm talking about," Pescatore said. "Mr. Anbessa is in the house."

"Are you sure? The light could be better..."

The newcomer was small, trim and straight-backed in a buttoned sweater and pleated khaki trousers. He strode into the street to the driver's door. He spoke to the driver, a volley of words and gestures.

"It's him," Pescatore said. "Height, weight, age. Look how he carries himself, like a guy with military experience."

Judging from the contours of the arm propped on the door, the driver was a lot bigger than the Eritrean. Yet he listened impassively to the diatribe, glancing around as if to confirm he was really the target. The others watched. Solomon Anbessa stood like a sheriff ready to draw. The driver spoke to the women. The women climbed into the convertible without opening the doors, generous curves in motion, bare legs bending and extending.

"Looks like he told them to move the party elsewhere," Méndez said.

"I like him already."

The convertible sped off, trailing its sound track. Solomon glanced up and down the block. His gaze paused on the Fiat. He marched back inside.

Pescatore killed the engine. He and Méndez crossed the street.

The door triggered a warning bell. Pescatore smelled air freshener and bug spray. An aisle in the middle of the high-ceilinged space led through clusters of computer cubicles, two dozen in total, four of them occupied by three African men and a young Italian couple with faux dreadlocks and piercings. The equipment, partitions, and furniture were old but well kept. The carpet was green and clean. Signs announced services— long-distance calls, wire transfers, express mail—and warned against noise, litter, smoking, and assorted misbehaviors. A neatly organized bulletin board contained notices and flyers in Italian, English, French, and several African languages. Computers clicked and whirred.

*Shipshape,* Pescatore thought. *And there's the captain on deck.*

Solomon Anbessa was visible in the rectangular window of a back office a half a story above the rest of the place. Seeing Pescatore and Méndez in the aisle, he descended a short steel staircase built against the back wall.

*"Buona sera."* The voice was cultivated and accented.

"Excuse me," Méndez said in English. "Mr. Anbessa?"

They had decided Méndez would take the lead. He was less likely than Pescatore to be mistaken for a local cop or criminal.

Solomon stopped near the bottom of the staircase, head and torso visible over the wall-like railing.

"Yes."

He stood poised on the stairs, a fight-or-flight stance.

Pescatore couldn't see the right hand. He wondered if it held a pistol or, as had occurred to him during the dispute in the street, if there was a gun beneath the sweater. Pescatore bumped Méndez slightly sideways, thinking he could push him into the cover of a cubicle if necessary.

Méndez said, "Please forgive the intrusion, Mr. Anbessa, but we are investigators from the United States. I am Leo Méndez. This is Valentine Pescatore. It concerns your sister Abrihet."

The stern brown eyes narrowed.

"You are not American."

"I am Mexican, but based in the United States. Mr. Pescatore is an American working for the government."

"What is your name?"

"Méndez. I am—"

"Leo Méndez? You are the writer of the articles about the Blake Acquisitioning Group?" He pronounced the words like someone who read English more than he spoke it.

*There we go,* Pescatore thought with relief. He saw the right hand appear. Empty.

"I am," Méndez said.

"But you are investigators of the American government?"

"It is a complicated situation."

"And you are looking for my sister."

"We have been for weeks. We are very concerned about her."

Solomon asked them to wait. Politely but firmly, he herded out the clients with promises of free computer time for their next visit. He locked the front door and invited Méndez and Pescatore up into his crow's nest. The presence of the three of them made the little office feel full. Anbessa sat in a chair at a desk that contained a ledger, a pen, a phone, and a laptop and gave him a view of the computer area below. Pescatore perched on a corner of the desk, letting Méndez take a second chair. In a framed photo next to a wall cabinet, Solomon Anbessa posed in uniform and dark glasses with a woman and two children who squinted into sunlight in front of a white, flat-roofed house. On another wall, a bank of closed-circuit screens showed security-camera views of the interior, the street, and a side gangway.

"Total coverage," Pescatore said, gesturing at the monitors.

"Severe security problems," Solomon said. "Drugs. Prostitutes. Criminals. When I begin here, they are selling cocaine from inside the place. They are always bothering, making trouble, threatening. I must watch."

Méndez explained what had brought them there. Solomon grimaced with concentration. He had coffee-colored skin, small refined features, and close-set ears. The hair at his temples was gray. He was whip-thin and five six at most. His shirt, sweater and pants were crisply ironed. The loafers gleamed. He glanced repeatedly at the screens.

"And that's why we are here," Méndez concluded. "We hope you can help us find her, ensure her security, and advance our inquiry."

"I see."

"Do you know where she is?" Méndez asked.

"I do."

"In Mexico?"

"I prefer not to say now."

"Is she safe, at least?"

"For the moment, she is safe."

"What good news," Méndez said.

"Thank God," Pescatore said.

The Eritrean studied his visitors, looking back and forth between them. His expression softened. Pescatore saw the resemblance to his sister's bright-eyed smile in a photo Méndez had showed him.

"I can communicate with her," Solomon said. "But it is risky."

"I assume she is not in the United States?" Méndez said.

Solomon said nothing. Pescatore resisted the urge to grab him by the lapels and bark questions.

"Mr. Anbessa," Méndez said patiently. "We have the resources and ability to bring her to the United States, where she will be safe. You can trust us."

Solomon looked at the security monitors again. They showed two vehicles rolling slowly by. He watched until they disappeared from view.

Méndez talked more about the importance of protecting Abrihet. Once again, he asked where she was. Abruptly, Solomon turned to Pescatore and asked, "Who in America will ensure my sister safety?"

"The Department of Homeland Security. I'm an investigator for them."

"You have a badge?"

Pescatore reached for his credentials. He started to explain what a contract investigator was, but Solomon ignored him. He was fixated on the screens. The two vehicles had returned. They stopped in front.

Scowling, Solomon rose to his feet.

Shown from multiple angles, grainy figures piled out— four, five, six men. Hoods, upturned collars. Pescatore spotted a brawny African in a watch cap. He held a pistol.

"Gun," Pescatore said.

*"Bastardi,"* Solomon snapped. "I am ready."

Confirming Pescatore's suspicions, Solomon drew a semiautomatic Beretta pistol from the small of his back beneath the sweater. He placed it on the desk and took keys from a pocket.

The man on-screen aimed up at the camera. His gun flashed, the shot sounded, and the screen went dark.

"Are you armed?" Solomon demanded.

"No," Méndez said.

All three of them were on their feet now. All of the men outside had produced guns.

Solomon's glare conveyed contempt for the kind of useless chickenshit so-called investigators who could waltz into Palazzo di Sabbia without weapons. As the gunmen shot out the external cameras, the screens dying one after another, Solomon unlocked the cabinet and removed a Taurus .38 revolver, a Remington pump-action shotgun, and ammunition. He stuffed shells into his pockets, his movements quick and deft, and looked hard at Pescatore.

"Now I must trust you," Solomon said.

He handed Pescatore the Beretta and extra clips. He gave the revolver to Méndez. The men outside banged on the front doors. Glass broke. Solomon pump-loaded the shotgun.

"Is there a back door?" Pescatore asked.

"Side door," Solomon said, hunching to stare from a corner of the internal office window. "But near the front, impossible to go now."

Pescatore felt a strange mix of adrenaline and satisfaction. His foreboding had been right. He noticed a small back window next to the cabinet, a fogged-glass aperture for light and ventilation.

"I can go through that window," he said.

Méndez shook his head doubtfully. "You'll break your legs."

More glass shattered at the front entrance.

"It's not that high." Pescatore checked the safety on the Beretta. "I'll circle around and come at them from the right side. We gotta divide their fire, triangulate on these fuckers, or we're history."

Solomon nodded fiercely. "Good."

"Watch out for cross fire," Pescatore said. "And call the cops."

"I am calling," Solomon said, punching numbers on the phone on the desk. "But they are very, very slow."

Solomon spoke Italian into the phone as he opened a fuse box and worked switches, plunging the place into darkness. The front doors gave way with a crash. Clambering through the window, Pescatore felt bad about leaving Méndez.

"Leo, use the stairs for your firing position," he said. "Good cover."

"Be careful, *hermano.*"

The window was a tight fit. He slithered out feet-first and hung from the sill. The ground was barely visible in the dark. As he let go, the shooting started inside.

It was a long drop. He did his best to bend his knees to absorb the impact, but it hurt. Pain shot through his legs and especially his left ankle, which had been injury-prone since the Patrol. He fell sideways with a grunt, rolled in grass and mud. He stumbled to his feet in a lot enclosed by ruins. Hurrying to his right, he searched for the gangway that ran alongside the cybercafé. His ankle buckled and throbbed. He entered the passage in a combat crouch, gun out in front of him, left hand gripping right wrist. He limped toward the streetlights and maneuvered around a row of smelly garbage cans at the side door, nearing the end of the narrow space between cinderblock walls.

The gun battle echoed: the crack of pistols, the blast of the shotgun, glass exploding. What scared him most was the rattle of an automatic weapon. He heard shouting, cries of pain. He took a deep breath, anchored his shoulder to the wall, and peered around the corner.

A body lay sprawled on the sidewalk.

*One down,* he thought with savage elation. *Nice work, fellas.*

Three gunmen were firing from behind the cars into the cybercafé. The one closest to Pescatore had an AK-47. A white guy with a flattop haircut, Arab-style scarf around his neck, wide frame in a suede jacket.

Pescatore's position was about fifty feet away and at an angle. The sedan gave only partial cover to the man with the AK-47 and the hooded gunman next to him. The white guy straightened from his crouch and unleashed a barrage into the storefront. Pescatore had to put that thing out of action. In the streetlight, he saw the rifleman's teeth gleam, his mustache curling down to his jaw, his arms tensed against the kick of the weapon. Pescatore saw all this as he took aim and fired four times. The rifleman staggered. He fell in stages, the weapon in his hands still chattering, slugs sparking off the street in a half circle as he went down.

The surprise flank attack spooked the hooded gunman. He scuttled away along the car and ran toward the other car. Pescatore darted a few feet onto the sidewalk to shoot at him. The gunman fell face-first, his pistol flying up out of his hand; Pescatore couldn't tell if it was due to his fire or shots from inside. The hooded gunman was on his hands and knees, groping around for the pistol.

Rounds fired from behind the second car whizzed past Pescatore. He dived back into the gangway, slugs chewing the wall close to him. His right forearm stung. His breath came in heaves. He got down low, reached around the corner, and returned fire blindly. There was more shouting. The shooting in the street abated. A motor roared.

Pescatore popped his head out in time to see that someone had jumped behind the wheel of the car, which Pescatore now recognized as the yellow Maserati from before—with the top up. The convertible lurched from the curb, the passenger door swinging open. An African bolted out of the building, shooting wildly over his shoulder, and tumbled into the moving car. Pescatore heard yelling. He realized it was his own voice, a roar that strained his throat as he emptied his pistol at the Maserati. The car screeched and swerved, gunfire puncturing windows and doors. It ran over the hooded man kneeling in the street, dragging him as it made a U-turn. Leaving the crumpled, mangled body behind, the Maserati zoomed away down the Via Domiziana.

In the gangway, Pescatore sagged back against the wall. His ears rang. His ankle ached. Blood seeped from his right sleeve. But he didn't have time to inspect the damage.

He reloaded, crept out, and made sure the bodies on the street and sidewalk weren't moving.

"Leo!" he yelled. "Mr. Anbessa. All clear?"

He yelled several times more. Finally, Méndez called from inside, "Clear!"

"Anybody hit?"

"Mr. Anbessa."

"I'm coming in."

"I will turn on the lights."

Dar es Salaam First Class Internet Service fit better with its surroundings now: all torn up. Blood, glass, smoke, debris, toppled partitions, demolished computers. An African huddled on his side in a cubicle, bleeding and unconscious. Hobbling on his swollen ankle, Pescatore hauled himself up the stairs into the bullet-shredded office. He found Solomon in his chair, head back, with Méndez pressing a towel to the Eritrean's abdomen. Solomon's breathing was steady, his eyes closed.

Méndez's glasses were cracked and askew. He held the .38 in his free hand. The air was thick with smoke and powder. In the distance, sirens approached.

"You all right, Leo?" Pescatore asked. When he got no answer, he asked again.

"My ears are ringing," Méndez replied, gesturing at an ear. "But I am all right."

"We lucked out. They weren't expecting our little arsenal. Let me get a look at him."

Pescatore assessed Solomon's wounds.

"He needs an ambulance right away," Méndez said.

"I think they're here already."

The sirens were loud and close. Lights flashed outside.

Solomon opened his eyes. He smiled crookedly at Pescatore.

"Good fighting," the Eritrean muttered. "Bravo. *Grazie.*"

*"Grazie a te."* Pescatore patted the lean shoulder. "You're a bona fide warrior, my friend. Just hang on, Solomon, we're gonna get you help."

"Listen," Solomon whispered. "Before the police are coming. My sister is in Mexico."

"Where in Mexico?"

"I have important information. About Blake. The company. Bad activities. In the safe in the cabinet."

"The pen drive your sister took?"

Solomon nodded. Fading in and out of consciousness, he managed to give them a combination. Méndez opened the safe, removed a pen drive, and slipped it into his pocket. Solomon's eyes were closed now.

The police ordered them to come out with their hands up.

"Pescatore." The prosecutor raised a hand with the fingers cupped together. *"Chi cazzo sei?"*

Although Pescatore's Italian was improving, it took him a moment to translate in his head: *Who the fuck are you?*

"I don't understand the question, Dottore. I told you who I am."

Giancarlo Maio rolled his eyes. His sigh sounded more like a growl. He came around and leaned against his desk. He looked with a mock-imploring face at the detectives and bodyguards. Gray morning light spilled into the office through the slats and bars of a window that showed the stained and discolored walls of an air shaft. And more barred windows.

"It is not satisfactory, what you told me," Maio said. "Who you work for in reality? *La* CIA? Intelligence?"

"No, sir, like I said: Homeland Security."

"If I call *il mio caro amico* Philip, the FBI attaché in Rome, he will know you?"

The prosecutor spoke what Pescatore's Uncle Rocco would have called "spaghetti English." Pescatore switched to Italian, thinking it might win him a little respect.

"No, he won't know me. Nobody in the embassy knows me. I'm working for Washington headquarters on a case."

"What case are you talking about?" Maio seemed happy to follow his lead and speak Italian.

"I'd like to cooperate, but I have to get authorization to disclose that."

The prosecutor nodded, deep horizontal lines in his forehead creasing, as if Pescatore had just confessed to something serious.

"Your Italian is pretty good." He said it rather accusingly. "Half Spanish, but pretty good. Better than my cousin Domenico from Providence. All he says is"—he mimicked a gravelly American-ginzo accent complete with mangled grammar and Sicilian dialect—*"Nun ricordu come si dissi."* I *don't remember how to said.*

Pescatore shifted in his chair. His ankle burned. He had read about Maio, who was kind of famous. He had started out as an anti-Mafia magistrate in his native Sicily, then prosecuted Islamic terrorists. It was a surprise to find him investigating a shootout in Camorra-Land. Maio looked the part of the hotshot crime fighter: leathery complexion, rugged build, thick in the middle; a guy in his fifties who tried to take care of himself. Kind of fair-haired for a Sicilian. The aquiline nose, unshaven face, and stylish baggy suit with no tie gave him an old-school quality.

*Vittorio Gassman, but shorter and in a bad mood.* That was what Pescatore had thought the night before when the prosecutor arrived at the crime scene. Two unmarked Alfa Romeos had purred up with blue lights turning. Bodyguards fanned out holding machine pistols, their look a blend of plainclothes cops, male models, and pirates. They escorted Maio, who was puffing meditatively on a cigarette, into the scrum of police and emergency personnel.

Pescatore had drifted through the aftermath of the gunfight as if he were in a hyper-realistic dream that he could stop by waking up but found interesting. An ambulance rushed Solomon to the hospital. Cops put Méndez in a car. Paramedics bandaged Pescatore's forearm, which had been cut by wall splinters from a bullet strike, and wrapped his sprained ankle. Then the police took charge of him too.

At the brutalist concrete courthouse guarded by soldiers with berets and rifles, Pescatore had napped in a locked office before his police interrogation. The detectives kept him separated from Méndez. They were vague about whether Pescatore was being detained as a witness or a suspect. They asked if he knew his assailants. They recited names: Kingsley, Celestine, Precious, Florian the Albanian. Pescatore answered some questions but refused to say why he was in Italy. His requests to call Washington were denied. At six a.m., the detectives gave him a cup of vending-machine espresso and a sweet roll before taking him — in a groaning, graffiti-scarred elevator — up to see the prosecutor.

"How many men you kill last night, Private Investigator Pescatore?"

Back to English again. Maio's question jangled his nerves.

Pescatore contemplated the fact that he might be in serious trouble. Thanks to Fatima Belhaj, he knew European authorities could be outrageously unreasonable anti-cop wussies when it came to judging the use of deadly force.

"It was self-defense, Dottore."

"That's not what I ask."

Despite Maio's exasperation, he treated Pescatore with a certain relaxed familiarity. He seemed impressed by the outcome of the gun battle.

"I shot two guys I know of," Pescatore said in a monotone.

"And how many killed in total? In your, eh, career?"

"What kinda question is that?"

"I want to know who are you. Answer."

"Jeez." He struggled to focus. He wondered if he was experiencing post-traumatic stress syndrome. When he closed his eyes, he saw a spatter of images: the gunfight, the corpses, previous gunfights, previous corpses, at the border and Europe and South America…

Opening his eyes, he said, "Anyone I ever shot was in the line of duty. Including the individuals last night. I count seven. And…"

"And?"

"There was a paramilitary mission. The Middle East. I was like a scout. But it's classified."

"*Minchia*. Classified. A real double-oh-seven."

Pescatore berated himself. *Why the hell did you give that up*, pendejo? *What's wrong with you?* But it was beyond his control. The situation had put his mind on autopilot witness-stand mode: the truth, the whole truth, and nothing but.

"Look, man—I mean, Dottore—I'm not some kind of CIA black ops guy, if that's what you're driving at. This is a legitimate international investigation. People's lives are at stake.

That's why I have to be careful. If you let me call DHS-HQ in Washington for approval, I might be able to talk."

"How do you permit yourself to make such a demand?" Maio had switched to Italian again. His voice rose, his arm waved, his fist pounded. "I don't depend on the whims of Washington! I can charge you with homicide, assault, illegal use of firearms. Espionage, if I get inspired. I don't like this situation. An American and a Mexican present themselves at a cybercafé in godforsaken Palazzo di Sabbia. A team of lumpen Camorra associates choose that precise spot and moment for a punitive commando expedition. Five dead, two wounded. Yes, five! We found two subjects—Martins, Sunset, and Adebayo, Alphonsus—in a Maserati, executed at close range. I ask myself: *What the hell is going on?* My first theory, considering that Spanish-speakers are involved: drugs. But your profile is atypical. This Mexican journalist is atypical. This Eritrean is a decent workingman, a soldier. A big mystery. I don't like it. You—"

A ringtone interrupted—an opera singer belting out an aria. Maio rose, pulled a phone from a pocket, and strode toward the window to answer. The caller must have asked how he was, because he declared, *"Incazzato."*

Pescatore knew that word; it meant "pissed off." The prosecutor who holds your fate in his hands is not someone you want *incazzato*. Things did not look good for Valentine Pescatore, jail-wise. If this blew up into a big scandal, it would hurt everybody, especially Isabel.

While Maio talked on the phone, Pescatore glanced around. Three detectives sat at a conference table covered with folders, piles of documents, and a box of old-fashioned ink-stamper kits. Two bodyguards—one balding, the other with shoulder-length, soccer-star hair—flanked the prosecutor's desk. They watched Pescatore like sleep-deprived pit bulls.

The wall above Maio's chair displayed a black-framed photo of Giovanni Falcone and Paolo Borsellino, the Sicilian anti-Mafia judges assassinated weeks apart in 1992. The legendary duo sat at a table leaning toward each other, as if sharing a private joke. Their smiles had a weary dignity.

In other photos on the wall, Giancarlo Maio examined a cargo container full of cocaine and perp-walked a kingpin with a coat over his head through a gauntlet of police and photographers. Framed press clippings and photos depicted Maio's role in foiling a terrorist plot in Milan to fire a bazooka at a chemical refinery outside Lyon, France. Fatima Belhaj had told Pescatore about that case, a joint French-Italian investigation of a cell of European jihadists returned from Iraq…

An idea flashed in his head. He must have reacted physically, because the long-haired bodyguard gave him a look. As soon as Maio sat back down, Pescatore threw the Hail Mary pass.

"Dottore," he said. "I know you are frustrated. I don't blame you. But there's someone who can vouch for me. I think you know her. Commissaire Fatima Belhaj. With the DGSI in Paris."

Maio's face registered disbelief and curiosity. Pescatore's hunch was right. Maio knew Fatima. And, being a healthy self-respecting Italian male, he was probably not indifferent to her charms.

"Fatima Belhaj," the prosecutor said slowly.

"Yes, sir."

"You know Fatima Belhaj."

"I've investigated terrorism with her."

"An exceptional investigator. A *cara amica* of mine."

"Mine too. In fact, she's"—he searched for the word—"my *fidanzata.*"

Even if marriage had never been mentioned, Italian men called a steady romantic companion a *fidanzata* —fiancée.

"Bullshit." Maio spat the word in English.

"Call her. Ask her. Here's her phone number." Pescatore recited it from memory.

The prosecutor shrugged, the corners of his mouth turning down in grudging admiration.

*"Complimenti,"* he said.

Pescatore started to repeat the number. Maio raised an imperious hand at him and worked his phone with the other. "I have it right here."

When Fatima answered, Maio laid it on thick. In French, he apologized profusely and playfully for waking her up so early on a Sunday morning. He murmured as if he were sitting on her bed with a hand on her shoulder. He said *bella, bellissima,* and *carissima* so many times that Pescatore wanted to say, *Okay, pal, cut the hound-dog crap and get down to it.* After a few minutes, Maio walked across the office to the window again and lowered his voice. The conversation lasted a while.

Finally, Maio came back. With a flourish, he gave Pescatore the phone. He did it as if he were bestowing the grand prize in a lottery and said the word Italians use when they hand you something: *"Toh."*

Fatima's voice was husky with sleep but alert and concerned.

"A big shooting," she said. "You are hurt, *mon amour?*"

"I'm okay," he said. "Mainly bad guys got shot. I just hurt my ankle. The one I twisted that time we went running on the beach in Normandy."

He said the last sentence loudly so Maio could hear.

"I am glad, Valentín." She chuckled warmly. "How is my dashing Sicilian friend treating you?"

"Not great."

201

"A good man. One of their best in antiterrorism. A bit flamboyant, but serious."

"Okay."

"I told him he has to take the utmost care of you. I told him you are highly respected and have done valuable things for the security services of Europe and the United States, and I have total faith and trust in you and whatever you are doing."

"Thank you."

"I also told him you are the most important man in my life, and if anything happens to you, he will have a big problem."

Warmth flooded Pescatore's face. She had stepped up without hesitation when he needed her. He was not alone in the world after all. Given the circumstances, he refrained from asking if her description of him meant she had made a decision or if it was just a figure of speech intended to get him out of a jam.

Keeping his voice low and even, he said, "That's the best thing I've heard in a long time."

"Take care of yourself. I hope to see you soon. *Bisous*."

Pescatore hung up. Maio leaned back in his chair and folded his hands on his midsection. He raised his eyebrows.

"So," the prosecutor said. "Now I know who you are."

# Chapter 12

The worst thing about the gunfight had happened before it started.

After Pescatore went through the window, Méndez hurried out of the office to position himself at the bottom of the staircase. It was pitch-dark because Solomon had killed the lights. Halfway down the stairs, Méndez stumbled. He caught himself on the railing, but his glasses fell off. As he searched for the glasses on the stairs and floor, all hell broke loose: Solomon's shotgun booming in the office, the curses and screams of the attackers, the deafening return fire. Méndez was myopic. He couldn't see a burro at three paces, as the Mexicans say. With bullets flying around him—thank God for Pescatore's advice to shelter behind the wall-like metal railing—he tried to do his part. He fired the revolver desperately into the blur of flashes, voices and shadows.

*If I die, I will die like a man,* he thought. *And if I live, I will set foot outdoors again only if I'm wearing contact lenses. No more getting caught off guard like an idiot, carajo. Nadie muere en la víspera.*

While he concentrated on killing and not being killed, his mind raced. Despite his near-blind, near-deaf state, he quickly understood several things. The attack was no coincidence. Operatives working for the Blakes had been shadowing him and his family. Either they had tracked him to Palazzo di Sabbia or they had been watching Solomon Anbessa already. Or both.

During the interrogation Sunday, Giancarlo Maio had become friendlier when he learned about Méndez's past as a police chief. He soon released Méndez and Pescatore and offered them bodyguards. Somehow, Pescatore had averted disaster and transformed the prosecutor into an ally. He had been reticent with Méndez about how he had done it, mumbling about a "mutual friend."

It was Monday evening. The three of them were in Maio's office talking in the Spanish-Italian-English patois with which they had become comfortable.

"As in Tecate, they hide their role by enlisting local gangsters," Méndez said.

"We gotta find a connection to the Blakes," Pescatore said. "Beyond the fact that Solomon is Abrihet's brother, which is a pretty good start."

"You should look hard at Louis Krystak, the corporate security chief," Méndez told the prosecutor.

Sitting behind his desk, Maio said he would have investigators check the name. He followed Méndez's gaze to the photo of the slain judges Falcone and Borsellino on the wall above him.

"I know that picture," Méndez said. "I have done research about the Sicilian Mafia wars."

"You will find that photo in the offices of most magistrates in Italy, Dottore Méndez." He pronounced it "Mendetz." "They are our martyrs."

When Maio had let Pescatore call Washington, Isabel gave instructions to cooperate with the Italians. Whether Isabel liked it or not, Maio had inserted himself into the case. Better to show good faith. The gunfight had forced her hand. She would have to tell her bosses about her secret investigation. Pescatore had said she sounded glum.

Two problems contributed to her pessimism. Solomon Anbessa was recovering from surgery and too weak to talk, so they still didn't know exactly where his sister was. Moreover, they hadn't seen the information in the pen drive that had been in Solomon's safe. The police had taken the device from Méndez while searching him.

Although Maio's involvement was a complication, Méndez saw it as a benefit too. The Italian justice system gave the prosecutor the power to pursue evidence across international borders. After hearing why Méndez and Pescatore were in his dominion, Maio was champing at the bit. The fact that the Blakes were fabulously influential American magnates made him more avid, not less.

*We had to come to Italy to find a guy who doesn't have an accident in his pants when he hears that name,* Méndez thought.

"So you haven't found any foreign links to the shooters?" Pescatore asked.

Maio lifted his head and shoulders with a grumpy "Eh" noise. "Not yet. There are suspicious things, like the survivor, this Nigerian hoodlum Celestine. He claims the shooting had nothing to do with you. His gang hated Solomon because he harassed dealers and prostitutes around the Internet place. He says they wanted to punish Solomon for being disrespectful in front of their whores. But I don't believe that."

Méndez recalled the incident in the street with the two women. "You think the confrontation was staged? To create a fake motive?"

"Yes. Someone was behind them, manipulating. These Nigerians are mean, but they don't kill that often. Not on the spur of the moment, and not without authorization from the Camorra boss who taxes them. The Camorra boss denies any role, and we corroborated that independently. Somebody else—an outsider—hired this bunch of low-level soldiers. He paid well, judging from the cash on them. We had wiretaps and informants in place for various investigations. It turns out this Albanian and the Nigerians were talking about you two, and mentioned Solomon's name, soon after you landed at the airport. They followed your trail."

*Nothing like cold confirmation to nourish your fears,* Méndez thought. His first move after the investigators returned his phone had been to call his wife. She and the police in San Diego hadn't spotted further surveillance, which was a relief. Méndez also called Athos and Porthos. They had not made progress searching for Abrihet in Tijuana. Méndez had told them he hoped to have more information about her soon.

"Who hired the Nigerians?" Méndez asked.

"We don't know," Maio said. "There is chatter about a special job for a big shot. We think he killed the guys in the Maserati to shut them up. Or to punish them for botching the job. Some clues place him in an area near the NATO base in Naples." Maio checked his watch. "*Allora.* It's late. Let's eat. I know a fantastic place. Remember, you are my guests. Don't reach for the check; my *scorta* are on high alert."

The *scorta* was the swashbuckling seven-man security detail. They escorted Maio, Pescatore and Méndez to the cars, jogging back and forth, stuffing pistols in belts, talking into radios. The two Alfa Romeos rocketed along the Via Domiziana, weaving through traffic, the sirens and lights clearing the way. The sunset lit up the Mediterranean.

Pescatore grinned gleefully and said, "Your boys drive like maniacs, Giancarlo."

Sitting next to his driver, the prosecutor turned and raised his chin emphatically. "Going slow makes me nervous, Valentine. Once I got stuck in a traffic jam. Palermo. We couldn't move, even with sirens. Just when we decided to get out and walk the last few blocks, the Mafia sent an assassin running up to the car. I was opening my door. He got off one shot before my guys neutralized him."

"What happened?" Pescatore asked.

"This." Maio pulled open his white shirt to reveal a scar near his collarbone amid gold chains and religious medals on a matted, tanned chest. "A reminder to keep the doors closed."

The hotel was an insipid brown tower on a spectacular promontory. Striding through the marble-floored lobby, the bodyguards carried their machine pistols in plain view. Maio paused at the entrance of the restaurant. His rakish grin made him look younger.

"My friends, I am happy you have joined me. In this part of the world, a magistrate has to keep his distance from everyone. The local elite go to this restaurant—the elite whose city councils are dissolved because of Mafia infiltration. Whose fortunes, one way or another, have roots in crime. Not my favorite dining companions. But the food is fantastic."

Maio patted his receding brown hair into place. He smoothed the lapels of his snug double-breasted blazer.

"Come on," he said. *"Facciamo la bella figura." Let's make a good impression.*

The corner table overlooked the water. The lights of fishing boats twinkled in the distance. Maio ordered a prodigious variety of cold and warm antipasti, pasta and seafood. Méndez did not love Italian cuisine, but the enthusiasm of his tablemates—especially Pescatore—was contagious. Méndez drank his share of the muscular Nero d'Avola red wine.

The conversation flowed between the personal—families, childhoods, studies—and the professional. Méndez explained in more detail how his reporting and Pescatore's sleuthing had converged. Pescatore told Maio that Isabel Puente looked forward to meeting him. The prosecutor loosened his tie. His brow relaxed.

Getting rapidly outside a plate of cannoli, Pescatore asked why Maio had switched from prosecuting mafiosi to prosecuting terrorists and back again.

"Good question, Valentine."

After the September 11 attacks, Maio explained, many anti-Mafia veterans shifted to antiterrorism. He transferred from Palermo to Rome.

"It was exciting, different. Glamorous. Politicians threw resources at us. International press coverage. Travel. How vanity makes us weak, eh? For a while, it was fantastic. But you know what? I never really found the beef in antiterrorism."

Méndez liked the phrase and the elegant pantomime: thumb and fingertips rubbing together, a hint of a chewing motion with the mouth.

The prosecutor paused while a waiter poured limoncello liqueur.

"I got disillusioned after a trip to Algiers," he continued. "We did an inquiry, months of wiretaps, on a terrorism-financing network linked to Algeria. I went to ask the Algerians to help identify suspects. My colleagues received me with exquisite courtesy—we had lunch on the Corniche—but they told me they couldn't do much. Essentially, the Algerians said, 'Listen. We lost two hundred thousand in our civil war. Car bombs, villages destroyed, terrorists slashing the throats of families like sheep. We are still very busy. We don't have time for your *indaginetta,* your little investigation.' I realized something: They were on the front line. I was scratching the surface. Even when I captured real terrorists, they weren't the bosses. They were fanatics, criminals, idiots, sadists—manipulated from afar. Sometimes by masterminds, sometimes just by Twitter, Facebook, all that crap. You understand?"

"Pawns," Méndez said. "Remote-control killers, like robots."

"Exactly. Never bosses. There was no way I was going to get those guys unless I went to Pakistan or Syria or Libya. And even then, only if someone loaned me the Delta Force."

Maio sighed. "A year ago, I transferred back to anti-Mafia. I found myself here. The style is different. In Sicily, the model is the Catholic Church: silent, secret, disciplined. A pyramid. One boss rules for decades and no one has taken his picture since 1978. Meanwhile, the Camorra is Neapolitan. An archipelago of clans, and there's always a hurricane. Loud, ostentatious, always fighting, always rising and falling. But I can arrest a boss. And his father was in the Camorra. His grandfather was in the Camorra! A profound cultural thing. Do you know the foundational myth of the Mafia, Dottore Méndez?"

"Osso, Mastrosso, and Carcagnosso."

"Bravo." Maio toasted him, impressed, the corners of his mouth turning down.

"Who?" Pescatore asked.

"Three Spanish knights in the fifteenth century who avenged their sister's honor and went into exile in Italy," Maio said. "According to the legend, anyway. They founded the Sicilian Mafia, the Calabrian 'Ndrangheta, and the Camorra. There is even a song about it."

Before Maio could sing the song, Pescatore's phone rang.

"It's Isabel, my boss, calling from Washington," he said, standing up.

Pescatore returned to the table ten minutes later. He looked like someone had died.

"Giancarlo," he said. "I need to talk to Leo in private. It's an emergency."

Méndez followed Pescatore into the lobby, thinking in a panic that it might be bad news about his family. Pescatore led him into the driveway of the hotel, favoring his injured left ankle. He stood with his hands in the pockets of his jeans, shoulders high, teeth clenched.

"Washington just shut us down."

"What?"

"Isabel went to the bosses and laid out what we have. They got mad. They said she was insubordinate, she didn't have any business investigating the Blakes."

"But we connected the two cases!"

"Yeah, well, that's as far as we go."

Méndez felt as if he had walked into a wall. His thoughts swirled. Standing behind Pescatore were two of the prosecutor's bodyguards. They leaned on a parked Alfa Romeo, keeping a vigilant eye on their guests.

Isabel had been curt and careful on the phone, Pescatore said. Her superiors wanted Pescatore and Méndez to stop what they were doing and come back.

"I said, 'Isabel, somebody just came damn close to killing us over here. And it's gotta be related to what we're doing. They can't just ignore the attempted murder of two U.S. persons.' She said the FBI will get a briefing from the Italians and talk to us eventually."

"What about the Tecate investigation?"

"The Justice Department says we're overreaching. Some of the DHS and FBI supervisors want to hammer the Blakes, but their hands are tied. The heat is coming from way above them. The problem is, we don't know who El T is. And we don't have Abrihet, the victim, the key witness. We don't have a statement from her brother. So Isabel had to tell the truth: we can't nail Blake for the massacre."

"Perhaps not in court, not yet. But still... there's circumstantial evidence. This is obscene. Isabel acted courageously, and they punish her. Has she lost her job?"

"They told her to take a couple days off. They're, uh, reviewing her situation."

Méndez ran a hand down his face. He relived the blind whirl of the shootout.

"It's like Mexico," he said disgustedly. "The public mafia protects the private mafia."

"It sucks, no doubt about it." Pescatore tilted his head, a challenge in his look. "But Leo, there's a big difference. The U.S. feds aren't a mafia. People don't get away with stuff like this in the United States. Even rich people."

"Oh, they don't?"

"Not mass murder. No way."

*He wants to believe,* Méndez thought. *So do I. But I'm starting to wonder.*

"I should publish an article about this," he said. "Right now."

"I told Isabel the same thing. Unleash Leo."

"And?"

"She said we gotta think hard before going public. Because of Abrihet. If you do a story, it could endanger her more and blow our chances of finding her."

"True."

"What do we do, Leo? Washington wants us to stop working with the Italians."

Méndez smiled his wolflike smile. He took Pescatore by the arm, turning his back to the bodyguards, and lowered his voice.

"I assume, Valentine, that your instinct is the same as mine. We do the opposite. Above all, we stay very close to our new friend the prosecutor."

As Méndez had hoped, Maio did not take the news well.

Méndez and Pescatore did their best to paint the picture that the authorities in Washington wanted to push him out of the case.

During the ride back from the restaurant, the prosecutor sat by the window in silence. It was interrupted by his cell phone.

"*Ciao,* Philip," he said. "No, for me it is not very late. *Dimmi tutto.*"

As the prosecutor talked, Pescatore leaned toward Méndez. He whispered that he believed Philip was the FBI attaché at the U.S. embassy. It soon became clear Pescatore was right. Maio said it was early in the investigation. He wouldn't have anything to share for days. No sense in Philip coming down from Rome. Maio listened as the agent spoke at length.

"Excuse me, excuse me, Philip, my friend," Maio said in English. "Let me remind you one thing. This is not a hotel. I am not the man you call for room service…Exactly…Well, that's what it is sounding like. Whether you meant or not…yes…fine. Apology accepted. Yes, I prefer you wait there…the American and the Mexican? They are cooperation witnesses under jurisdiction of the magistrate. They stay as long as I need…It doesn't matter, your instructions to send them home. If necessary, I confiscate their passports. *Hai capito?*…Calm down. Go have a nice lunch tomorrow and watch the *belle femmine* at our place on the Piazza del Popolo. We talk soon."

Maio hung up. He watched the coast rush by in the night. He undid his tie knot completely, muttering to himself in dialect. Pescatore gave Méndez a furtive elbow in the ribs.

*So far, so good,* Méndez thought. *Fortunately, we teamed up with a Sicilian. In Italy, that's as Mexican as you can get.*

The cars returned to the courthouse. Maio said he wanted to show them something inside.

The dilapidated elevator groaned its way to the top floor. The doors opened onto a short hall. A sleepy young uniformed cop sat at a desk. He had slicked-back hair and wore an armored vest. The desk contained textbooks and a machine gun. The cop stood at attention, then unlocked a steel-reinforced door.

The apartment had apparently been fashioned by knocking down walls and combining offices. It had a linoleum floor, fluorescent ceiling lights, and dull green walls. The grillwork on the windows looked better suited for resisting a bomb blast than letting in light. The furniture consisted of Ikea basics and office castoffs. They sat down at a table in a long rectangular space with living, dining and kitchen areas. There were a few personal touches: plants, a Sicilian warrior puppet on a hook.

As Maio prepared espresso in a machine that sounded like a helicopter taking off, he explained that his ex-wife lived in Palermo. His children were grown. The easiest, safest option had been to set himself up in these makeshift quarters above his office.

"A short commute," he said.

The place smelled like coffee, cigarettes, and solitude. It felt familiar to Méndez. While leading the Diogenes Group, he said, he had sent his family to live in safety in California. He had often spent the night in a bedroom in the unit's headquarters.

"I think I would be at home in Tijuana," the prosecutor said, rubbing his thick stubble. He had lapsed back into Italo-Spanish. "It's strange, Dottore. People think this life is glorious—fame, power, press conferences, bodyguards. They don't see the reality: eating alone, living in shitty rooms, indoors all the time, unable to walk in the sun or sit in a café without a paramilitary deployment. *La vita blindata.*"

"In Latin America, we call it *la vida blindada.*"

The armored life. Assassination plots, grinding menace, a suffocating security cocoon. Méndez had endured it. He had gone into exile to escape it.

Maio sipped coffee. "And the pressure, the envy. I remember telling a colleague about a trip to the United Nations. He says, 'Ah, how nice. Did you take a plane? Or just put on your cape and tights and fly over?' It's like they are waiting for you to fail, to be humiliated. Sometimes I think the best thing would be to die violently. That way, at least, they will speak well of you."

"I've had that feeling myself," Méndez said. "But I prefer criticism, humiliation and dying peacefully of old age in bed."

Maio leaned over, retrieved a thick accordion folder from his briefcase, and plunked it on the table.

"*Allora,*" he said. "I propose a pact of honor. I have a print-out here of documents that were in Mr. Anbessa's pen drive. Strictly speaking, I shouldn't show this to you. However, I wouldn't have it if it weren't for you. Also, I think you know my mood after talking to the FBI."

Hesitantly, Pescatore said, "*Incazzato?*"

"Exactly. I don't appreciate being told how or what or when to investigate. The FBI wants me to send you home. They want to participate in my investigation because it has sensitive repercussions. I'm not averse to cooperation, but I consider the request to be unacceptable interference."

Maio lit a cigarette and narrowed his eyes.

"These Blakes…" he continued. "They are megabosses. White-collar American bosses. The kind of criminals you dream about getting your hands on. A once-in-a-career, once-in-a-lifetime opportunity." He accompanied his words with jabs of the cigarette. "These *figli di puttana* made an enormous mistake—they tried to kill you on my turf. They gave me a shot at them. They opened a door, and I don't intend to let it shut. The pact I propose is this: I share with you, you share with me. We collaborate and coordinate. Agreed?"

"Agreed," Méndez said.

*"Assolutamente sì,"* Pescatore said.

Maio pulled a pile of papers out of the folder. He selected two sets of stapled documents and gave one each to Méndez and Pescatore.

"This comes from the pen drive that Anbessa's sister took from Perry Blake. We found a receipt in Solomon's office for a FedEx package she sent from New York. These are interesting items. Please give a look. I will make more coffee."

A half hour later, Méndez was wide awake, and it had little to do with the caffeine. One document was a roster of individuals, companies, and government agencies, mostly in Mexico. He recognized names of Mexican officials and businesspeople, including, to his satisfaction, his old nemesis Senator Ruiz Caballero. There was a list of "service charges" and "administrative payments" to law firms in Houston, San Diego and cities in Mexico. The total was in the millions. Méndez tried to contain his excitement.

"I am not a forensic accountant, but I believe it is a record of bribes paid by the Blake Group," he said.

"We think the same," Maio said.

"They're in the shit now," Pescatore said. "The Justice Department prosecutes Americans for payoffs overseas. That's what the Foreign Corrupt Practices Act is for."

"As brazen as it looks, there are precedents," Méndez said. "Walmart was involved in a massive bribery scandal in Mexico. The mechanism was similar, and the executives were accused of documenting kickbacks this way. And there is a huge Brazilian construction company that even had an international department of bribery."

"I remember," Pescatore said. "They were paying out all that cash. They had to keep track of it, right?"

"In the Walmart case, the bribes went to local officials around the country for things like zoning and construction permits. I see some of that here, mostly a few years ago, when the Blakes were expanding in Mexico. The difference is the names in the federal government, in national politics. The merger has needed backing at high levels in Mexico City."

*"Bellissimo,"* Maio said.

They discussed the second document, a series of internal reports and e-mails analyzing the progress of the merger and the political and regulatory process.

"An expert writing to a client," Méndez said. "Discreet enough not to identify the author or the recipient. But who else can the client be? It's the Blakes, or someone close to them."

The most incriminating passages were accounts of using campaign contributions and "other expenditures" to cultivate power brokers and bureaucrats in both nations. There were profiles of critics of the proposed merger. Other reports described, with great specificity, the developing investigations of the Blakes in both Mexico and the United States, and outlined defensive strategies.

"Whoever put this together had privileged information about what the investigators were doing," Méndez said.

"Damn right," Pescatore said. "Inside sources."

"It is a manual for obstruction of justice." Méndez turned to the prosecutor. "Giancarlo, could you give us a copy?"

Maio patted him on the arm. "Not yet, *caro*. You can take notes, but I can't give you anything. When it is possible, I will."

"Fair enough."

Maio yawned and stretched. He suggested they get some rest. The next day he would talk to Anbessa's doctors about allowing a visit.

A uniformed driver and two plainclothes officers drove Pescatore and Méndez to their hotel. A plainclothes officer escorted them into the lobby, said good night, and settled into an armchair with a newspaper.

In his room, Méndez typed up his notes and everything he could remember from the documents. When he checked, it was four a.m. Almost dinnertime in San Diego. He called home. Renata talked to him about Kermit the Frog. Juan reported that he had landed a starting position on the school soccer team and asked him for a vintage Naples jersey with Maradona's name on it. Estela said everything was calm. The San Diego Police checked in now and then. She asked how he was doing.

"A roller-coaster day."

"Go to bed, Leo. You have to sleep. Are you eating, at least?"

"Never fear. The Italians shovel food into me at all hours."

With one hand, he pulled open a curtain to look at the sea. His reflection, grim and haggard, startled him.

His wife was silent. Although hearing about the shootout had muted her anger, things between them had not returned to normal.

"Estela," he said. "How is the house? Does the yard need mowing?"

"What? Since when do you care about the house or the yard?"

"Well, I've been away for a while…"

"As if that makes any difference."

It was true. He was useless in the domestic arena. He called a handyman or a gardener for the slightest chore. Estela was better than him at assembling furniture and setting up appliances.

"I was thinking what it would be like to spend time working around the house."

"Your office is in the garage, in case you forgot."

"No, not journalism. Puttering around, using my hands, planting a garden. A calm, simple activity. What would it be like to have a regular anodyne job: normal hours, no drama, no insanity? Spend time thinking about mortgages and gas mileage and home improvement and the stock market. Whatever normal people think about."

"What would it be like? Like being a different person. And therefore you'd be married to someone else."

"*Vaya.* You prefer me the way I am."

"What are you having over there, a predawn existentialist reflection?"

"When people shoot at you, it makes you philosophical. I was thinking about when Juan was little, two or three years old. I was a reporter. You were finishing your dissertation. I remember those years vividly."

"I remember we didn't have any money. Not that we do now."

"Things were pleasant, though, Estela. Kids that age force you to focus on the basics. They make things simpler. And happier, don't you think?"

"Renata is the same age now that Juan was then."

The sharpness in her voice stung him. He thought about Renata, about reading to her the last time he had seen her.

"You are right, *mi amor,*" he said quietly. "During my existentialist reflection, as you call it, I came to a conclusion. I have been struggling with something. I'm a journalist who prefers being a policeman. Even though I became a policeman only because I was a certain kind of journalist. A hopeless dilemma. Then I had an epiphany. I need a drastic change. I don't need to slow down. I need to stop altogether. Maybe I should teach. Or write a book. Or be a househusband."

"Or a fading Mexican gigolo."

He laughed gratefully. The humor was like a peace offering.

"An excellent suggestion. What I should—"

"What you should do, Leo, is stop talking now. Get some sleep...*mi amor.*"

She said the words as if she were giving him a gift she had been holding behind her back.

He slept three hours. When he went down for breakfast, the plainclothesman was still in the lobby. The squad car was still parked in front.

Whatever his future, Méndez thought, for now he was back in the past. Back in the armored life.

# Chapter 13

In the medical center, statues and murals of saints, Christs, and Madonnas stared down as if they knew how long it had been since Pescatore's last confession—and his last checkup.

High ceilings amplified the hubbub in the halls. The chief doctor was a white-coated woman with a stylish auburn helmet of hair and a sophisticated northern-sounding accent. Heels clicking on tiles, she led a small parade through the intensive-care ward: Maio, Pescatore, Méndez, detectives, bodyguards, orderlies, nurses. A policewoman hurried by in the opposite direction leading three East Africans: a woman in a white gauze shawl in her forties, a teenage boy, and a woman in her early twenties. The youths were sad-faced and slender, dressed in the stylishly casual, brand-conscious uniform of young Italians. They held the arms of the older woman as if she were weak on her feet. The group had disappeared around a corner by the time Pescatore realized they were Solomon Anbessa's wife and children.

Two uniformed police officers flanked the door of the room. The doctor told the visitors to keep it brief. Maio ushered in Pescatore, Méndez and his chief investigator. He instructed the others to stay outside.

Propped up by pillows, Solomon Anbessa resembled a statue of an Abyssinian noble in repose. He nodded gravely at Maio, who wore a beige sports jacket with jeans. Maio addressed him as Captain Anbessa. He said he did not expect full testimony, but he had to ask some urgent questions.

"We believe you acted in legitimate self-defense," Maio said. "Of course, there remains the issue of illegal possession of firearms. What you do to help us now will be taken into consideration."

Solomon's nod said, *I've survived a gun battle, a death-boat, and a dictatorship. Excuse me if I don't get all anxious about a charge of packing heat.*

Maio skipped the throat-clearing biographical-type questions. "Where is your sister?"

"At this moment, I do not know." His Italian was tinged with the broad Neapolitan accent. "She was in Tijuana. With the priests. They are hiding her. They were going to move her to a new place."

The priests, who belonged to Padre Bartolomeo's religious order, ran a shelter for migrants in Tijuana similar to the one Pescatore had visited in Tapachula. Pescatore was impressed that they were harboring Abrihet. Apparently Padre Bartolomeo wasn't the only stand-up guy in the outfit.

Solomon's breathing was labored. He said Abrihet had emigrated illegally two years earlier, going from Eritrea through Sudan, South Africa, Brazil and Mexico before she finally reached New York. Solomon was already in Italy. They did not communicate frequently. She was busy with work and studies, he with work and family. But she had called in July, sounding traumatized. Perry Blake had assaulted her; his security officers were hunting her. She said she would send her brother something important. The FedEx package arrived two days later.

"Where did she obtain the pen drive she sent you?"

"His office. I read the documents. I did research. Some things I did not understand, but I thought it was valuable, confidential information about bad activity. We could use it to protect her."

"Did you? Have you told anyone about the documents?"

"Only you."

After reaching Tijuana, Abrihet had called and e-mailed. She wanted to join him in Italy to put as much distance as she could between herself and Perry Blake. Soon, however, she found out that it was too complicated and expensive to obtain a fraudulent passport good enough to get her to Europe. Brother and sister went over their options. They decided she should return to New York and go to the police.

"Even if she was arrested at the border, at least she would be in custody in the United States, not a Mexican prison," Solomon explained. "We could try to get a lawyer, refugee status."

Solomon scraped together five thousand dollars and wired it to Abrihet for the smuggling fee. After seeing press reports about the Tecate massacre, he couldn't reach her for days. Finally, she called from the migrant shelter. She was even more traumatized.

"Now it was very dangerous. We have avoided using the phone. The priests say the Mexican police and mafiosi are good at communications interception. She has access to a computer. I set up an account and we write draft e-mails to each other."

"A digital dead drop, like al-Qaeda," Maio said. "Of course, you could just talk on WhatsApp or Signal. Full encryption. Not even the NSA can hear you."

Solomon's attempt at a grin showed an appreciation for the nuances of tradecraft.

"Yes, but she depends on the priests for access to communication. And what they let her use is the computer."

Solomon closed his eyes a moment. As if on cue, the doctor bustled in. A dispute ensued between her and the prosecutor, but Maio succeeded in wrangling more time. He pulled his chair close.

"*Capitano.* You must help us contact your sister and see what we can organize to extricate her from this situation. *Va bene?*"

Solomon turned to Méndez, who looked up from his notebook.

"You can get her out?"

"We will do everything in our power. We think she will be safe if we can bring her to the United States."

Solomon looked at Pescatore, still wary. "The Mexican police are helping the criminals who want to kill her."

"I know," Pescatore said. "But there are good people down there too. Listen, Leo is from Tijuana. He was the chief of a police force. I've worked there myself. It's not gonna be easy, but I think we've got as good a shot as anybody. And you know you can trust us."

"Yes," Solomon said. "I do."

# Chapter 14

The Madrid airport, three days later.

A gleaming terminal. A cascade of sunlight. Pescatore and Méndez sat at breakfast. On edge, all talked out, waiting for their flights.

For Pescatore, from Madrid to Mexico City to Tijuana.

For Méndez, from Madrid to Chicago to San Diego.

Méndez was in a foul mood. Avoiding his eyes, Pescatore concentrated on cutting a potato omelet. Méndez had resisted arguments about the risks involved in his participating in the operation in Mexico. He had started to weaken after the phone conversations with Athos and Porthos, who rarely contradicted him but who had agreed with Pescatore's concerns. Méndez had finally relented when Pescatore convinced him that his presence would endanger the others. And the success of the plan.

*Like it or not, you're a public figure in Mexico, Licenciado,* Pescatore had said the day before. *Especially in Tijuana. Especially after you made a splash with the article and on TV and everything. Putting on a cap and sunglasses is not gonna do the trick. The minute you hit Mexican soil, it'd be like a ticking bomb. Forget about the bad guys a minute. What if some cop or flight at-*

*tendant or reporter recognizes you? What if you're a story by the time we land in TJ? This is a high-risk, long-shot op. It's gotta be fast and clandestine.*

Shrugging in defeat, Méndez had quoted a line from *The Harder They Come,* a Jamaican reggae/gangster movie he had seen in his youth: *"Every game I play, I lose."*

Pescatore went to get espresso. Méndez opened his laptop. When Pescatore brought him the coffee, Méndez drained his cup in a gulp. Once again, the story he was writing had kept him up all night.

"Making progress, Licenciado?"

"I will have a rough draft when I land. Except for the material from Giancarlo Maio."

"He'll send it to you when he files the court papers, right?"

"I have no doubt he will keep his word."

The prosecutor's strategy struck Méndez as bold, clever and creative, though stronger on style than substance. Maio had prepared a criminal complaint against Celestine Njoku, the surviving Nigerian gunman. The complaint laid out an ambitious theory of the case: Celestine's crew had acted on the orders of unknown suspects affiliated with the Blake Acquisitions Group of the United States. The prosecutor had sketched out the chain of events that had brought Pescatore and Méndez to the cybercafé, arguing that the attack on them was part of a continuing criminal conspiracy. Maio would name the rip-crew chief known as El T as an investigative target along with Louis Krystak and Perry Blake, and he would ask the U.S. Justice Department to find and make them available for questioning. His charges relied heavily on circumstantial evidence: the testimony of Pescatore, Méndez and Solomon; the fact that Solomon had incriminating material about the Blake Group. But the smoking gun, a direct link between the Blakes and the attackers in Tecate or in Palazzo di Sabbia, was still missing.

*Would it convict them at this stage?* Maio asked, pacing his office as if in front of a jury. *No,* signori. *Is it a legal house of cards? Sì,* signori. *But there are certainly grounds to request further investigation by the Americans.*

Maio's security team had driven Pescatore and Méndez to the Rome airport at a speed that defied any possibility of someone following unnoticed, then escorted them through VIP entrances directly to their flight to Madrid.

A text message beeped on Pescatore's phone.

"Facundo has landed," he said.

"Now all they need is the fourth musketeer," Méndez said morosely.

Maio had placated the FBI attaché by sending him the statements Méndez and Pescatore had given. But the prosecutor had withheld Solomon's testimony and the information about Abrihet's whereabouts. Before the Italians could pull the trigger on the criminal complaint and unleash an international commotion, there was the problem of getting Abrihet out of harm's way. With Solomon's help, they had established contact with her by phone and e-mail, then dispatched Athos to guard her in her hideout. Although the American embassy in Mexico had relationships with trusted Mexican police units, the police forces in Baja were complicit in the Tecate massacre and had blocked the investigation. It seemed impossible to involve Mexican authorities without turncoats finding out. Better not to send Italian investigators or ask for help from U.S. agencies, which were unlikely to attempt a secret unilateral operation in Mexico for this case.

"I'm glad Maio agreed to hold off while we take our shot," Pescatore said. "Now we just have to figure out how to do it."

"What we need," Méndez said, "is a private army."

A screen on the wall announced Pescatore's flight. He slung his bag over his shoulder. Méndez stood up. He scratched his three-day-old stubble. Looking in the mirror that morning, he had discovered that his beard had gone from salt and pepper to completely gray.

*I've aged five years in three weeks,* he thought.

"All right, then," Pescatore said.

"My people and I will be in position and waiting for you," Méndez said.

"We'll be in touch as soon as we can."

"If the FBI approaches me when I arrive, I will invoke my status as a journalist. I have nothing to add to my statement to the Italians."

Pescatore and Méndez embraced. To Méndez's surprise, Pescatore reached into his leather jacket and handed him two sealed envelopes. The names of women were written on them. Isabel, which wasn't a surprise, and a Fatima Belhaj. Méndez assumed she was the Frenchwoman with whom—according to a passing comment from Isabel—Pescatore was romantically involved. Pescatore looked uncomfortable.

"I hate to be all melodramatic, Leo, but if anything happens to me…"

Méndez patted Pescatore's shoulder. He felt as if he were sending a son off to war. A strong, resourceful, loyal son confronting huge odds. Méndez couldn't believe he wouldn't be joining Pescatore, Athos, and Porthos in this battle. Although he had accepted the decision, it broke his heart.

"Of course, Valentine," he said, forcing optimism into his voice. "Rest assured. But you are young, you have a bright future…*Nadie muere en la víspera.* Nobody dies before his time."

He said the words automatically. It was actually a statement that Carlos Menem, a roguish Argentine president, had made after surviving a helicopter crash in the 1990s. Although the president was not someone he admired, Méndez had liked the defiant self-assurance of the phrase. It had stuck with him. On the occasions he had come close to death—and there had been a number of them—he repeated the words to himself like a protective incantation.

Nevertheless, it occurred to him that the mantra might be a double-edged sword. The Argentine president had a reputation for being *mufa,* or cursed, a man who had providential good fortune while spreading catastrophe among those around him. Méndez worried now that saying the words to Pescatore might end up bringing him bad luck.

Not that Méndez was superstitious. But they were going to need all the help they could get.

# Chapter 15

Facundo had told Pescatore to fly business class; he wanted him well rested.

Pescatore let the Iberia crew pamper him. He drank a glass of Segura Viudas cava, ate a seafood and rice dish accompanied by a glass of Ribera del Duero, and finished with flan and Cardenal Mendoza cognac. If his last meal was to be airplane food, he had done it up right. Perusing the touchscreen music system, he found a recording of Astor Piazzolla, his father's favorite tango composer; Pescatore had rediscovered his music while living in Buenos Aires. He put on the headphones, lowered the seat to full horizontal mode, and curled up under the blanket. The bandoneon and strings unspooled their lament. His thoughts drifted like clouds.

Hard to believe it, but Pescatore was the driving force behind this gambit. After the bad news from Washington, he had appealed to Facundo to stick with the mission. Facundo agreed. He saw a positive angle in a new ally, an Italian prosecutor with a taste for high-profile cases. Like Pescatore, Facundo refused to abandon Abrihet. *Ungentlemanly and unthinkable,* he said. His biggest motivation, though, was basic. The enemy had tried to kill Pescatore. Facundo would gladly foot the bill—and swoop personally into harm's way—to retaliate.

Pescatore glided in and out of a shallow sleep. Isabel and Fatima floated through his dreams; faces, voices, erotic images. He had tried to call Fatima the day after she'd saved his bacon with Maio, but she was traveling. As for Isabel, they had talked only once—a short, stilted conversation. International calls were open season for intercepts, and Isabel was in batten-down-the-hatches defensive mode.

In the notes to Isabel and Fatima, he had told each woman how much she meant to him, how lucky he was to have been in love with her. He was sorry time had run out before he could clear up any confusion or conflict. Although it was like writing from the grave, he was glad to have done it.

Because he had guarded a border for a living, Pescatore always tensed up when he crossed one. He knew the balance of power: nonexistent for him, absolute—if narrow—for the gatekeepers. Standing in the immigration line in Mexico City, he wondered if the influence of the Blakes reached into airport border agencies. Méndez had said he doubted it. It was one thing to have powerful Mexican allies who could facilitate smuggling people and things. It was another to have the real-time capacity to identify and track Pescatore when he arrived. Still, you never knew.

The immigration officer stamped the passport so fast that Pescatore felt ridiculous about his apprehensions. After a two-hour layover, he caught the flight to Tijuana. He landed at eight p.m.

*Ahora sí, cabrón,* he told himself. *Aguas.* Now be paranoid.

Not that the terminal was menacing. He saw Mexican families, an Asian business delegation, a sprinkling of tourists in shorts and sandals. He was received by a security officer named Davila who worked for Porthos's company. They hur-

ried out to the pickup area, where Facundo and Porthos •
waited by a Suburban. They were dressed in dark clothing.
Their greetings were like a bloodless mauling by friendly
bears.

"*Buona sera,* muchacho," Porthos said, giving him a swat on
the back of the neck. "All that jet-setting in Italy, I thought
you'd forgotten us humble peasants."

"It wasn't that fancy, believe me. They fed us to death,
though."

"Compensation for being ambushed," Facundo rasped, sliding into the backseat next to Pescatore. "How is your ankle?"

"Better, thanks. I've got it wrapped. We plan on doing some
running?"

"Don't rule it out."

The U.S. border fence appeared as they sped away from the
airport on the highway that paralleled the international line.
Pescatore saw the rusty steel barrier in the night, the taller
secondary fence of transparent metal mesh, the floodlights on
masts. The glow seemed incredibly bright, an incandescence
stoked by his memories and dreams and nightmares.

Facundo reached back, lifted a blanket, and handed
Pescatore an armored vest and a Beretta in a shoulder holster. Pescatore spotted automatic rifles under the blanket.
He removed his leather jacket and strapped on the holster
and vest.

"How many guys?" he asked.

"Fifteen including us," Porthos said.

"Not bad."

It turned out they did have access to a private army: the
security force at Porthos's factory. The team did internal investigations and executive protection. They were trained in
countersurveillance and anti-kidnapping tactics. A few of the
officers were veterans of the Diogenes Group, most were

ex-cops, and all of them had been screened by Porthos and were fiercely loyal to him.

The route curled south and west into urban sprawl. Davila did evasive maneuvers to ensure they weren't being tailed. Pescatore spotted the concrete levee of the Tijuana River, and the towers of a high-rise hotel that had changed names over the years. Tijuana's scruffy energy appealed to him, but his image of the city was forever shaped by the weeks he had spent undercover in its underworld. The memory reminded him of a song by Silvio Rodríguez, the verse about Death walking at his side so long that she had become his sister.

Porthos turned around in the front seat with a big grin. He handed Pescatore two pieces of paper. The first was the sketch artist's rendering of El T based on Chiclet's description. The second was a Mexican mug shot of a U.S. citizen named Vincent Robles. They looked like twins.

"You identified him!"

"All credit to Athos. He thought about it, talked to the right friends and lowlifes, and there you have your man. We have already sent this to Licenciado Méndez, and he sent it to your Italian friend."

Robles was from Riverside, California, Porthos said. A *pocho,* or Mexican-American, he had served in the U.S. Army and earned combat decorations in Iraq. He did not appear to have a criminal record in the United States. During the past three years, the Mexican federal police had arrested him on a weapons-possession charge that had been mysteriously quashed, and the Baja state police had questioned him about drug-related murders that had stayed unsolved. As Chiclet had told them, Robles led a crew that specialized in robbing drugs and kidnapping migrants from smugglers.

"It appears this *cabrón* moves back and forth across the border with ease," Porthos said. "A heavyweight. Well connected. Gunmen at his disposal. But he keeps them at a distance."

"Was he a lieutenant in the army?"

"A sergeant. But perhaps he aspired to be a lieutenant. They call him El Teniente as well as El T. You were right about that."

"If only we could get this photo to Chiclet for confirmation, damn it," Pescatore said. His first instinct was to contact Isabel—impossible given the circumstances.

"We have confirmation. Athos showed the photo to sources. They said Robles has been talking to people in the state and municipal police about helping him find the young lady, Señorita Anbessa. We think a guy from his crew infiltrated the migrant shelter posing as a deportee from Los Angeles, snooped around. And municipal police officers came by to ask questions. The priests were clever. They didn't deny she had been there, but they said she had left for Mexico City."

*They're breathing down our necks,* Pescatore thought. *The rip crew might find her before we get there. Or find us instead.*

The prospect of going to the mat with Vincent "El T" Robles did not seem to faze Porthos and Facundo. Of course, Porthos had tangled with just about every species of animal the border could throw at you. Facundo had experienced combat in the Israeli army and clandestine action since then. Pescatore was no neophyte himself, but he didn't see how they could be so upbeat.

Clouds wreathed a low moon over the Pacific. The Suburban cruised along a clifftop coastal highway. The ride took about an hour.

Ensenada was a port town that lived off tourism, fishing, agriculture, and a smaller, tamer version of Tijuana's nightlife scene. Pescatore had been here once. He remembered cruise ships, strolling expatriate gringos, the smell of the Pacific.

The convent took up half a block on a side street. An arched double door opened in a high wall. The Suburban rolled onto the flagstones of a courtyard. Athos was waiting with an assault rifle at the ready, the brim of his cap pulled low over his eyes. He led the way to a house between a chapel and the main building of the convent.

"Where's our team?" Pescatore whispered to Porthos.

"They are set up at strategic points around the neighborhood. Keeping watch, but not so close they draw attention."

A nervous priest with square glasses and narrow shoulders opened the door of the house. An elderly nun hovered in a dim sitting room that smelled of cigarettes.

It was a guesthouse for visitors, mostly clergy. The priests had disguised Abrihet in a full-length habit and moved her to Ensenada in a bus full of nuns returning from the shelter in Tijuana.

*Pretty good tradecraft,* Pescatore thought.

There was a hushed conference. Athos told Pescatore it was the room on the right on the second floor.

Pescatore trudged heavily up the stairs in the armored vest. A whiff of faulty plumbing hung in the dark cool hallway. As he knocked, he felt a rush of anticipation similar to the one he'd experienced before finding Chiclet in the diner in Palenque. Except now he came as a protector, not a hunter.

Abrihet Anbessa opened the door.

As he'd imagined, she was small and slight and agile. She wore faded green jeans, gym shoes, and a hooded San Diego Chargers sweatshirt—no doubt acquired on the run—that was too big for her.

"Miss Anbessa, I'm Valentine Pescatore, the American investigator. It's a pleasure to meet you."

She hesitated before shaking his hand. Her thick medium-length curls were held back with a headband. Her features

234

had the angular, regal cast of her brother's, but softer and more youthful. Frozen dread glittered in her eyes.

"Come in," she said.

She sat in an armchair next to a round table with rosary beads on it. He took a hard wood chair. He saw a painting of the Virgin of Guadalupe, figurines of angels on shelves, a crucifix over the narrow bed in the corner. The fat-backed television was decades old. The room also had a sink, a microwave and a teakettle.

He said it looked like they were treating her well. She said they were. Her diction was clear and precise. She perched in the chair as if ready to spring out of it. Legs crossed, hands gripping the upholstery, she regarded him steadily.

"So..." he said.

"Would you like tea?" Her smile acknowledged the strangeness of the moment. It was a sweet and unexpected smile, and it lit up her face.

"Are you gonna have some?"

"Yes."

"Then I'll join you."

"It calms me down. I have trouble sleeping."

"I can imagine."

It was hard to imagine, though. On her own, not knowing whom to trust, so far from home. The world beyond the walls was hostile turf prowled by armed strangers working for her enemies. Now a new set of armed strangers had shown up promising to help.

He told her the story of how they had found her. She cupped the steaming mug of chamomile tea with both hands, warming them.

"Your brother sends his love," he said.

"How is he?"

Given everything that was going on, he had intended to

avoid mentioning that Solomon had been wounded. He found that impossible now.

"Tell you the truth, there was an incident. He's okay, but he got hurt. We got attacked a couple days ago when we were with him. We think it's all connected to your situation."

She stiffened, eyes wide. She asked questions. He assured her that Solomon was recovering. He asked how much she knew about the plan.

"Mr. Athos told me a few things."

"He doesn't talk much, huh?"

"He has been downstairs for two days," she said with a kind of grateful awe. "I don't think he has slept."

He pictured Athos smoking cigarettes in the shadows, a sentry waiting to waste the first sorry bastard of an intruder who showed his face.

"He's the guy I'd want guarding my door, believe me," Pescatore said.

She asked more about her brother, about details of the plan. He answered to the extent he could.

"We think it's the best option," he said.

"When?"

"In a few hours."

She nodded, eyes wide again, nostrils flaring.

"I have to warn you," he said. "There are risks."

"I understand. I want to get out of here." She emphasized the last three words, her tone strained.

They sipped tea. She toyed with the rosary beads. He asked if faith had been a comfort to her.

"In fact, I am not religious," she said. "But in a situation like this…"

"I know what you mean." He rested his hands on the table. "Listen, Miss Anbessa. You should rest up, get ready. But first, there's one thing. I'd like to record a statement. Your allegations against Perry Blake and the others. Later you'll give formal testimony and everything, and we'd have a female investigator present for that. But this way, we have the basics on the record. I'll send it to associates in the U.S. and Italy. Just in case."

"Just in case we are dead?" Her voice was hollow.

*Exactly,* he thought. "God forbid. But this gives us insurance. You think you're up to it?"

Without hesitation, she said she was.

He lifted his iPhone and framed the image. Her supple hands rose to smooth her hair. Her expression was diligent, like a student about to take a test. He started the video. Guided by his questions, she identified herself. She was from Asmara, had studied nursing, and had been in a medical unit during her compulsory military service. She described how she had come to work at the headquarters of the Blake Acquisitions Group in New York.

Her story tracked with what Zoraida Padilla had told Méndez. In the spring, Padilla had given Abrihet an unofficial promotion. She took responsibility for the executive floor, where Perry Blake made life miserable for anyone in his vicinity, including the cleaning crew, with his complaints, demands, and generally abusive and chaotic behavior.

"The first time I saw him, I knew he was trouble," she said bleakly. "His manner with people was sometimes quiet and friendly, sometimes agitated—yelling, insulting. Erratic. Like on drugs."

True to his reputation, Perry Blake spent the summer working around the clock along with his staff. Abrihet occasionally overheard conversations. She started following financial news about the Blake Group.

"I was taking business courses in the day, along with nursing classes, to major in hospital administration. Business is a new kind of English for me. It was interesting to read about the company and see them in real life. Sometimes there were reports lying on desks, and I would read. I was curious, I admit."

Pescatore nodded at her to keep going.

She said Blake began talking to her when she cleaned his office suite and when he saw her in the hallways.

"I didn't like it." Her gaze shifted from the camera to Pescatore. "Short conversations. Where I was from, what I studied. Not exactly flirting. But I didn't like the way he looked at me. How he said my name. Nothing specific to complain about. A bad feeling, that's all."

July was busy. Blake was wound up. His father, a rare presence at the office, arrived from California. Obese and irritable, Walter Blake was accompanied by Krystak, the security chief. Father and son spent hours behind closed doors. Voices were raised. Abrihet ate meals and studied during her free time in a kitchen area, which was connected by a vent to a conference room. She heard bits and pieces of meetings among the Blakes and others. There was tension between Walter and Perry Blake. They were worried about an investigation. The employees were worried about Perry Blake's moods.

Activity on the executive floor followed a pattern, she said. A crescendo during the week: meetings, phone calls, visitors, nights spent at computers. On Fridays Blake partied, often with a few executives, in his apartment in the building and at restaurants and clubs. Sometimes they started at the office or returned late to the office for a nightcap, raucous and belligerent.

One Friday night, she came across Blake snorting cocaine in his office with a blonde. They were half dressed. Abrihet turned away fast, but she believed Blake had seen her.

"That was the night it happened," she said.

"You don't have to talk about it. Whatever you're comfortable with."

She kept going. Her voice grew clipped and angry. He could see the fight in her now.

*He picked the wrong victim,* Pescatore thought.

Abrihet said, "I waited until very late to clean his office. About four in the morning. I thought he had left. The office was empty. I was working when he surprised me. Very fast."

Blake was staggering, red in the face, his tie askew and shirttails out. He said her name, then threw himself on her without another word. He tore at her clothes. She fought back. The struggle moved from his office to an adjacent conference room. It went on for what seemed a long time.

"He is a big strong man," she said. "But he was so drunk, or drugged. Barely standing up. That saved me. He hit me, I hit him back. He kept going, like the *Walking Dead* on television."

Her voice didn't waver, but tears began. Pescatore had bought a packet of Kleenex at the Mexico City airport with this possibility in mind. He offered the packet. She took a Kleenex and wiped her eyes.

"He passed out in the conference room. On top of me. Totally out. I thought he died, a heart attack. But he was breathing. I ran. In his office, I saw his laptop computer on the desk. I wanted to call the police. But I was thinking no one would believe me against him. Also, I don't have immigration papers. If I took the laptop, I could prove I was in his office and this happened. It sounds strange, I know. My mind was not clear."

He handed her another Kleenex. She caught her breath.

"I thought: *No, taking the computer is stealing.* I saw the pen drive sticking out from the computer and I took it."

"Why?"

"As I say, my mind was not clear. I wanted evidence. Also,

I did have the idea the information could help me. Or hurt him."

"Did you know it was documentation of criminal activity?"

"No. I thought it was perhaps important. He was careful with the laptop. He carried it with him or locked it in a safe. And I heard the talking about investigations. Definitely I thought he had things to hide."

The idea of using the information in the pen drive had come later, she said. It took shape in the long-distance conversations with her brother, who had a chance to examine the documents more carefully. But they weren't sure how to go about it.

"You hadn't looked at the computer before?" Pescatore asked. "You said you read reports sometimes."

"No. I looked at papers in the open. I never went into a computer or a drawer, anything like that."

"Did you take anything else?"

"No."

"Good. I'm just trying to reconstruct events. Do you have the photos Zoraida took of your injuries?"

"No. They were in my phone the kidnappers stole. At the motel."

She slumped, the chair making her seem smaller, her eyes averted. He waited, leaning forward.

*If we can get her in front of a jury, she's gonna be great,* he thought.

"After New York, this is the first time I talk about it," she said quietly.

"I'm real sorry I had to put you through that." He stood up. "Let me get you some more of that excellent tea."

She smiled, dabbing at her eyes. She said that after she left Padilla's house in Queens, a neighbor called to warn her that Krystak had come looking for her and had searched her studio apartment. Abrihet withdrew her savings, about three thousand dollars. She used the cash to ride Greyhound across the country.

"Why San Diego?"

"It was far from New York. And I knew Eritreans there. They helped me come to America through Mexico. I thought they could hide me, help me go to Italy. But they had moved. I couldn't find them. Then my neighbor from New York called. Krystak had come to my building asking more questions. She was trying to help me, but I was worried they could follow her call to find me. I went down to Mexico to find smugglers."

She stayed in a hotel in Tijuana while she tracked down a smuggler she had dealt with years before on her way to the United States. The smuggler told her the plan to go to Italy was unworkable. Abrihet told Pescatore about her attempt to cross north again, the kidnapping by the rip crew, the massacre in Tecate, her escape with Tayane Pires, the weeks in hiding. She identified photos of suspects and victims.

At about one a.m., as he was wrapping up the interview, she surprised him by asking if she could add a final statement.

"Of course," he said.

She took a breath and looked solemnly into the lens.

"I would like to say I want justice. That's all. Punishment for...for the people who hurt me and other people, many worse than me. Also, I cannot go home. I don't have a country. I don't have a passport. At this time, there is nowhere safe for me in the world. I would like a home where I can be safe. Thank you."

"We're gonna make that happen," Pescatore said.

He went downstairs. In the sitting room, he slumped onto a couch and bridged his eyes with his hand, kneading his temples. Facundo asked how she was doing.

"Better than I'd be doing, I'll tell you that. A real lady."

The conversation had drained him. He was in charge of this

expedition. Her fate was in his hands. With his iPhone, he sent the video file to Méndez and Maio using the WhatsApp messaging app. No matter what happened now, her story would see the light of day.

Next, Pescatore wrote a brief note to Méndez. Within a few minutes, a WhatsApp response from the Mexican appeared: *All set on this end. Good luck, brother.*

The plan was to roll at dawn. Pescatore and the others reviewed contingencies and prepared their gear. Pescatore dozed on the couch.

At five thirty a.m., Abrihet came downstairs carrying a small backpack. Athos, Porthos and Facundo treated her with great gentleness and courtesy. The nun served a breakfast of eggs, tortillas, fruit and coffee.

Pescatore helped Abrihet put on an armored vest. He sat with her and went over instructions.

"Ready?"

She nodded.

"Everything's gonna be fine," he said. "A Sunday-morning drive, that's all. Be over before you know it."

*"Orale,* muchachos*, a la chamba,"* Porthos said, hefting a rifle. "Let's get to work."

The nun and Abrihet exchanged tearful embraces and whispers. Before going outside, Abrihet raised the hood of the sweatshirt over her head. Pescatore held the armor-plated door of the Suburban for her. He climbed in and pulled the door after him, a ponderous dragging weight. It thudded shut.

Pescatore and Facundo flanked Abrihet. Davila drove. Porthos rode shotgun. Athos was in the lead Suburban in front of them. The three-vehicle convoy cruised through empty streets and headed north on the coastal highway. The sunrise illuminated a wall of cliffs. Rows of whitecaps flowed onto beaches. Seagulls swooped above occasional joggers and surfers.

"Beautiful," Abrihet said. The hood gave her an elfin look. "Sure is."

He wondered how long it had been since she had ventured out in daylight. He watched the roadside, the sparse traffic, the toll plaza when they stopped to pay. Everything seemed suspicious to him, everyone a potential *halcon,* a street lookout of the cartels.

*Car to car. That's what we need to worry about. A drive-by ambush.*

At the convent, Porthos had gone over the risks. Porthos knew a lot about road shootings. He had spent time studying them with Leo Méndez, who was obsessed with them. Méndez could rattle off statistics and cases from across the Americas: The vice president of Paraguay assassinated in a SUV. The Tijuana police chief peppered at the wheel by a shooter so accurate the bodyguard was killed by rounds that went through the chief. The Argentine folksinger riding with a cartel-connected promoter when *sicarios* struck en route to the Guatemala City airport.

*Speaking of Guatemala, watch out for motorcycles,* Porthos had said. *Interesting fact: Thousands of people have been killed by shooters on motorcycles in Guatemala. Licenciado Méndez told me it got so bad they banned motorcycle passengers. Our Mexican hit men like bikes too.*

Pescatore's fingers tapped the barrel of the AK-47. *I don't know how Leo sleeps at night with all that morbid shit in his head.*

The trip was uneventful. Soon they were rounding a curve from Playas de Tijuana and heading east on Calle Internacional, the border highway. The fence came into view again, topping the line of hills that led to the San Ysidro port of entry. Pescatore nudged Abrihet. He pointed at the U.S. Border Patrol vehicles on the north side of the fence.

"That's San Diego," he said. "We're almost there."

She nodded. Porthos's radio came to life. It was Athos in the lead Suburban.

"Checkpoint."

As they crested a rise, they saw police cars and red cones blocking the right lane at a point where the road leveled off. Half a dozen cops in jumpsuits and body armor stood with long guns across their chests. A few wore ski masks. It looked to Pescatore like a checkpoint run by the tactical unit of the Tijuana municipal police. A commanding officer watched the traffic go by in the left lane. Raising a black-gloved hand, he pointed imperiously at the first vehicle in the convoy. The other hand held a pistol, muzzle down. The officer directed the three Suburbans to pull over.

Abrihet swiveled toward Pescatore, starting to speak.

"Don't worry," he said with feigned tranquillity. "Not a problem. We'll take care of it."

Porthos murmured instructions into the radio. Davila eased the Suburban into the area marked by the traffic cones and came to a halt. Pescatore and Facundo put the rifles on the floor.

The officer in charge spoke to the driver of the lead vehicle and examined documents. Then he approached the second vehicle. Pescatore watched him. A crusty old-timer with self-importance in his stride. The officer had a furry brown mustache, a bald dome between neat half circles of hair, a high protruding rib cage beneath his armored vest. Stripes adorned the shoulder of the navy-blue jumpsuit. Removing his Ray-Bans with a flourish, he asked Davila for license and registration.

Abrihet clutched Pescatore's sleeve. He patted her hand. This was her third run at this border. The last one had ended in catastrophe. He couldn't blame her for thinking this time might not be the charm.

Porthos leaned forward. He spoke to the officer in a mild voice.

"*Que onda,* Chuy? What a long time it's been."

Pescatore's hopes soared. He wasn't surprised that Porthos and the cop knew each other. Porthos was something of a legend in local law enforcement. Pescatore liked how he had played the moment. He could have leaped at the opportunity, all eager and phony. Instead, his manner was breezy, casual, as if he were mildly amused at running into an old acquaintance. As if it weren't a life-or-death encounter.

The officer's smile was surprised. His stance became more relaxed.

"Look who's here," he declared. "*El mero mero.* Comandante Porthos, how are you?"

"Very well. And you, *mi* Chuy?"

"As you see. Working hard on the Lord's Day."

Porthos extended an arm to shake hands with Chuy. He held out a company identification badge, which the officer took, examined, and returned. To Pescatore's relief, Chuy holstered his gun.

Porthos said, "Us too, Chuy. Security never sleeps."

"You're working?" The deep-set eyes were quizzical.

"That's right. We have executive escort duty this morning."

The officer glanced again at the rest of the convoy. He peered into the back of the Suburban. Pescatore met his stare, feeling a new twinge of concern. Chuy sensed something.

"We'll have you on your way in a minute," Chuy said. "I just need to see identification for the rest of the passengers."

*Goddamn it,* Pescatore thought. *By-the-book bastard. He'll get us all killed.*

He had thought for sure the guy would let them go. Maybe he was just a ball-breaker. Maybe he had an old beef with Porthos related to the fact that the Diogenes Group had specialized in locking up cops. Or maybe he was in league with the rip crew that was on the lookout for an African refugee and would pay handsomely if some enterprising lawman came across her.

Abrihet didn't have a passport. Pescatore and Facundo had foreign passports that would draw attention. This couldn't go any further. Pescatore's hand crept toward his shoulder holster.

"Listen, my friend, I apologize, but unfortunately we're in a bit of a hurry," Porthos said. "I'd appreciate it if we could just get moving. It would be better for everybody."

The officer tilted forward in a wide-legged stance, his hard pate gleaming. Consternation spread across his weather-beaten face. Yes, Porthos had apologized politely and called him a friend. But Porthos's voice had grown colder, and he had paused before stressing the final word, *everybody*. Porthos was defying a command. It added up to a veiled threat, a verbal sword thrust.

Pescatore could tell that everyone was hanging on Chuy's reaction. Chuy was surely calculating the numbers and firepower of the occupants behind the polarized windows of the Suburbans. Did he want to go to war over an identity check? Did he want to breathe his last on Calle Internacional on a sunny Sunday morning?

Motionless, the officer looked through the window at Porthos. A stare as loaded as the words that had triggered it. Chuy's mouth tightened.

"Until next time."

He said it like a man with a long memory.

And he stepped back. And they were off again.

Nobody said a word as the convoy snaked through downtown streets. The traffic thickened. The Suburbans pulled over at the edge of the sprawl of ramps, bridges, and walkways that led to the concrete hulk of the U.S. border station. Reluctantly, Pescatore shed his guns and put them under the blanket in back. Facundo followed suit. Porthos turned to Pescatore and raised his eyebrows.

"Very good," Porthos said. "Time for the *licenciado*'s little show."

Remembering the instructions, Abrihet pulled off her hood. Pescatore helped her climb out of the vehicle. She looked excited, determined and a bit overwhelmed by the sun, the noise and the reception committee waiting next to the smoke and hiss of a taco stand.

Padre Bartolomeo was resplendent in his white robes and biblical beard, a cross on his chest. The tanned, scholarly-looking guy with him was an American lawyer friend of Méndez's, a human rights expert from Los Angeles and an adviser to the news website. The two Mexican hipsters were Méndez's reporters: a lanky, ponytailed young man who scribbled notes and a frizzy-haired woman in an army jacket who dictated into her phone. The photographer, an athletic American blonde in overalls, carried a camera that shot both photos and video.

A group of Porthos's men formed a perimeter. They had left the long guns in the vehicles with the drivers.

"*Giovanotto,*" Padre Bartolomeo said to Pescatore.

Pescatore made introductions. The priest clasped Abrihet's hands and murmured in Italian, beaming when she responded in the same language. He offered his arm nonchalantly, as if he were escorting her to brunch, and smiled with practiced ease while the photographer got up in his face, firing from multiple angles.

*The padre's kind of a media hound,* Pescatore thought. *In a good way.*

He had to give Padre Bartolomeo credit. When they had called from Italy, they said they needed his help for an emergency. That had been enough for the priest to rush up to San Diego from Tapachula.

The phalanx set off. Pescatore, Athos, Porthos, and Facundo formed a diamond. The priest and the lawyer walked on either side of Abrihet. She carried the backpack over one shoulder. The photographer and reporters backpedaled in front of her, making the most of the moment. The Mexican woman kept up a stream of narration.

*They better blur my face like Leo promised,* Pescatore thought. *I need to stay low profile.*

They advanced into the tumult of the border crossing. Heads turned. Kids ran alongside them. There was plenty of activity for a Sunday morning. Music echoed from shops and stands: banda, cumbia, bachata, mariachi, rock. Pescatore's eyes roamed over the crowd: vendors, beggars, tourists, migrants, partiers, commuters, miscreants. He watched for furtive moves, glinting gun barrels. The little procession crossed a bridge over hundreds of cars idling in the inspection lanes. Engines grumbled. Horns honked.

Moments later, Athos, Porthos and their men came to a stop. They were armed civilian foreigners, so they didn't want to get any closer to U.S. territory. Pescatore pulled out his passport, a private investigator's credential, and a card identifying him as a former Border Patrol agent. He spoke in Abrihet's ear.

"We're going into the port of entry," he said. "The padre and the lawyer will do the talking. You okay?"

"Yes." Her luminous eyes opened wide. "Big production."

"The more publicity there is, the safer you'll be."

She smiled tightly.

"Don't worry, the dangerous part's over," he said. "It's just bureaucracy now."

Lines of border-crossers on foot filled the sidewalk east of the traffic lanes. Pescatore led the way, feeling exultant, plunging into the throng enclosed by portable pedestrian control gates. He held aloft his credentials, declaring, "Sorry folks, law enforcement emergency, coming through!"

Accustomed to official types barking orders, people moved aside. At the entrance of the indoor pedestrian-crossing station, a group of blue-uniformed U.S. Customs and Border Protection officers hurried out to intercept Pescatore's group. They ordered the blond photographer to stop taking pictures. She made a fuss while the Mexican reporter kept filming and narrating.

Padre Bartolomeo and the lawyer identified themselves. The lawyer explained they were accompanying a refugee who wished to request political asylum because of urgent and imminent threats to her life.

Padre Bartolomeo addressed the camera and the inspectors.

"This is the young lady," he boomed. "Her name is Abrihet. It means 'She who brings the light.'"

# PART IV

# Chapter 16

*D*on't wake your father, *m'ijo. Renata, finish your juice. No, Juan, if you shut up and find your cleats we won't be late... Is Papá coming?... Let him sleep...* Corazón Espinado... *my ringtone... must be Porthos...* corazón... *My phone... Porthos said he'd pick me up...* espinado... *What time is the NYPD... My phone...* corazón... *Locked in the drawer with the gun... Forget it... Call him back...* espinado... *Porthos likes Santana as much as I do... We met at a Santana concert. The Tijuana bullring. Athos was in charge of security. He introduced us... Twenty years ago... Meet Leo Méndez. A trustworthy reporter, believe it or not. Leo, this big lug is Abelardo Tapia. He's partners with El Zorro Etcheverry at the state homicide group. And where is your partner today, Abelardo? You ate him?... Very funny,* guey. *A pleasure to meet you, Licenciado Méndez. I read your article about... Papá, are you awake?*

Méndez lay facedown. It had been his first real night's sleep since Abrihet Anbessa's exfiltration. Like a brush with oblivion. Like his brain had been wiped clean. Gradually, he remembered. He was home. It was Saturday morning. The somber boy in the soccer uniform next to the bed was his son.

"Mamá says you can't see the game because you're too tired and you have to work again," Juan whispered.

Méndez was impressed, even moved, that Estela had roused herself to drive Juan to the game. He scuttled his plan to sleep in.

"Absolutely false," he croaked. "I will be there by the second half."

"Great!" Juan lowered his voice. "The school coach says I have to use my right foot. He doesn't care what Maradona did."

"He's got a point. Now get going before you're late."

Renata darted into the room, kissed him on the head, and chirped her latest American expression—pitch-perfect, if not appropriate for the hour: "Good-night-sleep-tight. *Hasta luego,* Father."

A few minutes after they left, Méndez rolled to a sitting position. His head swam. He called Porthos and asked if he could come by earlier than planned so they could go to the game first.

"At your orders, Licenciado," Porthos said. "I was on my way to meet the guys for breakfast. We can catch up to them after."

"I don't want you going without breakfast."

"On the contrary, you do me a favor. If I go to the diner, I will eat waffles, and if I eat waffles, my wife will give me a sermon."

"If she finds out."

"She'll find out. She has a drone that follows me around monitoring what I eat."

"Are we set with the detectives from New York?"

"Yes. They interviewed Señorita Abrihet yesterday. We see them at eleven."

"Fine. What about Isabel?"

"Nothing new."

Isabel Puente was still in bureaucratic limbo in Washington. Méndez had avoided contact to protect her from any suspicion of collusion with the press. He asked how Abrihet Anbessa was doing.

"As far as I know, fine," Porthos said. "The FBI still has her in that fancy hotel."

"Good. See you shortly."

Méndez showered and shaved. Although it was especially onerous on a weekend, he put on a gray blazer, white shirt, blue slacks, and clunky black shoes with laces. Appropriate attire for a sit-down with the NYPD. His eyes felt raw, but— keeping the vow he'd made to himself in Italy—he put in his contact lenses. After mulling it over, he decided to carry his gun in a shoulder holster rather than in his belt. Less chance the soccer parents would see it and freak out. He ate a yogurt and a muffin in the kitchen and took a cup of coffee to his desk in the garage. The newsroom was strewn with the debris of an epic week: documents, printouts, notebooks, coffee cups, pizza boxes, dirty plates.

The story was still on the front pages. A British financial newspaper analyzed the damage to the Blake Acquisitions Group's image and stock prices. U.S. and Mexican newspapers reported the latest: the FBI had announced it would lead an investigation of the accusations in the Italian criminal complaint. A Rome correspondent had slapped together a profile of Giancarlo Maio, the crusading prosecutor who had "taken on a U.S. billionaire." An Italian magazine featured an interview with Padre Bartolomeo, "the Italian guardian angel of refugees in the Americas." The media in the United States and overseas continued to republish or write about the package of articles that Line of Investigation had posted Wednesday after a reporting, writing, and editing marathon by Méndez and his team. Fred Weinstein had donated hours of high-priced legal advice.

Although he had missed the rescue in Ensenada, Méndez was reasonably satisfied. He felt like a choreographer, a spymaster pulling strings. He hadn't wanted Abrihet disappearing into the labyrinth of the immigration system. That was why he had scripted out her public request for asylum, complete with a lawyer and a telegenic priest. The goal had been to make noise, and it had worked.

Méndez had coordinated closely with Maio in Italy. The reporting was built on the Italian criminal complaint, and Méndez posted his articles two hours after Maio filed the document. The sourcing had been a complicated exercise for Méndez because the Italian legal papers rested partly on his own actions and testimony. He had kept first-person details to a minimum. Abrihet's account of her odyssey appeared in a separate story, accompanied by excerpts of her videotaped conversation with Pescatore.

Méndez had also written a profile of Vincent "El T" Robles, the accused chief of the rip crew. The article was based on the Italian complaint, information from Athos and Porthos, and reporting by Santiago. With his usual aplomb, Santiago had managed to talk briefly to Robles's widowed mother through the screen door of a red stucco house in Riverside, a pit bull barking beside her, baleful homeboys watching from neighboring lawns and porches. Santiago had even tracked down a photo of Robles in his army days. The Italian prosecutor's report named him as a chief suspect wanted for questioning, though the investigators had not found a connection to Krystak yet. As agreed with Méndez, the Italian succinctly described the incriminating Blake Group documents in his report but did not reproduce or quote from them. *With this kind of* figlio di puttana, *you always want to have ammunition in reserve,* Maio had said.

Méndez reread his main article. It recited the Blake Acquisitions Group's litany of unpunished wrongdoing: taxes dodged, money laundered, markets manipulated, politicians bought, companies crushed, unions busted, jobs lost, lives ruined. All without sanction. Until, finally, if the allegations were true, Perry Blake had committed a vicious act against a woman who was not as powerless as she'd seemed. The aftermath had spiraled out of control. The article read, in part:

Gangs like the one that killed the migrants in Tecate are called "rip crews." They lack even the discipline and industriousness to traffic drugs, migrants or contraband. Instead, they rob those who do, slaughtering and violating at will. In the arena of the "legitimate" economy, the Blake Acquisitions Group is a predator. A rip crew. The U.S. and Italian authorities are investigating Blake and his company because of suspicions that he crossed the line into criminality that is easier to prosecute. In this complex case spanning four continents, different kinds of mafias have allegedly blurred together.

Méndez sipped coffee. He was still waking up. His euphoria mixed with uncertainty. Combined with all his reporting, the Italian court documents were a solid shield for his stories. But he had been forced to tone down allegations with caveats and questions. It was of course possible that forces connected to the Blake Group had tried to silence Abrihet without the approval of the executives. It was even theoretically possible, as Fred Weinstein had made him write, that the violent events in different countries were coincidental and unrelated. That was why the authorities had to, at a minimum, question Robles, Krystak, and Perry Blake. Responding to his articles and the Italian charges, the

Justice Department and the NYPD had publicly promised to get to the bottom of the affair. Yet they hadn't done much, as far as he could tell. He was impatient for results: a search, an arrest, something.

An e-mail pinged on his screen. Santiago had sent him a video. The subject line read Public Enemy #1.

Until now, the Blake Group had not commented beyond issuing a statement denying wrongdoing by any of its employees. The company promised to cooperate fully with law enforcement and respond vigorously to libel and slander.

The video was an interview with Perry Blake. The same big-haired, brassy reporter from the financial network, but in a new setting: the patio of a mansion in the Bel Air neighborhood of Los Angeles. Perry Blake and his father were meeting there to discuss strategies for responding to this controversy, the reporter said in a hushed and dramatic voice.

Perry Blake wore a tennis sweater. He sat erect with his hands clasped on a round glass table. His face was drawn. His tone was folksy and combative. He was going to fight this thing and win. The Mexican reporter and the Italian prosecutor were publicity hounds, antibusiness extremists. The indictment and the articles read like a gangland screenplay. It smelled like a foreign conspiracy.

"This Mexican reporter keeps talking about mafias," Perry Blake snapped. "He sure knows a lot about mafias. Isn't that interesting? I wonder who bankrolls him. We've got this awesome historic merger shaping up, unprecedented jobs and growth and profit for Mexico and the United States. And we're under attack. Lookit, maybe the cartels don't like me. The bad guys, the foreign competitors, don't want a cutting-edge American company doing positive transformational business down there. Maybe the Mexican and Italian gangsters teamed up. Well, here's news for you, Sophia: they picked a fight with the wrong guy."

The interviewer asked, gently, about the accusations of sexual assault by Abrihet Anbessa. A blood vessel flared in Blake's brow beneath the upswept crest of hair.

"I have sympathy for that lady. She's had a hard life," he said gravely. "I think she has serious psychological problems, and that's sad. But her allegations are outrageous. I never touched her. She worked in this building, I'm told. Frankly, I don't remember her. Lookit, she's an illegal alien. She had a fraudulent Social Security number. She's an identity thief. She got involved with bad people in Mexico and someone's using her to tell these false, hurtful lies."

Méndez shook his head with grim relish. The man was smooth, no doubt about it. The tremor of wounded indignation in his voice was convincing. But you could tell he was rattled. Blake had never experienced attacks like this on multiple fronts. He was on unknown turf.

The phone on the desk rang. Méndez stopped the video. He recognized the number.

*What do you know? Cardinal Richelieu on the landline.*

In the era of the Diogenes Group, the Secretary had often called Méndez from his home in Mexico City. There was always classical music playing in the background. Méndez heard "E lucevan le stelle," the doomed Cavaradossi's aria from the third act of *Tosca*.

"It's not every day I call you, eh, Leo?"

"It must be a special occasion."

The sleepy rasp of his own voice surprised Méndez. He cleared his throat, remembering Renata's words: *Father, go like this: Hem-hem.*

"I must congratulate you. A remarkable story. Perhaps the best you have ever done."

*You are ultimately congratulating yourself,* Méndez thought. *The twisted old wizard who waved his wand and set the whole thing in motion.*

"Thank you," Méndez said. "And thank you for your help."

"An absolute pleasure."

The Secretary sounded ebullient. The political repercussions must have redounded in his favor. Méndez was surprised that the man was having this conversation with him on the phone. Either he felt very sure of himself or he was slipping in his old age.

The Secretary wanted to share what he had heard in high places. The Blake Group's merger was dead—too much opposition and scrutiny in Washington and Mexico City.

"From what I hear, the documents that young woman pilfered are damaging. Expect casualties in Mexico. And in the Blake Group, executive level. Not that I will see the Blakes in prison in my lifetime."

Méndez frowned. He should have known the Secretary would use praise to set him up for a jab.

"Why not?"

"Too many buffers. Too many people in the chain of command to take the fall for them."

"The documents were in Perry Blake's personal computer."

"I am not contesting the merits of the case, my dear Leo. I am merely passing along what the U.S. embassy has told well-placed friends. There will be a response against the company, there has to be. But when it comes to the Blakes themselves, their defenses are robust. Does that surprise you? Since when do American executives go to jail?"

"We have a firsthand accusation of attempted rape."

"She's an illegal immigrant. An African. Wait until his million-dollar lawyers have at her."

"She is credible and compelling."

"I believe the expression is 'He said, she said.'"

Méndez was starting to get angry.

"Well, I think —"

The doorbell rang. Méndez asked the Secretary to hold.

Porthos was at the front door. He wore a black Toros de Tijuana baseball cap, a brown leather jacket, brown corduroys, and silver-toed cowboy boots. Méndez brought him in and told him to help himself to a cup of coffee and a muffin. Porthos declined the muffin. His hulking presence made the newsroom seem smaller. He leaned back against a desk and sipped coffee, grinning at the framed photo of the Diogenes Group on the wall.

"I'm on the phone," Méndez said apologetically. "I'll just be a moment."

"Take your time, Licenciado."

Méndez picked up the phone, marveling at the way Porthos and Athos insisted on acting as if he were still their chief. If he protested, they looked at him as if he were crazy.

"As to what you were saying," Méndez said to the Secretary, "let me remind you that there is an Italian investigation as well. That creates pressure."

The Secretary chortled.

"Do you know how long legal cases drag on in Italy? More than the *Inferno, Purgatory* and *Paradise* combined. Do you know how politicized their courts are? Surely you aren't suggesting that the Italians will succeed in having the Blakes extradited."

"And the multiple murders? Perry Blake can't wriggle out of that."

"Actually, that is where I note a weakness in your work."

The Secretary was warming to the challenge. Méndez heard him puff on a cigarette. He pictured him sitting in a study filled with books and smoke.

"I had the opportunity to talk to a friend in the Mexican security forces," the Secretary continued. "A senior operational friend. The federal police have taken over and reactivated the Tecate investigation, and they are working with the Americans now. My conclusion, based on what he said and what you wrote, is that the circumstances are suspicious. But making the direct link to Blake will be difficult."

Not only did the Secretary not seem to care about intercepts, Méndez was starting to think he *wanted* eavesdroppers to hear him. To show that he was still a power player, a spider spinning webs, retirement or no retirement.

"Give the FBI a chance," Méndez said. "This is their forte. Tracing money and communications, reconstructing movements. Once they get a case in their teeth, they don't let go."

"Perhaps. I believe the crucial target is Robles, the, eh, *pocho* who was chief of the rip crew."

"That's right."

"Your thesis is that someone, let's say the Blake security chief, transmitted the order to Robles. Logical, perhaps, but purely an unsubstantiated thesis at this point. Anyway, you will find this interesting. My friend said Robles had strong allies in police forces in the states of Baja California and Sonora. But his protection has come to an abrupt end."

"Really?" Méndez reached for a pen and notebook.

"The word is: Get Robles. Soon. But not alive. The police and the criminal underworld are both hunting him. Particularly groups aligned with the Ruiz Caballero clan."

"The Blakes asked their Mexican cronies to bump him off."

"No need for a request. Everyone knows many interests will be served if the man is erased from the equation. Mexico is no longer a refuge for Vincent Robles. Consider him, as the Americans say, 'a dead man walking.'"

The Secretary affected a posh accent when he spoke English, sounding like a Mexican newscaster auditioning for the BBC.

"He could try to make a deal here."

"He could. But my friend mentioned another thing. The police in Mexicali found a cadaver in the municipal dump. An American. They strongly believe it is the missing border inspector in the Tecate case. The one who let the smuggling van cross the border and who tipped off the rip crew."

*Good God, this is a story,* Méndez thought, scribbling notes.

"Mario Covington," he said.

"The name I don't know. There is evidence implicating Robles, which would automatically expose him to the death penalty in the United States for the murder of a federal official, even if the official was a criminal. But the crime was committed in Mexico, so it's our jurisdiction. Complicated, eh? No matter how you look at it, Robles is doomed."

Santiago had said he would come to the office at noon. They could call federal contacts to try to confirm the story, though it sounded like the Mexicans hadn't told the Americans about the corpse yet.

Méndez saw Porthos glance at his watch.

*The soccer game,* Méndez thought guiltily. He had forgotten.

"Robles may be a highly trained soldier and a top-notch pistolero, but he has nowhere to run," the Secretary said. "He's the buffer, the key link to the masterminds. If they eliminate him, I don't see a case."

"This is not just going to fade away," Méndez said. "This is a high-profile case in the U.S. justice system."

"For some quaint reason that escapes me, you have fervent faith in that system. I fear you will be disillusioned."

Méndez told the Secretary he had an urgent appointment. He thanked him and ended the call. Rolling his eyes at

Porthos, he grabbed his blazer. They hurried out to Porthos's pickup truck.

Méndez waved at the San Diego Police car parked outside his house. A tanned arm in a uniform shirt waved back. The police were still doing intermittent guard duty, but Méndez felt a lot safer now that the story had been published. His foes were out in the open, preemptively identified as suspects. Moreover, Athos, Porthos, Facundo and Pescatore were guarding him when he left the house. They had armed themselves from a north-of-the-border arsenal that Athos kept at his son's home in Chula Vista.

"That was the Secretary," Méndez told Porthos. He filled him in on the latest from Mexico City. The big man whistled.

"The news never stops," Porthos said. "Listen, where is the game? The others are going to meet us there. They want to see Juan play. Then we can all drive downtown to meet with the detectives from New York."

"Great. It's the Miramar area." Méndez pulled out his cell phone. "I'll tell Valentine."

Pescatore reported that he, Athos, and Facundo were close to the freeway and would be at the park soon. Méndez leaned back, watching the sun seep through the cloud cover. He felt groggy. Porthos put a Santana CD in the disc player—*Amigos,* a classic from 1976. Méndez recognized the acoustic guitar solo of "Gitano," the first song on the second side of the record, back when sides and records existed. He tapped his foot as the percussion came in.

They exited the freeway and headed northeast. The farther Méndez ventured from the coast and the border, the more uncertain he became. He directed Porthos onto a road along a row of subdivisions. They pulled into a walled housing tract, slowing for a speed bump.

"The park isn't far," Méndez said. "I think we want to go to the right here...No, that's not it. Keep going."

The lots were deep, and the houses large. There was a repetitiveness to the designs, a lot of blues and pastels. He saw lawn sprinklers, bicycles in driveways, American flags.

*Like a Spielberg set, or like* The Truman Show, *he thought. I couldn't live here, but it looks pleasant and civilized and safe.*

Porthos leaned over the wheel, glancing down cross streets. He grumbled good-naturedly. "Tijuana is chaos, disorganized, the street numbers are meaningless. Americans complain, and they're right. But San Diego is too organized, too orderly. Everything looks the same. I get lost up here."

"Let me check the map."

Méndez was peering at his phone when it rang. It was Pescatore.

"We're at the park, Leo," he said, "but Juan's game isn't here."

"What do you mean?"

Méndez gestured at Porthos to pull over. The truck came to a stop.

"No sign of your family," Pescatore said. "Just one game, and they're little kids. Kindergartners."

"Strange," Méndez said. "Oh, wait. I remember. Juan's summer league plays in the park. The game today is the school league."

Looking at his side mirror, Méndez noticed a blue car stop in the street a block behind them.

"So where are we going?" Porthos asked, drumming the wheel. "Not the park?"

"Sorry about that." Méndez chuckled. "I think they're playing at a school nearby."

"Leo, should we wait for you?" Pescatore asked.

"No, hang on. I'll give you the name of the school. We'll

meet there. Porthos, we should turn around and go back to the entrance of the subdivision."

He looked for the school on the map in his phone. Glancing at the mirror, he saw the blue car start up when they did. It followed as Porthos went around the block, left and left again. The blue car increased speed, gaining ground. A Buick Regal. Two occupants visible in front.

On the phone, Pescatore said, "Leo, what's the name of the school?"

Méndez stared at the mirror, a cold sensation filling his gut. He unclicked his seat belt.

"Porthos," he said, "are you seeing these guys behind us?"

The Regal accelerated fast, suddenly almost even with them. Méndez dropped the phone and drew his gun from his shoulder holster.

"Yes, I..."

As the truck entered the intersection, a white sedan hurtled out of the street on the left. Porthos cursed and swerved to the right. The sedan struck them a glancing blow, the truck rocking to a halt. The Regal swooped around on the right at an angle, brakes shrieking, boxing them in. Gunmen spilled from the sedan and the Regal.

Méndez raised his gun with both hands. He aimed mechanically at a man in a backward baseball cap and oversize white T-shirt who appeared in the street in front of him. A man armed with a pistol and framed in the windshield like a villain in a video game.

Méndez shot him through the windshield.

Then everyone was shooting. His world erupted in a frenzy of noise and glass and smoke.

*An ambush. Car to car. I've been thinking about and preparing and planning for this for years. And it is happening. Now. Here. Not in Tijuana or Juárez or Acapulco. Here.*

The firefight shattered windows with dull crunching sounds. Méndez heard Porthos yell at him to get down. He saw Porthos's gun arm swing back and forth. The gunfire was even louder than in Palazzo di Sabbia. Méndez kept firing. A substance like flying sand assaulted his eyes, ears, nose and mouth—the gunpowder spraying from their pistols along with ejected cartridges.

"Sons of bitches, sons of bitches, sons of bitches!" Porthos roared.

Bullets slammed into Méndez. His body jerked and shook. His gun jumped out of his hand and thudded to the floor. He tried to reach for the gun. His arm didn't respond. It hung from his side, a useless and inanimate object. An impact in his neck punched him back against the headrest.

Blood spattering off his chin, firing wildly, Porthos lunged to his right to shield Méndez with his body. Porthos snarled and grunted as rounds hit him. He screamed, "Get down, get down!"

He grabbed Méndez by the collar, yanked him horizontally onto the seat, and jammed him down behind the dashboard.

Méndez huddled on the floor. He was aware of Porthos writhing above him. The gunfire slowed and stopped. Porthos slumped heavily sideways onto the seat. A brawny protective arm descended onto Méndez's back, pressing him down in a contorted position.

Méndez discovered that he was covered in blood. He didn't know how much of it was his blood and how much was Porthos's. The realization wasn't as hideous as it should have been. It was curiously abstract.

In the sudden silence, Santana launched into the slow sweet overture of "Europa."

A wave of sleepiness descended over Méndez. A door closed in a room in his head, leaving only darkness. Like in Lampedusa when he'd collapsed. Like the way he'd slept last night. Blissful, overwhelming oblivion.

New bursts of gunfire. A car, running feet, screams, commands. It all seemed far away...

*Sons of whores... Don't move,* maricón, *I'll blow your head off... Robles... Careful... Watch that one, Facundo... Sons of whores, fuck your mothers... Porthos... My God, they shot them to pieces... It's bad... Abelardo... My God, look what they've done to them... Sons of whores, fuck your mothers... An ambulance... Licenciado. He's alive... Facundo, help me... Easy... Ambulance... His neck... Leo... Can you hear me...*

*I hear you, Athos. Can't talk though. Strange sensation. Porthos is dead. No one survives that many bullets, not even Porthos... It's my fault. I befriended him, recruited him to the Diogenes Group, pulled him into this shit... I named him Porthos... My fault...*

*Officer, Officer... What's the gentleman's name... Leo. He's law enforcement... Mexican police... Calm down, Athos... Homeland Security... Easy now, sir... Move aside, please... Leo. Leo, my name is Leticia. I'm a paramedic. Can you hear me... Let's lift him... One, two, three... Critical. Multiple gunshot wounds... On our way... Go, dude, haul ass...*

*Sirens... lights... fast... Too late. I named him. I killed him... Dumas... Dumas killed Porthos.* The Man in the Iron Mask. *The grotto on the island. Porthos battles a swarm of enemies. The biggest and best of the Musketeers goes down fighting... Dumas cried after he wrote that scene...*

*Faster, dude... vitals... pulse... oxygen... Leticia, he's speaking Spanish. What did he say... He said he killed somebody... Dude, that crime scene. Never saw anything like it... Leo... Leo...*

*Dumas died old and content, surrounded by his children... My children... I'll miss the game. Juan will score a goal. I'll miss it. He'll think I slept in... Tell Juan we're on our way. Estela, we're on our way... Renata... mi niñita...*

*Almost there, Leo…Just a couple of blocks…Stay with me, buddy.*

*Dumas didn't die young. Too much to do, too many books, too many battles…I keep telling you: Nobody dies before his time…* Nadie muere en la víspera…Nadie muere en la víspera…Nadie muere en la víspera.

# Chapter 17

Pescatore would never forget the moment he heard the ambush begin. The experience was too traumatic, impervious to time, like a recording he could not erase.

During a convivial breakfast Saturday at a diner near the I-5 freeway, Athos had been unusually talkative. Facundo told war stories about his military service and operations for "the Institute," as he called a certain branch of the Israeli government. The three of them were still savoring the thrill of a mission accomplished. They had spent several days briefing agents from the FBI and Homeland Security Investigations. Pescatore looked forward to talking to the NYPD detectives, who were negotiating with Perry Blake's lawyers about interviewing him on Monday.

Isabel had called Friday night to report that the FBI and HSI were consulting her as they formed a task force for the Blake case. They were moving slowly, however, apprehensive about the political snake pit that awaited. And it wasn't clear if they would bring Isabel aboard. Her bosses had hard feelings about her secret investigation using Pescatore, his collaboration with the Italians, and his unilateral operation in Mexico. Even though the braver bosses—and Isabel—had to admit that things had worked out pretty well.

*Hopefully, this will be over soon,* Isabel said on the phone. *We will have a lot to talk about.*

Arriving at the park, Pescatore realized they were not in the right place. He got out of Athos's Dodge Charger to ask people at the soccer field if they knew where the eleven-year-olds played.

The freshly trimmed grass gleamed. Little kids swarmed the ball in a determined flurry of short legs. As Pescatore talked to Méndez on the phone, he felt lazy and mellow. He wondered what it would be like to be a father watching his son play soccer. He was thankful to be back in San Diego in one piece, taking it slow for a change.

Then the sounds of the gunfight blared from the phone in his hand.

Pescatore ran back to the car. Athos sped toward the entrance of the subdivision, looking around wildly. Pescatore yelled for Méndez to give him a location but heard only shots and screams. They spotted activity down a street on their right. The Charger roared up to the intersection. Facundo and Pescatore leaned out their windows, guns at the ready.

There was a white sedan slewed across the street. Near it was Porthos's GMC Sierra, which had been intercepted coming from the right. A blue Regal was angled in front of the pickup truck on the other side. The truck's windshield was a riot of bullet holes and jagged cracks. Smoke hung in the air. Méndez and Porthos were not visible. A man in a backward baseball cap lay facedown on the concrete. The head and arm of another fallen man protruded from behind the Regal. A Hispanic gunman in a yellow T-shirt knelt behind the white car. He was reloading while glancing fearfully over the hood at the pickup. A gunman in a black shirt crouched in a combat stance by the Regal. He was tall and lean and had a crew cut. He was definitely Vincent Robles.

Robles covered a fifth assailant, a short black guy with braids and a buff physique in a Clippers jersey and baggy jeans. Armed with a sawed-off shotgun, Clippers Jersey crept toward the front of the truck. He hunched very low, as if expecting shots from inside at any moment.

The thing that terrified Pescatore was the lack of gunfire. Porthos and Méndez were incapacitated at best. The attackers were about to finish them off.

Athos braked, and Pescatore and Facundo opened fire. Clippers Jersey and Robles went down. Pescatore swiveled his aim to Yellow Shirt, who fumbled his gun. It clattered onto the pavement. Yellow Shirt stayed on his knees, thrusting up his hands in surrender, eyes shut. He shouted, "Don't kill me!"

Pescatore resisted the urge to shoot him anyway.

Pescatore, Facundo and Athos tumbled out of the car. Athos hurried toward the truck, pausing to ensure the fallen combatants weren't a threat. Facundo approached Yellow Shirt at gunpoint, bellowing orders and curses. Pescatore spotted movement beyond the Regal.

Robles was up and running. He clutched his belly with one hand and his gun with the other, but his loping, long-limbed strides covered ground. Pescatore hesitated. He wanted to help his friends, but he couldn't let Robles escape. And he was the only one with the foot speed to catch him.

"I'm going after Robles!" he shouted.

"Careful," Facundo said.

Sprinting around the cars, Pescatore calculated that Robles had a half-block lead. But the man was leaking blood, his shirttails trailing like a cape, his arm tight over the gut wound. Pescatore pounded down the street. His left ankle throbbed. People appeared on lawns and in doorways. A siren wailed faintly.

Robles darted to the right, up a driveway. Gaining fast,

Pescatore cut onto the sidewalk. Robles glanced back, brought the gun up, and slung a shot at him. The bullet whined wide to the left. Pescatore ducked and cursed. He didn't shoot back because he feared hitting civilians in the background. He followed the blood up the driveway, his gun out in front of him, and entered a yard in time to see Robles clambering over a back fence. Reaching the fence, Pescatore heard the deep bark of a big dog. It turned into a snarl and, after a gunshot, a whimper. In the yard on the other side of the fence, he came upon a dead Rottweiler with bared fangs. Someone yelled inside the house. The blood trail led him down a driveway, across the street, and up another driveway. More sirens wailed.

He passed the house and went into the backyard, seeing no cars or residents, and spotted his prey running alongside a pool deck. Robles zigzagged around garden furniture. His gait was uneven, his head drooping lower and lower. Pescatore veered to a spot with a clear sight line. He stopped and took careful aim at Robles, who was staggering toward the back fence.

"Drop the gun!" Pescatore yelled.

Robles whirled. Pescatore fired. Robles banged into the fence and slid along it, leaving a smear of blood on wood.

His heart pounding, Pescatore advanced in a two-handed crouch. Robles had come to rest with his head and part of his back against the fence. Pescatore stopped about ten feet from him. He put his foot on the pistol Robles had dropped. The chorus of sirens sounded closer, as if they were approaching the scene of the ambush.

Robles was alive. His belly wound had pumped blood across his unbuttoned black shirt, olive T-shirt, and camouflage pants. There were more wounds in the left thigh and right side. The hit man had the long-muscled, narrow-waisted build of a basketball forward, his forearms corded and veined below rolled-up sleeves. He was clean-shaven and square-faced, a light complexion contrasting with thick, spiky, very black hair receding at the temples. He was not breathing as hard as might be expected after all that shooting, running, and bleeding.

"Don't move," Pescatore said. "Don't even twitch."

Mindful of the veteran's reputation for hand-to-hand skills, Pescatore stooped warily. He pulled aside the shirt and patted around for extra weapons. Robles's face was a mask of hate and pain.

Pescatore straightened and stepped back. In a panic, he remembered the bullet-riddled pickup truck. Keeping the gun on his prisoner, he called Facundo. The Argentine answered, his voice full of exertion and emotion, a jabber of voices and vehicles in the background.

"Are you all right, Valentín?"

"I got him. Alive. What happened?"

Facundo's pause told him all he needed to know.

"Porthos is gone, son. May he rest in peace." Facundo choked up. "And Leo is very gravely wounded."

Anger flashed like heat lightning in Pescatore's head.

"Where are you?" Facundo asked.

"No." Pescatore made eye contact with Robles. He raised his voice. "No, don't send the police over here. No ambulance either. Give me time with this fucker."

Pescatore hung up. He put the phone in his pocket. Robles's eyes got big. Pescatore rammed the Glock into his brow, pinning the head back against the wood.

"Lord give me strength." The words came out in a sob. "Lord give me strength to blow this motherfucker's brains out."

"The fuck you doing? You crazy?"

The voice was deep and harsh—battlefield sergeant with a hint of barrio hoodlum. Despite the barrel digging into his forehead, Robles sounded more annoyed than frightened.

*Stone-cold bastard,* Pescatore thought.

"Open your mouth, Robles," he snarled. "Taste this Glock before your skull explodes."

"*Pendejo*, you'll do time."

"I don't give a...no, you're right. Wait."

Pescatore took three long paces backward. Robles pushed himself up to a sitting position, grimacing. Pescatore glanced around. No sign of police yet. He didn't think anyone was in the house. But someone would follow the blood. The phone buzzed in his pocket: Facundo calling. He ignored it.

"I'm gonna shoot you from here," Pescatore said. "Then I'm gonna put your gun in your hand."

He wasn't sure what he was doing. He wanted to terrorize the man, put the fear of God in him, use the threat of violence to extract information. But when he had Robles in his sights, rage shuddered through him. It wasn't an act anymore. He wanted to execute him. Impose immediate justice.

Robles held his stare.

Pescatore squeezed the trigger. The bullet hit the fence a foot above Robles's head. The seated figure reared in surprise.

Moving very slowly, Pescatore adjusted his aim downward. His voice was strangled.

"The next one is going in your chest."

He saw fear in the eyes at last. Robles shouted, "Don't do it!"

"Why not?"

"You need me."

"For what? Who can you give me?"

Robles moaned. He was turning pale.

"If I get a deal, and——"

"Fuck that." Pescatore stepped forward and took aim again. "No deals, no pleas, no lawyers and shit. I'll kill your ass right now and get some real revenge. Give it up!"

His wild-eyed roar was only partly a bluff.

Robles coughed. An ugly sound. He contemplated the blood pooling around him in the grass, then looked up.

"Jimmy Noonan," he muttered. "Master Sergeant Jimmy Noonan. In the Antelope Valley. The middleman."

"For who?"

"Krystak."

"Who gave the order to kill Abrihet Anbessa?"

"Krystak."

"Why did you whack everybody?"

"Make it look like narco activity."

"Who set up the hit in Italy?"

"I don't know shit about Italy."

"Does Noonan?"

"Maybe. I know this: You got a leak. Krystak gets intel from DC."

Pescatore absorbed that statement, trying to make sense of it. He remembered reading the Blake company documents in Italy, the reports by someone with inside information. He thought about Isabel's run-ins with forces in the government protecting the Blakes.

"Why are you telling me this?"

"They fucked me. Used me and fucked me."

Robles pressed both hands to his belly, trying to stop the blood flow. Moaning, he drew up his knees.

Pescatore heard voices in the street. He didn't have much time. He stepped closer.

"And today," he said. "Krystak ordered the hit today?"

Robles shook his head, eyelids lowered.

"No."

"Whaddaya mean, no?"

"Méndez was my idea."

Robles was mumbling now. Pescatore bent toward him.

"What? Why?"

The eyes closed. Pescatore kicked the wounded leg. Robles gasped through clenched teeth. The eyes opened.

Pescatore repeated, "Why?"

"Fucker put me all over the news. Everybody chasing my ass. Bothering my mother. He had to pay for that shit. I hired some *vatos*. Discount dumb-fucks, but we took care of him good."

It sounded true, and it explained the sloppy ambush. Robles had been forced to recruit second-stringers. Why would he lie after the things he had confessed? Pescatore felt like throwing up.

Robles groaned. His eyes fluttered shut.

"Hey," Pescatore said. "Don't die yet. Looks like you—"

Robles pulled a spring knife hidden in his right hiking boot and propelled himself up off the fence with startling power and speed. Pescatore flinched. The long lethal arm swept the blade at his jugular.

Thinking about it afterward, he had to admit the move was masterful. Robles had given up golden information, exaggerated his agony, drawn Pescatore close until he sensed his guard was down. If Robles hadn't been wounded, if he could have snared Pescatore with his free hand, it might have worked. But Robles was too far from him and too weak.

Pescatore reared away from the slashing knife. He stumbled backward, firing repeatedly, bracing his fall with his left hand on the grass, still firing. Half a dozen rounds stopped Robles in midlunge—a collision with an invisible counterforce. He jerked stiff and upright, dead on his feet, a vertical corpse. He toppled sideways and rolled onto his back.

Pescatore got up and caught his breath. He saw the dead man's lips stretched above the front teeth, like the Rottweiler's.

Vincent Robles. El T. The killing machine. The sergeant who wanted to be a lieutenant. The chief executive of the rip crew. The material author, as Méndez would say, of the butchery at the border.

The thought of Méndez, and then Porthos, brought tears to his eyes. Two more names on the casualty list. Pescatore was lucky not to be on it himself. He had assumed Robles would want to cooperate and try to swing a deal. But the guy knew he'd go to prison for years no matter what. Concluding that Méndez's article had doomed him, he had decided to bring down everyone he could. That's why he had fingered Noonan and Krystak. That's why he had tried to keep killing until he died.

Pescatore heard brakes, sirens, doors slamming. He holstered his gun. He didn't want to get blown away by rattled cops.

Because he had things to do.

The first officers who ventured into the backyard were a youthful Asian and a blond guy with the look of an ex-surfer. They came in warily, with drawn guns and a lot of adrenaline.

"Show me some hands, man!" The quaver in the Asian's voice indicated that it was the first time he'd seen the results of a Tijuana-style gunfight up close and personal.

Pescatore's hands were already up. His tone was reassuring. "Easy, Officers. I'm on your side. Pescatore, Homeland Security Investigations. Those are my partners who got shot in the pickup."

Once he had been disarmed, things calmed down. The officers had come from the scene of the ambush, where Facundo had explained the situation. Thinking fast, as always, Facundo had conveyed the impression that Pescatore's affiliation with the Department of Homeland Security was more formal than it really was. The Asian officer even called him "Agent Pescatore" as they questioned him in the street. They requisitioned his gun as evidence. Pescatore asked about Méndez. His condition was critical.

Half an hour later, the officers dropped him off at the hospital, where they said detectives would interview him. As Pescatore got out of the squad car, the Asian cop said he had read about Méndez and his police squad that had tried to clean up corruption in Tijuana. He said he was sorry for Pescatore's loss.

*My loss,* he thought, entering the lobby of the hospital. *What did Leo say in Madrid? Every game I play, I lose.*

He had intended to rush to the emergency room. Instead of following the signs to the right, though, he obeyed a sudden impulse and kept going straight. Down a hall, through glass doors, into a courtyard off a cafeteria. Doctors, nurses, orderlies, and visitors ate at outdoor tables. There were benches beneath vegetation. He sat on a bench in a corner and pulled out his phone. A quick Internet search found three Noonans in the Antelope Valley. The most likely candidate was a J. Noonan in his forties who owned a security business in Palmdale.

Pescatore got up. He wanted to find out how Méndez was doing. As he walked back through the glass doors, three men strode purposefully through the street entrance and into the lobby. A blue windbreaker, a certain style of khaki pants, sunglasses dangling from a neckband, a fanny pack big enough for a service weapon. The details told him they were law enforcement even before he recognized an FBI supervisor named Deming who had interviewed him after the rescue of Abrihet Anbessa.

Pescatore averted his eyes and ducked into a newsstand on his right. Hiding behind shelves of candies and magazines, he watched the agents hurry toward the emergency room.

He waited thirty seconds. Head down, he went out and hailed a taxi in line at the curb. He gave the driver the name of his hotel in Mission Beach. In the backseat, he slid down low.

If he had gone to check on Méndez, he wouldn't have been able to leave. The FBI and the police homicide unit wanted to talk to him. That would take time. And he would be forced to decide whether to disclose Noonan's name. He believed Robles had told the truth about Krystak having inside federal sources. Once Pescatore gave up the information, he couldn't control it. He didn't want Krystak or his bosses finding out that the good guys had identified Robles. Right now, Pescatore didn't trust anyone in the government except Isabel.

In the cab, he did more research on his phone. Not much data on J. Noonan, but he was originally from Riverside, like Robles, and known as James and Jimmy. Noonan's firm in Palmdale was called Master Sergeant Security Consulting. Robles had referred to him by that rank. It had to be the same guy. His company supplied home-protection systems and security personnel to individuals and businesses. There were records in the Antelope Valley of a divorce three years ago and the purchase of a home seven years ago.

Pescatore congratulated himself for having asked for a backup piece when Athos had handed out guns at his son's house. The Bersa Thunder .380 was locked in the hotel-room safe. Pescatore put the pistol in his computer bag with the laptop, ammunition clips, and a pair of handcuffs. He threw clothes in a suitcase, grabbed water bottles and chocolate bars from the mini-refrigerator, got in his rented Impala, and hit the I-5 freeway going north.

Missed calls and texts beeped on his phone. Facundo wanted to know where he was. Pescatore sent a text message: Busy. Talk soon. Anything he told Facundo would put his boss in a bad position if the FBI asked about Pescatore. He preferred to keep Facundo in the dark rather than expose him to problems with the feds.

The Camp Pendleton Marine base in north San Diego County was coming into view when a radio station gave a report about the gunfight. Days after making news with bombshell accusations against the Blake Acquisitions Group, Mexican journalist Leo Méndez had been wounded in an ambush. He was in critical condition and undergoing surgery. He had been shot eight times.

"Jesus Christ." Pescatore wiped away tears.

Three suspects had been killed along with Méndez's driver and bodyguard, Abelardo Tapia. It took Pescatore a moment to remember that was Porthos's real name. Two suspects were in custody, one of them wounded. The radio report didn't name the slain and captured gunmen, but he knew it would soon become public that Vincent Robles had surfaced, dead in San Diego rather than on the lam in Mexico.

That news had the power to send dominoes tumbling. He needed to exploit it.

# Chapter 18

Pescatore hunched behind the wheel. His legs and arms ached from physical tension. Adrenaline, grief and anger rattled around inside him.

He felt like a human missile soaring solo across the map—and off the turf governed by rules, laws and common sense. He was taking an enormous risk. The consequences were ominous for his job and for his relationships with Isabel and Facundo. Not to mention there was a strong chance he would get himself killed. But he couldn't figure out any other way to play it.

The trip north took another two hours. He crossed hills and valleys, coastal vistas and suburban sprawl. Orange County, Los Angeles, the San Fernando Valley, Santa Clarita. The Impala hummed at speeds close to ninety. He eased off the gas now and then, worried about police pulling him over.

After he made the steep uphill slog on the Antelope Valley Freeway, mountains gave way to desert. Billboards welcomed him to Palmdale and touted real estate developments with rustic names. The blue sky and distant ridges recalled a cavalry Western—John Wayne in a mustache, blue uniform and yellow bandanna around his neck. The landscape unfolded in a lunar monotone of sand, rock and brush, an expanse of shopping centers and housing tracts.

The Antelope Valley. The high desert plateau. The final frontier of Los Angeles County.

Pescatore had once met an LA County sheriff's deputy who worked up here. The locals called the rest of the county "down below."

Master Sergeant Security Consulting occupied a narrow storefront in a strip mall on an avenue lined with malls and fast-food places. Pescatore parked in front of a doughnut shop two doors down. The neon sign in the window of Noonan's company was on. A sleek Ducati motorcycle was parked in front.

Pescatore called the number for the company. A deep male voice answered.

"Master Sergeant Security."

"Jimmy."

"Yeah. Who—"

Pescatore hung up. Sitting behind the wheel, he finished a water bottle and a Milky Way. The latest news report on the radio said Méndez was out of surgery, in critical but stable condition. Speaking to a reporter by phone, a spokeswoman for the Blake Group condemned the attack on Méndez. Although the Blakes categorically denied the allegations in his articles, they wished him a full recovery.

Keeping an eye on the storefront, Pescatore did more research on his phone: the location of Noonan's home, background on the company. He reviewed accumulated voice mails and texts. Facundo had left a voice mail asking where he was and saying that the FBI and the police wanted to talk to Pescatore. The message was in English, meaning that Facundo had called in front of the investigators. In another voice mail, FBI Supervisory Agent Frank Deming urged Pescatore to return his call. Deming spoke in a relaxed drawl. He said Pescatore's failure to make contact might impede the investigation. And no one wanted that.

Pescatore considered calling him, gaming out the conversation in his head. He decided against it.

Another message on his phone was from Isabel, who was en route to the airport to catch a flight to San Diego. She had heard about Méndez and was horrified. She wanted to talk to Pescatore right away.

He didn't call back. Any communication between them at this point would pull her into what he was doing now. If he implicated her, it would be the final nail in the coffin of her career.

Twenty minutes later, the radio reported that police had identified Vincent Robles, a wanted fugitive, as one of the attackers killed in the gunfight in San Diego. Police believed his motive was revenge. Méndez had named Robles in an article as the chief suspect in the rip-crew murders.

Pescatore checked the time: two p.m. He was betting the news would generate movement among the suspects. If not, he'd have to initiate contact with Noonan and take his chances. But sure enough, twenty-five minutes later the lights went out in Master Sergeant Security Consulting. Jimmy Noonan emerged, wearing a short leather coat and carrying a black helmet, and locked the front door. He resembled his photos on the Internet: a neck-length reddish-gray mane, balding in front. He had a slope-shouldered, thick-limbed walk with a slight limp. As Noonan mounted the Ducati and pulled on the helmet, Pescatore caught a glimpse of a pudgy face and a toothpick protruding from a goatee. Noonan seemed agitated. No doubt he had heard about Robles by now.

Pescatore trailed the rider down the avenue. Noonan followed a route that Pescatore had anticipated, heading east toward home. He owned a ranch-style property near a hamlet called Littlerock.

In the open land outside Palmdale, Noonan unleashed the Ducati. Pescatore remembered the sheriff's deputy telling him about desert driving, how the car crashes up here looked like plane crashes. He sped up to keep his prey in sight. Rows of Joshua trees whizzed by. Isolated homes with landscaped grounds and horse corrals alternated with trailer parks. He passed a junk-filled compound formed by a shack, a yellow school bus, and a water tower tipped on its side. The sight made him think of biker gangs, survivalists, methamphetamine labs.

*Desert-rat territory,* he thought. *This guy is gonna have guns and dogs. Alarms and cameras too, being a security expert.*

The Ducati turned onto a long lonely road alongside a cyclone fence. Noonan slowed; Pescatore accelerated. Noonan must have activated a remote control, because a gate slid open between stone pillars topped by twin statues of bison. When the motorcycle turned up the driveway and went through the entrance, Pescatore overtook it.

The helmet swiveled toward him. A gloved hand darted under the coat, and a gun appeared. Pescatore snarled and spun the wheel.

Bike and rider tumbled, raising a spray of dirt. Pescatore screeched to a stop and leaped out of the car. He jabbed the Bersa into the prone man's spine just below the helmet.

"Don't fucking move or you're dead!"

Noonan grunted unintelligibly. Pescatore handcuffed him, closed the gate behind them with the remote control, and retrieved the fallen pistol. He confiscated Noonan's wallet, a cell phone, keys. Telling himself he wasn't going to fall for the same trick twice, he checked the man's boots for concealed knives. When he was done, he yanked off his captive's helmet and shoved him face-first into the backseat of the Impala. Pescatore slid behind the wheel. Noonan stirred and groaned behind him.

"Sir," he mumbled. "You don't have to do this. I won't rat anybody out."

"Shut up."

"I'm totally reliable, bro. The Major knows that. I won't—"

"You wanna live a few extra seconds, shut the fuck up."

Pescatore nodded with feral satisfaction. Noonan had come to the same conclusion that Pescatore had reached while standing over the corpse in San Diego. The death of Robles had changed the calculations. His solo kamikaze strike had transformed Noonan into the weak link in a chain that led directly to Krystak. So Noonan was convinced that Pescatore was someone sent to whack him.

The driveway was a long, semi-paved, internal road to a rambling one-story house with a barn and garage. A white horse stood in a fenced enclosure. A Jeep Wrangler and a Honda sedan were parked in front of the garage. Unseen dogs barked. No neighboring houses were visible. A bona fide high-desert hideout.

Pescatore stopped the car. Noonan had flopped onto his back in an uncomfortable position atop his cuffed arms. His barrel chest rose and fell. His hair was disheveled.

Leaning over the seat, Pescatore touched his gun to the bridge of the nose where the bushy, rust-colored eyebrows almost met.

"You gonna get slick with me?"

"Negative."

"You gonna answer my questions truthfully?"

"Affirmative."

"Anybody home?"

"Negative."

"Are those noisy-ass dogs running loose?"

"That's negative. They're in a pen by the barn. Sir, is Major Krystak coming? He said we'd talk in person. I can't believe he'd do me like this. Let me talk to the Major. Man to man, eye to eye."

"Shut up. Give me the code to your phone."

"All I want is—"

"Gimme the code!"

Noonan recited numbers. His voice had a cigarettes-and-whiskey warble. His eyes stared at the gun barrel with unblinking acceptance. They had seen death up close before.

*Not quite as tough as Robles,* Pescatore thought. *But he'll do. He knows when he's beat. He's focused on surviving.*

His mind raced. Things were moving fast, making him dizzy. Noonan's phone had logged incoming calls marked *Major* at noon and at 1:47. Krystak had probably phoned after learning about the ambush and again after hearing about Robles—either from the news or from a federal source.

Pescatore hurried his prisoner into the house. He put him facedown next to a wall of screens showing security-camera views of the interior of the house, the ranch and the road.

"Sir?" Noonan raised his head, still staring down at the floorboards. "What happens now?"

Pescatore let the question hang. Sliding into a masquerade that Noonan had inspired, he pretended to make a phone call.

"Major? Yeah...All set here...Roger. Yes, sir, Major. See you soon."

Pescatore acted as if he had hung up. He bided his time. When he saw Noonan turn his head toward him, he said: "Now we wait."

"Roger that." Noonan didn't speak for a while. Then he added, "Thanks, bro."

Pescatore did his best to come off like a dutiful underling. He said, "The Major's a man of his word."

"Sure is."

"What did he tell you, exactly?"

"We have to talk about the new developments. In person. ASAP. He said he'd be here by three o'clock…Is he still coming?"

"Yes."

"You were surveilling me." Noonan sounded dismayed. "I thought he trusted me better than that."

"Things are getting complicated. Maybe he thought you'd pull some shit."

"Negative. Not me." Noonan craned his head toward Pescatore, who stood out of sight behind him. "Were you with him in Afghanistan? Kandahar, or—"

"Enough yammering. Eyes front."

Krystak hadn't wasted time, Pescatore thought. He knew he might end up under surveillance or in custody after the Méndez shooting, even if they couldn't pin it on him. Krystak would be worried that the investigation in San Diego could lead to Noonan. Perhaps it was true that he just wanted to talk to Noonan. But Pescatore was convinced Krystak would want to eliminate a potential witness and dispose of evidence while he could.

Pescatore pulled Noonan to his feet. He forced him down a staircase into a semi-finished basement, where he handcuffed him to a pole. He found an old shirt and tore it into strips that he used to gag and blindfold the prisoner. Noonan cringed, as if fearing his time had come.

"You pull any shit," Pescatore said, "and I'll put one in your head, Major or no Major."

He went upstairs, locking the basement door behind him, and did a quick search of the house. The furniture favored Southwest colors and motifs, expensive but sparse, with a feel of postdivorce depletion. The military memorabilia included a photo of Robles and Noonan looking young and hard in fatigues in front of palm trees and sand dunes.

Pescatore unlocked a gun room. It was well stocked. Just about everything short of a howitzer. He helped himself to an AK-47 assault rifle. Something else caught his eye: a riot shotgun modified for less-than-lethal beanbag ammunition. He grabbed that too, and a backpack. He scooped up ammunition and several pairs of handcuffs, put them in the backpack, and toted his arsenal to the living room.

The security monitors showed no activity outside, not even a passing car. With a jolt of apprehension, Pescatore spotted Noonan's motorcycle. It was still lying near the front gate. The sight would put Krystak on guard.

"Shit."

Pescatore went outside carrying the assault rifle. He ran the length of the internal road, a good quarter mile. He inhaled the crisp cool air, enjoying the physical effort, powering through the twinges of discomfort in his ankle. Alert for approaching vehicles, he got the Ducati started, zoomed back, and parked it by Noonan's cars. Then he drove his Impala behind the house and out of sight.

Back inside, he checked the video monitors; nothing new. He loaded and readied the beanbag shotgun, put his Bersa in his shoulder holster and Noonan's gun in his belt. In the front room, he assessed the entrance and chose a window looking onto the porch from the right of the door. He opened the window halfway.

At 3:12 p.m., a buzzer sounded in the console by the security screens. The vehicle at the gate was a black SUV, probably an Escalade. Pescatore knew Krystak was big and bald; the moonlike head was shiny and oblong behind sunglasses in the grainy image on the screen. Krystak gave the camera a thumbs-up from the driver's seat. Surprised and elated, Pescatore saw no other passengers.

*He didn't bring help,* he thought. *Maybe he doesn't plan on whacking Noonan right this minute. More likely scenario: He does plan on whacking him, but he had to move fast, and he doesn't want more witnesses to worry about. These fuckers are running scared, man. Just like you.*

He pushed the button. The gate slid open. He watched the screen until the gate shut.

Sweat seeped out of his curly hair. Crouching at the window, he wiped his forehead and upper lip with his sleeve. The barrel of the beanbag shotgun was propped on the sill and pointed at the porch. The assault rifle leaned against the wall next to him.

The dogs barked. The Escalade approached. Tires crunched over rocks and sand. The motor died. A door slammed. Krystak appeared. Pescatore took aim, tracking him in three-quarters profile. Krystak's boots thumped as he climbed the steps to the porch. He wore a checkered lumberjack shirt beneath a gray down vest that increased his girth. His catcher's-mitt hands clenched and unclenched. He was less than fifteen feet away.

"Hey!" Pescatore bellowed. "I'm pointing a shotgun at you. Raise your hands and hold real still."

Krystak froze.

*Just fucking follow orders,* Pescatore implored silently.

Krystak's hand whipped aside his vest, reaching for a holster on his hip. Pescatore wasn't taking any chances with this giant pumpkin-head war fighter. He emptied both barrels. Dust and sound and fabric erupted off the down vest. The big man flew backward in an epic fall, made a thunderous impact on the wood. He didn't move.

*I killed him,* Pescatore thought. *That ammo's supposed to be nonlethal, goddamn it.*

Krystak was only stunned. By the time he regained consciousness, Pescatore had cuffed his wrists, and his ankles for good measure. He added Krystak's sidearm, a SIG Sauer, to his gun collection.

The Major grunted when Pescatore dragged him into the house. It was like towing a beached whale. Pescatore's thighs and biceps strained against the weight. In the living room, he used the remnants of the old shirt to gag and blindfold Krystak.

Leaving his new prisoner on the floor, Pescatore went out to the Escalade. The rear storage space contained rope, lime, gloves, duct tape, a shovel, a pickax, chloroform, galoshes, and a folded tarpaulin. Only a Grim Reaper's hood and scythe were missing. The goal of Krystak's expedition seemed pretty clear: kill Noonan, then take advantage of the area's plentiful supply of clandestine gravesites.

Back in the house, Pescatore sank into an armchair. The cushions were soft. Sunbeams slanted through a skylight. Dogs and birds made noise outside. Gradually, his pulse and respiration returned to normal.

Contemplating his prisoner, he thought about revenge and justice and luck and fate.

# Chapter 19

B efore going downstairs, he called Isabel.
Although he was still afraid of creating problems for
her, the fact of the matter was that she had already called him.
There was no hiding that. Moreover, the time had come to tell
her about his situation and ask what the hell to do next.

No answer. Her flight had taken off. She wouldn't be reach-
able until she landed in San Diego—another five hours or so.
Facundo and Athos were probably still at the hospital, and the
FBI and police were probably still around. He thought again
about reaching out to the FBI supervisor who had left the
voice mail. His doubts stopped him. How many allies did the
Blakes have in law enforcement? At what level? How quickly
could they counterattack if they learned what he was up to?

Pescatore was on his own. But he was in control. He didn't
intend to relinquish it until he had answers.

He went downstairs. In the basement, Noonan sat on the
linoleum with his legs crossed, his hands cuffed behind him to
a wooden floor-to-ceiling post. His pose conveyed the patient
resignation of a man for whom such a predicament was not
unthinkable. A Ping-Pong table and a washer-dryer set were

visible behind him. The room smelled like firewood, detergent and plumbing.

Pescatore removed the gag and blindfold. Noonan shook his head, his stringy hair bobbing. He squinted against the light. Pescatore held out a bottle of water so Noonan could drink from it. Noonan thanked him, a trickle dripping from his goatee.

"There you go," Pescatore said.

He pulled up a chair. The Bersa was in his shoulder holster, the confiscated pistols were in his belt and jacket pocket, the AK-47 and riot shotgun lay within arm's reach.

"All right, Noonan," he said. "We need to have a conversation."

Noonan studied him mournfully.

"Where's the Major?"

"Upstairs. Cuffed up and in custody, just like you. You mighta got the wrong impression earlier. I don't work for Krystak. I didn't come here to murder you. But you were half right—he definitely came here to murder you."

Pescatore showed him cell phone photos of the captive Krystak and the equipment in his vehicle. Noonan shook his head, dismayed but not surprised.

"Who are you?"

"Valentine Pescatore. Homeland Security."

"The USG."

"Yep."

"Why'd you run me down?"

"Why'd you pull a gun? I just wanted to talk to you."

Pescatore scowled. In fact, he had hoped to pressure Noonan to join forces with the good guys, but he had waited too long before deciding to make the approach. The encounter had escalated in a way he hadn't been able to control.

"I investigated that massacre at the border you organized,"

Pescatore said. "I was there today when Robles ambushed Méndez, who's a friend of mine. The cop who died was my friend too. I smoked your boy Robles. Personally."

Noonan's eyes turned incredulous and desperate, a boxer on the ropes.

"Fuck..." he muttered. "I..."

"Tell you the truth, I'm having trouble working up sympathy for him. He pulled a boot knife on me. Did you know he carried one? Yeah, I can see you did. Good. Now you know I'm not bullshitting."

"Sir, I swear, I had nothing to do with Vincent shooting your friends. That's on him. He was supposed to be hiding in Mexico or Guatemala somewheres. He was pissed. He felt like he got screwed over, and he went crazy. He did it on his own."

"Yeah, he told me that before he died. A big fucked-up joke on everybody, huh? If it's true."

"It's true, bro."

"He gave me your name. That's why I beelined up here. I figured Krystak would whack you. You're lucky I got here first."

"What happens now?"

"All this media heat, the feds need a big fish. The Blakes have money and political yank and hotshot lawyers. The U.S. attorney will need inside testimony. Looks like you're the star witness. Krystak would be better, but he's too high up the ladder. If they flip you, they've got a shot."

"Are you making an offer?"

Pescatore frowned. "Everybody wants an offer today. I'm an off-the-books guy. Low profile. Kinda like you. Except I don't set up executions of helpless women. That's a big fucking difference."

Noonan grimaced. Pescatore continued.

"The feds'll give you a speech. They'll tell you a story and say you can write the ending. You served your country. You made life-and-death decisions on the battlefield. Time to make another one. Get with the USG again. If you don't, you're looking at the death penalty, life without possibility, blah-blah. You see how bad your situation is?"

"Yes, sir."

"Well, listen to this: Nobody knows I'm here right now. Absolutely nobody. And I'm disgusted and furious. Even if Robles did today on his own, it's still your fault. Even if you didn't pull the trigger in Tecate, you're still responsible for that fucking bloodbath. I'm tempted to put a bullet in your head, you and Krystak both. Make it look like you did each other. Set up the scene, leave the bodies, let you rot. If you don't answer my questions right now, the death penalty won't be a theoretical punishment. Am I making myself clear?"

Looking punch-drunk again, Noonan said he was making himself clear.

Pescatore turned on the recorder in his telephone.

"First question: What's the connection between you and Robles and Krystak?"

Noonan said he had gone to high school with Robles in Riverside. They'd joined the military together, did basic training together. Noonan went off to fight in Afghanistan, where he met Major Louis Krystak. Later, Noonan did a tour in Iraq and reunited there with Robles, now a fellow sergeant. In the mid-2000s, Noonan left the army and opened his security firm. Meanwhile, Krystak became security chief for the Blake Group, dividing his time between coasts. He hired Noonan for jobs in California.

"Background checks, surveillance. Discreet stuff."

"Rough stuff?"

"Nothing like this summer."

In the flat declarative sentences of an after-action report, he recounted how Krystak had summoned him to Los Angeles. An employee of the Blakes had stolen sensitive material and fled to Mexico. Krystak wanted to track her down. Could Noonan help?

"I'd stayed in touch with Vincent. I knew he was deep into cartel activity at the border. Making coin. You heard of the Kaibiles? The Zetas?"

"Guatemalan and Mexican commandos who work for the narcos."

"Vincent Robles could scrap with any Kaibil or Zeta you got. And he was American, so he had mobility across the border. When he left the military, he did wet work for hire. Then he put together a rip crew. A squared-away setup. Mexican law enforcement protection. We subcontracted him for our op."

"Communications and money went through you?"

"Affirmative. Compartmentalized. For opsec."

"What?"

"Operational security. Robles talked to me, I talked to Krystak. Face to face or using messengers."

"And?"

"The Major had urgent intel: The African girl was coming back to New York to extort the company. The order was take her out, recover compromising information if we could. It couldn't look like a targeted hit. We had to erase connectivity back to us."

"These directives were from Perry Blake himself?"

"I think so. Vincent said he'd locate her. He'd stage it like a cartel thing. A rip-crew job gone bad. They smoke aliens all the time. I reported back. The Major said they liked that strategy. Nobody'd think we did a dozen to do one."

"'They' being the Blakes?"

"I think so."

"Listen, it's real important to confirm that. Otherwise the

Blakes could try to pin it on you or the Major. Play it off like you guys went rogue."

Noonan shook his head reluctantly. "I've never met the Blakes. The Major talked like he was relaying orders, like it was Perry who wanted this girl dead. But he didn't come out and say those words."

"Did he tell you Blake tried to rape Abrihet Anbessa?"

"No. I heard that on the news. I'm not surprised. Perry's like that. Chasing tail, putting his hands on girls, expecting the Major to clean it up. Ain't the first time."

"What happened in Tecate?"

"A cluster-fuck. Vincent's crew didn't deliver. The girl got away. Vincent kept looking for her in Baja and down south in Chiapas."

The errors seemed to bother him more than the bloodshed.

*Glad you're all broken up and remorseful about it,* Pescatore thought. *A real sentimentalist.*

"Did you do surveillance on me and Méndez?"

"Just Méndez. And his family. After he wrote about the Blakes."

"Somebody tailed me on the East Coast."

"Krystak's operators, I guess."

"What about trying to kill me and Méndez in Italy?"

Noonan steadfastly denied having anything to do with the attack in Palazzo di Sabbia. He hadn't known about it until the articles by Méndez. He looked Pescatore in the eye.

"The Major has a buddy in Italy," Noonan said. "A Brit he met in Kabul, special forces vet. He's a mercenary now, active in Africa. A gun seller too. Does business with the Mafia."

*That fits the profile,* Pescatore thought. *Another subcontractor.*

"You got a name?"

"Might have it somewheres."

"What did the Blakes pay you?"

297

"For me and Robles both, about a quarter million total."

"Through banks? Traceable?"

"You kidding? Straight cash, bro."

"Who are the sources Krystak has in law enforcement?"

"Sources?"

Noonan shifted his position on the floor, extending his legs. He winced in discomfort. His gaze lowered. Pescatore tilted his head impatiently.

"Don't get slick on me. I know for a fact the Blakes get inside intel."

Noonan shrugged. "Shit, you'll find out sooner or later. The Blake Group has a law firm in Washington. One of the lawyers was at the Justice Department before. Financial crimes. He still has access. Serious access. He passes info to the Blakes and the Major."

"Name?"

Noonan knew the name of the firm, not the lawyer, and that was only because Krystak had gotten talkative over drinks. Pescatore had heard of the law firm. He recalled the dapper black prosecutor who had overseen the Ruiz Caballero case and who was friendly with Isabel and Méndez.

"Sylvester Daniels works there. Used to be at Justice. Is he the guy?"

"Negative. The Major mentioned Daniels. Arrogant prick. Won't lift a finger for us."

"Who else in the government?"

"The Major knows people in the military, intelligence, drug task forces."

"Active, not just retired."

"Yeah."

"Here in California?"

"I'm pretty sure, yeah."

"Operational? Street level? Supervisors?"

"I don't know."

"Do Perry or Walter Blake know who you are? Would they know Krystak is here now?"

"Perry might."

"What's Krystak's relationship with the Blakes like?"

"He pretty much hates Perry. He says all the dope and drink and pussy is ruining his judgment. But the father wants him to clean up Perry's mess, so the Major does it. The father's a mean prick. The Major is too, so they get along. He's been working for Walter ten years. Shitload of money."

"Would the Major flip?"

Noonan laughed mirthlessly. "He wouldn't rat out Walter Blake, anyway. Hard to hurt the son without hurting the father."

"The Blakes calling the shots, that sounds logical. Your testimony is important. But what's some corroborating proof that Perry gave the order to kill Abrihet Anbessa? Phone contact, e-mails, money?"

"Not much, bro. The Major's big on opsec. It's not like there's anything putting everybody in the same place at the same time."

"Huh."

Pescatore ran a hand through his curly hair. He stopped the recorder.

"Okay," he said.

"What happens to me now?"

"Sit tight. Maybe you get to live."

# Chapter 20

The ranch had become his private little interrogation center. A secret outpost. A black site. He was climbing the stairs of the conspiracy: Robles, Noonan, Krystak. Basic investigative techniques. Organized Crime 101. The higher you rose, the better—and tougher—it got.

Pescatore hauled Krystak upright and pushed him into the armchair. Off came the gag and blindfold. Krystak accepted a drink of water. He didn't say thank you.

The Major was assembled like a mountain range: head, deltoids, shoulders, arms. The jut of his jaw suggested steroid use in the past. The polished scalp shone. As he sat with his wrists and ankles cuffed, his manner was stolid, almost sleepy.

Pescatore asked, "You know who I am, right?"

Krystak nodded.

"Then listen up," Pescatore said.

He laid it out. Evidence from witnesses, communications and documents put Krystak at the heart of an ongoing criminal conspiracy. He had ordered the kidnapping and attempted murder of Abrihet Anbessa, causing the murders of a smuggler in San Diego, ten migrants and three kidnappers in Tecate, and a CBP inspector. As well as the attempted murders in Italy of Solomon Anbessa, Méndez and Pescatore. He had covered up the assault on Abrihet Anbessa and obstructed a federal investigation.

"Plus the killings today in San Diego, which can be attributed to the continuing conspiracy. Death-penalty offenses, Major. The one thing in your favor, the one single thing, is that you weren't the top guy. But unless you help us go to the next level, you're gonna be the fall guy. The goon gone rogue. Is that a role you wanna play? Sacrifice yourself for Perry Blake?"

"Fuck yourself." The bass voice was affectless. "I want a lawyer."

Pescatore said this wasn't that kind of situation. He explained that he was there clandestinely. He repeated the threat he had made to Noonan: he could shoot them, then stage it so it looked like they had killed each other.

"Better start talking while you can," Pescatore said.

Krystak's thick eyebrows climbed the wall of his forehead. His breathing was slow and audible.

"Fuck yourself," he said again.

Pescatore nodded. "Noonan said you wouldn't rat them out because you're loyal to Walter Blake."

Leaving him in the chair, Pescatore walked down the hall to the gun room. He unlocked it, went in, came back out, and locked the door behind him. He returned to the living room holding a twenty-two-inch Monadnock expanding baton made of alloy steel. It was similar to the collapsible straight baton issued to agents by the U.S. Border Patrol.

He caught a glimpse of himself in one of the security screens on the wall console. The camera angle was from the side and above. The screen showed a compact, powerfully built, dark-haired figure in a leather jacket. The figure held the baton down along the right leg. The face was not visible.

"All right, then," he said. "I'm not gonna waste time. I respect your decision not to talk. But there's one thing you have to do. We're gonna call Perry Blake. You do some acting; you tell him you whacked Noonan, but he shot you. You're wounded. You need help. Perry has to get up here and save his soldier."

Krystak didn't say anything. Sweat slid down Pescatore's arms and sides. He shifted the baton from one hand to the other so he could wipe his palms on his jeans.

"How about it, Major?"

Krystak shook his shaved head. Pescatore walked across the room to the security console, located a master switch, and turned off the camera system. The screens went blank. He returned to his spot in front of Krystak.

"If you don't do it," Pescatore said very softly, "I'm gonna beat the shit out of you. Maybe beat you to death. Don't test me, Major. Not today."

"Fuck yourself."

The voice was hoarse.

Pescatore thought, *Now what?*

He remembered the stifling Saturday night in Mexico when he had questioned Chiclet. He had imagined brutalizing the smuggler. He had told himself that he had never tortured a suspect and wasn't about to start.

He paced back and forth, the baton over one shoulder, like a batter on deck. Memories assailed him. Disjointed images: corpses in a motel room; Blake in front of a skyline; blood on the carpet of a cybercafé; Abrihet Anbessa in a sweatshirt hood; the shattered windshield of a pickup truck. He stopped pacing.

"How do you live with it?" he demanded. "What the fuck is wrong with you? All those people hurt and killed. Just because some perverted billionaire wants whatever he can get."

Krystak's eyes were steel-colored. They studied Pescatore now. Probing, calculating. The gruff voice turned cagey. "You ever serve in the military, kid?"

"The Border Patrol."

"Seen combat?"

"Firefights."

"Kills?"

"Yeah."

*First he wouldn't talk,* Pescatore thought, a rivulet of sweat leaving a tang of salt on his tongue. *Now the suspect is taking over the interview.*

"You spend enough time in combat, you understand the world is shit," Krystak said. "Kill or die. Win or lose. Most people lose and die. You spend enough time around people like the Blakes, you find out about a whole different world. A sweet life. Hardly anybody gets to live it, though."

"That right?"

"Not unless you're tough and smart."

One side of Krystak's mouth turned up in a semblance of a smile. It occurred to Pescatore that Krystak was accustomed to command. He had experience leading soldiers into harm's way. He could talk up a storm if he had to.

"You must be tough and smart, kid," Krystak continued. "Because you're in control of this situation right now. A one-time opportunity. Take advantage of it."

"Meaning what?"

"Killing me would be stupid. I have access to unlimited funds. A life-changing amount of money. You know that. So name your price."

Pescatore spoke quietly, through clenched teeth. "Is that an offer?"

"Say the word. I can make it happen."

Pescatore tilted his head. There was a long silence.

So that was the bottom line. If Krystak couldn't kill him, he could still buy him. None of it mattered, all the lives lost and ruined. Krystak had money and that meant he could get away with anything.

"Fuck yourself," Pescatore said.

Fury overwhelmed him. He gripped the baton with both hands. He swung it at the left side of the man's body. Swift hammering blows: arm, ribs, knee, arm, ribs, knee. He was sickened by the impacts, the cries of pain, his silent punitive efficiency. There was a roaring in his ears, a metallic taste in his mouth. He saw more than heard Krystak scream in surrender.

Both of them took a while to catch their breath. Krystak looked straight up at the ceiling, his chin jutting high, the sinews of the neck straining. You could see him ride the pain, absorb it, dominate it.

"Okay," he said, his face pale and twisted.

"You'll make the call?"

"Yeah." And then, grudgingly: "Didn't think you had it in you."

"Me either. Till you disrespected me."

He put Krystak's phone on a side table next to the armchair. He told him what to say and how to say it.

"Where is Perry right now?"

"Bel Air."

"Does he know you came here to kill Noonan?"

"Yeah."

Pescatore drew the gun from his shoulder holster and pointed it at Krystak's face. He activated the speakerphone.

"Use Signal," Krystak muttered. "He won't talk unless it's encrypted."

"Okay."

After four rings, they heard rock music. The percussive

chug of a treadmill or a StairMaster. Fast breathing. Perry Blake was working out in his home gym.

"What's up, Major?"

Krystak didn't have to pretend to sound hurt.

"Issue resolved," he rasped. "But there's damage. I need assistance."

"Shit, Major..." The voice was imperious and exasperated. "How bad?"

"Bad. Not mobile."

Krystak was following Pescatore's script.

"The location we discussed?"

"Yeah."

"That's far..."

The music faded. A door slammed. Blake was walking and thinking.

Blake said, "It's isolated?"

"Affirmative. A ranch."

"There are some fucking press photographers hanging around outside. But we can give them the slip. Lookit, I could helo up to your location. It's a lot faster if it's secure."

Krystak glanced up over the gun barrel at Pescatore, who nodded.

"Good idea," Krystak mumbled.

"Excellent. The pilot's on call. I'll bring Danny for you. Can you hold out?"

"Uh-huh."

"Everything resolved otherwise? With the...issue?"

"Affirmative."

"On our way. Hang tight, Major."

Blake hung up.

"Where's the helipad?" Pescatore asked Krystak.

"Beverly Hills."

"So what's their ETA, maybe an hour?"

Krystak nodded. Pain distorted his face. He leaned to his right, keeping weight off his injured side.

"Who's Danny, a bodyguard?"

"Yeah. Medic. Served with me."

"I gotta ask: You and Blake trust each other, right? You have no doubt about his intentions?"

Krystak regarded him coldly.

"You really fucked me up," he growled. "My arm, my knee. Busted ribs too."

"Yeah, well, your subcontractors damn near killed me in Italy. Not to mention what I been through today."

The raised eyebrows appeared to concede the point. Krystak asked, "Do you know what the hell you're doing?"

"Pretty much."

"What are you doing?"

"Blake's presence with you and Noonan is gonna be incontrovertible proof of his involvement in the conspiracy. No way to deny it, finesse it, no matter how many lawyers he's got, how many moles in the government. I'm taking him into custody and turning all of you over to the feds."

"By yourself?"

"Listen, you decided to whack Noonan because he was a link to Robles. I'm asking if Blake might get the same idea. Whack you too. Erase connectivity."

"That's a bunch of crap."

"Why? Because you're tight with his father? Because you've done dirty work for the family? Killing people, covering up rapes?"

Krystak snorted in disgust. "You talk too fucking much."

Pescatore thought he saw a flicker of doubt in the broad face. He looked at his watch. A few minutes past five. He got to work. He prepared his weapons, mapped out his plan, and turned the security camera system back on. With his iPhone, he sent the recording of his interrogation of Noonan to Maio in Italy with a note asking the prosecutor to hold on to it for the moment.

Next, Pescatore wrote an e-mail to Facundo. He explained very briefly where he was and what was going on. He attached the file of Noonan's recorded confession and asked Facundo to send the cavalry, but he held off on hitting Send.

Pescatore stood near Krystak at the bay window, looking out at the Joshua trees, the afternoon sky. He waited. He sent the e-mail to Facundo at 6:17 p.m., when he heard the helicopter, and then saw it, emerging out of orange and purple cloudbanks in the distance.

He crossed himself and lifted his crucifix to his lips. Then he dialed 911.

"What's your emergency?"

The soft twang of the sheriff's department operator's voice fit nicely with the landscape.

Pescatore gave his name and talked fast. "Ma'am, I'm an investigator with DHS. I need assistance. I'm about to engage armed and dangerous suspects at the following address…"

The helicopter approached. Glass and metal glittered in the low sun.

Pescatore continued, "My suspects in custody are James Noonan and Louis Krystak. I'm about to engage another homicide suspect named Perry Blake, and accomplices. They are armed and dangerous. I need backup as soon as you can."

"Mr. Valentine, that location is remote. We're dispatching a resident deputy, but other units will take time."

"Ma'am, I'm sorry, I gotta go. Just send 'em quick. Thank you."

The helicopter circled high above the ranch. It was a medium-size, aquamarine-colored craft with room for half a dozen passengers. The pilot narrowed the circles, then widened them again.

*He's doing reconnaissance before they land,* Pescatore thought.

After another five minutes, the helicopter descended near the parking area. Sand swirled. Dust geysered. The dogs barked and barked.

The rotors came to a stop. Two men emerged from the helicopter. The pilot followed. He wore a blue flight suit, a belt holster, and a helmet with headphones. The three of them hurried toward the house.

Perry Blake was the tallest. His walk verged on a charge, like he was getting ready to throw a punch. He wore a dark red designer warm-up jacket, matching sweatpants, and gym shoes, looking as if he had left straight from the workout. The third man was black, medium height, bull-necked in a bomber jacket and dress slacks.

"Is that Danny?" Pescatore asked.

"No." Krystak sounded weak and defeated. "Jackson."

"Is he a medic too?"

"No. A thug."

*Bad sign,* Pescatore thought. *Maybe medical care isn't on the agenda.*

"All right," Pescatore said. "Just do what I say."

Moving as if in a dream, he pushed Krystak—short shuffling steps because of his cuffed ankles—toward the entrance. Krystak groaned and grunted. Pescatore positioned him at the end of a hall-like vestibule that extended about fifteen feet from the front door. Pescatore carried his Bersa and the assault rifle as well as the pistols in his belt and jacket pocket. He wore the backpack.

Footsteps reached the porch. Pescatore crouched, sheltered partly by Krystak's massive back and partly by the wall at the end of the vestibule. When the men entered, they would be hemmed in the narrow space without cover.

A knock.

"Major?" Blake's voice was nasal and urgent. "You there?"

Pescatore jabbed Krystak in the neck with the muzzle of the Bersa.

"It's open," Krystak called.

The door opened, and they stepped into the vestibule. They saw Pescatore behind his hostage, pointing the rifle at them with his right hand and the pistol at Krystak's head with his left.

"Hold real still," Pescatore ordered. "Hands up."

Blake's face tightened with surprise and anger. Sunglasses were propped on the upswept crest of hair. He was chewing gum, the long tanned jaw working rhythmically.

"What the fuck? Who are you?"

In person more than on television, Blake looked and sounded like an aging frat boy.

"Hands up, goddamn it," Pescatore said.

"Perry," Krystak said. "Take it easy. Let's do what he says."

Blake raised his long arms. He glared down at Pescatore. His well-plucked eyebrows arched in recognition.

"I know. Pescatore, the low-rent private investigator."

Pescatore felt oddly honored. Blake had probably seen his face in photos. Most likely when he'd given Krystak the green light to have him killed.

"Bingo. Pilot, close the door behind you. Easy. Lock it. Now, all of you, step into my parlor. Real slow."

Jackson's mouth twisted. He was in his forties. He wore an earring. His hair was shaved on the sides but not on top. His right hand drifted downward.

"Jackson, don't move!" Pescatore snapped. "This AK isn't gonna miss."

Jackson complied. Blake threw a sidelong glance at the pilot, who had removed his helmet and held it under his left arm. The pilot's thick brown mustache dominated features that were a mix of canine and porcine. He stared straight ahead.

*Something's going on,* Pescatore thought. His heart was thumping.

"Perry..." Krystak sounded imploring and reproachful.

"Get moving, fuckers," Pescatore snapped. "There's an army of cops on their way."

"Okay, guys, you heard him," Blake declared. "Everybody relax and follow orders."

Then he gave Pescatore a jagged smile. "Your call, Pescatore. I'm ready to talk business."

"Do me a favor, Blake. Don't bullshit me."

Blake's jaw hammered the gum.

Still using Krystak as a shield, Pescatore swiveled, covering the newcomers as he directed them into the living room.

"On your knees first. Hands on your heads. Then your bellies."

Pescatore removed the backpack. He pushed Krystak to his knees in the vestibule. Holstering the pistol, he advanced toward the prone trio. He disarmed the professionals first: Jackson, the pilot. After stuffing their guns into the backpack, he started toward Blake, who was on his stomach near a couch. Pescatore had seen the bulk of a pistol in the right pocket of Blake's warm-up jacket.

A foreboding nagged at Pescatore. Beyond the tension of the moment, there was something strange about the body language of his captives.

*Like they're expecting something...*

Hesitating a few feet from Blake, he glanced around. A ripple of movement on one of the security screens caught his eye. And saved his life. The screen showed the back of a figure entering a window from the porch. Pescatore spun around to see a redhaired man in a denim jacket clambering through the open window and pointing a pistol at him. Flame leaped from the pistol at the same time that Pescatore pulled the trigger of the rifle, stitching holes across the front of the jacket. The man collapsed. Pescatore felt pain radiating through his left side.

Then he was confronting a roomful of enemies, a nightmare whirl of converging threats. Jackson rolled and kicked, trying to sweep Pescatore's legs out from under him. Pescatore sidestepped, twisting away, and sprayed volleys back across his body at Jackson on the floor, at Blake with a gun scrambling behind the couch, at the oncoming pilot who hurled his helmet as he lunged. It caromed off Pescatore's left shoulder, which was preferable to a direct hit in the face but hurt like hell. The pilot tackled him, grunting, grabbing for the rifle. They went down in a heap and rolled back up, still struggling for the weapon. Pescatore pulled hard, then released his grip. The pilot crashed back against a coffee table. He was fumbling with the rifle when Pescatore yanked the pistol from his belt and shot him repeatedly.

Pescatore rolled away, shooting wildly at where he'd last seen Blake, gunfire sounding. He dived through a doorway into the dining room. He pulled another of his pistols, reached around, and pumped bullets back through the doorway. There was no return fire. Seconds went by. Gazing through smoke, both guns out in front of him like a bandit, he surveyed the battleground.

Jackson lay facedown, moaning.

The pilot sprawled on his back on the coffee table.

The red-haired gunman remained in the spot near the window where he'd fallen.

Krystak's manacled legs protruded, horizontally, from the vestibule.

Blake was nowhere to be seen.

*Now what?*

The cell phone clipped on Pescatore's belt was ringing. In

fact, it had been ringing for some time, an incessant subliminal buzzing during the melee. Probably the sheriff's department. Pescatore holstered a gun while keeping the other at the ready. Reaching with his left hand for the phone, he touched blood on his shirt above his hip. He answered in a whisper.

"Hello?"

"Mr. Valentine, this is the 911 operator. The deputy is three minutes from your location. What's your status?"

"Shots fired. Four down. I'm hit. One suspect unaccounted for."

Pescatore gave her a description of Blake and hung up. Crouching, he padded into the living room and retrieved the AK-47. Through the bay window he saw Blake outside, a pistol in his hand, by the Ducati motorcycle. Blake was frantically checking the ignition and the saddlebags, no doubt hoping to find the keys. He didn't find them, because they were in Pescatore's pocket. Blake took off running down the internal road away from the house.

*He plays the hard-ass,* Pescatore thought. *But he's not exactly a gunslinger.*

Pescatore pushed the button on the security console to open the street gate for his reinforcements, though he didn't see any yet. Hurrying through the vestibule, he glanced down at Krystak. The Major's forehead had been shattered by a point-blank bullet.

*Not one of my rounds,* he thought. *Blake must have capped him on his way out. Blake came here to kill Krystak. That's why he brought three guys. They weren't taking chances with the Major, wounded or not. That's why the last guy hung back, hiding in the copter, and sneaked up to the window. He was backup.*

Feeling woozy, Pescatore walked out onto the porch. Blake kept running. His gait was uneven. Pescatore had not missed entirely.

Pescatore went down the steps. Planting his feet, he raised the rifle. He sighted on the tall receding silhouette. He tracked it.

*Now's the time,* he thought. *Fleeing felon. Armed and dangerous. Justifiable. Do him. Get some revenge. Street justice. Do him. Make a contribution to society, addition by subtraction. Do him. Now's the time.*

With more relief than regret, he realized that he didn't have it in him. Not now. Not after everything that had happened in that house. His finger stayed on the trigger, his sights on Blake's back.

A cloud of dust announced the arrival of a Los Angeles County Sheriff's Department mini-truck. Lights flashing, the black-and-white vehicle sped through the pillars flanking the gateway. The driver swerved to the left and stopped in a defensive angle. He slid out fast and pointed a long gun.

Blake faltered to a stop. He looked at the deputy and then back at Pescatore, who was still aiming at him. Blake dropped his gun. The deputy shouted orders. The deputy peered down the road at Pescatore, who put the rifle on the ground and waved. The deputy signaled at him to advance.

Keeping his hands visible, Pescatore started forward. One step at a time, tottering now and then. He was deliriously tired. He felt like a zombie. As he trudged, he became aware of his surroundings. The beauty of the sky awed him, a symphony of light, clouds, and colors.

A resident deputy was an officer who lived in the vast turf he patrolled, a home substation arrangement, the only law for miles. In his green cap and uniform, the deputy looked the part: raw-boned, cowboy boots, graying whiskers. He stood with a shotgun covering Blake, who was on his knees with his hands on his head. The deputy's stance was alert, his voice hearty. "What's your name, son?"

"Valentine Pescatore. I called 911."

"Valentine, right, outstanding."

"I'm a contract investigator for DHS."

"Yeah, we just got a call from San Diego PD. And the FBI. They said you were in a situation up here."

*Facundo moved fast,* Pescatore thought. "Been a long day," he said.

The deputy went to work searching and cuffing Blake. Pescatore found it necessary to lean against the vehicle. He applied pressure to the wound at his hip. The deputy glanced at him.

"You hit, son?"

"Yeah. There's casualties in the house. And a handcuffed suspect in the basement."

"The fire department is rolling."

The deputy placed a pistol, phone, wallet, sunglasses, and bottle of pills on the hood of the vehicle. He and Pescatore stood looking at the handcuffed man lying facedown in the road.

The prisoner's hair was rumpled and dusty. He emitted a kind of humming sound—between a moan and a sigh.

"Who's the suspect?" the deputy asked.

In Pescatore's light-headed state, a memory took shape. A gangster film on late-night television. *The Roaring Twenties.* Tuxedos, tommy guns, fast money, Cagney and Bogart, rise and fall.

"Perry Blake," he said. "He used to be a big shot."

# Epilogue

Méndez felt that the English translation didn't do justice to the word *rematar*.

The concept is clear: To finish off. Administer the coup de grâce.

But some ideas do not cross borders unscathed. *Matar* means "to kill." *Rematar* implies a repetition of the act as well as its completion—to kill the same person again. Execute an irrevocable sentence, extinguish a life that is for all intents and purposes over. He had investigated and reported on crimes in which assassins in Mexico—and Central America, Venezuela, take your pick—returned to *rematar* their wounded and doomed victims, to repeat and complete the crime with savagery and impunity, storming into homes, police stations, ambulances. And hospitals.

After surgery, Méndez spent two days in intensive care. He drifted in and out of consciousness. His dreams were no longer speculative. He knew now the exact circumstances of his demise. A gunfight on a Saturday morning in the heart of America's Finest City. The film of the ambush in the subdivision played and replayed in his head with small variations but

315

the same events. Ending in his death on the floor of Porthos's pickup truck. Which was strange because, officially, he was still alive.

His assassination had happened despite layers of precaution and protection, despite the fact that he had accused his foes on the front pages, despite laws and institutions intended to prevent such savagery and impunity. In the final analysis, he was a dead man. His enemies wouldn't stop now. He dreamed that the killers were charging into the hospital to kill him again.

*"Me van a rematar,"* he yelled, sometimes out loud, sometimes in helpless silence. *They are on their way. In the building. No time to lose. I don't have a gun. Give me a gun, Athos. What are you waiting for? I'm going to fuck them up with a fuckload of gunshots,* un chingo de balazos, *sons of whores.*

When he thrashed awake, shouting and struggling against sheets and wires, faces appeared to console him: nurses, his wife, Athos, Facundo, a uniformed San Diego policeman guarding the room.

On Monday evening, Méndez was moved out of intensive care. The nightmares subsided. His condition improved. The wounds in his neck and chest had almost killed him, but the worst pain was in his right arm, which was immobilized, strapped and wrapped. The arm had been pulverized by four bullets, taking the brunt of the impacts because his hands had been raised to shoot back.

On Tuesday morning, he was groggy but awake. He had his first real conversation with Estela. They clung to each other, cried and laughed.

"I didn't die because of you," he said. "You and the kids. I had to be there for you. I went into a dark room on the other side, but then I came back. For you."

"You didn't die because you are stubborn and incredibly annoying," his wife said. "A wolf that can't be killed. My wolf."

"They did their worst, and here we are," he said. "We survived."

The children were with Estela's mother, who had come up from Tijuana. Estela would bring them to the hospital later. Isabel Puente and Valentine Pescatore would visit when they returned from Tijuana, where they had gone to a memorial service for Porthos. Athos and Facundo were tending to Porthos's family.

Méndez ate soup and fell asleep. He awoke in the afternoon. His wife had left. Isabel and Pescatore sat at his bedside.

They were both in black. Isabel wore a long skirt, a short jacket, and a high-necked blouse, her lustrous hair pinned back. Pescatore wore a suit and tie. They looked good—and good together—in a fierce melancholy way.

Isabel kissed Méndez on the forehead. Pescatore patted his arm. Méndez had never seen Pescatore in a suit before and had never seen him cry before. He commented on the former.

"Very elegant, Valentine."

"I bought it this morning." Pescatore returned to his chair, regaining his composure. "Isabel picked it out. I wanted to show respect."

"How was the memorial?"

"Lovely," Isabel said.

"You shoulda seen it," Pescatore said. "Cops. School kids. University students. Just plain citizens."

"Porthos was known and admired," Méndez said.

*Because of the Diogenes Group*, he thought. *Because of me. And look what happened to him.*

"He's all over the news," Pescatore said. "The plaza in front of city hall was packed. They called his name, and everybody yelled, *¡Presente!* A big roar went up. Gave me chills."

It took a while before Méndez was able to speak.

"Ay, Porthos. The best of all of us."

"All heart," Pescatore said.

"He sacrificed himself for me. I don't know how I can repay that."

Méndez spoke in Spanish—he didn't have the strength for English. Isabel and Pescatore slid back and forth between languages. After some small talk, Méndez got down to it.

"My dear friends," he said. "I would feel better if someone would tell me what is going on."

"Are you sure?"

"Isabel, it would be like medicine."

Isabel said her bosses had relented and appointed her cochief of the task force investigating the Blakes. She told him what had happened after the attack on him. It was quite a story. Méndez concentrated in a haze of pain and medication. While Isabel spoke, Pescatore sat low in his chair with a hand over his mouth. He avoided her eyes. There was a silent dynamic between them: affection, reproach, wariness. Isabel recounted Pescatore's actions in the Antelope Valley—which sounded valiant, reckless and remarkable—without comment or emotion.

Perry Blake had been charged in California with the murder of Krystak and in New York for the attempted rape and assault and battery of Abrihet Anbessa. A slew of further state charges were pending. On Monday, federal prosecutors had indicted Blake for violations of the Foreign Corrupt Practices Act in conspiracy with his father and others. In addition, American, Italian and Mexican prosecutors were sorting out who would charge whom with what in relation to the massacre at the border and the shootout in Italy. The FBI had arrested Walter Blake in Bel Air on the foreign-corruption charges. The investigators were still examining his degree of involvement in the violent crimes.

"Get this," Isabel said. "The father wants to cut a deal in exchange for testifying against Perry. And Perry thinks he can help himself by dropping a dime on his father. He says he knows about insider trading, money laundering, political corruption. Going back years."

"Let me understand. The Blakes did *not* order Robles to kill me? He acted alone?"

"Correct."

"What about Italy?"

The Italian police had arrested a British mercenary living in Naples, an associate of Krystak's involved in arms trafficking. Krystak had enlisted him for the ambush in Italy.

"You led them to Abrihet's brother," Isabel said. "They knew the brother lived in Italy, but not where. You guys were about to blow things open. Perry wanted to wipe out the three of you and recover the documents. Looks like he told Krystak to use the same script as Tecate, disguise it as a Mafia hit. I think by then Perry was desperate, half crazy. And he only got worse after Robles shot you."

Isabel glanced at her phone. She was late for a meeting at the federal building.

"Isabel, I'm gonna sit with the *licenciado* for a while," Pescatore said. "Unless you guys need me."

"Stay," Isabel replied tersely. "Leo, take care of yourself. Sorry, but I have work to do. A big mess to clean up."

The final words were directed at Pescatore. Isabel gave Méndez another kiss, her cinnamon-tinged scent a welcome respite from the odors of the hospital and his battered body.

On her way out, she put her hand on Pescatore's shoulder. Pescatore put his hand on hers and clasped it tight.

After she left, Pescatore grinned wryly.

"*Mi querido* Valentine," Méndez said. "My God, you were wounded too. How do you feel?"

"Sore." Pescatore patted his left side. "I really haven't had time to think about it. I've been giving statements to multiple agencies, prosecutors. And getting some grief, tell you the truth."

"From Isabel."

"Yeah, she's pretty mad. So is the FBI."

"And Facundo?"

"He wasn't overjoyed. But he's cool. Practical. He figures it's the results that count. Don't get me wrong, I know I made mistakes. For a while, I thought they might charge me with something."

"And?"

"Isabel wouldn't let that happen. Funny how the government works. She's sitting pretty because she was after the Blakes from the start. Her bosses are the ones in the doghouse now."

"Good."

Pescatore sighed. "Look, when Robles gave up Noonan, I ran with that info. I was scared that if I told anyone, the Blakes would find out. I thought the Blakes had pretty much infiltrated law enforcement."

"To some extent, you were right."

"To some extent. The FBI arrested a lawyer in Washington, at Sylvester Daniels's firm, and people in government connected to him. Justice, DHS, Congress. A network. He's an ex-prosecutor. They were passing him sensitive information for the Blakes and interfering with the investigation. The Blakes were paying them with money and favors. Isabel thinks a congressman might get indicted."

"Wonders never cease."

"The Blakes threw their weight around. But Krystak didn't really have informants in field offices or anything. Isabel says I should've just called the FBI and they would've taken care of business. But she understands why I got paranoid."

Méndez nodded. He felt a wave of weakness.

"You okay?" Pescatore asked. "Want to rest?"

"No, it's fine."

Méndez remembered the moment at the Madrid airport when Pescatore had given him two envelopes.

"If I may ask, Valentine," he said. "How are things with Isabel? And, eh, Fatima? I have the impression your life is…complicated."

"You got that right. As soon as I can, I'm going to Paris. I need to resolve some issues. There and here."

Méndez said that sounded like a good idea.

"It's hard to believe, Leo," said Pescatore. "All these people hurt and killed. All because of one rich sociopath."

"In that sense, a simple story."

"It messed with my head. I did things I'm not proud of."

"Such as?"

Pescatore looked down.

Méndez added: "Not that you have to tell me."

"I killed people, for one thing."

"You didn't have much choice."

"I guess." Pescatore sighed. "But that's not all. There came a point when I needed something from Krystak. He resisted. And I lost it."

Haltingly, Pescatore described how he had beaten a hand-cuffed prisoner.

"I was angry. Out-of-my-mind angry. About you, Porthos, Abrihet. Still, I crossed a line. I don't know if that's a line I can cross back. What do you think?"

Méndez had heard this kind of confession many times over the years, voluntary or under duress. Cops asking him for absolution, or condemnation, or wisdom. Never an easy task.

"I don't know, Valentine. I am not going to judge you. You

are your sternest judge. And that's a good thing. What did Isabel say?"

"She doesn't necessarily know the details just yet."

"I see."

Pescatore leaned back with his arms folded. After a while, he said, "It was scary out in the desert. Not just the shooting. The worst part was feeling all alone. Like I couldn't trust anybody or anything. You know?"

"Yes. On the morning they shot me, I spoke to an old acquaintance in Mexico—an influential, cynical man. He predicted that the Blakes would never go to jail, that the American justice system couldn't touch them. I told him he was wrong. But I admit I was worried."

"I'm glad you stuck up for the U.S.A." Pescatore brightened. "Hey, listen. I brought you something." He pulled a gift-wrapped object from a pocket. "A souvenir," Pescatore continued. "From when we caught Blake."

"How thoughtful. I—"

Noises in the hallway interrupted. Voices, running feet. Juan and Renata rushed into the room.

Ignoring the pain, Méndez held his son and daughter as close as he could with one arm. His heart soared. He had never felt so alive.

His wife came in. She warned the children to be careful with the wires and bandages. But she ended up wrapping her arms around the three of them.

By the time the family had calmed down and dried their eyes, Pescatore was gone.

He had unwrapped the gift and left it on the chair.

A pair of handcuffs.

# Acknowledgments

I want to thank my editor, Asya Muchnick; my agent, Bonnie Nadell; and my trusted readers, Carmen, Carlo, and Sal. And, as always, Valeria and my parents, and our family near and far.

Any expertise I have I owe to the real experts. I'd especially like to thank Alan Bersin, Stefano Dambruoso, and Enrique Degenhart. There are quite a few other people in the Americas and Europe whose help, insights, and experience contributed to this book in some fashion. But they must remain anonymous because of what they do for a living.

Finally, I want to thank Steve Engelberg, the editor in chief of ProPublica, and my other colleagues there for their support, wisdom, and inspiration.

# About the Author

Sebastian Rotella is the author of *Triple Crossing,* which the *New York Times Sunday Book Review* named favorite debut crime novel and action thriller of 2011, and *The Convert's Song* (2014), as well as the nonfiction book *Twilight on the Line* (1998). He is an award-winning foreign correspondent and investigative journalist whose reporting has taken him across the Americas and Europe and to the Middle East, South Asia, and North Africa. He is a senior reporter for ProPublica, where he covers international security issues. Previously, he worked for the *Los Angeles Times,* serving as bureau chief in Paris and Buenos Aires and correspondent at the Mexican border. His honors include a Peabody Award, Columbia University's Moors Cabot Prize for coverage of Latin America, Italy's Urbino Press Award, and awards from the Overseas Press Club. He was a Pulitzer finalist in international reporting in 2006 and an Emmy nominee for his work on the *Frontline* documentary "A Perfect Terrorist" (2011). His reporting at the Mexican border inspired two songs on Bruce Springsteen's album *The Ghost of Tom Joad.*